PROFUSION

STAN C. SMITH

Mbaiso
Production

To those who look to the future not with despair but with anticipation.

PROFUSION

Definition:

An abundance or large quantity of something. A pouring forth of something in great quantity.

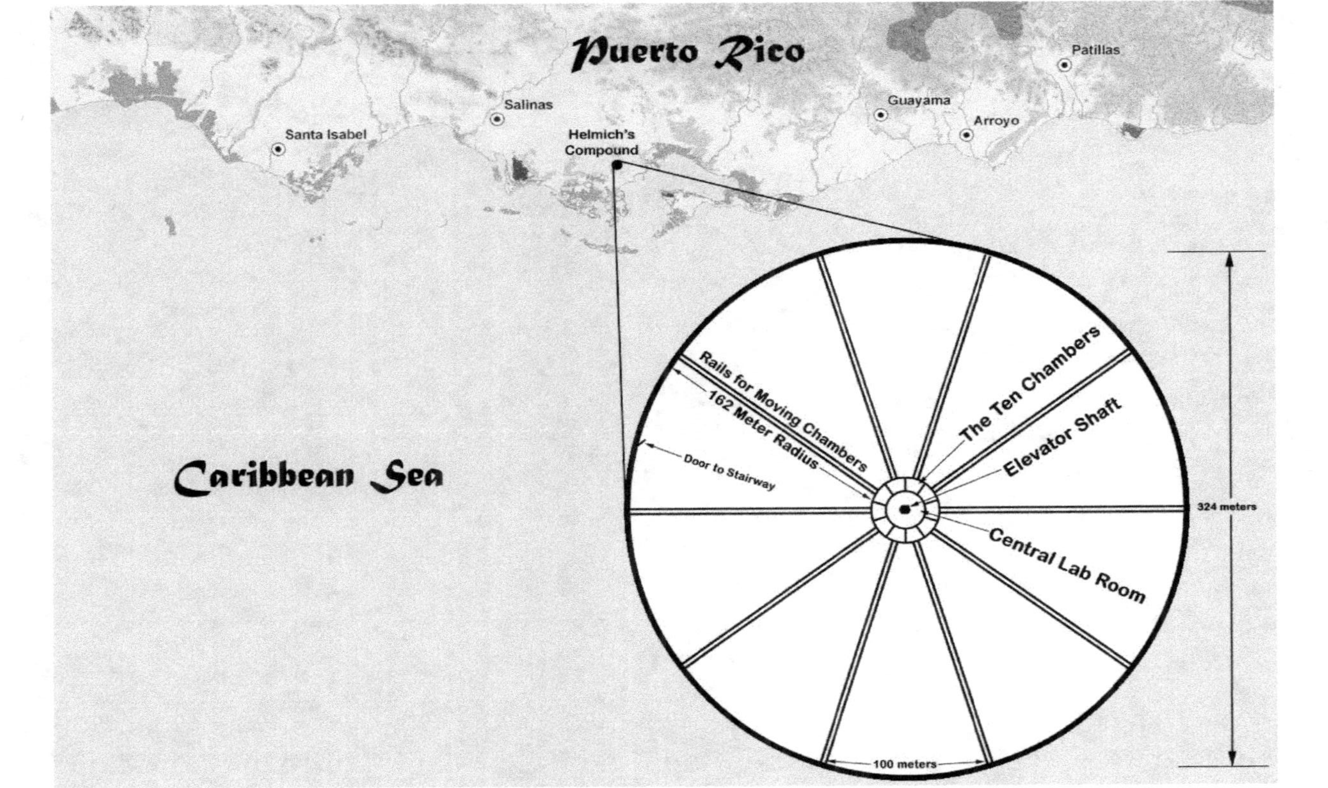

Puerto Rico
Patillas
Salinas
Guayama
Arroyo
Santa Isabel
Helmich's Compound
Caribbean Sea
Rails for Moving Chambers
162 Meter Radius
Door to Stairway
The Ten Chambers
Elevator Shaft
Central Lab Room
324 meters
100 meters

SAMUEL INWOOD TRUDGED up a densely-forested hill, slipping in mud from a recent rain and bearing a heavy pack made from woven sago leaves that had been softened by chewing. He stopped at the hill's summit, hefted the pack to the ground, and sat beside it. His bare arms and legs were scratched and bleeding, but they would heal soon enough. He inspected his spider silk vest and fingered a ragged hole. That would have to be mended.

The sound of claws scuttling on tree bark made Samuel glance up quickly. A tree kangaroo, locally known as an *mbolop*, was clambering up a tree a few yards away. The creature had followed him from the village. Samuel frowned. He would have preferred to do this without being observed, even by the mbolop.

The surrounding trees upon the hill's crown were relatively sparse. Many years ago Samuel had been on a hill similar to this one. It had been his first hunting excursion with the Papuan savages who had long ago captured him and killed his companions —savages he now considered to be friends.

Today, though, Samuel had not come here to hunt.

"I estimate the village to be nearly three miles distant," he said, not necessarily to the mbolop nor to anyone in particular. During eighty years living with the tribe, he had developed a habit of speaking aloud when he was alone.

He opened the pack. Inside were twelve pouches, each of them made from the skin of a bandicoot, and each of them containing a lump of clay slightly smaller than his fist. He pulled forth one of the pouches. He held it upside down until the lump of clay fell out onto the ground before him. He then pulled forth a second pouch and dropped a nearly identical lump of clay next to the first. This was followed by a third lump, and then a fourth. Eight lumps still remained in the pack, contained within their own skin pouches.

Samuel had discreetly collected the lumps over a period of three months, carefully storing them in his hut. Each was contained within a pouch so the lumps would not touch, as his purpose would be ill-served were they to be mixed together before this particular day. He had pinched off the lumps, one at a time, from a much larger source, a mass of clay over two feet in diameter. The Papuan villagers called the clay *Lamotelokhai*, which meant *the end of the world*. Eighty years before, Samuel had briefly believed the clay might have been a portal to God. Since then, however, he had seen that it was something even more astounding.

Samuel studied the four lumps before him. A pinch from any one of them could be used to perform seemingly impossible tasks. If he wished to cause an object to dissolve into soil, he would need only to apply the clay to the object. If he or a companion were injured, applying the clay would heal the wounds—even if the wounds would otherwise have been fatal. If he wished to cook a meal or fire-harden a spear tip, he could apply the clay to the wood before burning it, resulting in a smokeless fire that would not reveal his location.

Unique tasks requiring more specific instructions, however, could only be performed by the larger source of the clay, the Lamotelokhai. Or so Samuel had previously believed. Recently, however, an idea had been circling about in his mind. What if it were possible to combine bits of the clay into a mass smaller than the Lamotelokhai but large enough to carry out complex tasks? If this were possible, the benefits would be numerous beyond imagining.

The question was this: how large would the mass need to be?

He looked again at the sparse hilltop trees. "Am I alone?" he shouted, and then again in the language of the villagers. "*Nu bai-khokhüm?*" There was no response, although he sensed the mbolop watching him from above. Returning his attention to the lumps of clay, he shifted his position on the ground and straightened his back, attempting to drive away his misgivings.

"Let no man deceive himself," he muttered. "Let him become a fool, that he may become wise." He then pushed the four lumps together and molded them into one.

He plucked a river stone from the pack and placed it next to the clay. Then, he placed his hands on the clay and closed his eyes to create a clear vision of his request. He stirred up a well-rehearsed series of thoughts, running them through his mind in a specific order: a vision of the river stone becoming smaller and taking on a golden color; a silent explanation that the rock had turned to gold, the heaviest of metals; a vision of a gold nugget tipping a scale, outweighing a stone on the opposite end.

Samuel opened his eyes, pinched off some of the clay, and smeared it upon the stone. He then sat back and waited.

Nothing happened.

He pulled four more skin pouches from the pack, removed lumps of clay from them, and pressed the lumps into the larger mass. He placed his hands on the clay, repeated the series of thoughts, and smeared another pinch of clay on the stone.

Again, nothing.

"God blind me! Have I embarked upon another fruitless path of inquiry?"

He pulled the last four skin pouches from the pack, extracted the clay lumps from each of them, and pressed them into the mass, resulting in a lump that was now as large as his head. If this didn't work, he would have to conclude the experiment was a failure, as it was impractical to gather more. He placed his hands on the clay and repeated the sequence of thoughts. After anointing the stone, he sat back and watched, softly singing an old song from his childhood to calm himself.

"A-hunting we will go, a-hunting we will go, we'll catch a giraffe and make him laugh, and then we'll let him go."

The stone shifted. Or did it? Perhaps it was just his imagination.

"A-hunting we will go, we'll catch a bear and cut his hair, and then..."

The stone shifted again. This time it continued changing. It was becoming smaller. Its edges seemed to soften, and its surface turned to shimmering golden yellow. Samuel held his fingers above it to be sure it wasn't hot, and then he picked it up. The bottom of it had conformed to the twigs and soil, as if it had melted and cooled, although no debris was stuck to its surface. Its weight indicated that indeed it was gold. He looked more closely. It was imperfect, with speckles of minerals showing on its surface. This was peculiar. He had made this same request of the Lamotelokhai many times, always resulting in perfect, pure gold specimens. Nonetheless, the results were encouraging.

He proceeded to the second experiment he had prepared. He placed his hands upon the lump of clay, closed his eyes, and conjured another sequence of thoughts. In his mind's vision, the gold specimen transformed its shape. First it elongated and formed a head, thorax, and abdomen. Then two broad wings sprouted from each side of the thorax, gradually spreading wider until the entire object was an intricate gold sculpture of a butterfly. He opened his eyes and smeared a pinch of clay onto the impure gold.

He waited, softly humming the old song.

The gold began to change. It narrowed in two places, forming the three insect body regions. Then, however, the sculpting process went astray. Instead of delicate wings blossoming from each side, tendrils of speckled gold spewed forth into shapeless extensions. The insect body curled up and writhed, as if it were a malformed creature in great pain. Samuel watched, mesmerized, as the object's shape continued shifting. For a moment the gold resembled a giraffe, and then a bear, and then it even resembled the face of his beloved Lindsey, whom he had left behind in London and who had no doubt grown old and passed away years before. When he saw this, he glanced away, unwilling to be tormented by the sight. When he returned his gaze to the gold, the transformations had stopped, leaving an amorphous mass that bore no resemblance to a butterfly. He touched it with his finger, half expecting it to change again, but it was cold and solid.

"Most... extraordinary," he said. He turned to the lump of clay. "You seem to understand my requests but are hardly capable of granting them. Of what use are you? I shall have to endeavor to discover what you can and cannot do."

He got up and began searching the area for a beetle or other large insect, which he would need for his next experiment. After sifting through leaf litter on the forest floor for some minutes, a slight movement in a low bush caught his attention. He approached the bush and soon was eye-to-eye with a slender arboreal lizard perhaps two feet in total length. Its yellow-spotted black body sharply contrasted with a brilliant blue tail.

Samuel sighed and shook his head. This was yet another new species of the genus *Monitor*. He would have a most impressive collection of specimens, had his life not taken such a calamitous turn of fate.

He slowly inched his way closer and then thrust his hand out in a blur and snatched the lizard. He inspected the struggling creature, holding it out so that its lashing tail could not whip his face.

"If you are indeed new to science," he said to the lizard, "then I have the honor of naming you." He used his free hand to subdue the tail. "*Monitor cerulean* seems to fit you well, as your tail is as blue as the evening sky. Let us see what we can do to make the name even more fitting, shall we?" He then carried the lizard back to the lump of clay and sat upon the ground.

He placed his free hand on the clay, closed his eyes, and formed a mental vision of the lizard. Then, he imagined the blue pigment of the creature's tail spreading forward, transforming the scaly skin on the rest of the body from black and yellow to the same brilliant cerulean hue. He opened his eyes and smeared a pinch of clay onto the lizard's back. By this time the creature had stopped struggling, so he released it, keeping his hand ready above it in case it tried to run. The lizard tilted its head but remained where it was.

Samuel waited.

Soon his mental vision began materializing. Beginning at the base of the lizard's tail, bead-like black scales faded to gray and then became blue. This alteration progressed until its entire body and head were blue with yellow spots.

As the yellow spots began changing to blue, the lizard abruptly wrenched its head to the side. Its mouth snapped open and emitted a menacing hiss. Samuel pulled his hand back, thinking the lizard was about to lunge at him. Instead of attacking, however, the crea-ture spasmed and tumbled onto its side, its legs kicking desperately, as if gripped by seizure. Suddenly its body split in two, spewing forth blood and entrails.

Samuel rose to his feet. "What in God's—" He stopped short. The two halves of the lizard were now moving—transforming. Torn skin rolled up into itself and fell away from each portion of the carcass. The elongated rolls of skin then began crawling away, moving on their own like macabre grubs. Exposed organs detached themselves from the lizard's body. Some of them began oozing away, while others sprouted rudimentary legs and began crawling.

Horrified, Samuel realized he was stumbling backwards.

The lizard's tail broke free from the body and thrashed about. Its haphazard movements became more coordinated and deliberate, until finally it slithered away like a snake. The head portion of the body was still floundering about, going through its own revolting transformation. As it rolled on the ground, its jaws snapped shut on some dry leaves and small plants, which then began changing, eventually assimilating into the creature's head. The unholy beast then began snapping up every living and once-living object within its reach, as if it had discovered a new life-sustaining food source. Each thing it clamped upon became part of its abhorrent and growing mass.

Samuel could hardly look away from this disturbing sight, but suddenly his attention was drawn again to the snake-like tail, which had slithered and spiraled its way up a sapling tree and was now at the height of his chest. The thing was tightening around the sapling like a snake constricting its prey. Carefully keeping his distance from the creature's voracious head, Samuel stepped closer to the sapling to observe. But then he stepped back again when the trunk softened where the tail was gripping it, the entire tree folding and collapsing toward him. The autonomous tail then somehow melded into the folded joint of the sapling's trunk and was gone.

And then the entire tree began to move.

"God save me," Samuel uttered.

The tree continued changing its shape as it slowly writhed about. Samuel backed away, but he tripped and fell over something. Sprawled on his back, his feet and knees rested atop a hulking mass that only moments before had been the head of a small lizard. The thing was now the size of Samuel's body, although its form was unrecognizable. No longer resembling the lizard it once was, it had grown body parts of many different creatures, all of them squirming and fighting as if they desired to escape from the horrifying conglomeration to which they were bound.

As Samuel tried to comprehend what he was seeing, a creature's head materialized from the mass and clamped its jaws onto his bare calf. The head was the size of a small dog's, but it appeared to be reptilian, with round yellow eyes and vertical pupils. Samuel kicked it with his free foot, tearing its teeth loose from his flesh. He rolled out of its reach and then sat up, pressing his hand against his bleeding leg.

The multifarious masses continued to squirm and grow before his eyes, including several smaller blobs that had originated from the lizard's entrails and hind legs. With every passing moment they grew larger as they engulfed leaf litter, soil, and living plants. The reptilian head that had bitten Samuel gaped and screeched as it fought to free itself from the jumbled body parts of a dozen or more different creatures, all of them squirming in the same frantic manner.

Several sharp cracks drew Samuel's attention upward. He rolled to the side just in time to avoid being killed by the trunk of a large falling tree. Smaller limbs on the now horizontal tree folded where they joined the main trunk and then broke off. The limbs began bending and cracking on their own accord, taking on new shapes. One of them emitted a dry, twittering shriek, unlike any sound Samuel had heard before.

He stared at the scene before him, too shocked to run or to try to stop the accelerating process. Suddenly he was aware of a curious sensation in his bitten leg. He looked down. The wound was changing. His skin was peeling back, exposing red muscle and pale fat. The underlying tissues were moving about, transmuting into something else. For a brief moment a three-toed claw emerged from the wound and grasped at the air before sinking back into his calf muscle. Another bulge formed, and a pair of eyelids parted. A rust-colored eye stared back at him.

Samuel tried to cry out in despair and crawl away from the transforming flesh, but he could not escape his own body. He curled up on his side and pummeled his leg with his fist, desperately hoping to stop the monstrous transformation by beating it to a pulp.

In his panicked frenzy, his flailing arm struck something beside him. It was the mbolop, the tree kangaroo. Samuel's inadvertent blow sent it tumbling, but it quickly righted itself and sat up on its haunches. The creature scratched at its belly. It then ripped open its own skin, plunged one paw deep into its abdomen, and extracted a bloody lump of flesh, which it held out as an offering.

Samuel stared at the mbolop, then looked down at his leg. The wriggling, transfiguring wound was steadily growing larger. It had expanded down to his foot. One of his toes was now six inches long and was thrashing about, looking much like a lizard's tail. His entire body would soon be transmogrified.

He snatched the lump from the mbolop's paw and shoved it into his mouth.

IN HIS DESIRE FOR HASTE, Samuel ran directly through a patch of *yalün*, or stinging nettles. The unnatural transformation of his leg had stopped, but the wound was still wide open, and the nettles pricked and lacerated his raw flesh, injecting their astringent sap. The pain nearly caused him to collapse, but dread and remorse pushed him onward.

He continued fighting his way through dense jungle for nearly two hours. At last, exhausted and bleeding, he arrived at the village. He made his way straight to where the Lamotelokhai was concealed. Soon he stood at the base of an enormous, buttressed tree. Wasting no time, he extracted a thin rope with evenly spaced loops—a rope ladder—that had been tucked away in the crevices of the tree's bark. He began climbing toward the hut, which was over a hundred feet above the ground. His leg was now nearly healed, and soon he ascended directly through a hole in the hut's floor and stepped away from the ladder.

To his surprise, three Papuan natives were there in the hut. One of them stepped away from the others and blocked Samuel's path. He was about Samuel's height, but he had dark skin and wore no clothing other than a sheath made from a gourd, fitted tightly over his sexual organs. A band of white paint, made from palm oil and the crushed shells of river clams, extended from one ear to the other like a mask. Green lorikeet feathers protruded in random directions from his frizzly hair. His name was Sinanie, and Samuel had lived with him and his fellow tribesmen since 1868.

Sinanie appraised the scratches and filth covering most of Samuel's body, a deep frown forming on his face. He said, "Samuel, *ge sumo abül lép-telo* (you have the smell of a man who is afraid)."

Samuel was still trying to catch his breath. "Sinanie, *nu khof-e-kha lamoda-Lamotelokhai tekhén-mo* (I must touch the Lamotelokhai)."

Sinanie furrowed his brow. He did not step aside.

There was no time to explain. Samuel walked around Sinanie and kneeled down before a low table. Upon the table was the Lamotelokhai, a shapeless lump of clay approximately the size and mass of a man's body. This was where Samuel had gotten the smaller lumps of clay he had secretly combined on the remote hill. And the Lamotelokhai was the reason Samuel had remained in this forest for eighty years. Without waiting to see if the natives intended to stop him, he placed his hands on the clay. He formed words in his mind without speaking them, although his lips moved slightly to facilitate the process.

"I must confess, I have again done something foolish and am in desperate need of your assistance."

CHAPTER TWO

Quentin Darnell stared at a brown water stain on the ceiling above the bed. He had been awakened at 4:30 by a loud call to prayer from the mosque across the street. The calling hadn't stopped, so there was no going back to sleep. Finally, he turned on his phone to check the clock—6:00 am. He had to do something—anything—to pass the time. Their flight to the inland village of Navera wasn't for another three hours. Lindsey was still sleeping, so he quietly got out of bed, slipped into his rumpled t-shirt and khaki trousers, and shoved on his hiking shoes. He plucked a thin, 4-inch bone from the nightstand and put it in his pocket. It was from a male raccoon, a bone called the baculum, also known as the penis bone. He liked to think it brought him good luck—his only superstitious habit. This one was a replacement, as he had lost the original eight months ago in a plane crash.

After visiting the bathroom, he went back to the bed and gently shook Lindsey's shoulder.

She stirred. "You're going somewhere?"

Quentin sat on the edge of the bed. "I just need to walk or

something. Maybe I can pick up a few things we'll need. I'll be back in plenty of time to make sure you're awake and to get ready."

She nodded slightly and rolled onto her side. In a barely-conscious whisper she said, "I'm sleeping. Makes time go faster."

Sleeping was not an option for Quentin. He left the room and walked down to the lobby of the Grand Bayliss Hotel. The lobby was actually impressive compared to most other hotels in the Indonesian province of Papua. But upon closer inspection, it was easy to see evidence that this was a business struggling despite its best efforts amidst Papua province's impoverished economy and Indonesia's interminable bureaucracy.

"Mr. Grayson, delivery for you."

Quentin turned. Grayson was the name his family now used in public. The speaker was a hotel counter clerk, the same young Indonesian man who had checked them in the night before. His nametag said *Rama*. He waved Quentin over to the desk and then hefted two internal-frame backpacks onto the counter. The packs looked expensive, and they appeared to be full. Rama then handed Quentin a sealed manila envelope.

"Arrived late last night," he said, smiling pleasantly.

Quentin thanked him and took the envelope. All it said on the front was:

To: Warren and Olivia Grayson
    Grand Bayliss Hotel
    From: SouthPacificNet

HE OPENED THE ENVELOPE. Inside was a *surat jalan*, or travel permit, already filled out and approved for Warren and Olivia Grayson. He zipped open the top of one of the backpacks. It was filled with premium, lightweight wilderness gear. Hiking shoes, clothing, a cylindrical water filter with a pump lever, a handheld GPS device, and other things he couldn't identify without pulling them out.

Quentin shook his head. How Peter Wooley's staff had managed to get the travel permit approved without his and Lindsey's presence was a mystery, and perhaps a bit disturbing, but it would save them from taking a last-minute minibus ride to the police station to get one. And the hiking gear was a godsend. He and Lindsey had simply had no time to shop for the things they might need.

He paused, allowing a depraved memory to resurface—a memory of watching his son Addison pick himself up from the floor of a hanging hut, battered and bleeding, and then fleeing into the trees. Addison had just had his memory wiped out by a substance Quentin himself had forced upon him. They'd searched for him with no luck, finally giving up and abandoning him to die alone in the wilderness. Now, what would it be like going back into the Papuan rainforest, and back to that same hut? It was all happening so fast. Fifty-five hours ago he and Lindsey had been awakened by a call from Samuel on their satellite phone. Samuel Inwood, who had been living in the wilderness of Papua for more than 150 years, was perhaps the most extraordinary man Quentin had ever met. He had called them with the news that their son, Addison, was still alive. Samuel had explained that Addison was no longer a normal boy, and that his appearance was rather shocking. But he was alive.

Quentin shook his head to rid his mind of these futile thoughts. He asked Rama to store the backpacks behind the counter until he came back, and then he walked through the glass and chrome doors onto the street. The street was officially named *Kemiri Raya*, but was often referred to as *Sentani Kimera*. It was the same road Quentin and four other survivors of a devastating plane crash had traveled months ago from the airport to a hospital in Jayapura. The hospital visit hadn't ended well: Quentin's group held captive,

Bobby asking the Lamotelokhai to help, the Lamotelokhai responding by killing multiple Indonesians and transforming them into enraged, bird-like dinosaurs that then killed even more people. Again Quentin shook his head. He wished he could forget the entire incident. But of course he couldn't—he couldn't forget anything.

Outside the hotel, the air smelled of fried rice, curry, and a poorly-planned sewage system. The proportions of these smells would shift in the wrong direction as the day's heat set in. The traffic was still sparse, mostly minibuses for hire and motorcycles. Bicyclists and pedestrians bustled about on the roads and side-walks. Although Quentin preferred tropical forests over tropical cities, this entire scene was invigorating and exotic, and he welcomed the chance to walk. Plus, he desperately needed the diversion.

The crowd on the street consisted of a diverse mix of various Indonesian ethnicities, such as Bugis and Javanese, as well as people of Papuan descent, indicated by darker skin and distinct facial features. Other than tourists at the airport, Quentin had rarely seen Americans here. No more than a hundred or so expats resided in Jayapura, most of them missionaries or health workers. The city had once been a minor trading settlement, but it was now home to more than 300,000 people. Nearly all this growth had occurred since World War II, when a massive invasion of Humboldt Bay by Allied Forces had driven out the Japanese. The site had then become General MacArthur's headquarters, estab-lishing it as a major base. A year after the invasion, the Dutch had designated the city as the capital of Netherlands New Guinea. To Quentin, Jayapura showcased a fascinating juxtaposition of cultures—a nexus for the diffusion of customs, languages, and beliefs.

As he walked east toward the airport and Jayapura proper, Quentin turned his thoughts to Bobby and Ashley. During recent months the two teens had become part of his family. In fact, they would almost certainly have been here in Papua with him and Lindsey if the teens hadn't left with Peter only hours before the shocking call from Samuel.

Quentin suddenly felt the need to make contact with them. He pulled out his phone, confirmed that he had a signal, and then tapped the country codes and selected Peter's cell number. He covered one ear to dampen the noise of passing motorcycles. The call went straight to voicemail.

That was unusual.

Quentin stopped walking. He called Bobby's phone. It went straight to voicemail. A moment later, a call to Ashley's phone gave him the same result. A sense of helplessness took hold of him. He and Lindsey would be flying to the interior in a few hours. They had to find Addison—they simply had to. This was no time for a second emergency. He turned and made his way back to the hotel, now oblivious to the bustling activity around him.

When he entered the room, Lindsey was sitting up in the bed with her phone to her ear.

"I understand," she said. "We'll be in the air in two hours. After that we'll be reachable only on Peter's satellite phone, but even that could be spotty. Please call back the minute you know something." She ended the call and dropped the phone onto the bed.

Quentin swallowed hard. "What is it?"

She turned to him with a benumbed expression. "That was Ardell Gray from SouthPacificNet. He's one of the three people in Peter's company who know what Peter and the kids are doing. Quentin, they've lost contact with them. No one knows where they are."

CHAPTER THREE

BOBBY PUSHED A BUTTON, and a silent motor drew the accordion shade up into a compact strip across the top of the window. He had never been in a Mercedes-Benz before, let alone a luxury Mercedes passenger van. He found it to be both fascinating and disgustingly excessive. After two hours of messing with various electronic gadgets, he was still discovering new surprises. He gazed out the window. It was April, and things were greening up, but the Oklahoma landscape outside was a desert compared to the shore of the Sittee River in Belize, where he had lived for the last eight months. He turned around and glanced at the clock next to the television mounted behind his head. It was after 8:00 am. They would arrive soon.

"Should we wake her up?" Bobby asked.

Peter was sitting in one of the two deeply-cushioned seats on the other side of the table they had folded out from a cubby in the wall. He looked up from the brown leather folder of documents he was reading and smiled. He nodded at Ashley, sleeping in the seat beside Bobby. "Be my guest."

Bobby hesitated.

Peter said, "Afraid to rouse her, aren't you mate?"

"I have a healthy respect for her temper," Bobby retorted. He shook her shoulder. Then he shook it again.

She rubbed her eyes. "Are we there?"

"Almost," Bobby said. "Just thought you'd want to be awake so we could go over the plan again."

She gave him a look. "We've talked about it twenty times."

Peter closed his leather folder and stuffed it into the matching leather satchel that was in the seat beside him. He moved the satchel onto the floor by his feet and then patted the empty seat meaningfully.

Bobby understood why. If everything went according to plan, there would soon be something that looked just like a human sitting there for the ride back to Oklahoma City.

Peter took a moment to tighten the elastic band that held his silver-speckled hair in a ponytail. He adjusted the collar of his white shirt, fastened the top button, and tucked the shirt into his blue jeans. Leaning forward, he grabbed the leather sandals he had kicked off two hours ago and put them back on. He took a deep breath and smiled at them.

"I am almost queasy, if you can believe it. I first encountered the Lamotelokhai four and a half decades ago. So much of my life has been spent thinking about it and preparing. I do hope I make a good impression."

Bobby laughed at this, partly because he was nervous too.

"It's just a machine," Ashley said.

Peter said, "And the prize goes to Ashley Stoddard, for the understatement of the year."

Ashley almost smiled. "I'm Hattie Grayson now, remember?" She pushed the button to raise the window shade on her side and turned to watch the passing countryside. Bobby wondered if she was thinking the same thing he was, that the grassy fields dotted with thick patches of trees brought back memories of outmaneuvering two fighter jets to avoid being captured or shot down, hiding in a patch of trees until the coast was clear, and then walking into the town of Pawhuska to find a motel room where they could rest until morning. It had been the most exciting time of Bobby's life and also the most traumatic.

"It's starting to look familiar," Bobby said to her.

Ashley continued staring out the window. "Yes it is," she said quietly.

Peter pressed a button on the arm of his chair. "Robert, progress report please."

A voice came back through the van's surround sound system. "Five minutes from our destination." The voice belonged to Robert Ramey. Not only was he their driver for the day, but he was also one of only three of Peter's employees who knew about this mission.

Perhaps Robert and the other two knew about it, Bobby thought, but he doubted if they really understood how important it was—or how dangerous.

Tall steel trusses suddenly punctuated the view on both sides as the van rolled over a bridge. Shortly after crossing the bridge, they slowed down and turned into a parking lot. Bobby looked past Ashley, and his eyes were drawn to the door to room 4 of the Economy Inn.

Peter said, "Does this look like the place?"

Bobby nodded. "I can't believe we're back here."

"You and me both," Ashley said. She was also staring at room 4.

Bobby saw that there were only three other cars in the parking lot. "He needs to park right there," he said. "In front of room 4."

Peter pressed the button and relayed Bobby's suggestion to Robert. The van pulled in, and Robert killed the engine. Peter moved to the edge of his chair and grasped the handle of the sliding door. He looked at Bobby and Ashley.

"I know you would like to be with your folks in Papua. The

timing of Samuel's call was unfortunate. After we've completed this mission, perhaps we can fly there so we can greet them when they come out of the bush. If all goes well, they'll have Addison with them."

Ashley glanced at Bobby. She was smiling. She and Bobby had talked about requesting this but were afraid it would be asking too much. "That would be awesome!" she said.

"It's the least I can do. For now, though, we have a most pressing matter to attend to. As you know, Quentin and Lindsey will kill me if you two get into any trouble. I want you with us when we go into the room, but wait until I come for you. Got it?"

"Got it," they both said.

Peter slid the door open, and Robert was waiting for him just outside. Robert looked to be older than Peter, but Bobby knew he was much younger, due to the fact that Peter hadn't aged in the forty-five years since he had first found the Lamotelokhai. Like Peter, Robert wore blue jeans, sandals, and a button-down shirt, although Robert's shirt was plaid. He even wore his gray hair in the same ponytail. Bobby and Ashley had spent the previous day with Robert deep inside the Kembalimo server facility. Peter had asked Robert to show them everything they wanted to see, including the top secret room that would be the Lamotelokhai's new home.

Robert was smiling as Peter got out of the van, which probably meant that Robert didn't realize how dangerous their cargo could be. Peter shut the door, and the two men walked to the motel's office.

Bobby and Ashley could see into the office through the large glass windows on its front. They sat in silence, watching Peter and Robert talk to the woman behind the counter. She looked like the same woman who had been here eight months ago—the woman who had called the police to report that six fugitives were hiding in room 4. She had almost caused Bobby and his group to miss the most important appointment of their lives.

"This doesn't seem right," Ashley said. "We should have brought bodyguards—like twenty of them."

Bobby said, "Why would someone scouting a location for a movie bring twenty bodyguards?"

"Peter could have come up with a different story. A group of actors coming here to actually film the scene. Or an FBI investigation."

"Or maybe a bodyguard convention?"

Ashley snorted a laugh. "At the Economy Inn of Pawhuska."

Bobby smiled. He was as nervous about this as she was, but he tried not to let it show. The plan seemed too simple. Peter had insisted that they bring only one vehicle, to be inconspicuous. The Mercedes van wasn't really inconspicuous, but it was a good match for a movie director looking for a scene location. Peter had made the point that if anyone knew the Lamotelokhai had been hiding at the motel, then they would have taken it already. Besides, there were only three other people in Peter's corporation, including Robert, who knew why they had actually come here. 'Secrecy is the cracker of the day,' Peter was fond of saying. And he had insisted that Bobby and Ashley could come on this mission only if they agreed not to show their faces in public. They had taken private flights from Belize to Houston, and then to Oklahoma City. They had exited the plane and immediately entered the van, which had then taken them to Peter's Kembalimo server headquarters. Peter hadn't allowed them to leave the headquarters until this morning. They hadn't even stopped to pee—Peter had told them to use the tiny bathroom in the back of the van. In spite of all this caution, Bobby was still nervous. What if someone—like Darron Mesner and the other feds, for example—suspected the Lamotelokhai was here, but they were just waiting for someone to show up and lead them right to it?

But Bobby understood it was crucial to move the Lamotelokhai to a safer place.

"Uh-oh, what now?" Ashley said.

Bobby looked. It appeared Peter was arguing with the lady in the office. Peter was typically calm and in control. Now his back was stiff, and he was talking with jerky hand movements. Bobby started to worry that the lady might call the police again.

Finally, Peter put something on the counter, the lady handed something to him, and then he and Robert came back out. Peter opened the sliding door and got in while Robert waited outside.

"What an extraordinarily disagreeable woman," he said. He held up a key attached to a red piece of plastic with a 4 stamped on it. "She seemed to believe the story of why we're here, but she insisted on personally giving us a tour of room 4." He forced a smile. "I had to pay for a night's stay in every room of the hotel to convince her to allow us to look about on our own. With any luck, we will conclude our business and be off the premises in a jiffy."

A lump rose in Bobby's throat. This was it. He would actually be face-to-face with the Lamotelokhai again. Horrifying memories began replaying with high-definition clarity in his mind. A monster that had once been his friend killing Miranda and at least a dozen Papuan villagers. Eight-foot dinosaurs ripping innocent people to shreds in a hospital. A huge passenger jet splattering against the ground, pulverizing everyone in it. The Lamotelokhai was an amazing thing, but carnage seemed to result every time someone tried to use it. If it fell into the wrong hands...

For the ten-thousandth time, Bobby shut this thought down before it could play out in his head. Instead, he put on one of the cowboy hats Peter had brought to disguise them and handed the other to Ashley.

"One more time for good measure," Peter said. "We'll all go in together. Bobby, you'll do your magic with the Lamotelokhai. Robert, Ashley, and I will come back out and get in the van. Then Ashley will go back in, and I will follow her ten seconds later.

Bobby and the Lamotelokhai will come out to the van, and then Ashley and I will come out."

Ashley started to shake her head, but Peter held up a finger and said, "Our researchers have proven that nine out of ten people observing that sequence will not notice there is an extra person."

Ashley snorted. "Seriously, who does research like that?" But she put on her cowboy hat and nodded that she was ready.

Seconds later they were standing inside room 4. Bobby looked around. The room was just as he remembered it, except for two things. First, the pod for wired Internet connection was no longer on the nightstand between the two beds. In its place was an upright card with a Wi-Fi password. The Economy Inn had joined the 21st century. Second, there was another nightstand in the corner of the room. It was scratched and worn, obviously older than the one between the beds.

Peter cleared his throat. Bobby realized they were all looking at him, waiting. He walked between the beds and knelt before the nightstand. This had to be it. He placed his hands on the small table.

"Is it you?" he said.

The surface of the table heaved slightly, nearly causing the lamp on top of it to fall over. Bobby grabbed the lamp and the digital clock that was next to it and placed them on one of the beds. The table then began to change. First the corners became rounded. The gap around the drawer vanished, and the drawer's metal knob melted into the wood. The entire nightstand then became a brown, clay-like lump with no particular shape. Bobby stood up and backed away to give it room.

"Holy crap," Robert muttered.

Bobby turned to him. "Don't be afraid."

Robert's eyes were round, and he had backed up to the closed door behind him. "I was told what to expect. But holy crap."

Peter's eyes were round, too, but his face looked the way Bobby imagined his own face used to look on Christmas morning. The Lamotelokhai affected people in different ways.

The brown lump of clay had begun forming into something. Indentations had appeared on the surface and were now becoming folds. The folds deepened, shaping the clay into something with arms, legs, and a head. The featureless body awkwardly got to its knees and then to its feet. To Bobby it looked like a humanoid clay figure created by a five-year-old, coming to life. The creepiest thing about it was that it didn't even have a face. There was no mouth or nose for it to breath through. Bobby turned around to make sure Robert wasn't completely freaking out. The poor guy was still frozen in the same spot. When Bobby turned back, bits of clothing were starting to appear on the clay, and a mouth, a nose, and a pair of eyes were taking shape.

A few minutes later the transformation was finished. Standing in front of them was Addison. Bobby's friend. Son of Quentin and Lindsey. But of course it wasn't really Addison. The thing gazed at them. It had every one of Addison's freckles, and it had the same dark, curly hair. It was wearing flip-flops, blue shorts, and a yellow t-shirt that said Jose Cuervo across the front—the same clothes it had been wearing the last time Bobby had seen it.

"Hello, Bobby," it said with Addison's voice. "Hello, Ashley. Peter, it is nice to see you. How is Rose, Peter?"

Peter hesitated for a moment and then stepped forward. "Rose is not feeling very well, I'm afraid."

The thing's eyes turned from pale blue to fiery gold. This was its way of showing people it was thinking about something.

"I understand," it said. It dug into its left palm with the fingers of its other hand and then held out a small brown lump. "You should give this to Rose."

Peter stared at the lump. He opened his mouth like he was going to say something, then he stopped. It looked like he was about to cry. Finally, he took it. "This is to help her?"

"Yes," the thing said.

He pulled a blue and white handkerchief from his jeans pocket and used it to wipe his eyes. He then folded it around the lump and put it into a pocket on the front of his shirt. "Thank you. Will it be okay if I carry it this way until I am with her again?"

"Yes, it will be okay," the Lamotelokhai said. It then turned to Robert, still with his back to the door. "You are Robert Ramey."

"It's an honor to meet you," Robert said.

"Why?"

Robert's eyes flicked toward Bobby briefly. "Well, um, because you're important. You've already helped us all so much. You may even be the one thing that prevents our extinction."

"The probability that I will cause your extinction is approximately equal to the probability that I will prevent it."

This was followed by silence.

Finally, Peter spoke. "If we have anything to say about it, there will be no extinctions taking place." He put a hand on Robert's shoulder. "As you probably know, Robert is with us today to help transport you to a new location." He held his hands out and looked around at the room. "This place does not suit your capabilities."

"I understand," the thing said. "Bobby has explained this to me. I will go with you."

Ashley spoke up for the first time. "You've been in this room for months. I bet you're sick and tired of it."

The copy of Addison looked at Ashley with a blank face. "I cannot be sick. And I am not tired."

Ashley sighed. "Dude, seriously?"

Bobby saw that the thing was now smiling slightly. Was it actually messing with Ashley—making a joke?

A vehicle could be heard on the road outside, and Robert pulled the curtain back to watch it pass by. "We should go. No reason to linger."

Bobby wasn't quite ready to go. He turned to the Lamotelokhai and spoke softly. "I'm kind of afraid."

"Yes, I see that you are," it said. "Why?"

"I know you didn't come here to hurt people. You proved that during the time you were hiding here. But before that, when you were with us, bad things kept happening, and people did get hurt. They have an awesome place for you in Oklahoma City." Bobby tilted his head back toward Peter and Robert. "They showed it to me yesterday. It's nice, but still I'm afraid of what could happen before we get there. Promise me you won't do anything that will hurt people, okay?"

Just briefly, the thing's eyes—Addison's eyes—again changed from blue to fiery gold. "I can promise you that I won't do anything that will hurt people. However, it is not possible to predict what might happen when I am with you and with others of your kind, as you are unpredictable. Therefore it is possible I would break my promise to you."

Bobby stared at the thing's eyes. "Then it's not really a promise, is it?"

It gazed back at him without answering.

Bobby wasn't ready to give up. "It will take two hours to get to Peter's building in Oklahoma City. Then maybe another hour to get you situated in the room they have ready for you. And then we'll leave you alone to do what you feel you should do. Just like you've been doing while you've been hiding here. Please promise me that in the next three hours you won't hurt anyone—even if someone asks you to."

The thing smiled slightly. "I understand."

It looked like that was the best Bobby was going to get. He was about to agree with Robert that they should go, but he thought of one more thing. "The van is right outside, but Addison's face is even more famous than any of ours. Can you look like someone else, at least until we get into the van?"

"Yes," it replied. It stood still with its arms at its sides. Seconds later its features softened and began to shift. Light skin became darker, bones shifted, and clothing dissolved. After several minutes, the transformation was complete.

The room remained quiet. Before them stood a nearly naked Papuan tribesman, wearing nothing more than a penis gourd and several cords around his neck, strung with stone beads, black beetle carapaces, and small bones.

"This is the body of Miok," it said. Its voice had the lyrical sound that Bobby remembered from the men of Sinanie's tribe, almost like singing.

Ashley said, "I remember Miok, but that's not going to work."

"I agree," Peter said.

Again Bobby thought the thing was smiling just slightly. Another joke? If so, its sense of humor might need some work in terms of delivery.

Miok said, "I can make myself appear to be objects and living things I have encountered. I have encountered Miok and the others of his tribe. I have encountered you, Peter. And you, Bobby. And I have encountered you, Ashley, as I am sure you remember. I have also encountered Miranda, Carlos, Quentin, and Lindsey." He turned to Robert. "I have not yet encountered you, Robert."

"No, I suppose not," Robert said.

Ashley said, "You've definitely encountered Miranda. You helped kill her. Why don't you change yourself to her?"

Bobby turned to look at Ashley, but she didn't take her eyes off Miok. He knew her well enough to sense that her anger was about to get out of hand if he didn't step in. "That's probably a good idea," he said. "Miranda wasn't on TV with the rest of us."

The Lamotelokhai nodded. Again it stood with its hands at its sides, and its features began shifting into something else. Several minutes later, Miranda stood before them. Her hair was a mess. Her skin was dark from mud and dried blood. Filthy scraps of jeans and t-shirts were crudely knotted together and arranged so they barely covered her chest and groin. It was Miranda in the same condition as when Addison had used the power of the Lamotelokhai to kill her.

"Jesus Christ!" Ashley blurted out, her voice choking. She turned away and faced the wall. "Bobby, please make it get this one goddamn thing right."

Ashley's pain cut into Bobby like a spear to his chest. He looked at the Lamotelokhai, but the sight was so disturbing that he had to swallow a few times before speaking. "Miranda was her best friend. I don't think she expected her to look this way. Maybe you could—"

"Perhaps we are overthinking this," Peter interrupted. "The van is ten meters from the door." He pointed to Robert. "You're wearing an undershirt. Can we please borrow your shirt?"

Robert quickly unbuttoned his green and white plaid shirt and handed it over.

Peter gave it to the Lamotelokhai. "Do you know how to put this on?"

Without answering, Miranda put on the shirt. Peter then gently asked Ashley for her hat. She plucked it from her head and threw it at him. He placed it on Miranda's head and stood back. "Good enough, I should think."

Ashley, Peter, and Robert went out to the van. Ashley came back in, followed by Peter.

Bobby looked at the Miranda copy and motioned to the door. "Remember, please be careful."

Miranda smiled at him and led the way out the door. Bobby followed and squinted in the morning sunlight. The same three cars were still in the parking lot. He could see the woman's head behind the counter in the office. It looked like she was watching them, but he couldn't tell for sure. They got in the van, and Miranda sat in the seat facing Bobby. Seconds later, Peter and

Ashley came out. Ashley got in, and Peter went to the office to return the key.

They watched Peter through the window for a moment, and then the Lamotelokhai said, "Ashley and Bobby, I am interested to hear about the status of your relationship."

Bobby stared at the copy of Miranda. He didn't look at Ashley, but he could tell she was doing the same thing.

"What are you talking about?" Ashley demanded.

"I have learned much about your kind during the time I was in that room. Some of what I have learned allows me to consider from a new perspective your behaviors I observed when we were together before. When I consider your previous behaviors, I am able to surmise that you, Bobby, had romantic inclinations toward Ashley. And you, Ashley, had romantic inclinations toward Bobby. And now, as I observe you again, I surmise the same inclinations. It is clear from many of the artistic creations of your kind, such as novels, songs, and movies, that many of you are interested in the status of the romantic relationships of others. And so I am interested to hear about the status of your relationship."

"I don't want you to be Miranda," Ashley suddenly said. She was glaring at the Lamotelokhai. "I wasn't even serious when I suggested it before. Please turn into someone else."

Without saying a word, the thing handed Ashley her hat, removed Robert's shirt, and began transforming right there in the seat. It was happening so close that Bobby instinctively tried backing away, but all he could do was push himself deeper into the leather seat.

Suddenly the van's door slid open.

"Bloody hell," Peter said when he saw the transforming mass. He seemed to gather his wits quickly, though. He got in and sat in the only open seat, beside the Lamotelokhai. As Peter pulled the door shut, Bobby saw that the lady in the office was standing closer to the front window now. She was definitely watching them.

When the transformation was complete, the thing was Addison again, complete with t-shirt, shorts, and flip-flops. It gazed at Ashley for a moment, and then at Bobby, but it remained silent.

Peter pressed the intercom button. "Robert, let's take our passenger to its new home, shall we?"

The van backed up and pulled out onto the road, headed north toward the bridge and Oklahoma City.

Seconds later, Bobby saw the blurred shape of a white car careening around them from behind.

"What the hell?"

Bobby had heard Robert's yell without the help of the intercom. The van screeched to a stop, nearly throwing Bobby and Ashley into the laps of Peter and Addison.

"Mr. Wooley!" Robert's voice came through the intercom this time. "Some woman just blew past us and then crashed into the truss of the bridge ahead. She's out of her car and walking this way. She appears to be hurt."

Bobby's heart felt like it was in his throat. He looked at the Lamotelokhai. The thing just looked back at him with no expression. Next to it, Peter rubbed his chin like he was thinking. Then he let out a nervous, frustrated growl.

"Please remain exactly where you are," he said to all of them. He then got out and slid the door most of the way shut behind him.

"Please help me!" It was a woman's voice.

"Good lord, ma'am, you're injured," Peter said. "We'll call an ambulance."

"No! My husband—he'll kill me!"

"I'm sure he'll understand," Peter said. "I'll call—"

"No! You don't understand—he's going to kill me. He's coming after me now! I can't wait here for an ambulance. Please, I need a ride. Anywhere. Anywhere but here! Please!"

There was a pause. Bobby couldn't see them, but he imagined Peter was rubbing his chin again.

"Alright, come with me," Peter said.

The door slid open. Peter held out his hand, and the woman stepped into view. Her face was covered in blood. She wore a pretty blue dress with little yellow stars all over it and blood running down the front.

"You can have my seat," Bobby said, and he quickly moved and sat in Peter's seat next to the Lamotelkhai.

She climbed in. "Thank you. I'm so sorry." After sitting down she wiped her face and stared at the blood on her hand.

Peter got in, closed the door, and kneeled on the floor next to Bobby's seat. He said, "Bobby, press the com button." After Bobby pressed it, he said, "Drive north, Robert. I'll locate a hospital." He looked at the woman as he dug out his smartphone. "Try to relax. We'll get you somewhere safe."

Bobby couldn't help staring at the poor woman. She moved her right hand from her side into her lap. There was something in her hand. It was silver, the size and shape of a water bottle. But it wasn't a water bottle.

The van started picking up speed, but then it abruptly stopped. Bobby heard Robert's muffled voice. He was talking to someone.

Suddenly there was an explosion right next to the van, like a firecracker or a gunshot.

"Robert?" Peter shouted.

Bobby reached for the intercom button, but then he saw the woman's hand move again. She had pulled the silver cylinder closer to her belly. Then her finger moved against the object. There was a harsh hissing sound, like air leaking from a punctured tire.

Bobby looked up at the woman's bloody face. She was staring right at him. But then her eyes closed and her head dropped, as if she had abruptly fallen asleep.

Suddenly, Bobby realized what was happening, sensing that he too was falling asleep, but he was out before he could warn anyone.

Bobby heard voices, as well as the clicking and whirring of electronics. The voices washed over him and then receded, and then washed over him again. Finally, they became louder and did not fade away.

He opened his eyes, and the voices stopped. He felt like he had been asleep for a long time. He stared at a ceiling that looked to be concrete painted white. A man's face appeared above him.

"Bobby Truex, it is a pleasure to have you with us. I imagine you would prefer to sit up." The man did something with his foot, and a motor slowly cranked the bed into a sitting position.

Bobby then saw that the walls were just like the ceiling—white concrete. Medical equipment was arranged around the bed, and there were more people there—two men and a woman—sitting in chairs and monitoring computer screens. The man standing next to Bobby was older than the others. He had short black hair and a mostly-gray beard. He wore glasses with red plastic frames—the kind younger people usually wore. All four of them wore pale green doctor-type shirts and pants.

"Where am I?" Bobby said.

The man beside him held up a finger. "Hold on a moment." He turned to one of the men. "Ready to test it?"

"Yes, sir," the man replied.

He turned back to Bobby. "Bobby, could you please repeat your question?"

"Where am—"

Everything went black.

Bobby opened his eyes. He sensed he had been asleep again, but only briefly this time.

The man with red glasses was still beside him. He was frowning. He held up a finger just as he had done before. Again he turned to the younger man. "Drop the delay by point five seconds, and drop sensitivity to 200 millijoules."

The man at the computer typed for a moment and then nodded.

"Okay then," said the man beside Bobby. "Could you please ask your question again?"

Bobby stared at him for a moment. He then opened his mouth to speak. "Whe—"

Everything went black.

He opened his eyes, again feeling he had been asleep only a short time.

The man beside him was gazing at Bobby's face as if observing a fish in an aquarium. "Seems to be working. Don't become distressed, Bobby. We have tried to make it as painless as possible. But we can't have you just saying whatever you wish when we reunite you with your extraordinary friend, can we?"

CHAPTER FOUR

Quentin gazed at the endless expanse of dense tropical forest 2,000 feet below. The de Havilland Twin Otter cruised at 170 miles per hour, so from takeoff to touchdown the flight to the village of Navera would be only thirty minutes. This made it all too easy to forget the impenetrable nature of this wilderness. Entire expeditions had disappeared attempting to traverse the region on foot.

Addison was down there somewhere. Somehow he had survived eight months, in spite of having his memory wiped clean and being left alone to die. Quentin tapped a rapid beat against his leg with his raccoon baculum. He glanced at Lindsey. They were the only passengers, and she had moved to the far side of the cabin to look out her own window. If it had been solely her decision, she probably wouldn't have left the jungle without Addison all those months ago. She would have stayed, searching for him until she was hopelessly lost. And so Quentin had convinced her to leave. There were valid reasons why leaving had been the logical choice. Three of the other students had survived the plane crash, and Quentin and Lindsey had needed to get them home safely. And they'd felt an obligation to bring the Lamotelokhai, the most significant discovery of all time, to civilization. Perhaps most importantly, Addison had been mortally injured in the plane crash. The Lamotelokhai had kept him alive, but Addison was no longer their son after that. He had become a murderous monster. But still, Quentin was sure Lindsey would've stayed and that his decision to leave would always be a wedge between them, even if they never spoke of it.

Now they had learned that not only was Addison alive, but he apparently had some memory of his past life. Quentin not only had a chance to save his son, but also to redeem himself.

The satellite phone chirped loudly, heard even over the roar of the Twin Otter's engines. Lindsey had been holding the phone in her lap and quickly answered it.

"Ardell, please tell me you found them."

Seconds later her features hardened. Quentin muttered a curse. Ardell had clearly not called with good news. He turned back to his window. The trees below were now closer. They were approaching the village.

"What? Oh my God!"

Quentin whipped around.

"It was empty? Where the hell did they go? Did you check the hospitals?"

"What's going on?" Quentin said.

She ignored him, listening instead to Ardell. "Jesus, this can't be happening." There was a long pause. "Okay. Well, we'll have the SAT phone, but we're landing soon. Thank you, Ardell." She lowered the phone into her lap.

Quentin waited.

"They found Peter's van. In the middle of the street. Near the motel."

"In the middle of the street?"

"And there was blood. In the driver seat and one of the passenger seats."

Quentin inhaled sharply. He realized his clenched fist was about to break the baculum, so he shoved the bone into his pocket. In recent months he had almost allowed himself to forget what terror felt like, but now he settled uncomfortably into it like an old habit. And it sharpened his focus.

"Lindsey." He waited for her eyes to lock onto his. "It's beyond our control. They're going to be okay. For them, shedding a little blood isn't as dangerous as it used to be. They've made it through far worse."

Her eyes were narrow and she shook her head slightly. But then her features relaxed. She took a deep breath. "Damn right they have."

Quentin nodded. "We'll do what we came here to do. We'll find Addison and take him home. And then we'll deal with this other problem." Quentin waited for her to respond, silently pleading for her to prop up his precarious resolve.

As if she sensed this, she gave him a confident nod. "We came here to find Addison."

FROM THE AIR, the landing strip looked even shorter than Quentin remembered. He gripped the seatback in front of him with white knuckles as the Twin Otter cleared the treetops at the forest's edge and then dropped abruptly into the clearing. The wheels hit the ground, and seconds later the plane bounced to a stop twenty yards from a small crowd of waiting villagers. Wasting no time, the two pilots walked through the bulkhead from the cockpit to the cabin and then lowered the hatch, which had stairs molded to the inside of it. The two backpacks were all Quentin and Lindsey had. They grabbed these out of the seats and descended to the grass and dirt airstrip.

Without speaking a word to them, the pilots secured the hatch, and then the plane revved up. When Quentin and Lindsey were barely clear of the plane's tail, it heaved forward and turned, facing the far end of the runway. It then throttled up to a deafening volume, tore down the runway, and at the last minute lifted to clear the treetops. This capability was what made Twin Otters ideal jungle planes.

Familiar Papuan faces abruptly surrounded them. Quentin and the other survivors had stayed one night in Navera on their trek out of the wilderness eight months ago, and the villagers were apparently as happy to have visitors now as they had been then.

The villagers displayed an odd mix of traditional and modern clothing and adornments. Some of the men sported penis gourds, and some of the women were bare-breasted, but just as many wore shorts and t-shirts. There seemed to be almost as many children as adults, and most of the children were naked. Several of the Papuans stepped forward and guided their guests to the simple shelter at the center of the smattering of thatch-roofed huts. The tribe spoke their own dialect that Quentin suspected was derived from the more widely used language of the Dani people.

Conspicuously missing was Obert, who had used his radio to help them call for help eight months ago, and who was apparently the only member of the village who spoke English. And Samuel was nowhere to be seen. He had told them when he'd called three days ago that he would wait here at the village for them to arrive. When asked where Samuel and Obert were, the villagers pointed to the forest beyond the huts.

As they waited, the villagers brought out fresh cucumbers, cooked red fruit wrapped in banana leaves, and some heavily-spiced sago cakes, made from the sago palm. Quentin and Lindsey sat on low benches beneath the shelter, eating the offerings and listening politely to the villagers, who were perhaps explaining events that had occurred since the last time they had seen them.

"You Yanks look a far cry better now than when you stumbled out of the bush some months back."

Quentin recognized the heavily accented, jovial voice of Obert before he even turned to see him. Obert approached them, looking very much the same, wearing shorts and a well-used t-shirt with a faded image of a stick figure in a hammock and the words, *No Worries, Mate!*

Beside Obert was a white man with a thick black beard. The beard was new, but there was only one man Quentin knew who wore a skin loincloth and a vest made from spider silk.

"Samuel!" Lindsey got up and rushed forward. "I almost didn't recognize you." She hugged him, which seemed to alarm him at first. He awkwardly patted her back until she released him. She then gave Obert a light hug. "Thank you. We wouldn't be here if you hadn't agreed to safeguard the satellite phone and keep it charged."

"Sorry I wasn't here for the landing," Obert said. "I heard the plane approaching and went to fetch your mate, Samuel. He's been hunkering down in the bush rather than here in the village." He hooked a thumb at Samuel. "Bit of a wild man, this one is."

"Wonderful to see you again, Samuel," Quentin said. "And you too, Obert." He decided against hugs and extended a hand. They both shook it firmly.

Samuel appraised both of them before speaking. "Three days heretofore, I spoke to you with the help of a most astounding contrivance, as if you were just beside me. And now, after a mere three days, you stand before me, having traveled from the northern continent of America. When circumstances allow it, I insist that you expound on how this is possible."

Quentin exchanged a glance with Lindsey, and then they both laughed.

"We'll do our best," Quentin said.

Quentin, Lindsey, and Samuel left the village of Navera an hour later. They had removed half the contents of each of the packs and given the items to Obert and the other villagers. It was mostly expensive gadgets they probably wouldn't need, but the villagers could use them. In return, the villagers had stuffed the packs with fruits and sago cakes, which would make the journey easier.

As soon as they were out of sight of the village, Lindsey turned to Samuel. "Please tell us everything you can about Addison."

Samuel gave her a brief quizzical look. "I fear that my knowledge of him will leave you wanting. I know little more than what I have already told you. Addison came recently to the hanging village of my indigene hosts. The villagers' first inclination was to kill him and destroy his body so that it could not be resurrected. I determined, however, that he held no murderous intentions, and I endeavored to convince the villagers to spare him."

"How did he look?" Lindsey asked. "Did he seem healthy?"

Samuel continued walking, apparently considering this. "As it does for you and I, the medicine of the Lamotelokhai sustains him." He then stopped and turned to them. "I feel I am obliged to remind you of your son's transformation—the transformation that you witnessed yourself when fateful events brought you to the village of my indigene hosts. Your son was distinctively suited to communicating with the Lamotelokhai, and without regard to consequences, he invoked taboo by making a request for *lu gamo*. This means to ascend and become strong. You and I, and the villagers as well, have all become improved with the Lamotelokhai's help. However, when requesting lu gamo, one becomes *very* improved. You witnessed this transformation in your son." Samuel looked to the trees in the direction they had been walking. "The transformation is apparently permanent."

Quentin glanced at Lindsey, but she wouldn't look at him,

fixating instead on Samuel. "He's still Addison, though, right? You said he asked about us—about his parents."

"Yes, he seems to remember you. There is certainly cause for hope. However, I wanted you to know what you should expect if we find him."

"*If* we find him?" Lindsey said. "You think there's a chance we won't find him at all?"

"Addison came to the hanging village, accompanied by the mbolop you call Mbaiso. That is when I prevented the villagers from killing him." Samuel paused for a moment. "His ability to express himself in words was, well, rudimentary. However, he was able to inquire about you, his parents. He was determined to show something to me, so I followed him. We traveled south for nearly half a day. What I found there was astounding, to put it mildly. A colony of mbolop, hundreds of them, living in hanging chambers similar to those of my indigene hosts. I attempted to convince Addison to travel with me to the village of our friend, Obert. Addison did not understand my words, or he simply was not inclined to do this. A few days after that I went back to the mbolop colony, but I was unable to find him. That is when I determined to travel to Obert's village without him, with hopes that I could somehow get a message to you. Now here you are."

Quentin considered this. He and Lindsey had lived for months in silent anguish, rarely speaking of the nearly impossible chance that Addison might still be alive. Samuel's brief call on the SAT phone had sparked a fierce—but perhaps blind—determination in both of them to come here, get Addison, and take him home. It hadn't occurred to Quentin that they might not even find him, or that Addison might be unwilling to go with them or incapable of understanding.

"We'll take it one obstacle at a time," Lindsey said. "First we have to find him. I assume we'll be going to this colony of tree kangaroos?"

Samuel started walking again. "Indeed. Three days of laborious traveling are upon us, I'm afraid."

A few hundred yards further into the forest they came upon Samuel's camp, which was little more than a sleeping shelter constructed from poles and rigid sago fronds. Standing beside the shelter, as if he had been patiently waiting for them, was Sinanie. Quentin immediately recognized him, although Sinanie now had several new cords strung with ornaments around his neck, and he no longer had white paint around his eyes. But he still wore his short penis gourd etched with Kembalimo symbols, as well as green lorikeet feathers in his hair, perhaps thirty of them sticking out in random directions. He smiled at them as they approached, flashing perfect teeth.

"It is good to see you are well, Sinanie," Quentin said, although he was aware Sinanie spoke little English. After having taken the Lamotelokhai from them, Quentin had often wondered what would happen to the villagers' health.

Samuel apparently understood what Quentin was actually thinking. "To be honest, without the Lamotelokhai's presence, I feared for my own condition as well, although the indigenes are very much older than I. But as you can see, the Lamotelokhai's benefits have not abandoned us."

Sinanie said, "Lindsey, Quentin, *gu laléo lai-ati-bo-dakhu lelé-mbol-e-kho-lo?*"

"He wishes to know if you are coming back here as a spirit," Samuel said. "I believe he is asking if you are in good health, or if you have died since he last saw you."

Quentin exchanged a glance with Lindsey. The fact of the matter was that they *had* died since they had last seen Sinanie. Their entire group had been disintegrated in a violent jetliner crash.

"Tell him we do not come as spirits," Lindsey said. "We are in good health, and we are happy to see him, too."

Samuel spoke to Sinanie in the Papuan's language. Sinanie then smiled at them again. Quentin was tempted to shake his hand or embrace him but suspected these gestures would only baffle him.

Sinanie opened a small skin pouch that hung from his neck, a pouch in which previously he had carried a supply of clay from the Lamotelokhai. He held the pouch out so they could see its contents.

"Quentin, *nu if-e-kha misafi gup-tekhé fédo-p.*" He then shoved the pouch toward Quentin.

"He wishes to give one of them to you," Samuel said. "As you take one, be careful to not touch the other."

Quentin plucked one of the two objects from the pouch. He recognized it immediately, a stone talisman, intricately carved to resemble a tree kangaroo—an mbolop. Matiinuo, the elder member of Sinanie's tribe, had once given the same stone to Peter Wooley. Peter had lost it, and then Quentin had found it over forty years later, only to lose it again.

Quentin hefted the stone. "This thing refuses to stay lost."

"Sinanie accompanied me when I returned to the place that your son Addison had shown me. He has seen what is happening there, and he now believes the talisman to be more important than ever before. Having seen the place with my own eyes, I am inclined to agree.

Sinanie held the pouch out to Lindsey. She took the other talisman. Quentin didn't have to look at it closely to know it was identical to his own. Eight months ago Samuel had duplicated the talisman in a fantastical demonstration of the Lamotelokhai's ability to shift time. Sinanie must have found both of the figurines in or near Samuel's tree house, which was the last place Quentin had seen them.

Quentin pocketed his copy of the talisman. "We're ready to go if you are." He then helped Lindsey adjust her pack to better fit her shoulders. Samuel kicked over the temporary shelter and scattered the sago fronds, leaving little evidence that the spot had been occupied for three days.

Just as they started hiking south, a movement in a tree above caught Quentin's eye. It was a tree kangaroo.

"Is that Mbaiso?" he asked.

Samuel looked up. "The mbolop you call Mbaiso was otherwise occupied. This is another I recruited to accompany us and help with collecting food. If you wish to call it by a specific name, you will have to create one, as I have never been inclined to do such things."

CHAPTER FIVE

Bobby's head hurt, especially behind his ears. He wanted to touch his scalp and feel for a wound, but his arms were restrained. And so were his legs. It seemed like hours since the man with red glasses had left the room, and Bobby hadn't been allowed to get up. The three doctors—or whatever they were—continued working with their computers, talking to each other about technical stuff and occasionally asking Bobby to do things that didn't make sense. To speak a certain word, for example, or to think about something that made him mad. Every time he tried to say something they hadn't asked him to say, he would black out. Then he would wake up, and the process would continue. He was scared, and it was taking all his willpower to hold back tears.

Now he had to pee and take a crap, and if they didn't let him up soon he would have to do both right here on the bed.

Finally, the windowless metal door opened, and the man with red glasses stepped in. He asked the others how things were going, and they all answered by nodding. He gazed into Bobby's eyes.

"I would like to speak to this young man," he said.

One of the doctors typed something on his keyboard and then said, "Go ahead, sir."

Bobby felt a sharp pulse behind both his ears.

The man said, "How are you feeling?" When Bobby didn't answer, he said, "You may speak freely now."

Still, Bobby was afraid to speak. He cleared his throat, but nothing happened. "Where am I?"

"You are in a research facility. A rather remarkable one, actually. My name is Hugo Helmich. You can call me Dr. Helmich. Or just Hugo, if you prefer." He spoke like he was an enthusiastic tour guide.

"Where's Hattie?"

"We know her real name is Ashley. No need to pretend."

"Where is she? And where are Peter and Robert?"

Helmich smiled. "They are here. Ashley and Peter are perfectly fine. Robert, unfortunately, is recovering from a gunshot wound. We have hopes that he will recover fully." He pushed his glasses further up on his nose and smiled again.

Bobby closed his eyes and swallowed. He couldn't wait any longer. "I have to go to the bathroom. Right now."

"I am not surprised," Helmich said. He began undoing the restraints on Bobby's legs and nodded to the woman doctor. She got up and left the room. She came back in immediately, pulling behind her a strange toilet on wheels. She shut the door and parked the toilet next to the wall. Helmich finished releasing Bobby's legs and started on his arm restraints.

"The floor here is very hard," Helmich said, with a look of real concern on his face. "If you do something unexpected, you will of course be rendered unconscious, resulting in a head injury when you fall. That would not be good for you or for us." He finished the last strap, stepped back, and held one hand out toward the toilet.

Bobby stared at it. "You expect me to go in front of all of you? I have to take a crap."

Helmich didn't move. "Do you like films, Bobby? Motion pictures, I mean. Movies."

Bobby frowned at him. The question made no sense, and he had to go so bad it hurt.

Helmich lowered his hand. "*Hollow Man*, with Kevin Bacon. Bacon's character develops a way to become invisible. An intriguing idea. Even more intriguing, he finds that he is willing to do many things while invisible that he would never have done otherwise. Interesting concept, don't you think?"

Again Bobby just frowned at him.

"I suggest you imagine yourself to be invisible," Helmich said.

Bobby wasn't happy with this response, but he couldn't wait any longer. He got out of the bed and then wobbled on his feet for a moment. He realized for the first time that he was wearing a green shirt and pants, just like those the doctors were wearing. The only things he had on that were actually his were his shoes. He walked to the toilet and turned around. All four of them were watching him. Probably at least one of them was ready to press a button that would knock him out. He closed his eyes, pulled his green elastic pants to his knees, sat on the mobile toilet, and did what he had to do.

As soon as he stood up, the woman wheeled the toilet out of the room and shut the door with a clang.

Helmich said, "Perhaps you would like to stand for a bit, stretch your legs. You have something important to do today. Need to be in tiptop condition."

Bobby paced the floor. His head still hurt, so he rubbed his scalp. Both sides of his head were shaved bald around his ears. He moved his hands backward. Behind each ear was something solid. They were small boxes, a few inches across, made of hard plastic or metal. He pulled on one of them. It wouldn't budge. It was actually attached to his skull. He pulled harder, and this made him wince from the pain.

"What are these?" he said. His voice cracked a little, and again he fought to hold back tears.

Helmich spoke calmly. "Wireless receivers, solid state lithium-ion batteries, neurostimulators, implanted electrodes." He shook his head. "You don't really want details, do you?"

"I can't pull them off. Why won't they come off?"

"They're well-anchored. But you could certainly hurt yourself if you try too hard. Again, that would not be good for you or for us."

Bobby looked at his hands. His trembling fingers now had blood on the tips. "I want to go home now."

Helmich approached him and put a hand on his shoulder. "And we would like to send you home, Bobby. But first we have some very important things to do. Will you help us out so you can go home?"

Bobby looked at him. He wanted to believe him. But there was nothing about this situation that suggested he would ever be allowed to leave this place.

"What do you want me to do?"

"Well, you can begin by telling me exactly what you would say if you were to ask your friend, the Lamotelokhai, to do something for you."

Bobby was back in the bed, his arms and legs secured. For at least an hour Helmich had told him to explain again and again how he would ask the Lamotelokhai to do different things. It wasn't like there was a trick to it. Bobby would just ask, and the Lamotelokhai would do what he asked. But asking it to do things was dangerous, which he had tried explaining to Helmich. Bobby had asked the Lamotelokhai to do something to help them at the hospital in Jaya-pura, and it had created rampaging dinosaurs that killed at least seven people. And that was just one example. Helmich had seemed fascinated by these stories, but Bobby doubted he really understood. No one did.

Finally, Helmich had stopped asking questions. Now he sat next to the bed, reviewing the video he had taken of Bobby's answers. He had just heard Bobby say these things, and now he was watching it all again. Bobby couldn't imagine his answers were that interesting.

The door burst open, startling them both. A woman Bobby hadn't seen before stepped in and said, "We're ready just outside, sir." She then retreated.

Helmich went to one of the other doctors and whispered to him. The man nodded and started typing on his keyboard.

Helmich came back to Bobby's side. "I'm afraid we need to ask you to not speak for a little while again. And you know how that works, don't you?"

Bobby felt a pulse behind his ears as the devices on his head were switched back on. He nodded to Helmich, afraid to make any sound with his mouth.

"We would like to reunite you with your friends. So that you will know we are taking good care of them. Does that sound nice to you?"

Bobby nodded.

The woman came back into the room, this time pulling a rolling bed. Lying in the bed was Robert. Bobby hardly recognized him because his neck and one side of his face were covered with bandages. He seemed to be barely conscious, his eyes half open.

The woman waited for a moment, then left the room and came back pulling another bed. Peter was sitting up on the bed. He looked around the room, and his eyes met Bobby's.

"Good Lord, what have they done to you?" He pulled at his restraints, but they held him to the bed. He turned to Helmich. "You wanking idiot! You have no idea what you're doing. If you think my people don't know where we are, you're delusional. They're probably on their way now."

Helmich ignored this. He looked at the doctor he'd whispered to. The doctor nodded.

The woman parked Peter's bed beside Robert's. She left and returned with a third bed. Sitting on this one was Ashley, her eyes wide with fear. When she saw Bobby her fear transformed into rage.

"You assholes, who do you think you are?" She yanked at her restraints. She then let out a fierce, piercing scream.

Even Helmich seemed startled by this. He looked at her with his mouth open.

"She's the one," the doctor at the computer said.

Helmich eyed him. "You're sure?"

The doctor glanced at Ashley, who was now glaring at them. "It's not even close."

Robert was then wheeled out of the room, and the woman returned and began wheeling Peter's bed out.

As he passed through the door, Peter cried out, "Bobby, try to hold it together. We'll get out of here, and they'll pay—"

The door slammed, cutting him off.

Helmich gazed at the closed door. "That is an optimistic man." He turned back around. "But honestly, if you folks simply cooperate, you will have nothing to fear." He looked at Ashley. "Ashley Stoddard. It seems you are the winner. Bobby's cognitive activity indicates he is very emotional when you are near him. Did you know that?"

"My name is Hattie Grayson," she said. "That's Wyatt. He's my brother. You've kidnapped the wrong people. Don't you feds ever get anything right?"

"Feds." Helmich said this like he was thinking about what it meant. He smiled. "Do you like films, Ashley? Motion pictures?"

She glared at him without answering.

He went on. "Consider Tarzan films. Do you know what Jane's purpose is in every Tarzan film that has been produced?" He didn't wait for an answer. "Jane is there because Tarzan loves her. He will always endeavor to rescue her. Perhaps Margot Robbie's Jane in *The Legend of Tarzan* stated it best: 'An ordinary man will do impossible things to save the woman he loves.'"

Ashley's glare began to give way, and Bobby knew she was afraid.

"Your name is not Hattie," Helmich said. "We all know who you are, Ashley. But perhaps we should call you Jane."

Helmich waved his hand at the doctors, and one of them carried some kind of headset over to Ashley's bed. The other two doctors followed him. When he tried to put the device on Ashley's head, she pulled away. The other two then held her still. She squirmed and cried out. She even spat at them.

Bobby instinctively pulled at his restraints. Everything went black.

He opened his eyes. The device was now on Ashley's head. The woman doctor was wiping away a trickle of blood that had run down Ashley's temple.

"You'll be fine," the woman said. "Just hold still so it won't tear your skin."

"What is this?" Ashley said. The fierceness was gone from her voice. "What are you going to do?"

The woman patted her shoulder and then returned to her computer.

Bobby's eyes met Ashley's. She was terrified, and there was nothing he could do. He couldn't even speak to her.

Helmich moved a stool to the side of Bobby's bed and sat. "Time may be of the essence. We will begin immediately. Bobby, I am an advocate of showing, rather than explaining. Very soon you will know exactly what it is that we need you to do." He held up a digital tablet. "Based upon what you have told us, these words represent what you would say to the Lamotelokhai in order to request something. Please say these words aloud, exactly as they are written."

Bobby looked from Helmich to Ashley and back. He had no choice, so he read the words.

"Addison, I need your help. Please just do what I ask, okay? I will explain later. I need for you to divide yourself into ten smaller but equal portions. Can you do that?"

Helmich smiled at him. "Very good." He put the tablet down so Bobby couldn't see it. "Now, please say it again."

Bobby brought up a perfect image of the tablet and repeated every word.

Helmich blinked at him. "Impressive short-term memory. Well, let's take a different approach. Repeat the sentences again, but change one or more of the words."

Bobby didn't like where this was going. "Addison, I don't need—"

Everything went black.

Bobby awoke to the sound of crying. It was Ashley. She was sobbing and trembling.

"You assholes!" she cried. "That hurt!"

Bobby was enraged. "You f—"

His world turned black.

This time he awoke to desperate screaming.

"Stop! Stop it, please!" Ashley's back was arched and she was thrashing her head back and forth, trying to dislodge the headset.

Bobby wanted to break his restraints and trash everything in the room. He wanted to kill Helmich and the other doctors. But he couldn't move, and he couldn't speak. Instead, all he could do was stare at Helmich, his gut wrenching tight and his heart beating so hard he felt it in his ears.

Helmich leaned closer to Bobby. He spoke over Ashley's cries. "Quite astounding, isn't it? It's all automated. A fraction of a second after you say or do anything we have not asked you to..." He nodded toward Ashley.

Bobby felt cool streaks on his burning cheek as his tears began to evaporate. He closed his eyes so he wouldn't have to look at Helmich's smirking face.

"Now that you understand," Helmich said, "it is time to move on from learning to doing."

CHAPTER SIX

QUENTIN HELPED Samuel fasten the last sago fronds to the frame of their crude shelter by tying them with stringy fibers of sapling bark that Sinanie called *khol*. An afternoon rain had already drenched them, so the shelter's purpose at this point would simply be to prevent rain from pelting them as they slept.

In spite of having bodies enhanced by alien technology, Quentin and Lindsey were worn out from the first day of hiking. Quentin let out a groan as he folded himself into the shelter and sat next to her. She was holding two grapefruit-sized stuff sacks and handed one to him.

"I'm not inflating both of them," she said.

Quentin opened his sack and pulled out a tightly-rolled sleeping mat. Judging by its paper-thin fabric and negligible weight, it was a top-of-the-line product. At one end, surrounding a one-way valve, was a thickened pad that served as a hand pump. Following Lindsey's lead, he twisted open the valve and started pumping.

Samuel and Sinanie tucked themselves into the shelter. Sinanie glanced briefly at the slowly-expanding mats and then turned his attention to a raw spot on one of his feet. Samuel, on the other hand, seemed fascinated by the inflating mats.

"We're not as accustomed to sleeping on the ground as you two are," Quentin said. "Unfortunately, we only have two of these,"

Samuel caressed the shimmering green material. "That is remarkable. There was a time long ago in which simple comforts were much more important to me. I fear that I have gradually descended into a rather savage state."

Quentin noticed Sinanie shoving some leaves into his mouth. After chewing them briefly, he pulled the wad of pulp from his mouth and spread it over the abrasion on the side of his foot. Quentin felt a pang of guilt. If he hadn't taken the Lamotelokhai from the village, Sinanie could have simply spread some of its clay on his wound, and it would have healed in a few hours.

"The indigenes have reverted to many of their old healing practices," Samuel said, apparently perceiving what was on Quentin's mind. "They are generally healthy, however they no longer have the means to heal deadly wounds, or to restore to life their companions who have recently died. If warriors from another tribe were to attack the village, the results could be grievous. Only thirteen of them remain at this time."

Lindsey said, "My god, only thirteen?"

Quentin stared at Sinanie and felt cold inside. Addison had killed half of Sinanie's tribe. Quentin had to remind himself that during the last eight months the Lamotelokhai had provided humanity with effective cures to several devastating diseases, including AIDS and diabetes. Far more lives had been saved than had been lost.

"Samuel," Quentin said, "can you tell Sinanie we are sorry, and we did not mean to do his tribe any harm?"

Samuel spoke to the Papuan, although he hesitated a number of times as if he did not have full mastery of the language.

Sinanie finished spreading the chewed leaves on his wound and then blew on it as if helping it to dry. He looked at them and spoke. "*Gu finop. N-mom-él nggé khil Lamotelokhai-alingga. Nokhu nggul-lekhé nokhu khokhün nokhu-amo-ba-lé laibo. Õkhu khatakh.*"

Samuel considered Sinanie's words for a moment. "He says that you, Quentin, are a compassionate man. His uncles and friends, meaning his tribe, are healthy, even without the Lamotelokhai. But they are discontented because they have abandoned their purpose—the purpose for which they were born. And thus they are ashamed."

Quentin looked at Lindsey and then at Sinanie. "Their purpose? You mean to hide and protect the Lamotelokhai?"

Samuel hesitated and then exchanged a few words with Sinanie. "That is correct, but there is more to consider than only that. Sinanie is referring to something he has not discussed with me in a long time. I am unsure that I can adequately describe it, as the very concept of it bewilders my thoughts. He told me long ago that the Lamotelokhai has placed a measured portion of its knowledge into the mind of each of the members of his tribe. When I asked what this knowledge was, he replied that he did not know, only that the knowledge was quite extensive. How one can have knowledge in his mind without understanding the nature of the knowledge remains a mystery to me."

Lindsey spoke up. "Sinanie believes that the main purpose of his life is to have some of the Lamotelokhai's knowledge in his mind?"

"The indigenes have told me that their tribe was *wakhatum* for the Lamotelokhai. Wakhatum refers to stories or knowledge, in this case referring to those who keep the knowledge. The tribe has traditionally had no more than thirty members because each member was given a portion of the knowledge. Thirty is approximately the number needed to carry the knowledge of the Lamotelokhai."

Quentin and Lindsey exchanged another glance, this time a grimmer one.

Lindsey said it first. "And Addison killed half of them."

"Addison killed sixteen villagers, including twelve men and four women. There were thirteen who survived, only half the number needed to carry the Lamotelokhai's knowledge."

"And so they believe they have abandoned their purpose," Quentin said.

Samuel nodded silently.

Lindsey said, "So what does that mean, that the Lamotelokhai was using the villagers' brains to make a backup of its data?"

Samuel shook his head, indicating that he failed to understand the question.

"Do you think Sinanie might tell us more about this?" Quentin said.

Samuel spoke again to the Papuan. Sinanie crawled out of the shelter and gestured for them to follow him. He led them through the dense brush until they came upon a fallen tree they had passed before stopping to set up camp. Molded to a fork in the tree's trunk was a brown mass the size of a backpack—a termite nest. Sinanie broke a club-sized branch from the tree and swung it at the nest, putting a dent in it. He swung several more times, splitting the nest open. He then dropped the club and placed his hand into the gash he had created in the nest. Within seconds frantic termites covered his hand. He raised it to his face and began licking the termites off. Samuel stepped forward and did the same thing.

"Try them," Samuel said as he licked the last crawling insect from his hand. "Their flavor may surprise you pleasantly."

Quentin didn't step forward, and neither did Lindsey. Quentin said, "I thought maybe Sinanie was going to show us something."

Samuel just smiled and loaded his hand up with termites again.

After several more minutes of this, Sinanie began speaking. He punctuated his statements by pointing at the swarming termites. Everyone watched him attentively until he was finished.

"I must say, his familiarity with these insects is impressive even to me," Samuel said. "He would like you to understand that the termite nest is one functioning colony, achieving its purpose with the collective actions of three different castes of termites." Samuel allowed more of the insects to crawl onto his hand and then held it out for them to see. "Those with the black heads are of the soldier caste. They are uniquely suited to protecting the nest. They are, in fact, biting my skin at this moment." He flicked a couple of them off. "The small, pale ones are of the worker caste. They build the tunnels and forage for food. And somewhere in the interior of the nest are the queen and kings of the reproductive caste. I imagine I hardly need to explain their function, though you may not know that they are the most delectable to eat."

"How does that relate to Samuel's tribe?" Lindsey said.

"I believe he is making the point that each member of his tribe carried a distinct portion of the Lamotelokhai's knowledge. If you destroy any of the three castes of the termite nest, then the entire nest will fail to achieve its purpose. If you destroy any of the portions of the Lamotelokhai's knowledge, the knowledge is no longer complete. The united purpose is no longer achieved."

Curious, Quentin summoned the courage to step forward and touch the nest's exposed interior, allowing some of the termites to crawl over his skin. The black-headed soldiers began biting, though, and he quickly swiped them all off. Finally, he spoke. "If it was important to the Lamotelokhai to place its knowledge into the minds of thirty people, what did it do when sixteen of those people were killed?"

"I know only what the indigenes have told me," Samuel said. He then turned and spoke with Sinanie. The Papuan continued eating termites as he answered the questions.

Samuel turned back to them. "In the years I have lived with my indigene hosts, I had never witnessed the irrevocable death of a villager. Until your arrival, of course. But I am told that in the past, upon the rare occasion of a permanent death, the dead villager's knowledge was placed into the mind of another villager. This sometimes would require one of the females to bear a child for this purpose."

"Jesus," Lindsey said in a whisper. Then more loudly, "That makes it seem like the Lamotelokhai has simply been using the villagers to suit its own purpose."

"I might remind you that the indigenes hold the Lamotelokhai in the highest regard," Samuel said. "They consider it a great honor to have served as its stewards."

"This still hasn't answered my question," Quentin said. "What did the Lamotelokhai do when Addison destroyed more than half the people carrying portions of its knowledge?"

Samuel slowly nodded. "Indeed, an interesting question."

CHAPTER SEVEN

Peter Wooley sputtered and then cried out. He pulled at his restraints, confused. He looked around at the stark white concrete walls, remembering where he was. A bizarre feeling of relief washed over him. He had just been dreaming, even though he didn't recall falling asleep or even feeling tired. In the dream he had occupied the body of his old friend, Samuel. He had hiked miles from the hanging village in order to carry out an experiment, with the goal of discovering what could be accomplished by piecing together small portions of the Lamotelokhai's clay. But the experiment had gone horrifically wrong, spawning an outbreak of creatures that were the stuff of nightmares. Even now that Peter was awake, he found himself shaking and fighting back tears.

This had been more than a mere dream. More detailed and lucid. This felt like the visions the Lamotelokhai had placed in his mind before. Peter could think of only one reason the Lamotelokhai would put such a disturbing vision into his head.

"Hey! Someone get in here! We need to talk!" He waited, but his shouts were followed by silence. He yelled again. He yanked violently against the restraints, actually rolling the bed a few inches toward the center of the room.

The metal door clicked as it was unlocked. It swung open, and the woman who had pushed his bed into the room stood in the doorway. A burly man stood behind her. They both wore green scrubs, like everyone else Peter had seen in this place. They entered the room, but the bloke remained by the door. The woman came over, pushed the bed back to the wall, and flipped a brake with her foot.

"You've got to listen to me," Peter said. "I think there's a possibility that something very dangerous might happen. I know you have Addison—"

"You mean the Lamotelokhai," she said.

Peter hesitated only briefly. "Yes, good for you, you know what it's called. But I'm pretty bloody sure you don't know what you're dealing with."

"What are we dealing with, Mr. Wooley?"

"And it seems you know who I am. Then perhaps you'll listen while I explain something."

She sat on the edge of the bed next to Peter's knees. "Absolutely. Our purpose here is to learn all we can."

"Are you with the United States government?"

She raised her eyebrows. "I thought you were going to explain something to me."

Peter glared at her for a moment. "I had a dream. More accurately, a vision. I believe the Lamotelokhai put it into my head as a warning of what might happen if you people are careless."

She raised her brows again. "What might happen?"

"It's difficult to describe. What I saw was apparently the result of attempting to work with a small portion of the Lamotelokhai, rather than with the entire entity."

The woman's eyes grew wide for a brief moment, and she glanced at the man by the door. "Go on," she said.

"I'm trying to tell you that the thing is dangerous beyond anything you can imagine. I know for a fact that the Lamotelokhai is programmed to do whatever we ask it to do, regardless of the consequences. Perhaps it's just studying us, watching to see if we destroy ourselves. If we do, it will simply watch it happen. Maybe a million years later—maybe fifty million—a more intelligent species might evolve on this planet. If so, those future beings will have the opportunity to make the same mistakes we did. It won't stop them, just as it won't stop us."

The woman waited patiently, apparently considering his words.

"It gave me a warning," Peter said. "But if you don't heed the warning, it won't interfere."

The woman nodded thoughtfully. "Why did the Lamotelokhai give *you* this warning?" She nodded toward the straps holding him to the bed. "You are not in a position in which you are likely to make a careless mistake, are you?"

"I don't know! It gives me these visions occasionally, maybe because its particles have been in my body for fifty years!"

She seemed to consider this before speaking again. "Mr. Wooley, since arriving at this facility, have you seen anything that might suggest that we are being careless?"

He stared at her, stewing in his anger. "I have seen little of this facility, perhaps because you drugged me and brought me here unconscious. Not to mention that you shot my friend. And the very fact that you are performing some sort of barbaric experiment on a mere child suggests that you are ill-suited to do anything at all scientific, let alone anything involving the Lamotelokhai."

"Well, you should see more of the facility, Mr. Wooley. I think you would be impressed, particularly since we constructed it in only half a year."

Peter said, "Can we get back to the impending catastrophe I'm trying to warn you about? Personally, I don't care if the

Lamotelokhai kills you and your other government lackeys in the most horrible way possible. But the danger is very much larger than that. I'll say it again, the vision I saw suggested it is a very bad idea to try to deal with a subset of the particles that make up the Lamotelokhai. God knows it's dangerous enough to use the entire thing intact."

She put her hand on Peter's knee, and he shook his leg to dislodge it. "Here's an interesting thought," she said. "If you were the Lamotelokhai, and you did not want us to divide the collective particles of your body into smaller portions, perhaps because such an act might allow us to learn the secrets of how you function, then wouldn't you be tempted to scare us by warning of the terrible things that might result?"

Peter was incredulous. "If you think the warning is a deception, then you have no—"

"This conversation has been helpful," she said. "In fact, we are counting on you being correct, that the Lamotelokhai will do anything it is asked to do."

She stood up and walked to the door. "Please let us know if you decide to share additional information. We wish to learn all we can. You may ask for me by name, if you wish. I am Sofia."

She and the bloke stepped out, and the door slammed shut.

CHAPTER EIGHT

T̲ʜᴇ ᴇʟᴇᴠᴀᴛᴏʀ's stainless steel doors whisked open and then were silent, waiting for Bobby to step through. He tried to control his breathing. Outside the elevator was a white floor. Beyond that was a glass wall with another white room behind it. He stepped forward, and the doors closed behind him. He was in a large circular room, empty except for the cylindrical elevator shaft in the center. He now saw that the glass wall before him was only one of ten glass panels that made up the outer wall of the room. Behind each glass panel was a smaller chamber. He walked around the elevator shaft, looking into each of the chambers until he found one that wasn't empty. Standing inside the chamber and gazing back at him through the glass was Addison. The Lamotelokhai.

Bobby stared at it, terrified that he might make a mistake.

Addison smiled. He then spoke, and his voice came through speakers somewhere in the ceiling. "Hello, Bobby. You are wearing an interesting hat."

Bobby swallowed. "It's a protective helmet, in case I fall." This was exactly what he had been told to say, and it was true. "I like it, so I wanted to wear it today." This part was a lie, but if he hadn't said it, Ashley would have been hurt again.

Addison stepped closer to the glass. "I have observed some interesting events since I last saw you. It is difficult to predict what behaviors your kind might exhibit next."

Bobby kept his mouth shut, waiting for a pulse behind his ears. None came, so he didn't dare speak.

"You are afraid," Addison said. "Why?"

This wasn't going the way Helmich had told him it should. After several long seconds of waiting, Bobby felt the pulse. The device was off, and he was now allowed to answer the Lamotelokhai. But he knew what would happen if he said anything Helmich didn't like.

"I'm not afraid. I'm just kind of nervous about everything that's happening. Sometimes it's hard to tell the difference." Bobby held his breath, half expecting to wake up on the floor. But nothing happened. Helmich was waiting for him to say what he'd been instructed to say.

Addison gazed at him with no expression.

There was no point in trying to put it off. Bobby had no idea if it would work, and he silently hoped it wouldn't, particularly after the terrifying vision he'd seen in his mind less than an hour ago. But he had no choice.

"Addison, I need your help. Please just do what I ask, okay? I will explain later. I need for you to divide yourself into ten smaller but equal portions. Can you do that?"

Addison's eyes turned from sky blue to fire gold. They stayed that way for many seconds, longer than Bobby had seen them do it before. Finally they turned back to blue.

"That is an interesting request," it said.

Bobby gave the response he was allowed to give. "I'm sorry, but it's important. Can you do it for me?"

Addison looked down at his own body and then back up at

Bobby. "If I do, it will affect my ability to function as a collective entity."

Bobby felt faint. The Lamotelokhai was actually considering doing it. Why in the hell did these people want to split it up? Did Helmich think he could destroy it this way? Bobby wanted to stop this, to warn the Lamotelokhai. But he knew that he wouldn't be able to finish his warning and that Ashley would have to suffer. He had to trust that the Lamotelokhai would not allow itself to be harmed.

"I'm sorry, but it's important," he repeated. "Can you do it for me?"

Addison lowered his head, like he was praying.

Don't do it! Bobby opened his mouth to say what he was thinking, but then he stopped himself. It was too late.

Addison folded over at the waist. But instead of bending forward like a person would, his upper body folded straight back, until his head touched the floor behind his feet. The motion was so unnatural and sickening that Bobby barely stopped himself from crying out in surprise. He stared, helpless.

Addison's left arm and part of his shoulder detached and fell to the floor beside his inverted head, which was still attached to the folded body. Bobby heard the thump on the floor through the ceiling speakers. There was no blood or gore, just a smooth, pink surface where the arm had been attached. The other arm and shoulder tumbled away from the body. Next came the head, with a portion of the chest still attached. It fell and came to rest facing away from Bobby. Without the head propping it up, the rest of the body fell into a heap. Each of the legs detached just above the knee, followed by the two thighs. After that, the jumble of body parts made it hard to comprehend what was happening. But Bobby knew Addison's torso was being split into three sections. The Lamotelokhai was doing exactly what he had asked it to do—just as it always had.

A low beep sounded in the earpiece that had been fitted to Bobby's left ear. He then heard people cheering and congratulating each other. It sounded like a NASA control room after a successful Mars landing.

"Very well done, Bobby." It was Helmich. "You have convinced even those of us who have held the most skepticism. Now, as you know, you have another task to complete. Please be most careful. We do not want to have to hurt you or your friends." The earpiece beeped again, and the radio went silent.

Suddenly the floor vibrated as a large machine somewhere beneath kicked on. The machine's hum rose to a higher pitch, and then the ten chambers surrounding the room began pulling away from the room's center. They moved steadily outward, and Bobby then saw that each chamber was on two metal rails. The rooms stopped after receding about ten feet outward, and the machine fell silent. The rooms had been pulled out from the center like pieces of a pie, and now there were gaps between them.

Bobby listened for a moment to his own breathing and the blood rushing through his ears. He had to do something to stop this. Maybe he could surprise them. Maybe they were so busy congratulating each other that he could enter the chamber, shove the Lamotelokhai's pieces back together, and order it to zap itself out of here—to the motel room or anywhere else. Bobby looked around at the strange array of chambers and then at the pile of Addison's body parts, and he knew it was too late. Any opportunity he may have had was now past.

He walked through the gap that now existed beside Addison's chamber. The chamber's door was there, just as Helmich had said it would be. The door looked like an airplane's emergency hatch. Bobby stood before the hatch as he had been told to do until the lock clicked. He pushed down on the lever and pulled hard. This broke the airtight seal, and the hatch opened. He stepped in and closed it behind him.

He stood over the ten portions of Addison's body. This wasn't going to be as easy as he'd hoped. He had assumed that, if the Lamotelokhai actually did what he asked, it would transform itself into ten pieces of featureless clay. The pieces before him looked like the result of a chainsaw massacre, minus the blood. Each body part still had Addison's clothes on it. Bobby could now see the thing's face, and he was relieved that the eyes were not moving or staring at him.

Following the instructions he'd been given, he picked up one of the pieces, an arm with the shoulder attached. It was heavy, maybe fifteen pounds, and he decided the best way to carry it was to grip two of the fingers and dangle the arm at his side.

He carried it to the hatch, waited for the click, opened the door, stepped through, and went to the next chamber's hatch. The lock clicked, and he took the arm inside. He moved toward the middle of the chamber to put the arm on the floor.

"Hello, Bobby."

Bobby froze. The voice had not come from his earpiece or the speakers above. Instead, it had come from within him, sounding very much like his own voice.

The voice spoke again. "Perhaps now you can explain."

Bobby glanced up at one of the cameras in the ceiling. If he did anything other than what he was supposed to, Helmich would press a button and knock him out. If he spoke, the implants behind his ears would knock him out. But he had to do something.

He tried forming silent words. "Is that you?"

Everything went black.

He awoke to a voice in his earpiece. "Please get up, Bobby. You must finish your task. Your friend Ashley is not a happy camper at this moment. If she were capable of speaking coherently, I think she would ask you to avoid talking, even in a whisper."

Bobby was flat on his back. His head hurt, especially where the implant was attached behind his left ear. The helmet they'd given him hadn't done much to protect that area. He sat up. Addison's arm was on the floor beside him.

"Leave it where it is and attend to the others," Helmich said in his ear.

Bobby got up, stepped out of the chamber, and closed the hatch. He returned to the first chamber while imagining several ways he'd like to kill Helmich. One of them involved a baseball bat. He re-entered the first chamber and picked up the other arm.

"For me to speak this way, you must have your hand upon a portion of me." The voice was in his head again. "Your thoughts are many, and they are without singular meaning. Perhaps if you speak aloud."

Again Bobby looked at the ceiling camera. He couldn't just stand there. It would look suspicious. So he carried the arm to the hatch and left the chamber. He entered the center room, passed by the second chamber, and waited by the door of the third chamber. He clamped his lips shut, determined this time to form mental words without involuntarily mouthing them.

"I can't."

"I understand you now," it said. "Perhaps now you can explain."

The door clicked. Bobby had no choice but to enter the chamber. He concentrated on forming silent words. "I'm sorry for what I asked you to do."

"You said that you would explain. I am curious."

Bobby was standing in the middle of the third chamber. "I will, but first I have to let go for a second." He placed the portion on the floor and quickly returned to the first chamber. He picked up another portion, this time a lower leg, and carried it to the fourth chamber.

"Are you going to be okay?" he said silently, still careful to keep his lips clamped shut.

"My portions are in close proximity, and therefore they can

work together to accomplish cognitive functions, such as speaking to you."

Bobby deposited the leg and returned for the other lower leg. When he picked it up, the voice continued where it had left off.

"It is not possible, however, for me to perform mechanical functions."

"I'm sorry. I didn't want to ask you to do this."

Bobby left the piece in the fifth chamber and returned for one of the thighs.

"I do not understand," the voice said.

"It's hard to explain. If I didn't do it, Ashley would get hurt."

"Why?"

Bobby left the thigh in the sixth chamber and went back for the other thigh. He was starting to sweat from the work.

"It's because of something they attached to my head," he said silently. "If I say something I'm not supposed to, it automatically hurts Ashley. I have to do what they tell me to. That's why I had to tell you to split up into parts."

There was no voice for some seconds after that. Bobby paused before placing the piece on the floor of the seventh chamber. He scratched his neck with his free hand, trying to look like he had an itch.

Finally it spoke. "You are faced with an interesting dilemma."

"It's not interesting, it's terrible. Just a second." He put the piece down and returned to the first chamber. There were four more pieces, one of which had to be left where it was. He decided it would be the head, because he didn't want to pick it up. He grabbed the piece that used to be the butt and groin.

"I need your help," Bobby thought. It was getting easier to make clear statements without using his mouth. "We need to get out of here. But these people have Ashley. And they have Peter and Robert. We all need to get out of here, including you. Can you help with that?" He entered the eighth chamber and walked to the center.

"An interesting dilemma indeed," the voice said. "In this disaggregated state I do not have the capability to help you in a physical way."

Bobby put the piece on the floor and returned to the first chamber. He picked up the piece that had been the belly and headed for the ninth chamber.

"We have to do something," Bobby said. "There's only one more piece of you to move after this one, and then they probably won't let me touch you again. So we won't be able to talk."

"You would like to talk to me after that?"

"Yes! Even if you can't do your normal stuff, if I can talk to you maybe you can help me figure out what to do." Bobby was now standing in the ninth chamber.

"You will need to keep a portion of me with you," the voice said.

"I can't! They won't let me." Bobby could almost feel Helmich resting his finger on the knockout button.

"If you wish to talk with me, you must keep a portion of me with you."

"Bobby?" It was Helmich in his earpiece.

Bobby dropped the body part on the floor and returned to the first chamber. He avoided looking at Addison's head as he gathered up the chest portion. He moved as slowly as he could without causing suspicion, but his mind frantically struggled to form the right words.

"I can't keep this part! I have to put it in the last room!"

"You do not need the entire part," the voice said. "Perhaps you could take a portion of it."

Bobby stepped into the space between the chambers. As he waited for the hatch to the tenth chamber to click, he pulled off a chunk the size of his fist, hoping there were no cameras there.

"I've got some. Is it enough?"

"It is difficult for me to know now. We will know soon."

The door clicked, but Bobby didn't move. Helmich would see the chunk of Lamotelokhai in his hand as soon as Bobby stepped into the room. His pants didn't have pockets. Trying to be discreet, he squeezed the chunk against his leg to make it flatter. He then slowly raised the hand holding the chunk up under his shirt, used two fingers to lift the elastic band of his pants, and tucked the flattened chunk under the band. He turned the lever, pulled the door open, and stepped through the hatch. He stopped. His movements had caused the flattened chunk to slide down and almost come loose from his waistband. He shifted the larger chest portion he was carrying so that his arm held the smaller chunk in place.

"I don't know if I can do this! It's going to fall and then they'll know."

"The portion will not fall."

"How do you know?"

"It will not fall."

Bobby took a step. The chunk stayed in place, so he walked to the center of the last chamber. "I have to put this piece down now. If this doesn't work, I may never get to talk to you again."

"I will attempt to make it work."

"I'm really sorry," Bobby said silently. He waited, but the voice did not reply. He placed the piece on the floor. As he stepped back he casually rested his hand on his waist to prevent the hidden chunk from dropping.

The chunk was gone.

"Nicely done, Bobby." It was Helmich. "Now please return to the center viewing room. Close the door as you leave the chamber."

Bobby looked at the floor. The chunk wasn't there. He took another step back. He didn't feel it inside his pant leg. He tried to gather his thoughts. "Lamotelokhai, are you there?"

There was no answer.

"Bobby, for Ashley's sake, please go to the center viewing room," Helmich said in his ear.

Bobby stepped out, closed the hatch, and went to the center room. He turned and gazed through the glass at Addison's head. "Are you there? Can you hear me?"

"Bobby?"

Bobby almost jumped with joy. "It's working! I can hear you!"

"I have successfully patterned my cognitive activity so that I may speak to you with the smaller portion of me you removed."

Bobby thought, "I can't find the piece I took. Where is it?"

"Its particles have moved into your body."

Suddenly the room shook as the machinery below the floor kicked on again. Almost immediately the ten chambers began pulling further away from the center room.

The voice was in his head again. "The distance between my portions is becoming greater. If the distance continues to increase at this rate, my cognitive functions will stop in twelve seconds."

"No!" Bobby screamed within his mind. He turned to one of the cameras and waved his hands over his head, but he knew it would do no good. The chambers were now at least fifty yards out into a vast dark space, and they were still rolling away.

"If you wish to have my help, you will need to decrease the distance between my portions. My cognitive functions will stop in three seconds."

Bobby could only stand and stare at the receding chambers. Finally, the machinery stopped churning and fell silent. The chambers were now small rectangles of white light in the distance, evenly spread in a wide circle around the center room.

"Lamotelokhai? Addison?"

There was no response.

The elevator shaft in the center of the room opened. Men and women in green doctor clothes spilled out, each of them carrying a computer or some other device, and they quickly started setting them up in the room. Helmich came out of the elevator last. He grasped Bobby's shoulders and smiled at him, as if he were a proud father.

"What an invigorating and successful day!" he said. "You have been most helpful. Come, I will take you to see Ashley. You may want to apologize to her for what you have put her through."

Bobby followed him into the elevator, his thoughts silent as well as his mouth. The doors slid shut, and they were alone.

"I believe we deserve a treat." Helmich said. Suddenly he clapped his hands together. "Say, do you like ice cream?"

CHAPTER NINE

THE FIRST LIGHT of morning drove away the opaque blackness and then the murky shadows of the forest near the river the local humans called *Méanmaél*. This was Mbaiso's favorite time for activities that served no purpose other than amusement—activities that distracted the tree kangaroo from the tasks that would fill the rest of his day.

With no particular destination, Mbaiso made his way along the river, sniffing and pawing at anything interesting. Each time his path took him close to the water's edge, he became acutely alert to the possible presence of crocodiles. Due to Mbaiso's own actions many days ago, crocodiles were now more abundant in the area.

A slight movement in the leaf litter caught his eye. Cautiously, he stepped closer. The moving object appeared to be a brown worm. Now this was an interesting distraction. Mbaiso had seen worms like this before. Many other creatures never had the opportunity to learn to avoid such a worm, as their first encounter was nearly always their last.

The tree kangaroo circled to one side of the worm and then to the other, carefully investigating the arrangement of leaves and soil around it. The worm continued wriggling back and forth as Mbaiso looked for the most promising angle of approach. He did not intend to eat the worm or even to kill it. He desired only to touch it. Finally, based upon the area's spatial parameters, Mbaiso selected a position, dug his hind claws in for leverage, and lunged forward. His intent was to jump past the worm with enough speed to avoid danger, touching the worm in the process.

The leaf litter around the worm exploded. In a fraction of the blink of a tree kangaroo's eye, a broad head shot out, jaws gaping, and two long fangs slammed into Mbaiso's abdomen, injecting a lethal dose of venom. The head immediately pulled back, releasing him.

Mbaiso tumbled on the ground and slid to a stop. He got up on his haunches and gazed at the creature, no longer hidden beneath the litter. The worm-like tail, which typically acted as a lure, was attached to a large snake, much larger than Mbaiso had predicted—and much faster. The villagers called the snake *malan*. Samuel called it a death adder.

Mbaiso scurried up a tree to avoid a second dose of venom. A strange sensation began emanating from the bite, spreading to his legs. Soon his legs began shaking, and it became difficult to maintain his balance. This was followed by numbness. Gradually, the lack of feeling became so complete that Mbaiso had to use visual cues to be sure he was still grasping the tree's bark. He remained in the same position until the numbness passed. By this time, low shafts of sunlight were beginning to cut through the forest canopy. Although unintentional, the encounter with the snake's venom had been an interesting and unique experience. Mbaiso had existed for thousands of years, and unique experiences were not easy to come by. Mbaiso decided he would do it again when he had the opportunity.

Finally, the tree kangaroo descended to the ground and returned to the bank of the river to quench his abnormally strong thirst. He scanned the water's edge for evidence of waiting crocodiles. Satisfied that it was safe, he took a long drink.

Suddenly a wave of agitation washed over him. He sat up on his haunches, ears cocked, listening. Nothing unusual. But the agitation persisted. He focused his attention inward, probing his mind for the source of the sensation. His consciousness extended fingers of thought, systematically peeling away layers of his processing centers, finally examining the subtle changes that had taken place during the first moment he had detected the uneasy feeling. Disaggregated pieces gradually came together, bringing the feeling's component parts into focus.

The uneasy feeling had nothing to do with the residual effects of the snake's venom. Instead, it was linked to an abrupt cessation of an incoming signal. The signal had previously been so faint that Mbaiso hadn't even been aware of it until it had stopped. Further probing revealed that the information processing centers that had detected the sudden absence of the incoming signal were those that had previously allowed Mbaiso to communicate with the Creator.

He climbed to a comfortable spot in a tree so he could contemplate this in safety. He sprawled on his belly on a thick branch and closed his eyes. Apparently, without Mbaiso knowing it, a faint signal from the Creator had continued after the Creator had departed. The signal had been too faint to contain information or instructions, but it did signify that the creator had existed somewhere beyond the forest that had always been Mbaiso's home.

But for some reason the signal had stopped. Perhaps the Creator had moved much farther away. Possibly it had even left the great forest of this world. Or perhaps the Creator had ceased to exist. Mbaiso rested upon the limb, considering the implications of each scenario, until the sun was at its highest position of the day. The abrupt end to the Creator's signal would almost certainly impact the preparations he had supervised for many days. He did not know if the preparations were yet sufficient. But after analyzing possible consequences of waiting for further preparation, he decided it was time to move ahead with his plans.

Driven by renewed purpose, Mbaiso left the Méanmaél and made his way up a gently sloping hill, sometimes leaping from tree to tree and sometimes hopping on the ground. Upon the hill's broad plateau was a dense stand of uncommonly tall *khaim* trees. Although nearly invisible from the forest floor, an elaborate network of tunnels and chambers hung in the canopy of the trees, a small-scale version of the hanging village of the humans where Mbaiso had once lived.

He stopped between the buttress roots of a tree just beyond the border of the hanging tunnels. He twitched his nostrils, sniffing the air, and detected the scent of a creature that was mostly human. In addition to the scent, he heard a faint sound, the creature's voice. Mbaiso leapt onto the tree's trunk and dug his claws into the bark to keep from sliding back down. He pumped his hind legs, thrusting himself a full body-length higher, and dug in again. He repeated this until he entered a hut far above the forest floor.

In the center of the hut, a dark figure sat with his back vertical and his legs folded beneath him. He was human, but not quite like any human Mbaiso had encountered before. The other humans had called him *Addison*.

Mbaiso cautiously padded closer but then sat back on his haunches to wait. The creature did not appear to be aware of his presence yet. His eyes were closed, and he was speaking, though in an unusual way, his voice rising and falling rhythmically. The almost-human creature held his arms in the air before him, bouncing his fingers up and down with the rising and falling of his voice.

"Deels um bus go down um town,
down um town, down um town.
Deels um bus go down um town, All round town.
Wiper um bus go wish um ish,

Wish um ish, wish um ish.

Wiper um bus go wish um ish, all round town."

Addison opened his eyes and looked at the tree kangaroo. "Baiso."

Mbaiso hopped closer, still cautious, until his nose was just before Addison's. Addison leaned forward, and their noses touched. It was a ritual that reassured Mbaiso and seemed to calm the almost-human creature.

The tree kangaroo sat back and began talking to Addison, using the forepaw gesture language he had always used with the villagers. Addison quietly watched. He continued to sit and stare for some time after the gestures ended. Mbaiso waited patiently, aware that visions were playing out in Addison's mind to facilitate his understanding.

Addison abruptly jumped to his feet and slapped his belly with both hands, indicating he was ready and willing. He then stepped to the hole in the floor of his hut and dropped through it. Mbaiso crawled through the hole more cautiously. When the tree kangaroo emerged beneath the hut, Addison was already several trees ahead of him. The human slapped his belly again, this time conveying impatience.

When Mbaiso arrived at the central hub of the miniature hanging tunnels, Addison had already squeezed through one of the openings. He was stretched out on his side, propped up on one forelimb because the room's ceiling was too low for him to sit up. He lay near Tupela—too near for Mbaiso's comfort. Tupela was important to Mbaiso's plan, and Addison could be unpredictable.

Three shapes stretched and undulated on the floor next to Tupela. They were new tree kangaroos in various stages of formation. The largest of them would be fully mature by the end of the day. Each of them had originated when Mbaiso had added a small portion of his body to a portion of Tupela's. Other tree kangaroos entered and left the hub, engaged in various errands and tasks.

After surveying the chamber, Mbaiso decided it was not suitable for what he needed to do.

He stopped a tree kangaroo that was entering the hub carrying a *layop* fruit in his mouth. The creature paused and stared as Mbaiso signed instructions with his forepaws. The tree kangaroo dropped the fruit onto a pile of other fruits that had been gathered and then delivered the same instructions to a third tree kangaroo, which then turned and delivered the message to a fourth.

By the time Mbaiso and the human creature descended to the forest floor, a group of over a hundred tree kangaroos was waiting for them. Soon after that the entire colony had arrived except for Tupela and the three unformed young.

Mbaiso let out a hailing bleat. The tree kangaroos stopped fidgeting and watched him. With Addison towering above him at his side, Mbaiso began a sequence of gestures, describing the purpose of this gathering. The tree kangaroos were to learn the next phase of their purpose, a purpose that could not be fulfilled in this part of the forest. Soon they would journey to other parts of this world's great forest. And when they found a place where they could carry out their purpose, they would need to know what to do.

Occasionally, Mbaiso had seen Addison speak to one of the tree kangaroos who was now near the front of the gathered mass. Addison had given her the name *Newton*. Mbaiso signed for her to approach the human. When she was at Addison's side, Mbaiso pressed his snout against hers. His instructions were too extensive for conveying by gestures. A packet of information he had painstakingly prepared passed into her consciousness through the point of contact.

Before this moment, Mbaiso had transferred this packet of information to only one other tree kangaroo. The man, Samuel, had recently come to the mbolop colony and had asked Mbaiso to allow one of the tree kangaroos to go on a journey with him, to find the humans who were the parents of Addison. Mbaiso had given the information to the mbolop he had chosen to accompany Samuel.

Newton pulled away from Mbaiso. She turned to the human creature and gazed up at him. Addison made a strange facial expression, exposing his teeth, and then he sat down on the ground with his legs crossed before him. He extended one of his forepaws and placed the palm on Newton's head for a moment. It was something he had done to Mbaiso before, possibly a gesture of trust or affection.

Newton dug into her abdomen, breaking the skin with her claws. She pushed her paw in until it disappeared and then pulled it out holding a wet lump of her insides. She offered it up to the human.

Addison looked at the lump and then at Newton, hesitating. After a few moments he took the lump and placed it in his mouth. Mbaiso and the rest of the colony watched and waited. Mbaiso fretted, digging his claws into the soil beneath him and flicking his ears back and forth. Perhaps his plan wouldn't work.

Addison suddenly straightened his back. He rolled to one side and sprang to his feet. Newton and some of the other tree kangaroos grunted in alarm and backed away. Addison began walking away, but then he staggered. He fell to his knees. He turned and looked toward Mbaiso but seemed unable to focus his eyes. Addison then fell forward, and his face struck an exposed root with a thump.

Mbaiso, Newton, and the others gathered around the body. Mbaiso sniffed the back of Addison's head and then shoved it with his snout. Addison didn't respond.

Mbaiso signed some instructions to Newton and then to the others. One of the tree kangaroos hopped forward and touched snouts with Newton. The two remained in contact until a packet of instructions had been passed on—instructions that had now been augmented by Newton's encounter with Addison.

The two separated, and the tree kangaroo Newton had touched scampered off, presumably back to the task it had been engaged in prior to the gathering. Another came forward, and the instruction packet was passed on again. One by one, every member of the colony came forward and received the necessary information. Finally, when the shafts of sunlight penetrating the canopy were again at a low angle, Mbaiso and Newton were alone with the human's still body. The two tree kangaroos waited.

Addison rolled over slowly and sat up. Newton hopped up to him, and they touched snouts. The human then extended a hand and slowly stroked Newton's head.

CHAPTER TEN

Bobby gazed at the walls and ceiling as a woman wheeled his bed down a hallway. Everything here looked the same—white, painted concrete with nothing on the walls. The doors didn't even have numbers or names. The place was definitely not a hospital.

The woman stopped the bed before a featureless door that looked like all the others. She held out a key attached to a spiral lanyard around her neck, unlocked the door, and wheeled the bed into the room. Three more beds sat next to one wall, occupied by Ashley, Peter, and Robert. They were all awake and sitting up, including Robert, and like Bobby they were restrained. Helmich stood facing the beds, his arms folded. Behind him were four small cameras on tripods, all pointing toward the beds. The woman parked Bobby's bed next to Ashley's and left the room.

"Are you okay?" Ashley said.

Bobby looked at Helmich.

"You may speak freely," he said.

"I'm okay," Bobby said. "Didn't sleep much. I can't even turn on my side on this bed." He shot a look at Helmich.

Helmich nodded his stupid nod. "Have I asked you already if

you like films? Consider *Papillon*, with Steve McQueen. McQueen's character, a safecracker, is wrongly accused of murder and sentenced to life in prison in French Guiana. Worst conditions you can imagine—you should consider yourself lucky. But the character never gives up. He formulates one plan after another, sustained by his boundless hope. At last, after he has grown to be a much older man, he manages to escape." Helmich looked at Bobby with a smile. "Perhaps you might take heart in such a story, and in the hope that perhaps you will find a way to leave this place. Fortunately for you, that will simply require your complete cooperation. Say, I'll arrange a *Papillon* viewing for all of you. We'll make it a festive occasion!"

Bobby had no idea how to respond to this, so he just glared at the man.

"Who are you, and what the hell is this place?" Peter said.

"Yes, it is time for questions." Helmich gestured to the cameras behind him. "We are not alone today. I have invited my benefactors—my superiors, if you will—to join us. They are as excited to meet you as the rest of us have been. Please do not ask who they are. They would be here in person if they wanted you to know."

"Hey, freak," Ashley said. "Last I checked, real doctors don't torture people."

Helmich nodded his stupid nod again. "I am more of a freelance consultant. And yes, I am a medical doctor. A neurologist, specifically. I am also a somewhat accomplished psychologist. And I have a passing interest in exobiology, astrobiology, human-machine interfacing, American pop culture, and motion pictures. Some of those interests make me highly qualified to be here, others make me an interminable bore. Or so I am told." He raised his eyebrows behind his red glasses like he was waiting for the next question.

"I'd like an honest and detailed report on Robert's condition," Peter said.

"I'm doing okay," Robert said before Helmich could answer. His speech was a little slurred, and his neck and part of his face were still bandaged. "They've actually taken pretty good care of me. But I agree with Bobby about the damn straps on the bed."

"Robert was struck by a nine millimeter rubber bullet just above his right clavicle," Helmich said. "The round, which by the way was designed to be less lethal, did not rupture any major arteries, nor did it fracture any bones. I can now say confidently that he will recover fully, although the full range of motion in his neck may not be restored for some time. And although you haven't asked, the woman you met on the road at the bridge—her name is Sabrina—is going to be fine as well. Some of the blood you saw on her was simulated, but some of it was real. She mustered a praise-worthy performance, did she not? I suppose she would be considered a method actor." Again, he raised his brows, waiting.

Bobby spoke up. "What are you trying to do to the Lamotelokhai? Why did you want to split it up?"

"They split it up?" Peter asked.

Ashley said, "I had a dream yesterday, a vision that thing put in my head. If you idiots are trying to split the Lamotelokhai up, you need to know what I saw."

"Yes," Helmich said, "Bobby has told me of this dream. And I understand Mr. Wooley experienced the same dream as well. How do you suppose that is possible?"

"It doesn't matter how it's possible," Peter said. "What matters is why we had the dream."

Helmich pushed his glasses up on his nose and then stroked his chin. "I am beginning to suspect that you people have a profound lack of curiosity."

Bobby said, "You haven't answered. What are you trying to do?"

"Yes," Helmich responded, "that is the question, isn't it? You might say that our group has put all of its proverbial eggs into one basket. We have structured our efforts upon one primary premise, that the Lamotelokhai is nothing more than a collection of interconnected but potentially independent parts. If you separate those parts into subgroups—say ten subgroups—then the entity will be incapable of functioning as a whole. We also have hypothesized that the distance between the ten subgroups is important. That's why we have constructed this facility, with a circular, subterranean space 324 meters in diameter. It allows us to increase the distance between the subgroups under controlled conditions. In case you are interested, in the space below us we can move each of the ten subgroups 162 meters from the center. This places them into a circular array 324 meters in diameter, with 100 meters between the subsets around the perimeter. It's all quite fascinating, although I can't say I was at all instrumental in its design. I'm not much of an engineer."

Bobby shoved out a frustrated grumble from the back of his throat. "You need to put its parts back together. I still don't know what you're trying to do, but it's really dangerous."

Helmich sighed and frowned. "Perhaps you do not fully understand the idiom, putting all of one's eggs into one basket. Consider the 1981 film, *All The Marbles*, with Peter Faulk. Faulk's character is a sleazy manager of two female professional wrestlers."

"Seriously," Ashley said, "do we have to hear about another stupid movie?"

Helmich held up a finger as if he were lecturing them. "Patience. Yes, such films are often rubbish, but this one is an under-appreciated gem. The two wrestlers happen to be very good at what they do. But as you can imagine, the world of small-time professional wrestling is rife with drudgery, unglamorous gigs, and shady characters. This unlikely trio hits a low point when they are forced to accept a mud-wrestling match. But they finally manage, through one ruse after another, to obtain a chance at the tag-team title. The climax is a brutal, twenty-minute depiction of the match, one of the great sports scenes in cinema history. The two wrestlers, as well as their manager, know that this is their one and only chance. Nothing else matters. It is for all the marbles. They have put all their eggs into one basket."

Helmich fell silent and waited, as if he expected applause or something. When no one responded, he went on.

"And so, you see, we know that we have only one chance. We will either succeed or we will fail. But there is no turning back. You tell me this is dangerous, as if we were not aware of that. Yes, it is a high-stakes match. But we are already ahead of the other teams. We have found the Lamotelokhai before any of them."

Bobby, Ashley, and Peter exchanged confused glances.

"Other teams?" Peter said.

"Of course. There are at least sixteen other groups that I am aware of. We've even collaborated with some of them, although we certainly cannot reveal to them what we have accomplished here recently. They are scattered around the globe, funded by assorted governments and benefactors. Most of them have facilities as elaborate as this one, although with designs based upon entirely different hypotheses. One of them is even designed to convince the Lamotelokhai to construct a wormhole in space, so that the sponsors of the facility can be transported to other solar systems. Blithering idiots, if you ask me. Another I know of is designed to destroy the Lamotelokhai with a contained nuclear blast. I believe they are offended by its presence here." Helmich laughed as if this were funny. "Honestly, you should be happy our team found you first."

Bobby was too stunned by all of this to know what to say. Apparently the others were too. It was actually Robert who broke the silence.

"Why are you avoiding Bobby's question?"

Again Helmich sighed and frowned. He then glanced at a smartwatch on his wrist. "I am providing context. I joined this team voluntarily, because I believe there is much to be gained by understanding the technology behind the Lamotelokhai. I am one of millions who believe that humankind is *not* best served by allowing this remarkable entity to hide out somewhere, making its own decisions about what we need and do not need. You want to know what we are trying to do? We intend to understand how the Lamotelokhai works. Once we understand that, we will have the ability to achieve on our own what the Lamotelokhai may or may not have decided to achieve for us. We will make our own decisions about what is best for us. If we succeed, humanity will reclaim its position of authority and autonomy on this planet. If we fail, well, then it won't matter what happens. This is for all the marbles."

Bobby felt the small amount of hope he still had slipping away. It was one thing for Helmich to be clueless about the risk he was taking. It was a very different thing for him to understand the risk but not care about it. It would be a waste of breath to try to talk any sense into him.

Helmich looked at his smartwatch again. "I now have a few questions of my own. I would very much like for you to be forthcoming with your answers, as I am not keen on expending additional time extracting them from you under duress." He gave Ashley a meaningful look. "Can we all agree on that?"

After a moment of silence, Peter said, "Ask your questions."

Helmich nodded and half-smiled. "Why were you moving the Lamotelokhai, and where were you planning to take it?"

Peter answered immediately. "We felt that it needed to be in a more secure location. We were taking it to a facility that I had constructed for that purpose."

Helmich nodded, apparently considering this. "I see. It is fortunate then that we found you before you accomplished that. Now for my second question. You people are, I suppose, the world's leading experts on the Lamotelokhai, at least for the moment. What role do you believe it should play in human existence? Please answer one at a time." He nodded toward Robert first.

Bobby could hear Robert swallow a lump in his throat from several beds away. "I believe it can be a repository of knowledge, perhaps a database we can tap into whenever we have an important problem to solve."

"So you think it should be a glorified encyclopedia, perhaps with an online interface like that of a search engine."

"Well, I don't know what it might—"

Helmich held up a hand to cut him off. "I get it." He then nodded at Peter.

Peter sighed loudly. "Okay, I'll play along. I don't know exactly what role it should play. I would suggest that a consortium be formed, with representatives from every country, culture, and way of life. This consortium then could decide what role the Lamotelokhai should play that would benefit everyone."

Helmich clapped his hands three times in fake applause. "Well done. You have described the most dysfunctional consortium imaginable, unable to make any decisions whatsoever due to the very human tendency to favor one's own interests."

Peter glared. "Okay, what is your—"

Helmich put up his hand again. "Let's move on." He nodded at Ashley.

"Go frack yourself," she said.

Helmich smiled. "Well said. I suppose you are confident that I am in too much of a hurry to arrange things so that I can coerce you to give an honest answer."

Ashley's defiant look wavered a little.

"I suppose you're right," Helmich said. "All of that nonsense is so tedious and messy. Let the record show that you simply have no opinion on the matter." He then turned to Bobby. "Your turn, young man."

Ashley spoke up before Bobby could open his mouth. "You act

like you don't care what happens if things don't go the way you want them to. But when it comes to not caring, the Lamotelokhai kicks your ass. That's something you people just don't get. You should probably listen to those of us who know."

Helmich gazed at her. "I *am* listening. And so are my superiors."

"Good," she said. "All of you go frack yourselves."

Helmich turned to Bobby.

Bobby considered backing up Ashley by repeating her words. But he didn't want to pass up a chance to say something that might make a difference.

"The Lamotelokhai is smarter than us. Smarter than all of us, even you. What you're trying to do proves it. You asked what role it should play. I think it should be hidden away somewhere so people like you can't find it, and it should help us the way it thinks is best for us. Like it has been doing." Bobby looked at the cameras and then at Helmich. "I think I understand what you're trying to do now. Have you seen the movie, 28 *Days Later*? It's a zombie movie."

Helmich smiled but still managed to look skeptical. "Now you're talking my language."

"Well, at the beginning these people break into a research lab to let some chimpanzees out of their cages. They think they're doing something good. They think people shouldn't keep animals in cages. But they don't know that the chimps have a disease called *rage*. Twenty-eight days after that, the main character wakes up from a coma, and he finds out almost everyone is either dead or has the disease." Bobby paused for a moment to make sure Helmich was listening. "I think you're the people freeing the chimps."

Helmich puckered his lips and adjusted his red glasses. "With one important difference. The animal rights activists in the film had no coherent plan. We, on the other hand, not only have a plan, but our plan is proving to be successful." He broke into a smile. "But extra points for effort, Bobby! Now, I have one more question for you folks. With the understanding that we intend to continue our course of action, is there anything you can tell us that might reduce the risks that you are so concerned about?"

"If you've split it up, put it back together," Peter said.

"I'm afraid our entire hypothesis is based upon segmenting it," Helmich replied.

Bobby realized this might be his last chance to say something. "Be careful what you ask it to do. It doesn't think like you do."

"Good advice," Helmich said. He waited for a moment. When no one else spoke up, he looked at his watch again. "Very well. This discussion is now concluded. It is time for us to discover how the Lamotelokhai functions. Bobby, I would like you to be a part of that."

"I want to be there, too," Ashley said. "I want to see what's happening, and I haven't been out of this bed except to go to the bathroom."

Helmich shook his head. "Not possible, unless you would like us to install implants in your skull, as we have done with Bobby."

Ashley just shook her head slightly and looked up at the ceiling.

Helmich walked over and rapped on the door. It opened, and several doctors came in. Helmich began to leave but then turned to them. "How about a double feature tonight? I will arrange for a viewing of *Papillon* and *All The Marbles*. Under the circumstances, however, and with all due respect to Bobby, we should pass on *28 Days Later*."

Bobby and Helmich took the elevator down to the room in the center of the array. The room was now completely filled with computer stations and racks of equipment. At least ten doctors or scientists worked at the computers or bustled around the machinery. The ten chambers were still at their farthest positions, which Bobby now knew to be 162 meters out. The chambers formed a distant circle of bright rectangles in the otherwise darkened space beyond the well-lit center room.

Helmich held a hand out toward a wheelchair parked next to the elevator. Bobby's protective helmet was in the wheelchair's seat.

"I'm sure you understand why we must activate your implants," Helmich said. "You may choose the helmet or the chair. Personally, I would choose both."

Bobby hated the helmet, so he moved it to the floor and sat in the wheelchair. Helmich nodded to one of the doctors, the same man who had been in control of Bobby's implants the day before. The now-familiar pulse in the back of Bobby's skull signaled that the implants were turned on. Helmich pushed the wheelchair to a position where Bobby could see out into the vast darkened space surrounding them, then he grabbed a rolling desk chair and sat beside Bobby.

"I wanted you to be here, Bobby, because it's possible you will have some valuable insight that we haven't considered. Please observe our procedures carefully. If you have a suggestion, raise your hand. Depending on the circumstances, we will allow you to explain. Is that clear?"

Bobby nodded, although he couldn't imagine these people would listen to any suggestions he might have.

"Very well," Helmich said. He then spoke to the entire room. "In your places, please. Let's waste no more valuable time. Systems reports, beginning with Bobby's hardware and software."

"Neural implants are activated and functioning normally," said the doctor who had turned on Bobby's implants.

A woman at the next computer station said, "Microclimate probes are functioning, and they indicate nominal variation during the last thirteen hours."

A man at the next station said, "All physical parameter probes functioning, with no variations detected."

The next guy said, "All biological parameter probes functioning. Nothing detected here, sir."

"Mechanical functions ready to roll, sir."

"Structural integrity probes are functional and indicate no changes."

"Chamber security locks and all alarms appear to be functional."

"Lighting and microclimate variables are optimal, unless you are uncomfortable, sir."

"All audio and video feeds are functioning properly."

This brought the reports full circle to the man at the station on Helmich's left. "Systems check on the four forty-four protocol indicates all systems go."

Helmich leaned in closer to Bobby. "I'm responsible for naming the 4:44 protocol. It's a reference to a film depicting the last day on Earth, which was to be destroyed at 4:44 AM. The protocol is a self-destruct safety measure. If things don't go as planned, we can activate it, destroying everything within the facility." He raised his brows and pulled back from Bobby's face a bit. "And you thought we were ill-prepared, didn't you?"

Bobby suddenly realized he was never going to leave this place. He was watching them start an experiment that would probably lead to his death within a few minutes. He raised his hand, resulting in a sharp pulse behind his ears. Helmich nodded for him to speak.

"I don't think this is going to end well. Can you let my friends and I go before you do whatever you're planning to do?"

Helmich smiled. "Forever resourceful, aren't you? But the fact of the matter is that we may need your help." He nodded again to the guy next to him, and the implants came back on.

Helmich stood up next to Bobby and addressed the entire

room. "Bring them in slowly. Alert me immediately to any change in any parameter, no matter how seemingly insignificant."

The machinery beneath the floor kicked on.

"Initiating convergence," a man said. "Point five meters per second."

In the distance the rectangles of light moved slightly.

"Alert me to any variation," Helmich repeated.

The man spoke again. "One-hundred forty-meter radius, eighty-eight meters between chambers."

Bobby sensed that everyone around him was nervous. Their eyes flitted a little too rapidly between their computer monitors and the approaching chambers. The machinery continued humming.

"One-hundred ten-meter radius, seventy meters between chambers."

"Stop," Helmich said.

The machinery beneath them fell silent, and the chambers stopped moving.

"Anything to report?" Helmich said. "Anything at all?"

The room was silent.

"Proceed."

The machinery started again.

"Ninety-meter radius, fifty-six meters between chambers."

The seconds passed like the wrenching of a spear in Bobby's flesh.

"Sir, I have something!"

"Stop," Helmich said.

The machinery stopped.

"I first saw it at eighty-five-meter radius, fifty-three meters between chambers," the man said. "A spike in EEG activity, common to all ten chambers."

"All ten chambers? Not just chamber one?"

"Common to all ten, sir."

Another man said, "At the same distance I detected slight mechanical movement. Not profound but certainly measurable."

A woman said, "Sir, at the same distance our unipolar grid indicates rather unusual activity with the high-density surface EMG."

"Hello, Bobby."

Bobby stiffened. He clamped his lips shut to avoid mouthing his words. "Lamotelokhai! Are you okay?"

"The proximity of my parts now allows me to function cognitively."

Helmich spoke to the doctors. "Expand the chambers to one-hundred meters. Tell me what you observe."

The machinery kicked on again.

The voice spoke in Bobby's head. "The distance between my parts is increasing, and soon I will not—"

The voice fell silent.

"That's the distance, sir. The activity has stopped."

"Same result here," the woman said.

"And here," another man said. "It looks like the critical point is eighty-seven meters radius, fifty-four meters between chambers."

"Lamotelokhai? Are you there?" Bobby tried to keep his face expressionless and still.

Helmich said, "Bring them back in to eighty meters."

The machinery hummed, and the chambers moved.

Several doctors reported that they were seeing something important again.

"Hello, Bobby. It appears that someone is attempting to understand the proximity needed for my parts to function collectively."

Bobby closed his eyes to concentrate on forming words. "Yes, I think that's what they're trying to do. They've got all kinds of probes and things, and they're trying to measure what's going on with your parts."

"Sir?"

Bobby opened his eyes. It was the doctor next to him, the one who operated the implants in his head. The guy was looking right at Bobby.

"What is it?" Helmich asked.

The man cleared his throat. "I wasn't sure at first, but it happened similarly both times. At the precise moment the others have reported physical and biological activity, the kid's brain has shown a significant increase in neural oscillations." The man hesitated. "It can't be a coincidence, sir."

The voice in Bobby's head said, "You are afraid. Why?"

Bobby didn't dare try to answer.

Helmich was gazing at him and frowning. He stepped over and kneeled down in front of the wheelchair, looking directly into Bobby's eyes as if he were searching for something.

"Bobby, are you talking to the Lamotelokhai?"

CHAPTER ELEVEN

QUENTIN LISTENED to a symphony of birdcalls as he relieved himself beyond sight of the camp. He recognized several doves and the screech of a cockatoo, but the other calls were unknown to him. The diversity of birds here was staggering. He looked up at the cloud of flies hovering above him. One of the benefits of the Lamotelokhai's particles was they somehow made his body invisible to biting insects. This benefit and numerous others still persisted eight months after his last contact with it.

He completed his task and returned to the campsite. Lindsey had finished stuffing the sleeping pads into one of the packs and was laying out the fruits and sago cakes from the Navera villagers. Quentin went to the stump where he had left the satellite phone the night before. It was the spot he had determined would have the best chance of receiving a signal in case Ardell Gray tried to call with news about Bobby and Ashley. They had to leave the phone turned off to conserve the battery, but it could be remotely turned on if the caller entered a specific PIN. He plucked the phone from the stump and powered it on. The phone refreshed its search for satellites and then showed a marginal signal, but there were no messages. He switched it back off, trying to convince himself that no news was actually good news.

Quentin, Samuel, and Sinanie sat down on the ground next to Lindsey and began eating. They would need the fuel for a long day of hiking, so they focused on chewing rather than talking.

Before long, the tree kangaroo, which Quentin hadn't seen since the previous evening, scampered out of the forest and stopped in the middle of their group. It began moving its forepaws, using its peculiar sign language.

Samuel said, "The mbolop has informed us that fresh water is available a reasonable distance from our camp. And apparently there is a breadnut tree near the water. The creature means to assist us, unaware perhaps that you have brought food and water with you."

Lindsey fished two water bottles from her pack, one half full and the other empty. "Perhaps we should fill these while we have the opportunity."

Sinanie got up and took the bottles from her. He stared at them curiously.

Lindsey took one back and screwed the lid off. "This is how it works," she said. She screwed it back on.

Sinanie frowned at the bottle, but then he took it from her and headed into the forest.

The tree kangaroo hopped closer to Lindsey and leaned forward, sniffing the air near her face.

"I think it likes you," Quentin said.

She gazed at it. "So this is one of the new mbolop from the colony you told us about?"

"Indeed," Samuel said. "The mbolop you call Mbaiso was quite willing to assign one of the creatures in the colony to assist on this journey."

Lindsey slowly extended a hand, palm down, and tried petting its head. The mbolop moved to one side to avoid her hand, but it didn't retreat. It then stepped even closer and pushed its snout within a foot of her nose. Lindsey's eyes grew wider, but she held her ground.

"What does it want?" she said.

"I have no idea of its intentions," Samuel replied. "The mbolop I have known have generally been helpful when needed, but rarely have they shown companionable tendencies."

Lindsey stared into the thing's eyes, a smile gradually forming on her face. "Is this a real flesh and blood animal, or is it made of Lamotelokhai particles like Mbaiso?"

"I'm afraid I do not know," Samuel said.

Lindsey fished her mbolop talisman from her pocket and held it out to the creature. "Look, this is you."

The thing sniffed the talisman. It then sat back on its haunches and began scratching its belly. This was a behavior Quentin had seen before, so he wasn't surprised when he heard a faint pop as the creature's skin ruptured. A moment later, the mbolop held out a moist lump of tissue with the obvious intention of giving it to Lindsey. It wanted her to eat it.

Lindsey accepted the lump. She glanced at Quentin. The look on her face was a bit alarming—she wasn't afraid. Not long ago, she would've been scared to death of this. Quentin sidled up to her and looked at the lump. Should he tell her not to eat it? Even though he had never seen anything bad come from such an offering, this particular mbolop was new, and they knew even less about it than they did about Mbaiso. Could the lump being offered help them find Addison?

He said, "Samuel, can you ask what it's trying to do?"

Samuel signed to the tree kangaroo. It faced him and signed back.

"I believe it intends no harm. I can't be completely certain, but it seems to believe Lindsey will soon need what it is offering her."

"I think it'll be okay," Lindsey said, half speaking and half laughing. She looked at Quentin. "But if you're not comfortable with it..."

Quentin was not at all comfortable with it. Yes, it had occurred to him that this might be something to help them find Addison. Or it might provide Lindsey with even more health benefits. Or perhaps it was the next step in whatever plans the Lamotelokhai had for them. But maybe he was wrong and it would kill her. There were too many possibilities to be comfortable with it.

He looked down at the lump of mbolop flesh in her hand. What he saw made him inhale sharply. It was gone. The last bits of it were disappearing through her skin and into her body.

"I guess it's too late," she said, staring at her empty palm. She turned to Quentin with a blank look, perhaps still processing what had just happened.

He took her hand in his and studied her face. "It's going to be okay. It'll be some way to make you stronger, I'm sure." But he wasn't sure.

She squeezed his hand and tried to smile. But then she squeezed his hand harder—far too hard.

"Quentin! I don't—"

She heaved, like she was going to throw up.

"Are you okay?"

She pushed his hand away and unfolded her legs, trying to get up.

Quentin was on his feet. "Lindsey!"

She let out an incoherent moan and collapsed onto her face.

"Lindsey!" Quentin shook her shoulder. She was unconscious. He rolled her over. Her eyes were half open, staring but not moving. Samuel rushed over to Lindsey's side as Quentin put his cheek just above her mouth. He felt her breath against his face. He grabbed her wrist, feeling for a pulse. He found it. It was strong and rapid. He shook her again. "Lindsey!"

No response.

Quentin gently pushed her eyelids shut to prevent her eyes from drying out, and then he sat back on his heels. Samuel said something beside him, but Quentin paid no attention. He should have stopped her. He should have immediately grabbed the lump from her hand and thrown it back at the tree kangaroo. Why in the hell hadn't he stopped her?

He turned to the creature, which was still sitting there watching. His first impulse was to grab the thing and tear it apart. "Samuel, what did it do? Ask it what it did!"

"I'll do what I can."

Quentin turned his attention back to his wife, but he saw Samuel and the mbolop exchanging gestures in his peripheral vision. Lindsey's eyes had begun to twitch beneath the lids, as if she were in REM sleep. Maybe that was a good sign.

Samuel spoke up. "I cannot determine if the mbolop is unaware of what it has done, or if I have simply failed to understand its meaning. Although the mbolop are more sophisticated than true wild tree kangaroos, still they are simple and brutish creatures, and I have long believed that they can do little more than follow elementary requests."

"Who would have asked it to do *this*?"

"I cannot say," Samuel replied. "I was not able to decipher all of its explanation. It seemed to be saying that Lindsey now belongs to it, or perhaps that they each belong to one another. I cannot be certain."

Quentin turned to Lindsey and watched her breasts rise and fall. Samuel's explanation made no sense and only heightened his fears.

Lindsey moaned. She opened her eyes and sucked in a lungful of air. Her eyes rolled around, searching, until they found Quentin.

"Are you okay?" he said, so softly he barely heard his own voice.

She blinked. "Was I asleep?"

"You were unconscious. For several minutes."

She rubbed her eyes. 'Oh god. I thought I was awake through the whole thing."

Quentin put his hand on her cheek. "Did you have a dream? A vision?"

She shook her head. "It was real. I know it was." She sat up and then rubbed her eyes again. She looked at Quentin. "It's inside of me. I felt it—I even saw it. It put itself into me and spread to every part of my body. Even into my head. It's still there. I can feel it."

He shook his head, confused. "What's still there?"

She nodded at the creature sitting a few feet away. "The mbolop."

"What?"

She didn't reply. Instead, she held a hand out toward the mbolop, palm down. The creature rolled off its haunches and ambled toward her. It sniffed her hand and then stepped even closer. She leaned forward and actually touched her nose to its snout.

Quentin said, "Lindsey?"

She turned to him and gradually formed a slight smile. As she gazed at Quentin, her hand moved to the mbolop. The creature held steady, allowing her to stroke its head.

CHAPTER TWELVE

Helmich was inches from Bobby's face, staring into his eyes with fascination. The central room had become very quiet.

"They know!" Bobby said with his thoughts. "They know I'm talking to you."

The Lamotelokhai replied, "You believe that is a bad thing. Why?"

Helmich nodded to the doctor next to them, and a pulse shot through the back of Bobby's skull as the implants were turned off.

"Well?" Helmich said. "Are you talking to it? Is it talking to you?"

Bobby didn't know what to do. The only thing in his favor up to this point had been that he could talk to the Lamotelokhai without Helmich knowing. Bobby said aloud, "I think it's trying to talk to me. It's kind of like a voice in my head." He then pursed his lips shut and thought, "They know we're talking! What should I do?"

The Lamotelokhai replied, "I cannot know what to advise you to do because I do not know the outcome you desire."

"What is the voice saying to you?" Helmich asked.

"It's kind of hard to tell. It doesn't think like us, so it doesn't really talk like us. Just a minute." Bobby wrinkled his brows, trying to look like he was concentrating on the voice in his head. Silently he said, "I want to put your parts back together so we can get out of here. I'm scared something bad will happen if we don't."

"In this situation, what is bad?"

"If people get hurt or killed, it's bad."

"With my parts separated into subgroups as they are, your fears are justified. With the subgroups of my parts near, as they are now, my consciousness functions collectively, although physical movement is limited. However, when the distance between the subgroups is increased so that they cannot function collectively, I cannot predict what might happen."

"So what should I do?"

"If you would like the others to understand this, perhaps you could explain it to them."

"They won't listen to me. Is there any way you can tell them?"

"If they wish to talk to me, they could recombine the subgroups of my parts."

"They won't do that."

"Then perhaps they can put their hands upon one of the subgroups of my parts."

This was an idea. Bobby turned to Helmich. "It's definitely talking to me. And it wants to talk to you."

Helmich raised his brows and smiled. "Well, okay!"

"It can't talk to you unless you put your hands on it."

Helmich frowned. "You don't have your hands on it."

"Some of its parts are inside me. So I don't need to touch it."

The voice spoke in his head. "Bobby, there is something I would like to tell you."

Bobby held a finger up to Helmich. "Just a minute. It's telling me something." And then silently, "I'm listening."

"You have told me you believe it is bad if people are hurt or killed. Since I cannot predict what might happen under the current circumstances, I have decided to give you some information. You should recombine the subgroups of my parts. If you cannot do this, you should convince the others to recombine the subgroups of my parts. If they cannot or will not do this, the following is information you may want to know. My ability to function cognitively is something you may think of as my consciousness, or perhaps my personality. Or perhaps you may think of it as my operating system. My consciousness, or my operating system, exists when my parts are together. As a precaution, I have previously duplicated and compartmentalized my consciousness into twenty-four packets of information. These twenty-four packets can be extracted and recombined to restore my consciousness if you ever feel the need to do so."

Bobby felt his gut tightening.

The Lamotelokhai continued. "If circumstances occur that make you feel the need to restore my consciousness, you will need to access and recombine the twenty-four packets of information."

Helmich sighed loudly and gazed at Bobby.

"Where are the packets?" Bobby asked silently.

"One of them is within you."

Bobby stiffened. "Within me? When did you do that?"

"Eight months, one week, and six days ago. Before that, the twenty-four packets of information were within men and women of the hanging village."

Bobby blinked, trying to process this new information. "Addison killed some of the villagers, so you put one of the packets in me?"

"That is correct."

"I didn't even know it was in me. Why didn't you tell me?"

"Putting one packet within you would have little effect on your awareness, and so I did not tell you. I would like to tell you now how to access and recombine the twenty-four packets of information if you feel the need to do so."

Helmich grabbed him by the shoulders. "Bobby, if you want me to believe the Lamotelokhai is talking to you, you'll need to tell me what you are experiencing at this time."

Frustrated, Bobby rubbed the itchy part of his scalp next to the implants behind his ears. "It's trying to tell me something. Please just give me a minute!"

Helmich narrowed his eyes and flared his nostrils.

"You need to tell me!" Bobby thought. "I'm running out of time. Where are the other packets? How do I do it?"

"In addition to your body, I have placed packets of my information within the bodies of the following people: Sinanie, Matiinuo, Ot, Jara, Rossa, Teatakan, Sirizo, Yerema, Korul, Kumbi, Kebuge, Anaru, Owa, Samuel, Quentin, Lindsey, Carlos, Ashley, and Addison."

Bobby had a hundred questions but no time. "Okay, how do I do it?"

Helmich shook his head. "I am unwilling to play this game any longer." He spoke to the entire room. "Move the chambers outward to ninety-meter radius."

The machinery below the floor kicked on, and the chambers began moving.

"Wait!" Bobby said aloud. "Just listen to me—it wants to talk to you! All you have to do is go into one of the chambers and put your hand on it. Then it'll send its particles into your body so you can talk to it in your head."

Helmich looked at the other doctors one at a time. It seemed like he was considering this.

The machinery stopped. "Ninety-meter radius, sir," a man said.

"It'll save you tons of time," Bobby said. "Instead of doing all these experiments, you can just talk to it. It'll answer all your questions."

"I'd like to volunteer to try it, sir." It was the woman who had reported unusual activity with the high-density surface EMG.

"Lamotelokhai, are you there?"

No response. The chambers were too far apart.

"Well, this certainly is an interesting turn of events," Helmich said. He was pacing back and forth now. He stopped in front of Bobby. "I suppose it's possible you are trying to trick us in some way. But are you capable of such a thing, particularly when you understand the consequences to you and your friends?"

Was Bobby supposed to answer this? "It told me it can't do anything physical while you have it separated. You know that's true. That's why you did it. I'm not trying to trick you."

Helmich started pacing again. He stopped in front of the woman. She got up from her workstation.

"I'd like to try it," she said.

Helmich said, "I'm impressed by your dedication to this project, Eunice."

"I've waited my entire life to do something like this, sir."

Helmich nodded at her. "Very well. Verbally report every detail of your experience. Nothing is too small." He turned to Bobby. "What does she need to do?"

"It said it wants to talk, so she just needs to put her hands on one of the parts."

Helmich shrugged and nodded at Eunice.

"Thank you, sir." She got an earpiece from one of the other doctors and walked out of the well-lit center room and into the huge darkened space, headed for chamber one.

"Wait a minute," Bobby said. "I thought you were going to move the parts in closer first. They need to be in closer for it to talk to her."

"One thing at a time," Helmich said while watching Eunice walk away.

"But she might get hurt!" Bobby had raised his voice without meaning to. "The Lamotelokhai told me the parts need to be closer, so it can think and talk."

Helmich finally took his eyes off Eunice and turned to him. "As I said, one thing at a time."

"But that's what it said! I'm trying to tell you what you need—"

"That's enough!" Helmich nodded at the doctor next to Bobby.

Bobby twitched at the pulse in the back of his head. He immediately raised his hand.

Helmich ignored him and returned his attention to the woman doctor. When she was almost to chamber one, Helmich sat down in his rolling chair, wheeled it to a computer monitor and said, "Display the feed from one of the cameras in chamber one."

Bobby lowered his hand. He got up from the wheelchair and walked to Helmich's side so he could see the monitor. Helmich glanced up at him and frowned but didn't tell him to sit back down. Chamber one was ninety meters out, too far to see much without the video.

"She's at the door," Helmich said. "Let her in."

The video was from a camera on the chamber's ceiling, and the wide-angle lens showed the entire room in high-def color. On one side of the screen, the hatch opened and Eunice stepped in. She closed the hatch behind her.

"I'm in the chamber. Video and audio check." Her voice came loud and clear from a speaker somewhere in the center lab.

"Video and audio confirmed," Helmich said.

"And confirmed here," she replied. "I'm going to remove the microchamber." She stepped over to Addison's head and neck. The body part was still on the floor where Bobby had left it, but a clear box had been placed over it. Wires and probes were attached to the box, and even more wires fed through a hole in the box directly to the body part itself. On each of its four sides, the box had a latch that had been bolted to the floor.

Eunice got to her knees and flipped open one of the latches. She moved around the box, flipping the other three. She carefully tipped the box on its side so that the wires were still in place. She sat there on her knees, staring at Addison's head.

Bobby had to try again. He raised his hand and waved it to get Helmich's attention.

Helmich glanced at him and then sighed. "Let him speak."

The pulse came quickly. "I really think you should move the parts—"

Eunice's voice came over the speaker. "I feel a strange tingling."

Bobby turned to the monitor. She had already placed her hands on Addison's head.

"The sensation is moving up my arms. Perhaps when it reaches my brain the entity will be able to speak to me."

"Please move the chambers in closer," Bobby pleaded.

Helmich studied Bobby's face, like he was trying to decide. "Okay, bring the chambers in." The machinery below the floor kicked on. "Eunice, remove your hands from the entity, please."

Eunice said, "The sensation is almost to my head."

'Eighty-five-meter radius," one of the doctors said.

"Hello, Bobby."

Bobby clamped his lips shut. "Lamotelokhai. Is everything okay?"

"It appears that particles of one of my portions have diminished somewhat."

"Eunice!" Helmich said. "Remove your hands from the entity now. We're going to try again after bringing the chambers in."

Eunice hesitated a moment longer, as if she really didn't want to pull her hands away. Finally she withdrew. "Yes, sir."

Bobby formed words in his mind. "A woman was trying to talk to you. Just now, when your parts were too far apart to talk to me."

"The results could be interesting."

Bobby stared at the monitor. "What do you mean, interesting?"

"I mean the results will be unpredictable. The results will be interesting to me, but they may be dangerous for you."

"Something's happening, sir." It was Eunice. She was feeling the sides of her face with her hands. "I think it's trying to communicate."

Bobby watched the video, his apprehension growing. "Why would it be dangerous to me?" he said with his thoughts, although he feared he already knew the answer.

Helmich said, "What exactly are you experiencing, Eunice?"

She didn't answer him. Instead she kept rubbing her face.

"Because my parts were designed to be used when they are together and fully functional," the Lamotelokhai said. "My parts are not fully functional when separated. If you wish to minimize your risk, you could rejoin the subgroups of my parts."

Bobby turned to Helmich again. "I really think—"

"Something's wrong," Eunice said. Still holding her face, she went to the chamber's hatch and tried to open it. "Please open the door."

Helmich gazed silently at the monitor.

"Sir?" one of the doctors said.

"Don't unlock it. Not yet. What's going on, Bobby?"

"I don't know. But it just told me we should put its parts together to make it less dangerous."

"Open the door!" Eunice shouted. She yanked frantically at the handle. "Open it! Open the goddamn door!"

"Do not unlock that door," Helmich said forcefully.

Eunice stumbled away from the hatch, holding her head. "Stop! Please stop it!" She started hitting her face with her fists. "Stop!"

One of the doctors said, "Sir, we have to help her."

Helmich rose to his feet and wheeled around, facing a man who was standing by the elevator. "Wesley, draw your sidearm. If anyone attempts to unlock that hatch, shoot them."

The man pulled a pistol from his belt and stepped forward to where he could see everyone.

"What the hell?" the man next to Bobby said.

Bobby turned to him, thinking the guy was upset about the gun being pulled out, but the man was staring at the video feed. Bobby looked at the screen, and a lump formed in his throat. Eunice was running in circles within the chamber. But it was the *way* she was running. Every few steps she would spin around, bending at the waist so that her hands touched the floor. She would flop over, spin in a circle on all fours, stand up, run another few steps, and then flop over again, like a broken robot doll. Everyone fell silent as they watched. The only sounds were the strange grunts from Eunice as she flopped and stumbled around and the pulsating motor beneath the floor as it steadily moved the chambers closer to them.

Bobby couldn't take his eyes off the screen. He had never seen anyone move like that. It was both horrifying and mesmerizing. "Something terrible is happening," Bobby said aloud. He had intended to say this silently to the Lamotelokhai.

"I am detecting disorderly cognitive signals in the vicinity of one of the subgroups of my parts," the Lamotelokhai said in Bobby's head. "If you wish to minimize your risk, you could rejoin the subgroups of my parts. Once rejoined, I might have the ability to minimize the danger to you."

Eunice stopped. She looked around the chamber as if she had no idea where she was. Bobby turned from the monitor and looked directly at the chamber, which had stopped less than ten meters out. Eunice's eyes fell upon the central room and the people in it. With no warning at all, she lunged toward them, apparently unaware of the two-inch glass on the front of the chamber. She hit it with a thunk and blood splattered from her nose onto the glass. The act was so violent that Bobby stumbled back a step and several doctors cried out in surprise.

Eunice fell onto the chamber floor so hard her head bounced twice. She tried to roll over, but her arms and legs jabbed around wildly, preventing any coordinated movement.

"Seal the air vents to that chamber," Helmich said. "Lock down the entire facility, now. Initiate alert phase of the 4:44 protocol."

Helmich lunged at Bobby and grabbed him by the head, using the two implants as handles. "Tell me what's happening or I'll call upstairs and have all three of your friends killed!"

Bobby cried out in pain. "I don't know! If you let me talk to it, I can find out."

"God almighty!" someone said.

Helmich turned to look at chamber one. He released Bobby's head and stared.

Bobby backed out of his reach. He looked at the chamber, and suddenly he forgot the pain in his head. Eunice's body had somehow broken into two halves. Bobby's eyes were drawn to the lower half, which was really just two legs held together by part of the hips. The legs were moving, bending at the knees and then pushing off against the floor, scooting the hips steadily across the room and leaving a wide, red smear. Suddenly the legs separated, and one of them moved in a new direction, dragging the other with it by the tattered remains of elastic pants.

The top half of Eunice's body was trying to crawl up the front wall of the chamber, but her hands kept slipping on the glass. She pressed her mouth against the glass like she was trying to use it as a suction cup. Bobby watched her bloody tongue rolling around against the glass.

Helmich walked out of the center lab and toward chamber one. He stopped a few feet from the glass and just stared.

"Sir?" It was one of the doctors. "I'd like to leave. I volunteered to be on this team, but this—this isn't what I signed up for."

Helmich didn't turn around. He just stared into the chamber. "The facility is locked down," he said, almost too quietly to be heard. "No one leaves."

"I agree with Kendrick," said another doctor. "We should be allowed to leave."

Suddenly Helmich jumped back from the chamber. He turned around, his eyes wide. "Get everyone with security status down here now! Go to critical phase of 4:44. No one leaves this room until we contain this."

And then Bobby saw it. Eunice's mouth had created a hole in the glass, as if her saliva had simply melted it away. And she was coming out through the hole. The red tip of her tongue had pushed through, and it just kept coming. It oozed down the outer surface of the glass, stretching and then thickening like a huge earthworm, getting longer by the second, until the end of it found the floor two feet below the hole. It began slithering across the floor as more and more of it emerged. As the worm grew, Eunice's face became shriveled and unrecognizable.

The entire center lab erupted into chaos. Some of the doctors tried getting in the elevator, but the security men Helmich had called for were pouring out of it, and they drew their guns to stop the doctors from leaving. Helmich barked out orders, but no one was listening. One of the security guys approached chamber one with an orange canister, kind of like a fire extinguisher, and sprayed the hole in the glass and the nightmare that was coming out of it. When the white cloud settled, the crawling thing kept wriggling ferociously, seemingly unaffected. Another security guy was taking flimsy-looking facemasks to everyone in the room, ordering them to put them on. As he passed Bobby, he hesitated, but then he handed him one of the masks. Bobby couldn't imagine how the mask could help, but he strapped it over his mouth and nose anyway.

He turned back to Eunice in time to see the worm detach from the remains of her head. The thing was at least four feet long, and it began squirming toward the center room. Suddenly Eunice's body shoved one of its arms through the widening hole. The arm groped the outer surface of the glass, and Bobby thought he heard bones cracking as it felt its way in a complete circle around the hole.

A gun fired, and Bobby reflexively ducked his head. It was one of the security guys. His bullet had struck Eunice's protruding arm and shattered it at the elbow. Her forearm dangled from the hole, swinging back and forth. The man shot again and the forearm came loose. It started flopping and squirming on the floor.

"Put your goddamn gun away before a ricochet kills someone!" Helmich said amidst the rising panic. He pointed to the parts of Eunice that had come out through the hole. "Get those things into containment bags!"

"Bobby, you are afraid. Why?"

Several doctors were placing pieces of equipment in front of the slithering thing that used to be Eunice's tongue, trying to stop it from entering the center room.

Bobby shouted at the Lamotelokhai, "Because everything's going to hell!"

"If you wish to minimize your risk—"

"I know!" Bobby cried. He made his way to Helmich's side. "The only way to stop this is to get its help. Please!"

Helmich was opening the seal of a large, silver plastic bag, and he ignored Bobby. He then shoved the bag into the hands of one of the security guys. "Get those things into the bag and incinerate them!"

Another man was already trying to put a bag over Eunice's severed arm, but the arm had somehow grown legs and was skittering in circles so fast he couldn't catch it.

Bobby looked again at chamber one. The hole was now larger, and the remainder of Eunice's upper body was crawling through it. But the body no longer resembled Eunice. It looked more like some kind of lizard, or maybe a lobster. Or maybe both. There was definitely a head, with two round eyes and a wide mouth, and the head had already crawled out the hole in the glass. The arm stub that had been shot off at the elbow now had regrown clawed fingers, which were digging into the glass, steadily pushing the chest through the hole. The longer arm didn't look anything like the stubby one. It was covered with a glistening exoskeleton that reminded Bobby of a huge insect or lobster leg.

The creature popped out the hole and fell awkwardly to the floor. Bobby then saw there was another head at its back end. The second head looked like a miniature elephant's, with a foot-long snout that whipped around as if the elephant were struggling to break free of the rest of the body.

Bobby had seen some terrifying things since he had met the Lamotelokhai, but nothing like this creature. A security man shot it twice, but the thing kept moving and changing. Another man made a desperate lunge at the creature, trying to enclose it in one of the silver bags. The bag went over the end with the lizard head but it got hung up on the legs. The creature whipped around and the weird elephant-like snout encircled the man's wrist.

"Kill it, it's biting me!" the man screamed.

The other man opened fire, shooting point blank at the creature until his gun only clicked.

The creature released the man's wrist, and the guy rolled onto his side, holding his arm. "You idiot, you shot me!" And then the elephant thing was on top of him, this time going straight for his face. The silver bag still covered half its body, and the bag began shaking violently like it was full of pissed-off cats.

Another creature the size of Eunice's leg crawled through the hole. This one resembled a crocodile, but it was still changing. A dog-like leg protruded from its side, just behind one of the front legs. The creature ignored the screaming man already under attack and started walking straight for Bobby. But then the extra dog leg kicked out swiftly and knocked the creature onto its side. It squirmed and then righted itself, but by this time the creature had transformed into a patchwork of reptile and mammal parts. The crocodile-like mouth gaped and let out a wet, sloshy growl, as if the transformation process were excruciating.

Doctors were now fighting to get on the elevator, and the two security guys who had been trying to stop them gave up and ran to help the man who had been bitten and shot. There were too many doctors to fit in the elevator, and the doors wouldn't shut. A fist flew from within the elevator and struck a man who was trying to push his way in. His head jerked from the blow and he fell to the floor. Angry shouts then escalated into a full-blown mob fight and the fallen man was trampled by scuffling feet.

"Bobby, you are still afraid. Why?"

Bobby blinked. The voice in his head had roused him from his horrified trance. "I don't know what's happening," he said, this time with thought-words. "But I have to do something."

"If you wish to minimize—"

Someone grabbed Bobby roughly by the shoulder and spun him around. Helmich leaned over, his face a foot from Bobby's. "Alright, do it!" he said.

Bobby shook his head. "Do what?"

"Put the parts back together! If you think it can stop this, then do it. I'll unlock all the chambers." He released Bobby and went to one of the computer stations.

Bobby nodded and said, "Okay," although Helmich was already too far away to hear him over the chaos. Bobby headed for chamber one, but he stopped when he looked through the glass. The last portion of Eunice's body—her other leg—had split into smaller parts, and the parts had become scurrying, climbing, slithering, and oozing creatures. They were all over the inside of the chamber, and at least one—a black thing like a huge mantis with extra-long legs— had found the hole in the glass and was crawling through it.

There was no way Bobby was going into chamber one.

He started for the next chamber. As he ran by the man who had been attacked, he realized the guy had stopped fighting. The elephant-like creature had released him and was rolling on the floor, trying to disengage from the now-shredded silver bag. The man was still lying on his back. He was alive, but instead of getting up to run away, he was staring in horror at his own body. His green clothing had been mostly torn away, possibly by the claws and fingers of whatever he was becoming.

Bobby backed away and then ran to the door of chamber two. Just as he reached for the hatch's lever, an arm shot over his shoulder and grabbed one of his hands.

"Open it!" It was Helmich reaching over Bobby's shoulder.

Together they lifted the lever and threw the hatch open. Helmich rushed in, knocking Bobby to the floor and falling on top of him. Helmich jumped up and quickly shut the hatch. He turned around, facing Bobby. Breathing hard, Helmich raised his hand and stared at it. Something had bitten off two of his fingers. Blood flowed out and fell onto Bobby's shoes.

Bobby kicked his feet out, pushing himself back from the dripping blood. He got up and looked through the glass front. The doctors, and now the security guys, were still fighting to get in the elevator, too panicked to organize a smaller group to go up first. Something the size of a dog darted past on the other side of the glass wall, too fast for Bobby to see what it was. It had run between the chambers into the vast dark space beyond. Bobby looked to where the transforming man and the creature in the silver bag had been. Now there were only smears of blood on the floor—they were both gone.

Suddenly another dark shape shot out from between two of the chambers and smashed directly into the mass of people fighting in the elevator. The creature, whatever it was, ripped into them in a blur of teeth and claws. The people erupted from the elevator in panic. Bobby could see they were crying and screaming, but it was all eerily silent behind the thick glass. Some of them ran between the chambers to the space beyond, while others fell where they were, struggling but too hurt to get up.

A grunt from behind caused Bobby to turn away from the nightmare beyond the glass. Helmich had pulled off his shirt and was wrapping it around his injured hand. A key card hung on a spiral lanyard around his neck, slapping his bare chest as he worked.

"Hello, Bobby," the Lamotelokhai said in his head. "You are still afraid."

Bobby tried to calm himself and focus his thoughts. "I was going to put your parts back together, but now I'm trapped. I don't think I can get to your other parts." Bobby looked at Helmich, who was now staring at the glass wall in a trance. "In fact, I don't think I can even stay in *here* for long."

"How many subgroups of my parts can you put together?"

"There's only one part in here. I can't get to the others."

The Lamotelokhai remained silent for several long seconds. "This is an interesting situation."

Helmich was now rubbing his face with his good hand in the same way Eunice had rubbed hers.

"Maybe it's interesting to you, but I'm about to die!"

"With the present arrangement of my parts, I cannot help you."

"Then I'm dead!" Bobby shouted aloud. Helmich didn't even glance over at him.

"Bobby," said the Lamotelokhai, "you have access to one of the subgroups of my parts, correct?"

Bobby looked at Addison's left arm and shoulder within the clear micro chamber latched to the floor. "Yes, but only one."

"At this moment I am doing what I can to reconfigure the functions of the subgroup nearest to you. Perhaps that subgroup can be of some use to you."

Bobby started unlatching the micro chamber from the floor. "I thought you said people shouldn't do things with just a part of you."

"I am doing what I can to reconfigure the functions of the subgroup. I believe I can reconfigure its functions so that it will not be as dangerous to you."

Bobby finished unlatching the microchamber. He shoved it

over and kicked it away, ripping out the probes and wires. "What can I do with it?"

"It is difficult for me to know."

Bobby stared at the arm and shoulder and frowned. "Okay."

A sound came from behind Bobby and his gut clenched tight. It was a large body hitting the floor, followed by the moist tearing of flesh. He wheeled around. Helmich was mostly gone. In his place was a hulking jumble of partially-formed animal parts, each of them pushing and straining against the others to the point of tearing flesh wide open. There wasn't much left that was recognizable as Helmich, other than some pieces of his green clothing. His red glasses lay on the floor to the side. And there, hanging from the creature's neck and head, which now looked something like a fruit bat, was the lanyard with the key card.

Bobby had to get out of there. With no plan in mind, he picked up the clear shell of the microchamber, raised it high, and brought it down hard on the mass of fighting creatures, halfway enclosing them within the box. He kicked it, rolling the entire box and writhing body onto its side. There was the key card, right on top. He lunged forward and grabbed the card, pulling it back just as the fruit bat tried to sink its teeth into his hand. The spiral cord stretched—it was caught around the bat's neck. Bobby yanked on it as hard as he could. The bat screeched, the cord came loose, and Bobby fell on his butt next to Addison's arm. He scooped up the arm and scrambled to his feet.

To get out of the chamber, he would have to jump over Helmich's transforming body. He couldn't risk that, so he circled to the side covered by the clear microchamber. He kicked the chamber again, which pushed the struggling mass an inch to the side. He sucked in a lungful of air and kicked it again and again, spitting out one word with each kick.

"Get...out...of...my...freakin'...way!"

One of the creatures within the mass—the fruit bat—seemed to be winning the battle for dominance over the others. A long, wing-like arm protruded from each side. The arms grappled with the floor, allowing the creature to turn the entire mass to face Bobby. It started to stand up.

It was now or never. Bobby kicked the microchamber cover one more time, pushing the creature back another few inches. He grabbed the hatch, threw it open, and jumped through into the space between chambers.

His ears were assaulted with cries of people in panic and pain. He glanced at the center room. The elevator doors were trying to close over and over, stopped by several transforming, fighting, screeching bodies. No chance of going that way. There had to be a stairway somewhere, but 162 meters of cavernous space surrounded the center lab in every direction. Bobby could see shapes out there in the semi-darkness. Some of them were on two legs—the doctors and security men who had so far avoided being killed or transformed. But other shapes had more than two legs, or they had wings, or flippers. And most of them were close on the heels of the panicked people.

Where were the stairs? He would have to make it to the outer wall and then search the perimeter until he found them. Or, he could stay here in the center and try to recombine the Lamotelokhai's parts. To do that he'd have to go into every cham-ber. But the area was crawling with monsters. Some of them were no bigger than mice, but that probably didn't matter. One bite or scratch and he would be transformed like all the others. The bodies in the elevator were starting to take shape. In fact, they had all merged together into one, and the massive things was getting to its feet—a creature with a long neck and head like an emu, but a body somewhere between a kangaroo and a velociraptor.

Bobby stood there between the chambers, key card in one hand and Addison's arm in the other. "I can't put your parts together," he said silently.

"I am detecting the cognitive functions of others. There are many of them. They seem to have my parts within them, but they are unable to communicate with me."

"That's because they're deformed animals! Can you make them stop?"

"It is not possible for me to control them. I can only attempt to speak to them."

Suddenly a dark shape filled the hatch to chamber two, which was hanging open. Bobby instinctively shrank away until his back was against the wall of chamber one. But this put only a few feet of space between him and the creature that used to be Helmich. Apparently the fruit bat had won the struggle for control over Helmich's body, and now the thing was crawling through the hatch directly toward him. Clawed wings longer than Bobby's body tapped and scratched against metal as the creature awkwardly grappled with the opening. As it emerged, it paused to look toward the well-lit center room. It then turned and looked out into the dark space beyond the chambers. Finally it looked at Bobby. It started scratching again, this time more violently. It was coming for him.

Bobby inched to his left, away from the center room. The thing's head was only three feet from his face. The creature fell the rest of the way out of the hatch and then steadied itself with its folded wings and two legs that seemed too long to belong to a bat. Now it was close enough that he felt its breath on his face.

"Help me!" Bobby thought. "I don't want to die like this."

"In my current state there is little I can—"

"I know! But this thing's going to kill me. Make it stop. Fry its brain or something!"

For several seconds the Lamotelokhai didn't reply. The giant bat leaned in closer, almost touching Bobby's nose.

Suddenly the creature lifted its head. It looked one way, then the other, like it was confused.

"I have sent information to the entity that is nearest you. It is likely the entity will need a short time to process the information. But only a short time. This is all I can do, but perhaps it will be useful to you."

Bobby bolted. He ran out from between the chambers into the vast, dark space. He felt increasing dread as every step took him farther from the light of the center room. He still heard terrified cries from a few other people, mixed with the sounds of monstrous things. At least he couldn't see any dark shapes moving around in the area directly in front of him. He cradled Addison's arm like a football and continued to sprint for the outer wall.

When he thought he was about halfway out, he heard claws scraping concrete behind him. And the sound was getting louder by the second. He looked back. The Helmich-bat was scrabbling after him, running on its hind legs and folded wings. Bobby almost cried out in fear but stopped himself. He didn't want to attract the attention of the other creatures. He gripped Addison's arm tighter and turned on every bit of speed he could.

Now he could see the outer wall, maybe fifty yards away. But the creature was only half that distance behind him and was still gaining.

Thirty yards to the wall. He saw now that it was just a blank concrete surface. He scanned left and then right. There was something there, in the distance, a faintly glowing rectangle halfway up the wall. Bobby veered to the right. It had to be an exit sign. The scraping claws got even louder as the creature also cut to the right, closing the distance at an angle.

"I need your help again!" Bobby screamed with his thoughts.

There was no reply, only the scraping of claws on concrete behind him.

"Lamotelokhai!"

Nothing. He was too far from the other nine parts.

The glowing rectangle was getting closer. It *was* an exit sign— he could see a door beneath it. But then he saw something else, a dark shape in front of the door. In fact, there were two shapes. He could see them now, the body of one of the doctors—a woman—and a creature crouched over her, chewing on her abdomen. They were right in front of the door.

"I need help!" Bobby thought, although he knew the Lamotelokhai couldn't hear him.

The Helmich-bat was right behind him, and he was ten yards from the door. He had no idea if he could open it, even if it weren't blocked by another monster.

The thing chewing on the body raised its head and looked at Bobby. It was dog-like, but its back end was more like a reptile's, and it had a bulging hump over its shoulders.

Suddenly the woman beneath it began struggling, and Bobby saw that her arms had already transformed into squirming, tentacle-like things. One of the tentacles encircled the reptile-dog's neck, and the two creatures began snarling and struggling.

Bobby skirted around them, the Helmich bat at his heels. He put his back to the wall and held Addison's arm in front of him to use as a shield. But the bat skidded to a stop beside the two fighting creatures. It paused there, watching the battle.

This would give Bobby a few seconds at the most. He swallowed hard and turned back to the door. The glowing rectangle above it said *Salida*. He saw a black key-scanning box on the wall by the door's handle. He pressed Helmich's key card against the box as he had seen the doctors do.

The door clicked.

Bobby turned the handle and pushed it open. There was a dimly-lit stairway leading up. He started through the door, but then something grabbed the right side of his head and neck and held tight. He dropped Addison's arm and reached over his shoulder. His fingers found the bat's head, its teeth tearing into his flesh.

"No!" He tried gouging one of the creature's eyes with his

thumb. The teeth only sank in deeper, and a claw dug painfully into his arm.

Bobby twisted his body and lunged through the doorway to escape the bat's hold. The teeth ripped away from the flesh of his head and neck, causing pain so intense that flashes of light flooded his vision. He hit the floor hard. He put his hands to the back of his head, trying to stifle the pain. The implant behind his right ear was gone, torn off by the creature's teeth.

Blinding light was all he could see, but he felt the creature crawling over his legs, coming again for his head. He tried kicking, but the thing's weight held his feet down. He blinked, and now he could see the creature's hulking shape. His vision was starting to come back. The bat's head was now above his chest.

Bobby choked back a sob. There was no point in fighting now. The thing had already torn into him, contaminating his body with the same rogue Lamotelokhai particles that were killing and transforming all the others. Soon it would start in his body. In spite of his horror, for just a moment Bobby wondered what kind of creature would force its way out of his body, or if perhaps he would split into many creatures like Eunice had. Even if he could escape now, he would only be carrying the same fate to the people upstairs, including Ashley, Peter, and Robert.

He turned his head and saw Addison's arm on the floor next to him. His mind besieged by terror, he instinctively allowed the arm to represent a glimmer of hope.

Bobby grunted and pulled his knees up to his chest. He then kicked his legs out, sending the bat sprawling back. But it quickly gathered its wings and legs beneath it and started coming for him again. Bobby threw Addison's arm through the half-open doorway and then pushed against the floor with his feet, shoving the door the rest of the way open and scooting his own body through.

The bat lunged and caught Bobby's shoe with its teeth. He kicked the door with his other foot. The door struck the thing's head, tearing its teeth from his shoe. Bobby was on his feet in an instant. He pushed on the door, but it closed on the bat's neck and wouldn't shut. The bat let out a gurgle as he leaned into the door even harder. Its claws desperately raked the outside of the door and the wall as it tried to pull itself free.

Bobby was vaguely aware he could have opened the door slightly and the creature would have pulled its head out, but he didn't care. Instead, he slammed his shoulder against the door with all his strength. The creature gurgled again. Bobby put both hands against the door and leaned into it. He braced his feet against the bottom step and was able to push even harder. He heard himself sobbing, so he pushed with everything he had in a desperate, demented attempt to make the sobbing stop. Finally it did stop, and then he realized the bat's claws had stopped scratching the door. The creature was silent.

Bobby wasn't finished. He stepped back and then kicked the door. The creature's head slid down to the floor and didn't move. He kicked the door again, and he kept kicking until it latched shut, severing the creature's head in the process.

He sat down on the bottom step, wiping tears from his face and trying to catch his breath. The bat's head lay at his feet, mouth open and tongue hanging out. Blood had been smeared on the floor around it by the bottoms of Bobby's shoes. He held up his hands and stared at them. How long before they transformed into claws, or wings, or tentacles? He had to at least try to stop it. He hoisted Addison's arm into his lap. It still looked exactly like it had before, a human arm attached to part of a shoulder, still partially covered by the torn and grimy remains of a t-shirt. There was no blood where the arm had separated from the body, just jagged pink tissue. He placed both his hands on the arm.

"I don't know if you can understand me or not, but I really need help. I need to stop the stuff that got into me from turning me into a monster." He didn't know how else to say it. It would either work or it wouldn't. It might even make things worse. But what did he have to lose?

He tore some of the pink tissue from the ragged end of the arm. It was squishy, changing shape as he pressed it between his fingers. He rubbed some of it onto his arm where the bat's claw had punctured his skin. This hurt, because the wound was deep, but then the pain quickly faded away. That had to be a good sign. He worked the rest into the bites on the back of his head and neck. He winced as he touched the raw scalp where the implant had been torn off, but again the pain faded quickly.

A movement in front of him caught his attention. The bat's eyes were now open. They rolled back and forth like they were searching for something. The thing's tongue started moving. In fact, it was growing larger, actually crawling out of the bat's mouth like a huge slug.

It was time to go.

Bobby scooped up Addison's arm and bounded up the stairs. He turned a corner and climbed a second flight, ending at another door with a key card reader. He pressed Helmich's card to the reader, the door clicked, and he pulled it open. He stepped into a hallway, squinting against the harsh LED lighting.

A body slammed into him from the side, knocked him over, and fell on top of him.

"Oh god, I'm sorry!" It was a woman, the same woman who had taken Bobby to the meeting with Helmich earlier that day. She pushed herself off of him, her eyes wide. "It's you! How did you get here?" She grabbed his shirt by the shoulder.

Bobby sat up and pulled Addison's arm closer to his belly. The woman took a look at it then let go of his shirt. She got to her feet and backed away.

"Is that what I think it is? Why do you have that?"

Bobby got up. "We have to get out of here. Where are my friends?"

She stared at him like she was trying to comprehend. "Where's Dr. Helmich?"

"He's dead—they're all dead!"

Her eyes got wider. But then she turned her head. "What is that?" She was looking at the bottom of the door to the stairway.

Something was trying to crawl out through the narrow slit under the door. Three spider-like legs, each at least a foot long, grappled with the floor, trying to get enough traction to pull something larger through. Failing at this, they simply detached and began crawling away on their own. Seconds later more of them followed.

Bobby and the woman backed away from the door.

"Don't let them touch you," Bobby said. "We have to go! Where are my friends?"

The woman continued staring at the crawling things, either ignoring Bobby or too terrified to answer. The thin creatures were coming under the door five or six at a time now. They were spreading out across the floor. Some of them remained in the same shape, while others stopped, curled up, and began transforming. One of them became something between a scorpion and a spider the size of Bobby's hand. It took off running down the hall with unnatural speed. Another creature ran the other direction before Bobby could see what it was. Several others were forming insect-like wings.

"Where's Ashley!" Bobby shouted. "After what you've done to us, you can at least tell me where she is."

She pulled her gaze from the spreading creatures and looked at him. Her cheeks were quivering. "Follow me." She took off down the hall.

Bobby ran after her, eager to distance himself from the skittering Helmich-spawn.

They made a left turn and ran down a long hallway, apparently toward the center of the complex. They came to a T and turned left again. Ahead of them a group of doctors were gathered outside an open door. They all turned and stared.

"What's he doing here, Hannah?" one of the men said. They were all looking at Bobby and what he was carrying.

The woman with Bobby—Hannah, apparently—said, "We've got to leave now!"

"Like hell," another man said. "The 4:44 is at crisis level. Helmich isn't letting anyone out."

"Dr. Helmich is gone!" Hannah cried.

They all fell silent.

Hannah said, "Look, I believed in this project. We all did. But—"

A flying creature the size of a pigeon crashed into the back of her head. Her body lurched forward and the creature, still clinging to her hair, flopped over her head and onto her face. The next few seconds were strangely silent. Hannah reached up to her face in slow motion. She made only the slightest whimper as she grabbed the thing, pulled it away, and dropped it to the floor.

Bobby's gut tightened when he saw what it was. It had the wings and head of a wasp, but the abdomen more closely resembled a huge centipede, with numerous curved, sharp-tipped legs on either side. It twisted itself over and onto its feet, seemingly unharmed.

"Hannah, you're bleeding," said one of the woman crowded around the scene.

Bobby looked up from the creature to Hannah. Blood and clear fluid were running down her face from one of her eyes.

She put her hand to her eye. "Oh no," she said softly.

The creature spread its wings and flew up off the floor. At the same time, another creature buzzed right by Bobby's head and hit one of the men just below the chin, latching on tightly. He coughed and staggered back.

The doctors suddenly seemed to realize they were in danger. Some of them ran down the hall away from the source of the flying creatures. A few of them dashed into the nearest room, but the centipede-wasp flew through the door before they could close it. They poured back out, shrieking, and followed the others down the hall. Two women stayed behind, trying to help the man pull the other flying creature from his neck. Hannah stood where she was, probing her eye socket with her finger as if she couldn't quite believe what had happened. Bobby looked in the direction from which he and Hannah had come. Several rat-sized creatures were running toward them.

He stepped in front of her. "Where are my friends?"

She looked at him with her good eye. "This whole thing was a mistake, wasn't it?"

The creatures were approaching fast.

"Please," Bobby said firmly.

"This way." She turned and began shuffling down the hall. Bobby urged her to hurry and her shuffle turned into an ungraceful jog.

After making several turns and running far enough for Bobby to get winded, they entered a hallway with numerous unmarked doors. Hannah stopped in front of one of them.

"Your friend Ashley should be in here." Still holding one hand to her eye, she fumbled for her key card.

"I've got it," Bobby said. He pressed Helmich's card to the reader, and the door clicked. Bobby went in. Hannah followed, but she stayed by the door.

Ashley lay in her bed, apparently asleep.

Bobby set Addison's arm on the bed and started unbuckling her restraints. This woke her up.

"What?" she said. Her eyes met his. "Bobby?"

"We have to get out of here," he said. He finished freeing her wrists and then saw her ankles were already free.

She sat up. "Shit!" She was staring at Addison's arm on the bed beside her.

Suddenly he had an idea. He pulled another chunk free from the jagged end of the arm and held it out to her. "This might save your life."

She took it. "What do you mean?"

He shook his head. "I don't know. It's from the Lamotelokhai. Just eat it, or rub it on your skin or something. Please, we have to go."

She hesitated only a second and then rubbed the stuff on her arm. She got up from the bed. "What's wrong with her?" She was looking over Bobby's shoulder.

Bobby turned. Hannah was still by the door. She was looking down and rubbing her face with her hands. Bobby gathered up Addison's arm and then cautiously walked over to her.

"Where's Peter? And Robert?"

Hannah didn't look up. She muttered something that wasn't really words and didn't sound like her voice.

Bobby glanced at Ashley. "Don't touch her," he said. He grabbed Ashley's arm and led her out of the room. He pulled the door shut just as Hannah collapsed to her knees.

"What the hell was that?" Ashley said.

Shouting echoed from somewhere down the hall. There wasn't time to explain, but Ashley had planted her feet, and Bobby knew she wasn't going to budge until she got answers.

"They took the Lamotelokhai apart to figure out how it works. Something didn't go right and one of them transformed into these... I don't know, these *creatures*. It's like the dinosaurs that time at the hospital. They're attacking people and turning them into creatures too. So we need to get out of here."

She was staring at his face and neck. "Did one of them bite you?"

He sighed. "Yeah, but I think this stuff helped me." He nodded down toward Addison's arm. "That's why I gave you some. Please, Ashley! Where's Peter?"

"How should I know? I've been tied to—"

She stopped talking, and Bobby turned in the direction of her gaze. A mass of creatures—at least twenty—was moving toward them. Some were no bigger than rats, others were larger. One of them was the size of a cat. It crawled awkwardly on folded wings like a smaller version of the Helmich-bat. Another looked like a skinny tree kangaroo with bulging eyes and no tail.

Ashley started backing away from them. "Those are the creatures?"

"Don't let them touch you," he said. He went to the next door in the hall. He opened it with the key card. The room was empty.

The creatures were getting closer. He ran to another door. That room was empty too. The scratching and skittering of the creatures grew louder. There were more doors in the hall but no time to check them.

Ashley shouted, "Peter! Robert!"

No answer.

They had no choice but to run. They came to a T at the end of the hall and stopped.

"The place is a big circle," Bobby said. "There must be exits on the outer wall." The problem was, the halls were straight instead of curved, making it hard to tell which direction was out or in.

As Bobby was looking to the right, he glimpsed two people in green clothes running from left to right at the next T. If any of these people were as smart as they thought they were, they'd be trying to get out right now. From the way the others had talked, it sounded like at least some of them weren't crazy enough to actually carry out the 4:44 protocol. Unless they planned to do it as soon as they got clear of the facility.

"They're catching up!" Ashley said.

Some of the faster creatures were only seconds behind them.

"This way," Bobby muttered, and he took off following the doctors he'd seen.

He and Ashley turned right at the T and ran straight all the way to the outer wall. Next to a door with another sign above it that said *Salida* were six green-clad men and women. They were shouting at each other and didn't see Bobby and Ashley until they were only a few yards away. The doctors stopped shouting and stared.

Bobby spoke first. "Do you guys know where our friends are? Peter Wooley and Robert?"

For a moment none of them spoke.

"He's got part of it," a woman said. She was holding a tablet with her finger hovering above the screen. "We should initiate now!"

"Don't!" said one of the men. "I'm not willing to die here. Neither are you, Sofia, and you know it. Just open the door and we can leave."

It appeared that Sofia was the only one of them with a key card.

Bobby heard tapping and scuttling behind him just before the doctors saw what was coming.

"Sweet Jesus," one of the men said. "Open the goddamn door, Sofia!"

Sofia was shaking, her finger still hovering over the tablet.

Without warning, the man drew back and punched her. The tablet clattered to the floor, and she crumpled into a heap and began moaning.

The man ripped the key card from her neck. He went for the door.

"Hurry!" someone said.

The creatures were twenty yards away, and there was nowhere to go but through the door.

The door opened, and blinding sunlight poured in. The doctors ran out except for Sofia and another woman who had knelt down to help her up. But Sofia could barely even sit up. The other woman looked up at Bobby and Ashley.

"Please. Help me!"

The first creatures in the swarm were seconds away. Bobby exchanged a glance with Ashley, and then they both grabbed Sofia by the armpits and dragged her to the door. The door had already closed, so Bobby let go of the woman and pressed Helmich's key card to the reader. The door clicked.

"Oh Jesus," the woman said.

Bobby pulled the door open and turned around. The kangaroo-like creature had outdistanced the others and was now sitting on Sofia's lap, sniffing her face. Sofia was apparently too dazed to move.

"Pull her out the door," Ashley said quietly.

Bobby held the door open as they dragged her out. The kangaroo stayed on Sofia's lap until it was through the door. It jumped off and hopped away. Just as Sofia's feet cleared the opening, Bobby stepped through and slammed the door shut, but not before another creature—something the size of a rabbit but more like a lumpy, disfigured bird without wings—slipped through and ran off.

"Sofia, are you okay?" It was the second woman. She was on her knees, holding Sofia by the shoulders.

"Bastard," Sofia said, holding a hand to her forehead. "He hit me."

It occurred to Bobby that the air was warm. This wasn't what the air in Oklahoma had felt like. He turned and looked at their surroundings. There was a gravel parking lot with about ten cars in it. Several of the doctors were driving out of the lot onto a road, throwing dust and gravel in clouds behind them. Beyond the parking lot were open fields. Beyond the fields were scrubby green trees. And sticking up through those were several tall palm trees. He turned and looked at the compound. It wasn't tall, only one story, but the white walls extended far to the left and right, gently curving in until they disappeared. It was a concrete circle 324 meters in diameter.

"Where are we?" Bobby asked.

Sofia and the other woman looked up at him. Their eyes darted nervously to the object Bobby held against his chest—Addison's arm.

"Four miles east of Salinas," the other woman said. She pronounced it *suh-lee-ness*.

Bobby shook his head.

"Where's that?" Ashley asked.

Sofia spoke up, her voice still shaky. "The Caribbean side of Puerto Rico."

CHAPTER THIRTEEN

QUENTIN STOPPED WALKING when he realized Lindsey was no longer with him. She was a dozen yards back, waiting for the mbolop to come down from a tree. Quentin sighed and pulled off his pack. He started to set it down and realized he was standing over a slide, a smoothed-out trail entering the water of the *Méan-maél* river on his left. Under typical circumstances he would call Lindsey over to look at it, and they would speculate as to whether it had been created by a small crocodile or a large water-rat. But she hadn't been herself all morning, since her somewhat alarming encounter with the tree kangaroo. Not that she seemed ill or depleted in any way. Her condition was quite the opposite, in fact. Lindsey was more animated and enthusiastic than she had been in several days, which was strange considering the circumstances.

Quentin hefted his pack to his shoulder and walked back to her side. Samuel and Sinanie were already well ahead of them, but they were following the river's edge and would be easy to find. Quentin put the pack down and waited, uncertain of what to expect from the mbolop.

Suddenly the creature scuttled backward down the trunk of the tree. When it turned to face them it had a plum-sized fruit gripped in its teeth, perhaps some variety of avocado. It held the fruit in its diminutive forepaws and chewed a hole in it. Methodically, as if this were a practiced procedure, it placed the fruit on the ground, clawed its way into its own abdomen again, dug out a glistening lump of tissue, and shoved the lump into the hole in the fruit. It then picked up the fruit and offered it to Lindsey.

Quentin forced himself to remain silent as she ate it. This was the fourth time in four hours the mbolop had offered her something to eat, and she had long since made it clear that she considered the offerings to be safe and would not be dissuaded from eating them. Never mind that the first of them had rendered her unconscious.

Quentin sighed loudly.

She smiled as she finished the fruit and tossed the seed away. "If you knew how good I felt right now, you'd stop worrying."

"How do you know you're not just high on something that thing gave you? You have no idea what you've ingested."

"I know what it's giving me," she said. "It's giving me what I need. It's taking care of me, making sure my body chemistry is perfectly balanced. That's why I feel so good."

"How can you possibly know that?"

She stepped closer to him and gave him a long, deep kiss. She smelled the way she always did—desirable—even on the second day of hard hiking. She pulled back and gazed into his eyes.

"Do I seem out of balance to you?"

Quentin had to control his breathing. "Not really, no."

"Then stop worrying." She smiled. "Do you remember the first time you told me you loved me?"

"Of course."

"Mark Twain National Forest. We were in that old orange tent. When you said it that night, how did you know it was really true?"

Quentin frowned. "Are you actually comparing this to—"

She leaned in and kissed him again, this time for even longer.

Finally, she pulled back. "Look, I know why you're worried," she said. "But this feels right." She held up her hands, fingers out, and gazed at them. "I felt fine before. The Lamotelokhai's nanoparticles—or whatever they are—had been taking care of us. But this is different. In the last few hours I've started feeling better than ever." She shook her head. "If that's even possible."

Quentin studied her face. Her eyes were bright and alert. She certainly appeared to be herself.

Abruptly she furrowed her brows and sniffed the air. "Do you smell that?"

Quentin sniffed and shook his head.

"It's fresh soil," she said. "Like it's right in my face." She looked down at the mbolop. It was now snuffling around in the leaf litter on the forest floor, as if it were looking for something to eat. She then looked up at Quentin, her eyes wide.

"What?" he said.

She pointed at the mbolop. "Put your hand down there. Let him smell you."

Quentin crouched and extended his hand, palm down. The creature leaned forward to sniff it.

"That's you!" Lindsey cried. "I smell your skin. Right now. Right in my face!"

Quentin looked at her, confused. He felt the tree kangaroo lick his fingertips and he instinctively withdrew his hand.

"Oh my god!" Lindsey said. She put her hand over her mouth. "Oh my god." This time it was muffled. She turned away, still covering her mouth.

"Lindsey?"

She let out a burst of laughter. "It's incredible!"

"What is?"

She turned to him, flashing a delighted grin. "You're not going to believe this." She guided him by the shoulders a few steps and stopped. "Stand right there." She took several steps back and stood facing him, still grinning.

"You're starting to scare me again," he said.

"Put one hand behind your back."

He did.

"Now pick a number and hold out that many fingers."

Quentin gave her a look, but then he held out three fingers behind his back.

"Three," she said.

He stared at her. She raised her brows, waiting.

He changed from three fingers to five.

"Five."

Quentin turned and looked behind him. The mbolop was sitting there on its haunches, watching him. This was impossible. He tucked his hand against his body so there was no way Lindsey could see it, and then he folded all his fingers into a fist except for the middle one.

"Very funny," she said. "One finger."

He turned around to face her, speechless.

She smiled again and shook her head, as if she couldn't believe it either.

"Hold on," Quentin said. He walked over and kneeled down by the mbolop. He leaned in to within inches of its snout and cupped his hands around his mouth. He then whispered to the creature, so softly that Lindsey couldn't possibly hear from where she was. He said, "How much wood could a woodchuck chuck if a woodchuck could chuck wood?"

She giggled. "As much wood as a woodchuck could chuck if a woodchuck could chuck wood."

"I MUST SAY, the most peculiar things happen when you two are in the vicinity," Samuel said. "Enigmata are drawn to you as are ants to honey."

Lindsey pulled the last of the food from her pack, a half-dozen sago cakes, and passed them to Quentin to divide up. The mbolop was lying on its side next to her. "I know it all sounds strange. The funny thing is, it already feels normal to me, like this connection I now have with the creature is something that was missing in my life before. I feel... complete. Not alone anymore."

Quentin cleared his throat.

She put a reassuring hand on his. "It's not like that. It's more like—I don't know—like when we were kids learning to walk. Suddenly that's what we did, and it seemed like we should have always been able to walk, only we couldn't before that because it just wasn't our time yet."

Quentin exchanged a glance with Samuel, who seemed just as perplexed by this new development. Sinanie gazed thoughtfully at Lindsey. It was hard to say how much of Lindsey's explanation he had understood, but he had watched attentively as she had demonstrated to Samuel how the mbolop was now an extension of her senses.

After Quentin and Lindsey had caught up to Samuel and Sinanie, they had continued hiking for another hour before deciding to tell them about this. Samuel had suggested they stop to rest, and it had seemed like the time to bring it up. Neither of the men had seen or experienced this phenomenon before. It was becoming apparent the tree kangaroos were as full of surprises as the Lamotelokhai had been.

They sat in silence for some time, eating the last few sago cakes.

"I think I'll name him Rusty," Lindsey said. The mobolop raised its head as if it knew she was talking about him.

Quentin eyed the creature's mottled brown fur. "It suits him."

"Not just because of his color. There was this boy I met when I was a young girl. I was only six. In first grade. We lived too close to my school for me to ride the bus, so I would walk. The school was only five or six blocks away, but one day I was daydreaming about something. Suddenly none of the houses looked familiar. I got scared, and I froze. I just stood there on the sidewalk. Eventually a boy I had seen at school came out of his house. He asked why I was just standing there." Lindsey huffed out a brief laugh and shook her head. "When I told him, he said I wasn't lost at all. He said he'd seen me walk by his house every day. He was right. I hadn't taken a wrong turn. Suddenly his house and all the others looked familiar again."

"I suppose your hero's name was Rusty," Quentin said.

She laughed and put her hand on his again. "I could name him Quentin, but that would get confusing, now wouldn't it? But seriously, that kid somehow helped me see things in a new light. And so the name fits."

He squeezed her hand. "I guess the real question is, why do you feel compelled to name the thing in the first place?"

She frowned at this. "Bobby named Mbaiso."

"Bobby was fourteen then."

"Does it bother you that I'm naming him?"

It was Quentin's turn to frown. "Of course not. It's just that we came here to find Addison. When we do, we'll take him home, and the mbolop will stay here."

Her eyes narrowed. "There's no way in hell I'm going back without Rusty."

He stared at her, taken aback by this. "You can't take a tree kangaroo—"

"We'll figure out a way! Or we'll stay here."

Quentin had no idea how to respond. He shook his head. "You're joking, right?"

Her features softened somewhat. "No. Yes." Her lips showed

the slightest of smiles. "I wish you could understand what I'm feeling right now."

Samuel cleared his throat politely. "More than 150 years have passed since I first encountered the Lamotelokhai. I have witnessed many peculiar phenomena thenceforth. It is my opinion that it is wise to allow such a phenomenon to run its course before drawing conclusions. What seems inconsequential now may turn out to be of great consequence. What seems perilous now may turn out to provide unforeseen benefits."

Quentin and Lindsey stared at each other. Quentin nodded in acceptance.

The mbolop—Rusty—rolled from its side and sat up. It dug into its abdomen, produced another lump of flesh, and offered it to Lindsey. The fifth one of the day. She put it in her mouth without hesitating.

"Unforeseen benefits," she said, glancing at Quentin.

AFTER SEVERAL MORE HOURS OF hard hiking it started raining, so they stopped for the night. By this time, Lindsey was already fluent in the mbolop sign language. She had explained to Quentin that it was easy. When she saw Rusty sign something, a vision appeared in her mind. The visions helped clarify the meaning of the gestures. Bobby had once told Quentin he had acquired the same ability with Mbaiso eight months ago. He had acquired it in the same way, by eating a chunk of Mbaiso's body.

The group quickly constructed another lean-to shelter to sleep under. It was still raining when they finished the shelter, so they all sat in a row beneath it. The mbolop plopped into the mud next to Lindsey. Quentin was hungry, but the food was gone.

He nudged Lindsey. "Maybe Rusty can find some fruit we can eat."

She patted the tree kangaroo on the head to get its attention and then made some gestures with her hands. The creature jumped up and hopped away.

"You're an mbolop whisperer," Quentin said.

In spite of her haggard, soaked, and mud-covered appearance, Lindsey smiled at this. But then she pulled her knees up, wrapped her arms around them, and just stared at her feet.

Samuel was in the process of wiping mud from his lower legs by repeatedly sweeping his palm from his knees to his bare toes. He glanced at both of them. "Have you considered what you might say to your son if we are able to find him?"

Lindsey remained quiet as Quentin considered this.

"I suppose we'll know better what to say once we have a better idea of his state of mind," Quentin said.

Samuel took one more swipe at his leg and then flung the mud from his hand. "I would suggest that you refrain from excessive exuberance. He seems to me to be quite timid, and I fear he may retreat if frightened."

For months Quentin had subjected himself to three conflicting mental images of Addison. First, there was Addison as he had been before all this started—Addison his son. Actually, a copy of that Addison still existed. He was living an innocent, undisturbed life with his parents—copies of Quentin and Lindsey—and he deserved to be spared from this nightmare. Quentin's own copy of Addison, the original Addison, had been lost in a plane crash not far from where they sat at this moment. Following the ill-advised application of the Lamotelokhai's medicine, that Addison had turned into a murderous monster. That was the second version of his son, the version Quentin had tried so hard to forget. And third, there was the version of Addison that had actually been only the Lamotelokhai's disguise.

Now the second version of Addison, Quentin's own son, had apparently regained his memory, or at least part of his memory.

Surely no other parent had ever had to endure such an embattled emotional tug of war.

Quentin looked at Lindsey. She glanced at him and shook her head before going back to staring at her feet, perhaps unwilling to delve into the black abyss of the topic. Quentin didn't blame her.

Suddenly she spoke. "Samuel, how far are we from the hanging village?"

"I would guess that it is no more than three miles distant," Samuel replied. "We should arrive there tomorrow morning."

"I think I see it. At least I see where it is." She was still staring at her feet.

This was followed by silence. Quentin struggled to grasp the implications of her words.

She didn't take her eyes off her feet. "It's in an area with trees that are taller than the surrounding canopy, right?"

"That is true," Samuel said.

"Then I see it, a mile or so away. A broad area with much taller trees." She glanced at Quentin and saw him staring. "Don't look so startled. It's Rusty. He's looking for fruit. He just happened to climb high enough to have a view over the canopy."

She turned her attention back to her feet, although Quentin supposed she was actually watching the view through the eyes of the creature. Lindsey's eyes sparkled with intense curiosity, and the corners of her mouth formed a grin. It was an expression Quentin had not seen enough of in the past eight months. At least for the moment she seemed completely serene. But this was as disturbing as it was comforting. He had no idea what was really happening to his wife.

"Lindsey?" He waited for her to look up before going on. "You seem to be happy with whatever this is between you and the tree kangaroo."

"His name is Rusty."

Quentin hesitated. "Okay, Rusty. Maybe it's because I can't

really know what you're feeling, but it's freaking me out a little. It's almost like you're changing into someone else before my eyes. Can you see why I would feel that way?"

Again, the reassuring hand on his. "I'm not changing into someone else, hon. But I feel like I'm becoming a *better* me. Rusty is helping me do that." She paused for a moment. "You know what I think?"

Quentin raised his brows and waited.

"I think this isn't all that unusual. The oxpecker that lives on the zebra's back, eating bugs and parasites. The bird gets food, the zebra gets pest control. The bacteria living in our guts. They get food and a place to live, and we get help with digestion."

This took Quentin by surprise. "You're suggesting you've suddenly fallen into a new form of mutualism? Those relationships evolve over hundreds of thousands of years. This thing with that—with Rusty—started this morning!"

"All I know is this feels right. Besides, mutualism is the rule in nature, not the exception. And you know not all of those relationships took that long. Some of them happened overnight, by accident."

"Lindsey, that thing's not even a real animal!" He sighed. The last thing he'd intended was to start an argument. He looked to Samuel, hoping for some help.

Samuel nodded. "When I departed England, the word 'mutualism' was rather new, although the idea of symbiosis had been well known for centuries. It is my understanding that mutualism requires that both organisms in the relationship derive some benefit from it. Perhaps a question worthy of attention is, what benefit is the mbolop deriving from you, Lindsey?"

This was followed by silence.

Finally Lindsey said, "I don't know. But as you said yourself, for now the benefits may be unforeseeable."

Samuel looked at Quentin and shrugged.

They sat in silence for some minutes, each of them perhaps lost in their own thoughts.

"I have bad news and good news," Lindsey said abruptly. "Rusty didn't find any fruits we can eat. But he found something else on the bank of the river. Apparently the rain has driven the earthworms there to the surface. They're big ones—longer than Rusty's body." She held a hand up and formed a one-inch circle, apparently showing the girth of the earthworms.

"Excellent!" Samuel said. He turned to Sinanie and spoke to him in the Papuan's language.

Sinanie had been quiet since they had settled in under the shelter, but now he flashed a broad grin and said, "*Génggémop. Sikh!*" He got up and took off toward the river.

Samuel turned back to them. "Sinanie is particularly fond of the giant earthworms that inhabit the soil near the Méanmaél. They come above ground only occasionally, I suppose when precise conditions of moisture and temperature align." He gestured toward the sky. "This rain will not allow us to make a fire, but the giant earthworm is still quite palatable in its raw state."

CHAPTER FOURTEEN

ASHLEY BROKE THE SILENCE. "PUERTO RICO?"

"How did we get to Puerto Rico?" Bobby asked.

Sofia and the other woman glanced at each other. Sofia said, "It wasn't us who brought you here. We were simply told you were on your way and to get ready." She grimaced and got to her feet. She was half a foot shorter than the other woman. "If you don't remember, then you were probably brought here unconscious." She looked around on the ground. "Where's my tablet?"

"You dropped it," the taller woman said. "It's still inside."

"Then I have to go back in." She groped at her neck and chest. "Where's my key?"

"Sofia," the taller woman said, "you can't trigger 4:44. Some of our people are still inside."

"Dr. Helmich gave me the codes because he trusted me to do the right thing if circumstances required it. I need to get to my tablet!" She turned to Bobby. "That key is definitely not yours. Give it to me."

Bobby closed his fist around Helmich's key. "Our friends are in there. Besides, some of those things are already out."

She lunged at him. "Give me the key!"

Ashley stepped next to Bobby, ready to help push her away, but the taller woman grabbed Sofia's arm and held her back.

"Sofia, please! If Dr. Helmich wanted you to do it, he would have contacted you. He hasn't given the order."

"Are you blind?" Sofia cried. "Obviously something went wrong!"

Bobby decided this was not a good time to mention that Helmich was dead.

"Let go!" Sofia said, shaking off the other woman's grip. Then she froze for a split second. She rushed toward the parking lot, picked up something that had a spiral cord on it, and immediately turned back. Before Bobby registered that she had her missing key, she went straight for the door, unlocked it, and pushed it open.

She didn't even have to step all the way inside to pick up her tablet.

"No, you can't!" the other woman said.

But it was too late. Sofia tapped her screen several times. Seconds later an alarm went off inside the building, followed by more alarms from the outside, above the doorway.

"Five-minute warning," Sofia said, barely audible above the alarms. She then turned her back to them and threw her tablet through the open door and it clattered down the hallway.

Bobby glimpsed something large and dark beyond the doorway, and it was quickly getting larger. Sofia must have seen it, too. She stepped back and pulled the door shut. But before she could even turn around, the door exploded outward. It flew off the hinges, knocked Sofia to the ground, and landed on top of her. The creature that had demolished the door came barreling out with frightening speed, but then it grunted and its head snapped forward, flinging a string of snot into the air. Its shoulders couldn't fit through the door.

The creature was terrifying. Its head looked something like a black bear's, but the neck was hairless and as long as Bobby was tall. The portion of the body he could see was also hairless, and it seemed like there were more legs than should be possible. The thing didn't growl or screech—it just panted and grunted, barely audible above the alarms, struggling to push through the doorway.

"Sofia!" The taller woman rushed forward to help. Sofia was beneath the broken door, but the creature's gnashing head was in the way.

It was working its way through the opening, inch by inch. Puddles of dark blood formed at its feet as the rough edges of the broken door frame gouged its flesh.

The woman went to the top end of the fallen door. From there she was close enough to reach under it. She grabbed Sofia's collar and pulled, but Sofia wasn't moving—she was just dead weight.

Ashley grabbed Bobby's arm. "We have to go!"

Bobby's feet wouldn't move. Things were happening too fast for his mind to keep up. *Five minute warning*, she had said. How many of those minutes had already passed? How far away did they need to get? He stared at the struggling creature. It's head was changing, and it no longer resembled a bear. Now it was more like a dragon or dinosaur, with only patches of black fur remaining. Its shoulders slid forward again, and it started struggling even harder, as if sensing it was almost free.

Ashley punched his arm. "Bobby!"

"Yeah, okay! But we have to help them."

"Damn it, Bobby!" Ashley rushed to the woman's side and grabbed her shoulder. "Come on, we're getting out of here!"

The woman was still pulling on Sofia's collar. "I can't just leave her—"

With a sickening grinding of flesh the creature came loose from the doorway. It stumbled forward from the momentum and collapsed right on top of the door, crushing Sofia beneath it. Ashley and the woman fell back on their butts and scrambled backward.

The creature was larger than it had appeared when stuck in the door frame. Its back end was the size of a hippo and looked like nothing Bobby had ever seen. It squirmed, trying to right itself, but was unable to because arms and legs stuck out in every direction. Bobby couldn't even tell which side of it was the top or bottom. To his horror, he saw at least two legs wearing green elastic pants and running shoes.

The thing floundered for a few more seconds and then managed to stand up, still on top of the door and Sofia. It shook itself off and looked around like it had no idea what to do now that it was out of the building. Its head was still changing, becoming thinner, and the neck had grown even longer.

"Get up slowly," Bobby said, just loud enough to be heard over the alarms.

Ashley and the woman got to their feet. The creature saw the movement and stared. It straightened its neck, extending its head closer to them.

The alarms stopped.

"Oh no," whispered the woman next to Ashley.

The explosion started deep within the compound, a low *whump* that shook the ground, and a split second later it got louder. Bobby briefly saw an orange glow through the doorway behind the creature, and then he was knocked off his feet by a blast of hot air. But the creature caught the worst of it. Fire erupted from the building and then immediately receded. The entire back half of the creature was ablaze, and the smell of burning flesh filled the air. The creature panicked and took off, a fireball running through the open field, igniting the weeds.

Bobby was dazed and sitting on his butt, but he realized Ashley and the woman were in worse shape. He jumped up to help. The woman was trying to put out her hair. "Take it easy, I've got it," he said. He patted out the flames between his palms. He then looked at Ashley. The bottom seam of her shirt was burning. "Your shirt!"

Ashley slapped it, snuffing out the fire, and then blew on her hands to cool them. Bobby helped them both get to their feet, and they stood there for a moment, staring up at the compound. Its white, gently curving wall stretched out to the left and right. Other than the demolished door, the structure appeared to be intact.

He grabbed the heavy metal door and flipped it off of Sofia. She was dead—beyond dead. He approached the open doorway, but the heat coming from inside was so intense he had to move back.

"The 4:44 protocol was designed to sterilize the entire compound without destroying the structure," said the woman behind him. "There's nothing alive in there right now, not even bacteria or viruses. It will cook for at least a week, and then it will be another week before the place cools down enough for anyone to go in."

Bobby turned and looked at Ashley. She stared back at him. She blinked away some tears but didn't wipe them off. Bobby looked where the burning creature had run off. Some of the flames on its trail through the weeds had gone out, but others were spreading into larger fires. Beyond the field, smoke was rising from the trees. Either the creature had died and was burning up, or it had ignited some of the trees as it ran through.

"I have a car here," the woman said. "I'm going to drive to San Juan. I don't know what else to do. I'll get a flight back to the States. If I'm lucky, I'll be able to go home and no one will know I was involved in this whole mess."

Ashley said, "But *you'll* know, won't you?"

The woman nodded slightly and looked at the ground. "You can ride with me if you want." She turned and headed to the parking area.

Bobby was still holding Helmich's key card, but he had dropped Addison's arm—maybe the only remaining portion of the Lamotelokhai—in the scuffle. He draped the card's lanyard around his neck and picked up the arm. He and Ashley exchanged glances, but they didn't speak.

They followed the woman to her car.

***

Bobby was surprised the compound wasn't more isolated. Within a minute of pulling out of the gravel parking area, they were on a paved road driving by a cluster of short, blocky houses on the edge of a small town. A few minutes after that they were on a bustling four-lane highway.

No one in the car was talking, so Bobby stared out the window at the rugged hills covered in dense but low tropical forest as he thought about Peter and Robert. Had they suffered very long, or had the heat killed them instantly? Maybe somehow they were still alive. Maybe they'd escaped the compound before Bobby and Ashley had gotten out. Or maybe they'd found an insulated room or closet. Bobby thought about the key card hanging from his neck, and he considered telling the woman to drive back to the compound. He could figure out a way to go back in and open every door to see if Peter and Robert had somehow survived the heat. He wanted so badly for that to be possible. But of course it wasn't.

Bobby expected to have tears, but his eyes were dry. Why wasn't he crying? Maybe because he had seen so many traumatizing things. Maybe seeing so many people die in horrible ways had broken him, made him unable to care about anything.

"My name is Tiffany," the woman in the driver seat said. "Tiffany Travers."

"Ashley," Ashley said. She was sitting in the front passenger seat while Bobby was in the back with Addison's arm.

"Bobby," he said, although he figured she already knew his name.

They rode in silence for a few minutes.

Ashley turned to Tiffany. "Did it bother you that they kidnapped us and brought us here?"

Bobby watched Tiffany's eyes in the rearview mirror. She just stared at the road.

"I wasn't actually told that's what happened," she said.

"But you must have known. Did it bother you?"

"Yes it did. But it's not as simple as that. All of us came here because we believed it was important. I knew it was possible you'd be brought to the compound that way, but I was convinced our purpose was important enough to make that an acceptable transgression. I would have preferred you to come because you wanted to, because you agreed with us."

Bobby just shook his head and looked back out at the passing hills. He didn't have the energy to get mad at anyone. Ashley must have felt the same way, because she let it go.

"What were those things?" Tiffany said after a few minutes. "Those animals, or whatever they were. Where did they come from?"

Bobby said, "It's all because of what you guys did. The Lamotelokhai is dangerous, but everyone always wants to play god."

She glanced at him in the mirror. "But what *were* they?"

"They were your friends," he replied. "Dr. Helmich and the others. That's what they were turned into. You shouldn't have done what you did to the Lamotelokhai." Bobby watched her eyes. She was fighting back tears, and he actually felt sorry for her.

Ashley said, "They weren't all burned up. Some got out."

Until now Bobby had avoided thinking about that. He was the one who had allowed the creatures to escape the lower level. And he was the one who had opened the outer door of the compound. Now those things were running around the countryside. What if they went into the nearby town? His stomach churned at the thought of what might happen.

The Lamotelokhai was the only thing that could stop the consequences Bobby was envisioning. But the Lamotelokhai was probably gone—at least nine tenths of it. He looked at the remaining portion on the seat next to him. The Lamotelokhai had told him that if he ever needed to do so, he could access and recombine the twenty-four packets of information. Apparently, the packets were a way of making a backup of its own consciousness, or operating system. Things had been pretty chaotic at the time, and Bobby hadn't paid much attention, but now his perfect memory made every detail accessible, including who the Lamotelokhai had put those packets into. Bobby himself was one of them. And so was Ashley.

He pulled Addison's arm onto his lap. The Lamotelokhai had intended to tell him how to access the information packets, but then things had gone to hell, and there had been no time for it. He rested his palms on the arm. He was afraid of what might happen if he tried to communicate with the Lamotelokhai, but they needed its help to stop the death and destruction.

The Lamotelokhai had told him it would try to configure this arm so that it wouldn't be dangerous. It had stopped him from transforming into a monster after the Helmich-bat had attacked him, so maybe the arm was safe. He had no idea if it would work, but he started talking to the arm with his thoughts. "I know there's a packet of your information inside me. I want to download it from my body into yours. Can you do that? If you can do that, I'll find all the other packets and download them, too."

Bobby didn't have to wait long. His head began to tingle. It didn't hurt—in fact it almost tickled, and he felt a smile forming on his face. Soon the tingling feeling was on the move. It went from his head into his neck. It worked its way into his shoulders, down his arms, and into his hands. The last place he felt it was on his palms where they were touching Addison's arm.

"What are you smiling about?"

Bobby looked up and realized Ashley was watching. Before he could answer he felt Addison's arm move against his palms. Startled, he shoved it from his lap onto the seat beside him. The arm and shoulder began shortening and thickening. The fingers became little stubs and then disappeared. The torn shred of t-shirt melted into the shoulder until it was gone. The skin transformed into a rough brown surface as the entire object became an amorphous lump.

Bobby felt trapped. The car only had two doors, so it wouldn't be easy if he had to make a quick escape. He watched the lump, ready to yell at Tiffany to stop the car if it turned into any kind of creature. But it had stopped changing. It looked like nothing more than a lump of clay the size of a soccer ball. It was a miniature version of the Lamotelokhai's original form.

"What did you do?" Ashley said.

"I'm not sure yet." Bobby cautiously put his hand on the lump of clay. Images appeared before his eyes. He jerked his hand back. But some of the brief flashes had included symbols from Kembalimo. How was this possible? He put his hand on it again. The images flew by. They seemed random and too fast to make any sense. Bobby knew Kembalimo, perhaps better than anyone, because he was one of the few people who had used it to talk to the Lamotelokhai. But these flashes were nonsensical.

Of course they were. He hadn't downloaded the other packets of information yet.

"Put your hand on it," he said to Ashley.

She frowned at him. Tiffany eyed him in the mirror.

"You need to trust me. It won't hurt, I swear. I just did it myself. Just put your hand on it."

She twisted around far enough to extend her hand back between the two seats. Bobby held the lump of clay out so she could reach it.

She quickly pulled her hand back. "What is all that?"

"Kembalimo symbols. Just ignore what you see and leave your hand on it for a minute. You might feel something, but it won't hurt."

"You want to tell me what I'm trying to do?"

"If it works I'll explain the whole thing." He waited until her hand was firmly on the clay. Then he spoke with his thoughts. "Ashley has a packet of your information in her, too. I want to download it from her body into yours. Can you do that?"

He watched Ashley's face.

She obviously felt something, because she twitched her head like there was a fly on her nose. Then she looked like she was concentrating. Her eyes met Bobby's.

"It tickles," she said without smiling.

"Is it finished yet?"

"How would I know? It's in my arm right now." Seconds later she said, "Now it's in my hand." And finally, "I think it's done."

Bobby put the object back on the seat. Its surface began to ripple. Wide bumps formed and then moved, creating the illusion that the whole thing was rolling. Soon the rippling stopped, and the lump of clay looked the same as before.

Bobby put his hand on it. The visions appeared again, but now they were more stable. Kembalimo symbols appeared, remaining long enough for him to actually recognize them. And there were other symbols he had never seen before, and flashes of images, like stars and trees. There were even sounds in his head—snippets of some weird language or animal.

"What did you just do to me?" Ashley asked.

Bobby pulled his hand back. The visions and sounds stopped. "I downloaded some information from you into this." He nodded toward the lump. "It was a packet of data the Lamotelokhai put into you back when Addison killed the Papuans at the hanging village."

She opened her mouth to say something but then stopped and crossed her arms. Apparently she was waiting for him to explain.

"I know, I was kind of freaked out about that, too. Here's all I know about it. The Lamotelokhai is a computer, right? So it made a backup of itself. But that backup is split into twenty-four packets of data. We just downloaded two of those packets into this." Again he nodded at the clay. "The rest are in other people. The Lamotelokhai told me who they are. I think it knew it was about to be destroyed."

Tiffany said, "What are you two doing?"

Bobby looked at her in the mirror. She was shifting her eyes between him and the road. "You probably didn't know it," he said to her, "but you guys may have started a really big problem. The Lamotelokhai warned us of what might happen, but you guys wouldn't listen. Those creatures you saw that got out of the compound? Now they're probably going to kill more people and spread. And they'll keep spreading and killing more people. They may even spread over the entire planet. Do you understand what you've done?"

She was fighting tears again, and she didn't answer.

Bobby went on. "We need the Lamotelokhai to help stop it. But the Lamotelokhai is probably dead—or destroyed, I guess—because of your 4:44 protocol. And even if it survived, we can't get to it for at least two weeks."

"I'm sorry. I don't know what else I can say."

"I know what you're thinking," Ashley said to Bobby. "We need to get the other twenty-two data packets."

He blew out a puff of air. "Well, yeah. But most of them are in the Papuans in the hanging village."

"Oh. Well crap." She turned back around to stare out the windshield.

"Yeah."

She spun back around. "So let's go there and get the data packets."

Bobby stared at her. They didn't have identification, passports, or money, which would make leaving Puerto Rico almost impossible. But then it dawned on him that there might be another way. "Peter said there were two other people in his company who know what we were trying to do. He must have trusted them."

Ashley turned to Tiffany. "Tif, we need to borrow your phone."

Tiffany braked abruptly and pulled to the side of the road. The car stopped. Her arms were shaking, even though she was gripping the steering wheel.

They waited for her to say something.

She turned her head without letting go of the wheel. Much of the hair between her right eye and ear was burned away, making her look kind of pitiful. "I have to think for a minute," she said.

They waited.

Finally she spoke. "I know this project was a mistake. I think I knew it before, when I realized Dr. Helmich was, well, a little fanatical compared to the rest of us."

Bobby felt a surge of anger. "I have a box anchored to my skull. The other one was bitten off by a giant bat that used to be Dr. Helmich. Is that what you call *a little fanatical?*"

She turned around and actually studied Bobby's condition for the first time. "That wound's going to be infected soon. And you'll have to have the remaining one surgically removed. I'll take you to a hospital."

"I don't have to worry about infections." Bobby touched the remaining implant. "And this can wait. Do you have a phone we can borrow?"

She closed her eyes, like she was trying to decide. Then she opened them and nodded toward Ashley's feet. "Under your seat. They make us leave everything in our vehicles except one ignition key."

Ashley pulled out a tan leather purse and Tiffany reached for it. Ashley hesitated, then handed it to her. Bobby heard a zipper, and Tiffany held up a smartphone. "Before you start calling people," she said, "maybe we should talk about what we're going to do next."

Bobby and Ashley exchanged a glance. Bobby said, "Okay."

The woman half-turned in her seat so she could look at both of them. "I don't want to get in trouble. I really just want to go home. I have a family."

Ashley said, "A family?" Bobby recognized a fierceness in her voice that he had heard before.

But apparently Tiffany didn't. She said, "I'm going to San Juan and to the airport, where I'll try to get on the first available flight to the States. I can take you two to a hospital first, or you can ride with me to the airport."

Without warning, Ashley shoved her palm out and awkwardly smacked the woman on the side of her face. "A family! You want to talk to *us* about your fucking family?"

Bobby lunged forward to put his body between them. "Ashley, stop!"

Tiffany let out a whimper and fumbled with her seatbelt. She got it loose and started getting out of the car.

"Mrs. Travers, wait!" Bobby said. "Please."

She hesitated. Besides, where was she going to go?

"We really need your help," Bobby said. "Please."

She looked at Bobby. Even her hands were trembling now, and there were tears in her eyes. "I told you I was sorry. I'm not the one who did those things to you."

"We know you're not." Bobby turned to Ashley. "We need her help. Please."

Ashley's eyes were narrowed and enraged, and she was breathing hard. But she nodded.

Bobby settled back into his seat.

"I came here thinking I might have the chance to do something good for the world," Tiffany said. "I had no idea something like this would happen. I'm scared."

Bobby sighed. "We're all scared. Ashley and I have seen what happens when people make mistakes with the Lamotelokhai. The mistake Dr. Helmich made is worse than all the others so far." Bobby looked out the window. "We need your help. We don't even know where we are."

Tiffany seemed to consider this. "Are you going to go to the police?"

Bobby looked at Ashley and she met his gaze. Her eyes had relaxed.

"I think they might need to evacuate the area around the compound," Bobby said. "Maybe a really big area."

Tiffany nodded, but she was frowning. "So we need to call the police."

"Look," Ashley said, "we know you just want to go home to your *family*. If you call the police now—get someone who can evacuate the people near the compound—and then help us get to the airport, you can fly home and we won't tell anyone we know who you are."

Tiffany nodded again. "Okay. Um, okay. I'll do what I can." She turned on her phone and dialed 911. After several seconds she said, "English, please." There was another pause. "Yes, I need to report an emergency. Animal attacks, several miles east of Salinas, just north of Jobos Bay Estuarine Reserve." Another pause. "They have? I see. Okay, well please tell them to hurry. It's very serious. No, I'm sorry, I can't. Just hurry!" She lowered her phone. "My lord, they've already gotten calls."

Dreadful thoughts flooded Bobby's mind, and he tried to ignore them. He put his hands on the lump of clay and spoke aloud. "Lamotelokhai, I need your help. Can you understand me?" The same snippets of symbols, images, and sounds passed through his consciousness, but none of it made any sense.

Ashley snatched the phone from Tiffany's hand and started tapping. Then she looked at Tiffany. "How do I call the U.S.?"

"Puerto Rico's a U.S. territory. Just tap 1, then the area code and number."

Ashley tapped out a phone number Bobby assumed was the special number Peter had given them. Abruptly she handed him the phone. "You know a lot more about what's going on here than I do."

Bobby put the phone to his right ear, but that side of his head hurt too badly, so he switched to the left.

A man answered. "Benson here."

Bobby remembered the name. Jonathan Benson was the third employee of Peter's who knew about the plan to move the Lamotelokhai. Bobby hadn't met him.

"Um, this is Wyatt Grayson," Bobby said.

"Bobby! Is that really you? We've been losing our heads here. Where are you? Where's Mr. Wooley?"

"Well, it's kind of a long story, and I have really bad news about Peter."

There was a moment of silence. "What do you mean?"

Bobby explained the best he could without taking too much time, and the guy listened without interrupting. He told him about the experiment gone wrong and the rampaging creatures. He ended with their escape from the compound, the 4:44 protocol, and how it had burned up everything and everyone inside.

"Are you still there, Mr. Benson?"

"Yeah, still here. I just—I don't know what to say. Peter and Robert are dead?"

"There's another thing, and this is really big. Some of those creatures got out and ran away."

There was another pause. "I'm not sure I understand."

Bobby didn't understand either, and there just wasn't time to explain further. "Mr. Benson, you're one of the people in Peter's company he trusted the most, so you can probably arrange things like trips on his jets and stuff like that, right?"

"That's correct."

"Well, we need you to come get us. Like right now."

"I can certainly do that. Where are you?"

This was one of the many things Bobby had left out. "We're on our way to the airport in San Juan. Puerto Rico."

Yet another pause. "Why in God's name are you in Puerto Rico?"

Bobby had no idea. He tapped Tiffany's shoulder. "Why are we even in Puerto Rico in the first place?"

She shook her head. "We weren't told that, but I assume those funding the project had their reasons. Maybe to avoid scrutiny from the U.S. government, or maybe fewer regulations, but I don't know."

Bobby spoke into the phone. "No idea. Can you come get us anyway?"

"Yes, I can."

"I know this is asking a lot," Bobby said, "but if Peter were here he'd know we have no choice. After you pick us up, we need to go to Missouri to see my friend, Carlos Herrera. Then we need to go to Papua, Indonesia."

"That's... well, that *is* asking a lot."

"But you know how important the Lamotelokhai was to Peter. I can't even tell you how important this is to the Lamotelokhai. And to a lot of people around here, probably. Maybe everyone in Puerto Rico. You just need to trust me that Peter would want you to do this."

Jonathan sighed. "Okay, Bobby. I believe you. Will I be able to call you back at this number?"

Bobby considered this. "Yes."

"Good. You get to the Marin International Airport. I'll call you when I have more information about my arrival time."

"Mr. Benson, it's really important that we hurry."

"How important is it that you come back here to Missouri to see your friend? That's going to take considerable time."

"We can't save the Lamotelokhai without seeing him in person."

Jonathan let out a long breath, which sounded like tearing cardboard in Bobby's ear. "Right, then. Okay, I'll let the police know you guys have been found. Everyone's searching for you. And since it's you, Bobby, I think the feds are involved. But I'm not telling anyone Peter and Robert have been killed until I have absolute proof of that."

"Mr. Benson, I think it's just as important now as it was eight months ago that we can't let the government have the Lamotelokhai. Especially not a small part of it, which is all I have left now."

"Understood. Peter has given Ardell and myself the authority to leverage an impressive portion of the SouthPacificNet resources. You did the right thing, calling me."

Bobby ended the call. He looked up to see a string of blue and yellow cars and SUVs with *Policia* on their sides race past them in the opposite direction, sirens blaring. Tiffany started the car and pulled back out onto the road.

"We're an hour from the airport," she said. "We need to get some clothes for you two first." She gazed at Bobby in the mirror. "And you need to get cleaned up."

Bobby said, "Mrs. Travers, we're going to have to keep your phone."

She glanced in the mirror again but didn't say anything.

Bobby tapped the phone's screen and pulled up the web browser. He went to an international calling assistance site and looked up the codes to call a satellite phone in Papua, Indonesia from Puerto Rico. He tapped in the codes and then the number for the SAT phone Peter had given them months ago. He then tapped the PIN that would power on the satellite phone, which would probably be shut off to save the battery charge. He listened for a moment to make sure the call was routing through, and then he nudged Ashley's shoulder and stuck the phone in her face.

She turned and frowned. "What?"

"You're handling this one."

CHAPTER FIFTEEN

For Quentin, the second night of camping in the wilderness typically allowed more sleep than the first. But on this night every slight sound set him on edge. The forest floor was alive with scurrying creatures, most of them probably rats and small marsupials, but some sounding like they had more than four legs—large spiders or scorpions, most likely.

So when the SAT phone chirped, he flinched and shouted a curse, waking the others. He crawled from the shelter and stumbled to the fallen tree where he had placed the phone to maximize the chance of picking up incoming calls. Lindsey was right behind him.

He fumbled with the phone's buttons in the dark. "Hello, this is Quentin."

"Quentin, this is Ashley. I can barely hear you. Can you hear me?"

"Ashley!" Quentin turned to Lindsey, but her face was just a shadowy oval in the darkness. "I hear you. Are you okay? Is Bobby okay?"

"Well, we're alive. Look, it's really a long story, and I'm worried

I'm going to lose you, so first there's some really important stuff I need to tell you. Can you still hear me?"

Quentin held the phone out and tapped it to activate the speaker. "Yes, go ahead."

"Well, we have to come there. To the hanging village. And we have to do it soon. You're at the hanging village, right?"

For a moment Quentin was at a loss for words. Lindsey remained silent, but she gripped his arm, her nails digging into his skin.

"Um, no. We plan to arrive there tomorrow morning."

"Okay, can you just stay at the village until we get there?"

"Ashley, how could you possibly—"

"Listen! I'll tell you what I can. First just promise you'll stay there with the villagers until we get there. Promise!"

"Okay, I promise." Quentin pulled from Lindsey's grip and started pacing.

Ashley went on. "We'll get there as fast as we can. We were kidnapped. They took us... compound... Rico." Her voice started breaking up.

Quentin rushed back to where he'd had a better signal. "Ashley! Are you there?"

"I'm here, but I can hardly hear you. They took us to this place in Puerto Rico and they made... Lamotelokhai into... then things went really... got out in time but the whole building... and Robert were still inside... gotten out."

"Ashley!" Quentin stepped up onto the fallen tree and held the phone as high as he could. "Ashley, are you there?"

"I hear you. I just need to know you'll be at the village, okay?"

"We'll try to wait there, but what's going on? How are you going to get here?"

"We'll get there, don't worry. It's because of the Lamotelokhai." She paused and Quentin heard Bobby's indistinct voice in the background. Then Ashley went on. "Okay. We have to kind of put the Lamotelokhai back together, from twenty-four packets of data it created as a backup. That's why we're coming there. The people who took us divided it up into pieces. And, well, just about everyone died. We're lucky to be alive. But we have to come there. You'll be there, right?"

"We'll be there."

Lindsey spoke up for the first time. "Ashley, I don't know what's going on, but you and Bobby be careful, okay? You two are our family. We love you."

There was a moment of nothing but static. "We love you guys, too. We'll call again when we can. Maybe there will be a better signal. See you there." The line went silent as the call ended.

Quentin lowered the phone and stared at the screen. It said 4:42 AM. He stepped down from the fallen tree, powered the phone off, and set it back in its place on the log.

He and Lindsey stared at each other in the almost complete blackness.

Sinanie broke the silence. "*Mbakha-mo-f-é wofekha amo-mémo?*"

Samuel spoke to him in his language, presumably trying to explain how phones worked, although as far as Quentin knew, Samuel had used a phone only once.

Finally Lindsey said something. "Puerto Rico?"

"I think that's what she said." Quentin realized his hands were fists. The lack of information was frustrating. But his aggravation quickly gave way to relief. "At least they're alive."

Lindsey made her way back to the shelter. She mumbled something at the mbolop, and then pushed it off her sleeping mat to make room. The thing made a soft bleating sound. Quentin, Samuel, and Sinanie got under the shelter after her.

For several minutes they all sat in silent contemplation.

Samuel said, "The news from Ashley that I find to be particularly alarming is that the Lamotelokhai was divided into portions. What gave them such an idea, I wonder?"

Quentin felt his hands becoming fists again. "This is insane. How do they think they're going to get here? I assume Peter can help them get to Obert's village, but do we need to go back to Navera to meet them?"

Lindsey said, "Maybe tomorrow we can find Addison and take him with us back to Navera so we can all meet them together."

"That is not what Ashley has asked you to do," Samuel said. "Based upon her words, she believes she must come to the hanging village of my indigene hosts. She mentioned putting the Lamotelokhai back together. I believe she may be referring to the portions of the Lamotelokhai's knowledge placed into the minds of the indigenes. This concerns me greatly."

In the darkness Quentin couldn't tell if Samuel was looking at him or if his eyes were closed. "I'm not sure I really want to hear the answer to this, but why does that concern you so much?"

Samuel shifted his position as if he were reluctant to answer. "Ashley stated that the Lamotelokhai had been divided into portions. This would indicate that someone wished to have smaller pieces of it. For what purpose I can only imagine. Nevertheless, I have myself discovered that such an endeavor is perilous, to say the least."

"Perilous in what way?" Lindsey asked.

Samuel shifted again. "I discovered this in the most abhorrent and grievous way. It was more than seventy years ago. And it was due to my desire to learn whatever I could of the nature of the Lamotelokhai. I desired to learn if it were possible and practical to perform useful tasks with only a portion of the Lamotelokhai's clay. You see, such capability would have innumerable implications." He paused, apparently thinking.

Quentin and Lindsey waited.

"As with some of my other misguided attempts at experimenting with the Lamotelokhai's clay, the results haunt my dreams to this very day."

Quentin hesitated as dread began stirring within him. "What happened?"

"Well, it is first important to understand that the Lamotelokhai can be thought of as an *artist* of sorts. It is a creator of wondrous things. Every great artist has his favorite medium from which to fashion works of art. The painter has his palette of dyed oils. The sculptor has his stone or bronze. The Lamotelokhai works in many media, but in my opinion it is a master of the medium of life. It sculpts and paints living organisms as if it were a god. Additionally, it seems to have endless knowledge of every living thing it has encountered, both past and present." He stopped, as if he were giving them a chance to absorb this.

Quentin thought about the frightening transformation of Addison, as well as the events at the hospital in Jayapura eight months ago. It certainly hadn't occurred to him to think of the Lamotelokhai as an artist in those instances. Samuel never failed to surprise him with his unique way of looking at things.

Samuel continued. "But in order to effectively sculpt and mold living organisms, the Lamotelokhai must be in its complete state. A portion of it is ineffective in such an endeavor. Just as you would be incapable of creating a masterful painting with most of your brain removed." Again he paused.

"So what happened when you tried separating the Lamotelokhai?" Quentin asked.

"I attempted to command a portion of the Lamotelokhai's clay to sculpt a living creature. The results were wretched beyond imagining. Creatures were contrived with no concordance or harmony of parts. It was as if the devil himself had promulgated his madness in the form of a nightmarish menagerie. And to make matters worse, it seemed that everything these abhorrent creatures touched was then likewise transformed into a new and quite unique abomination. What began as a single creature soon became an overwhelming profusion."

Quentin tried to imagine the scenario Samuel had described. It made his skin prickle.

"How did you stop it?" Lindsey asked.

"I returned to the hanging village to call upon the Lamotelokhai. I spoke to it in my thoughts, describing the dilemma I had caused. It provided me with a handful of its clay. It placed a vision into my mind, a vision showing me what I was to do. So I took the clay to the site of my imprudent mistake. It was several miles distant, and by that time the profusion of ungodly creatures had grown to encompass such an extensive area that I could not imagine how it could be subdued. It required all of my courage to avoid fleeing to save my life. Following the instructions within the vision the Lamotelokhai had shown me, I scattered bits of the clay onto the ground. Soon the bits transformed into insects—flies to be specific. And those flies transformed fallen leaves and other organic matter into more flies.

"As I watched in wonder, an enormous cloud of flies swarmed from the ground and dispersed. They continued rising as more and more were created. Some of them alighted upon my skin, with no untoward effects. However, those flies that encountered the transforming creatures seemed to halt the creatures' transformations. In good time it seemed that all the transformations had stopped. I can scarcely imagine what might have occurred had I not enlisted the Lamotelokhai's assistance."

For some seconds the only sounds were the scuttling of nocturnal creatures and the cricket-like calling of tree frogs.

"What became of the transforming creatures?" Lindsey asked. "Were they killed by the flies or transformed back to their original forms?"

"Neither one nor the other. The creatures simply halted further transformation. Some of them were in such a state that they could not walk nor fly, and they eventually died where they were, presumably due to starvation or thirst, or to being preyed upon. Others were functional creatures, able to move about, some of them even able to procure food. Those remained in the area for some time. For years after the incident I occasionally returned to the region. Each year I saw fewer of the unnatural creatures. Finally, on the eleventh year, there were no more to be found, and I assumed that they had all perished."

Samuel could then be heard arranging himself so that he could go back to sleep. "Sleep well, my friends," he said.

Quentin gazed at Lindsey in the darkness, and he could tell she was looking back at him, perhaps pondering the same disquieting scenario that was playing out in his mind.

CHAPTER SIXTEEN

Mʙᴀɪsᴏ ᴘᴜᴍᴘᴇᴅ ʜɪs ʟᴇɢs, shaking the tree limb beneath him, which was barely thick enough to hold his weight. This disturbance flushed a cloud of insects, and he watched them spiral upward, their wings glittering in the unobstructed sunlight above the canopy. They dispersed to other, less trespassed-upon leaves and limbs. Mbaiso cautiously turned his body, searching in every direction until he spotted what he was looking for. It was another limb, several tail lengths below but at a distance slightly beyond any he had attempted.

He tilted his head downward and lowered his tail as a counterbalance. Below him was one of the hanging tunnels of his mbolop colony. And far below that was the forest floor, although only small glimpses of it were visible through the canopy foliage. A long fall. Long enough to kill a real tree kangaroo.

Mbaiso gathered his hind legs beneath him and positioned himself carefully. He bounced again to test the leverage the limb would provide. Not much. He considered finding a different limb, but it was too late for that—he had already envisioned the fulfillment this challenge would provide, and a lesser challenge would not do.

He began swaying, forward and back. He escalated the swaying, and suddenly, just as the limb began its forward swing, he took advantage of its momentum and launched himself out. He held his tail high, providing stability as he arced through the open space. His claws caught the target limb, and he flung his tail forward over his head to break some of his momentum.

He nearly toppled over, but he dug his hind claws in, shifted sideways, and wrapped his forelegs around the limb. He held tight but couldn't keep himself from slipping until he was hanging upside down from a limb no thicker than his tail. Having the heavy body of a real tree kangaroo, Mbaiso lacked the agility needed to quickly remedy this situation. So he simply hung there, allowing his excitement to dissipate.

As he gazed upward, something caught his eye. It was high above, moving steadily across the cloudless sky, leaving an almost perfectly straight white cloud behind it. It sparkled in the sun's light like a droplet of water. But the object was not made of water. It had a definite symmetrical shape. Mbaiso had seen such an object before. Months ago, such a thing had fallen from the sky. Humans had then emerged from it, and those humans had changed Mbaiso's existence by taking away the Creator. As the villagers would say, they had turned the world upside down.

Hanging with his belly toward the sun, Mbaiso watched the object move across the sky until it disappeared, leaving behind a cloud that gradually dissipated as it was pushed by the breeze into a serpent-like wisp. Still he clung to the limb, unmoving, processing the implications of the object in the sky. There was something about it he found discomforting. It gave him doubts. Perhaps his carefully nurtured plan might be inadequate. He had known there must be more humans in other parts of the great forest of this world, but seeing the object made him suspect he had underestimated how many. He considered all the mbolop in his colony, each of them painstakingly created from particles of his own body combined with particles from Tupela's. With this method of procreation, it was not possible to accelerate production.

Perhaps it was too soon to send his colony out to the great forest of this world.

Mbaiso clambered along the underside of the limb, paw over paw, until the limb was nearly vertical and he could maneuver to the larger trunk. No longer in the mood for amusing challenges, he made his way to the forest floor.

Mbaiso found the almost-human creature, Addison. As expected, the mbolop paired with Addison was there too. The two were engaged in a puzzling activity with several of the colony's other mbolop. Mbaiso found a comfortable spot in a low fork of a *wotuwo* tree where he could observe and think.

Mbaiso had been made soon after the human villagers had found the Creator. As the human, Samuel, would say, nearly 10,000 years had passed since then. During that time, Mbaiso had performed the functions he had been created for: facilitating communication between the villagers and the Creator, gathering data for the Creator, and assisting the villagers with various tasks. He had grown to appreciate the comfort of routine, the satisfaction of keeping the human village in balance. Unmet needs were to be addressed immediately in order to restore balance and therefore Mbaiso's comfort. When the Creator had gone away with the new humans, the village had been thrown into disarray, prompting Mbaiso to do something he had never done before—defy the Creator's instructions. He had been instructed to terminate his own existence, but instead he had formulated a plan of his own. His plan would restore purpose to his life, and a renewed sense of balance.

Mbaiso pushed aside his thoughts regarding the unknown number of humans in the great forest of this world. There were other problems he needed to address now. So he observed Addison and Newton.

Addison had recruited three of the other mbolop in addition to Newton, apparently pulling them from their duties to engage in an activity that seemed to amuse him. Mbaiso understood the desire for amusement, but there were certain aspects of the pairing of Newton to Addison that could be troublesome.

"Hide seek, hide seek, hide seek!" Addison said to the three mbolop. He pointed to the forest beyond them. Addison then turned his back to them and covered his face with his hands.

At Addison's feet, Newton gestured to the tree kangaroos, and they scurried off. Each of them concealed itself behind some vegetation.

After a brief wait, Addison turned around and ran straight to the nearest concealed mbolop. "Found you, found you!" he cried. He then went to the other two, repeating the same words.

The three mbolop came out of hiding and gathered before Addison and Newton.

"Hide seek, hide seek, hide seek!" he said. This started the routine all over again. Each time they did this, Addison covered his eyes, but Newton watched the mbolop as they concealed themselves.

It was obvious to Mbaiso that Addison was able to watch them through Newton's eyes. But the three hiding mbolop did not seem to understand this. Again and again they would conceal them-selves, only to be immediately found.

"Hide seek, hide seek, hide seek!" Addison cried again. This time he pointed upward.

When he turned around, Newton repeated the gesture, and the

three mbolop climbed into the trees. Soon they were all concealed high above, although Newton had observed their every move. Addison uncovered his eyes, ran to the nearest tree, and scaled it with the agility of a *silek*, the creature Samuel called the sugar glider. Newton followed him up the tree.

Addison quickly found the first mbolop. "Found you, found you!" He then turned and launched himself toward the next concealed mbolop.

Addison was in mid flight when Mbaiso noticed something was wrong. Addison's almost-human hands flailed as if he had lost sight of his targeted limb. One hand caught the limb, but it wasn't enough. His chest struck the limb, and he let out a high-pitched grunt. He bounced off and lost his grip, his hands thrusting out desperately as he fell. Halfway to the ground his head hit a larger limb. His body then tumbled loosely until it slammed onto the forest floor.

Mbaiso and Newton got to the motionless body at the same time. Addison was lying face up, and Newton nudged his head with her snout. There was no response. She sniffed his face and then released a nasally distress bleat. She looked at Mbaiso and bleated again, pleading for him to do something.

Mbaiso gazed at Addison's face. Blood was still flowing through the creature's nearly human body, and he was breathing. But the breaths were shallow, and there was no eye movement.

Newton bleated again.

Mbaiso hopped away and sat on his haunches a short distance from Addison's body. He waited.

Newton bleated and spun about in a circle. Again she nudged Addison's head.

Mbaiso didn't move. He wished to observe what she was capable of, as it was important to his plan.

Again she spun about. She hopped onto Addison's chest and

pushed her snout against his lip. She bleated, hopped off, and paced to Addison's feet and back to his head.

Still Mbaiso didn't move.

Finally, Newton became quiet. She scratched her abdomen until her claws broke the skin. She pulled forth a dripping lump of flesh, placed it on Addison's face, and then smeared it onto his cheek and one of his eyes. She glanced at Mbaiso then sprawled onto the ground next to Addison's shoulder and lay there with her head up. She waited.

Mbaiso processed this new information. If Addison quickly recovered from his fall, it would mean that Newton had adequate healing abilities and could likely care for Addison. And by extension, the other mbolop would be capable of caring for other humans. Perhaps this assumption could be invalidated by the fact that Addison wasn't like other humans, but this was the data currently available to Mbaiso. It was better than no data.

Mbaiso continued to watch as Newton rested silently beside Addison's body. Other tree kangaroos from the colony came forward to investigate, sniffing cautiously at Addison's still form and then wandering off. Addison's body twitched occasionally, sometimes with a faint pop, as cracked bones were pulled back into their original positions by the particles Newton had provided—the same particles that comprised the Creator as well as Mbaiso and all the mbolop of the colony. The Creator had not provided Mbaiso with an understanding of the secrets that allowed the particles to exist and function, but Mbaiso was aware of what the particles could do. He knew they could exert force upon objects such as Addison's bones by creating localized and incremental nudges to the most pliable of all the forces, that of gravity.

Mbaiso had been given some understanding of his heritage. The creators of the Creator existed in a forest far from the great forest of this world. They were seekers of knowledge. But nothing they had ever learned before could compare to their eventual mastery of localized control over the properties of time, space, and gravitational forces. This was achieved not by massive machinery, but instead by the creation of the tiniest of particles. The discovery of the particles marked a turning point in the history of the creators of the Creator, which then led to the making of the Creator, as well as many others like the Creator. These Creators were sent out to locate other great forests, carrying with them the particles, formulated into a package possessing the awareness necessary to judiciously administer the particles' power.

Mbaiso had also been given the knowledge that the particles composing him were the greatest achievement of the creators of the Creator, perhaps the greatest achievement possible. He existed as a result of the Creator's administering of the particles' power. For thousands of years Mbaiso's actions had been based primarily upon instructions from the Creator. But then the Creator had gone away, and Mbaiso had experienced a turning point in *his* existence. The Creator's absence from the hanging village had turned Mbaiso's world upside down, triggering something new and compelling within him. Instead of destroying himself, as instructed by the creator, he had formulated a plan. It was a plan that would allow him to carry out the same tasks that had always provided him with purpose—to assist humans.

More specifically, to assist humans in their interactions with the Creator. For 10,000 years, this assistance had been limited to a small village of humans. But now the Creator had gone away. Mbaiso was certain of what this meant. He had seen many things happen, and he was aware of the vulnerabilities of humans to the powers of the Creator's particles—particles that could nudge the properties of physical reality.

The humans of the great forest would need assistance. They would need protecting, as Mbaiso had protected the villagers. Without protection, they would surely perish.

While Mbaiso and Newton waited, the shafts of light piercing the canopy slowly changed angles as the sun moved across the sky. Eventually clouds blocked the sun, and the shafts of light were gone.

Finally, Addison opened his eyes. He sat up and rested his face in his hands, staring at the ground through the spaces between his fingers. He was alive and apparently healthy.

Mbaiso was satisfied with Newton's ability to care for the nearly-human creature. But he was not at all satisfied with the condition that had caused Addison to fall in the first place. The sharing of senses between humans and their paired mbolop had been a mistake. Humans were apparently not well-suited to such sensory duality. This would have to be fixed before the colony went out to the great forest of this world.

Mbaiso sat upright and signed to Newton, conveying what he wanted her to do next.

Newton snorted. "No!" she then signed back.

Mbaiso scratched his snout and thumped one foot against the ground. He was confident he could force Newton to do what he had asked, but there was something about her defiance that pleased him. It was his own defiance, after all, that had led to the realization of his ambitious plan.

He gazed at Newton and then at Addison, who was still staring at the ground through his fingers. Addison's next accident might kill him, in spite of Newton's assistance. But perhaps the colony no longer needed him. Most of the colony would be leaving this place soon, although Mbaiso intended to stay here with Tupela. Addison would not be needed for expanding the hanging tunnels. At this point his death would probably not interfere with Mbaiso's plan. Besides, there might be more to learn by observing Newton's reaction to the death of the almost-human boy.

But as for the rest of his mbolop colony, Mbaiso intended to remedy the situation. He waited until a pair of mbolop approached to check on Addison. They both had come earlier in the day, sniffing at Addison's body and signing to Mbaiso for an explanation. Mbaiso now stopped one of them and pressed his snout to hers. She received a packet of data, an addendum to the set of instructions regarding pairing with humans. She then turned to the mbolop at her side and passed the data packet to him. They both hopped away to repeat this with the other mbolop of the colony.

CHAPTER SEVENTEEN

PETER STARED at the microwave meal on his lap. Mashed potatoes, corn, and some kind of meat covered in brown gravy. Other than having a compartmentalized tray made of paper instead of foil, it was identical to the tv dinners he used to buy for a dollar at the Coles grocery in Cairns back in the 70s. He glanced over at Robert. The poor bloke was shoveling his meal into his mouth with a plastic spoon like a starving animal.

"Let's begin, shall we? We should have had this done already." The woman held a tablet and had barely looked up at them since unceremoniously placing the meals on their beds and unfastening their wrist restraints. Her name was Marleah, and apparently she was the one assigned to taking care of Peter and Robert's basic needs. Every time they had to relieve themselves, she had to undo their restraints, and she complained every time about how much easier her job would be if she didn't have to do this. If she were Peter's employee, he'd have her repeat the part of her training about taking pride and pleasure in her work.

"Please describe your first encounter with the Lamotelokhai," she said. She then held the tablet out, apparently having tapped a record button.

"Can't remember," Robert said with his mouth full of mystery meat. "I got shot. Traumatized, I guess."

Marleah glared at him. "I've got more than forty questions here. This will be over faster if you just answer them honestly."

"Can't remember," Robert repeated. "And why would I want this interview to be over? At least now I can scratch my crotch." He dropped his spoon and started scratching away.

Peter could't help but smile. This was a feisty side of Robert he had not yet seen, as his employer.

Marleah rolled her eyes and turned to Peter. "Mr. Wooley?"

Peter stirred his potatoes with his spoon. "My first encounter?" He looked up and met her eyes. "It was a long time ago, before you were born."

"Can you describe it?"

"It was a rather unusual experience. It's doubtful you could appreciate the intricacies of it, nor the implications. If you could, I don't believe you would be involved in this insanity."

"If you're implying that Dr. Helmich is insane, then you surely understand that he will take whatever steps are necessary to get honest answers from both of you."

Peter appraised her. "You're American—I can tell that. What is your profession, might I ask?"

Marleah sighed. "I'm an RN."

Robert snorted a laugh without looking up from his meal.

"A nurse," Peter said. "And somehow you have come to terms with the truthfulness of your poorly-veiled statement that we may be tortured."

"We're all here because we believe in this project. We believe you and your cohorts have made a terrible mistake in hiding the Lamotelokhai from the rest of us. As if it were entirely up to you to do such a thing."

Peter shook his head and looked at his food.

"My father died in November," she said.

Peter looked up at her.

"I loved my dad. Everyone did. And we now live in a world where a dear man like my father should not have to die because of a stroke. Sure, if Dad would have had diabetes, or maybe AIDS, he probably would have lived. Because the Lamotelokhai decided, for whatever reason, to give us cures for *those*. But strokes were not high on the priority list, I guess. Too bad, Dad, you're out of luck."

"I'm sorry for your loss," Peter said.

"Every one of us here could tell you a similar story. We all have good reasons to believe in this project."

A shout came from somewhere beyond the windowless metal door, followed by more frantic shouting.

Marleah frowned. She went to the door and used her key card to open it. She looked out. With the door open, Peter could hear more shouting, along with the distant drumming of feet against concrete. People were running.

Marleah stepped back in and slammed the door shut. She turned to face Peter and Robert, her eyes wide.

"What's going on?" Peter asked.

"There's something out there. I—I don't know what it is."

Peter and Robert exchanged a glance. This didn't sound good. Peter couldn't help but think of the dream he'd had, in which he'd witnessed unspeakable horrors through Samuel Inwood's eyes. "Was it an animal?" he asked Marleah. "One you couldn't identify? Maybe one that shouldn't exist?"

She furrowed her brows in confusion, nodding.

"Oh, bloody hell! I knew the dream was a warning."

With her back to the door, Marleah said, "What are you say—"

Her words were cut off by a blasting alarm, loud enough to startle Peter even though it came from beyond the thick door.

"Oh no!" Marleah said. She covered her mouth, her eyes darting around the room like a frightened animal's.

"What is that?" Robert shouted.

Her eyes narrowed, and she lowered her hand from her face. Determination was now chiseled into her features rather than panic. She rushed to Peter's bedside and yanked off the sheet, sending corn and mashed potatoes flying. She then began loosening his ankle restraints. "They've triggered the 4:44 protocol!"

Peter said, "The what?"

"You don't want to know. We have less than five minutes."

"What happens in five minutes?" Robert asked. When she didn't answer he threw his sheet off, meal and all, and fumbled with his own ankle restraints.

Marleah finished freeing Peter and helped Robert. Seconds later they were on their feet, following her to the door. Again she used her key card to open it. She stuck her head out but immediately pulled it back in and slammed the door shut.

"Oh Jesus!" she said.

"Open it," Peter said. "Let me see."

She sucked in some air and then unlocked the door. Peter stuck his head out. The alarm's volume assailed his ears, disorienting him. There was some kind of creature in the hall, moving away from them. At first its awkward scuttling limbs reminded him of a crab's, although the thing was as big as a German shepherd. But then one of its legs slipped on the smooth concrete and flailed to the side. He realized it wasn't a leg at all. It was a wing.

He pulled his head back in and closed the door enough to muffle the alarm without latching. "The hall is clear to the right. I think we can make a run for it."

Marleah shook her head. "We have to go left to get to the outer perimeter where the exits are. We probably have about three minutes."

"Then we have no choice," Peter said. "Are you ready?"

They nodded.

He threw the door open and they rushed out and started fleeing down the hallway to the left. But then they stopped. The creature had turned and was looking at them. Its eyes were mounted high upon a head that otherwise looked remarkably like that of a large sea turtle. And now beyond it was a swarm of several dozen smaller creatures. All shapes and sizes. Running, crawling, and slithering. And more of them were pouring into the hall from around a corner.

Peter threw his arms out to prevent Robert and Marleah from going any farther. If these creatures had anything to do with what he had seen in his dream, it would be wise to avoid them.

"Back into the room!" Peter shouted.

Marleah shook her head. "No, we'll die in there! This way!" She took off running in the only direction they could go—away from the building's exits.

Peter glanced at the approaching creatures. The turtle-headed animal with wings was now scrambling toward him, either to attack or to escape the horde that was quickly advancing. He turned and ran after Robert and Marleah.

They took a right and then a left. The hall opened into a circular space. In the center was a round elevator shaft. The elevator door was closed. Marleah ran for the elevator, but instead of going for the door, she circled to the back side of the shaft. Peter and Robert followed. When they caught up, she was already halfway up a vertical ladder bolted to the shaft and ending at a hatch in the ceiling five meters up.

Robert started up the ladder after her. Peter began climbing as soon as Robert's feet were at eye level. The throbbing alarm had become more intense, or maybe it was just louder in this room, and Peter had to fight the urge to let go of the ladder and cover his ears.

Marleah stopped at the hatch. Peter could hardly see past Robert's body, but he could tell that she was fumbling with some-thing. Her hand shot out with her key card, and she pressed it against a card reader on the ceiling. The hatch opened, and sunlight poured in. The hatch apparently opened onto the compound's roof. Marleah climbed through, then Robert.

Peter was almost to the hatch when something pulled on his foot. He looked down. The winged turtle had clambered up the ladder and its toothless jaws were clamped onto his shoe. Its featherless wings, each over a meter long, thrashed about, awkwardly trying to hold on to the ladder. Peter tried shaking the creature off, but its jaws were like a vice. So he pulled himself up, hoisting the monster with him. He looked down again. The smaller creatures were now swarming the room, running around like frenzied ants. The turtle gripped his shoe so tightly that Peter worried it might crush the bones in his foot.

He hooked his fingers over the edge of the opening and strained, dragging the creature up. Marleah and Robert leaned through the hatch and grabbed his shirt. They pulled him up until he was sitting on the lip of the hatch. He pulled his right leg out, but his left leg and the creature still dangled below him.

"Get off me!" he screamed.

Marleah and Robert grabbed his knee and pulled, forcing Peter onto his back. His foot and the creature's head came into view over the hatch's lip. Suddenly the thing forced its wings through the opening and found purchase. This took much of the weight off Peter's leg, but the creature still didn't let go.

The alarm stopped.

"Oh God!" Marleah cried. "Shut the hatch!"

Before anyone could act, a massive *whump* came from below, shaking the entire roof. This was followed by a roar that steadily got louder. Suddenly flames blasted through the hatch. Peter cried out as the creature was ripped from his foot. He rolled away from the hatch. His shoe and pant leg were burning, but for some reason he thought only of the creature. He looked up and there it was, in the sky. Its body was on fire, but nevertheless its wings were intact and it was flying. It circled aimlessly once and then took off toward the horizon, leaving a trail of black smoke drifting across the cloudless sky. It was a strangely beautiful sight.

Robert and Marleah pummeled Peter's foot and leg with their hands trying to put out the flames. Pain spread to his butt and back, and it steadily got worse. Peter realized the roof was heating up.

"Bloody hell!" he cried. He sat up and got to his feet in spite of excruciating pain in his leg.

"It's the heat from inside," Marleah said. She lifted one of her jogging shoes off the concrete roof. Strings of melted rubber extended from the shoe to the concrete. "It'll get even hotter. We have to get off the roof. Now!"

Peter looked around. They were in the exact center of a vast circular roof. The edges looked to be about 150 meters away no matter which way he turned.

Marleah started running, her shoes leaving a trail of melted goo.

Peter looked at Robert. The bandage on his face and neck had been pulled most of the way off, revealing purple bruising. He was lifting one foot and then the other to avoid being burned through his shoes.

"I know you're hurt, sir, but either you have to run or I have to carry you."

"I can run," Peter said. They took off after her.

When they were only halfway to the compound's outer wall, Peter knew they were in serious trouble. The soles of his shoes were nearly gone. Marleah was twenty meters ahead, but he could hear her crying out in pain. She kept running. They all kept running. There was no other choice. It was hard to breathe. Like inhaling fire. Peter imagined at any moment Robert and Marleah would burst into flames before his eyes.

About fifty meters to go. Peter was sure there was nothing left between the bare skin of his feet and the concrete.

Twenty meters. Now he was sure the skin of his feet had been burned away and he was running on exposed bone. Step after excruciating step, the edge of the roof drew nearer.

Marleah reached the edge first. She threw herself onto her belly, put her feet over the edge, and slid off, wailing in pain the whole time. For just a moment, her fingers were visible, hanging on to the roof's lip, but then she let go.

Peter and Robert arrived seconds later. Five meters below them, Marleah lay in the rocky dirt, moaning and holding her ankle.

"Give me your hand!" Peter said.

Robert nodded. "Once I'm down, I'll catch you when you jump." He took Peter's hand and dropped to his knees. A second later he was over the edge, pushing his feet against the wall to keep away from its heat. Peter sucked in a lungful of hot air. With the additional weight pulling him down, he couldn't shift from one foot to the other. He thought he could actually smell the flesh burning on his feet. Robert's eyes met his.

"Do it," Robert said.

Peter let go. Robert hit the ground with a grunt and rolled onto his side. Peter was tempted to simply launch himself from the roof to avoid the searing concrete, but such a desperate move would surely break his legs. He dropped to his belly and slid off the side as quickly as he could without losing his grip on the edge.

He heard Robert call from below, "I got you, sir!"

His fingers began to fry, so he let go. Robert broke his fall some, but when he hit the ground his knees buckled and his head flew forward and struck the wall.

"Sir! Peter!"

He realized Robert was looking down at him. He blinked. "I'm okay. I think."

Robert sat back. "God, I thought you were dead."

Peter sat up. He put his hand to his forehead, and it came away red. He tried to gather his thoughts. What the bloody hell had happened? It had been more than a fire. It was like a bomb had gone off inside. Perhaps the explosion had been in the lower, underground level. Maybe that's why the walls and roof were still intact.

Suddenly a wave of panic washed over him. "Bobby and Ashley! They're still in there!" His arms flailed as he tried to get up.

"You can't go inside," Marleah said. She was sitting a few meters away, still holding her ankle. "They triggered the 4:44 protocol. There's nothing left alive inside the compound. Not even microbes."

"What?" Peter said, collapsing back into the dirt. "Why would they do such a thing?"

She stared at her ankle. "It was a precaution. In case something went wrong with the procedures. Obviously something went wrong."

"Maybe they found a safe place," Robert said. "Maybe a closet or something."

She shook her head. "There's nothing alive in there. And it'll be weeks before the temperature drops enough for anyone to enter."

Peter couldn't believe what he was hearing. He had to get inside. Maybe the kids had somehow found a way to survive. Maybe they had even gotten out. He struggled to his feet. His left leg was seriously burned from the knee down, the flesh blistered and the pant leg partially burned away. He looked at the bottoms of his shoes. He had been right about the soles. They were melted, and blistered skin was fused with the remnants of rubber and fabric. He needed to move now, before the pain got so bad he couldn't walk.

He spoke to Marleah. "You said there were doors. Which way to the nearest one?"

She looked up at him. "You can't go in there."

"Which way!"

"I don't know. There are four. People only use one because that's where the parking lot is. It's probably that way." She nodded.

Peter held his hand out and Robert helped him to his feet. He started limping away.

"I can't walk," Marleah said. "My ankle is broken."

Peter kept walking. Without saying a word, Robert caught up and walked beside him.

They followed the gently curving outer wall. But before they were even out of sight of Marleah, Robert stopped. "What is that?" he said. He was staring ahead.

Peter squinted. A rabbit-sized creature was running beside the wall, headed for them. But it wasn't a rabbit—not even close. It was pink and hairless, and it ran on two legs like a flightless bird. Something strange was protruding from its side. Peter grabbed Robert's sleeve and pulled him away from the wall as the thing scampered past them, and he saw what was protruding from the creature's side. It was a human hand.

"I think I'm seeing things," Robert said.

Peter turned and watched the creature. "You're not. I saw it too."

The thing stopped when it saw Marleah sitting where they had left her. It approached her cautiously. Peter started to yell at her to avoid touching it, but he was too late.

She kicked it with her good foot. "Get away from me!"

The freakish animal tumbled away but was not so easily deterred. It approached her again.

"Marleah, move away from it!" Peter shouted.

Instead of backing away, she kicked it again. Again it tumbled away, and again it approached her, this time more aggressively. Another kick. It tumbled. And then it leapt at her and latched onto her leg.

"Get off! Get off!" She pounded it with her fists until it let go. But it attacked again.

"She needs help," Robert muttered, and he started limping back to her.

Peter hesitated. The dream he'd had flooded his thoughts again. "Wait!"

Robert turned.

"I don't think you can help her."

Robert frowned. "It's attacking her. I'll stomp on it."

Marleah continued screaming at the creature, trying to fight it off.

"Listen to me," Peter said. "It's more dangerous than it looks."

"How so?"

"The Lamotelokhai tried to warn us—"

Suddenly Marleah's cries escalated to sheer terror. "What is this? Oh no! What is it?" She was scooting backwards, pushing herself with her hands. But not to escape from the hairless creature—it was running away from her, still hugging the slightly curving wall.

Instinctively, Peter started toward her with Robert at his side. It was impossible to ignore someone in such desperate distress.

"What is it?" she cried over and over.

At ten meters away they both stopped. It was now obvious why she was backing away.

Peter became vaguely aware that Robert was retching. In the corner of his vision he saw him cover his mouth. But Peter couldn't take his eyes off Marleah. She was trying to back away from her own legs—because now they weren't legs at all.

"No! What is it?" Her cries were becoming little more than garbled screeches.

Her legs had lost their solid physical form. Instead, they had become shifting, wriggling masses of worms. Hundreds of them. Some were large, like snakes. But most were the size of spaghetti. The main mass of them was attached to Marleah—it was being dragged with her as she tried to escape. But many had broken loose, and she was leaving behind a trail of individual squirming earthworms as she pulled herself across the rocks and dirt.

"No! No!"

Something with wings fluttered by Peter's face. A second winged thing flew up from the ground and came for him. He swiped at it with his hand. He then realized the worms Marleah had left behind were changing, becoming other creatures. Some of them now had legs and were skittering about. Others were sprouting wings and taking to the air. One of these fluttered at his face and he ducked instead of trying to swat it, fearful that any contact might result in the same frightful fate as Marleah's.

"Robert, run!" Peter turned and ran as fast as the pain of his broiled leg would allow. A moment later he heard Robert grunting behind him, trying to catch up.

"No! Noooo!" Marleah's screams became muffled, and then they stopped altogether.

As they followed the curving wall, Peter saw a car speeding away on a gravel road, leaving a cloud of dust. After running a few more meters, a cluster of parked cars came into view. And then they were at the entrance to the compound.

The door appeared to have been blown off its frame. It lay on the ground in front of the entrance. Next to the door was the body of a woman. She had been crushed, possibly by the broken door.

While Robert stared at the woman's body, Peter approached the open doorway. At arm's length from the opening, he could go no closer due to intense heat. He could see nothing but darkness beyond the doorway. It was like the gaping maw of hell.

"Bobby! Ashley!" Of course there was no answer. There was nothing alive in there. *Not even microbes*, Marleah had said.

Robert stepped up beside Peter. "Maybe they got out. That psycho Helmich knew they were important. He probably took them with him when he evacuated the place. Don't you think?"

Peter didn't answer. He just stared into the darkness.

CHAPTER EIGHTEEN

BOBBY WATCHED Tiffany walk across the parking lot and through the gleaming doors of the Kmart. She had changed into shorts and a shirt she'd gotten from the car's trunk, and she'd combed her hair to hide the burned spot. Now she was going in to buy clothes for Bobby and Ashley.

"I notice she took the keys with her," Ashley said.

Bobby had noticed this too, but he was glad. If Tiffany had left the keys, at this moment he'd be talking Ashley out of driving off and leaving her here. They needed Tiffany's help. They had no money, or ID, or anything else—except a cellphone and an incomplete chunk of the Lamotelokhai.

Bobby closed his eyes and tried to gather some courage. There was something he had to do, and it couldn't wait—they would be at the airport soon. He touched the skin behind his right ear. The area still hurt, and it was crusted with dried blood. He moved his hand to the left side of his head and touched the box anchored to his skull. He had no idea how it was attached, but sheer force was probably the only way he could remove it. He had already tried pulling gently on it, but he'd had to quit because of the pain. So he decided to treat it like a Band-Aid—pull hard and fast, not soft and slow.

Before he could talk himself out of it, he sucked in some air and then yanked on the box. A cry escaped between his gritted teeth and his feet shot out and kicked the back of the driver seat.

Ashley whipped around. "Damn, Bobby!"

He clamped his eyes shut, enduring the lasting pain and trying to breathe normally. He hadn't pulled hard enough. The box was still attached, although now it jiggled a little when he touched it. He opened his eyes and looked out the windows to make sure his cry hadn't attracted attention. Tiffany had parked at the outer corner of the lot to change her clothes, and the closest people were too far to have heard.

"You need to wait and have a doctor do that."

Bobby looked at his hand. It was shaking, and his fingertips were red with blood. "A monster bit the other one off. I survived that. I just need to pull harder."

"Well, at least let me do it." She got out of the car, flipped the seatback forward, crawled in next to him, and shut the door behind her.

Bobby turned so she could get at the left side of his head.

She gripped the box with one hand and put her other against the side of his head. "Ready?"

Bobby closed his eyes again. "No, but I want it off." He waited. Seconds passed.

She let go. "I don't think I can do it."

Bobby exhaled.

"Why don't you use that?" she asked, nodding toward the lump of clay. "Or do you still think it's dangerous?"

Bobby considered this. So far this portion of the Lamotelokhai hadn't done anything disastrous. Maybe it *could* help.

"It might work." He looked at her. "But you should get out of the car, just in case."

She frowned. But then she crawled out, closed the door, and leaned in through the open window. "If you turn into a monster, I'm going to kick your ass."

Bobby put his hands on the lump of clay and decided this time to just speak out loud. "I need help getting this thing off my head. Can you make it come off without hurting me?" He waited for a moment then pinched off a pea-sized chunk and rubbed it into the box and the surrounding skin. He waited.

Ashley watched him silently, her elbows resting on the door.

Abruptly the box dropped to his shoulder and tumbled onto the seat. He picked it up. It was black and made of metal, featureless except for the side that had been against his skin. That side had a sticky gray pad and four shiny steel posts that looked like they'd been melted off at the ends. Was the rest of each post still stuck in his skull?

Ashley opened the door again and crawled into the back seat. "If it can do what you ask, it should also do what I ask, right?"

"I guess so, but—"

She put her hands on the clay. "I want Bobby's shaved hair to grow out. Like, right now." She pinched some off and smeared it gently onto the right side of his head. There was something almost magical about her fingers rubbing his scalp. He was tempted to close his eyes but decided that would look weird.

She finished and said, "Turn." He turned, and she rubbed it into the other side. She wiped the remaining bits onto the back of the seat in front of her. She then sat back and gazed at the side of his head.

This made Bobby feel awkward, so he looked out the window at the Kmart. It looked like every other big store he had ever seen, except some of the signs were in Spanish. And the shoppers were Puerto Ricans, most of them with dark hair.

The shaved areas of his scalp began to tingle.

"It's working," Ashley said. "I can't believe I did it right."

Bobby felt his head. It *was* working. Bristles now covered the previously smooth skin. And the bristles were getting longer by the second.

Ashley put her warm, magical fingers against his scalp again. "We've just discovered a cure for baldness."

Bobby smiled at this. "It came a zillion light years to help middle-aged men feel young again." But then he forced the smile away. It didn't seem right to make jokes when so many people had just died, including Peter and Robert. Maybe he could go back to the compound and use this piece of the Lamotelokhai's clay to bring them back to life. But it would be days before they could enter the compound. And besides, the bodies were probably burned to ashes. Maybe if he successfully restored the Lamotelokhai's consciousness, he could ask it to create a new copy of Peter's body and put Peter's consciousness in it. That wouldn't work for Robert, though, because the Lamotelokhai hadn't put its particles into him to learn about him.

Ashley finally pulled her fingers from his scalp. "What else do you think it can do?"

"No idea." He put his hands on the clay and spoke aloud. "I want to know what else you can do. Can you tell me?"

He didn't really expect much to happen. But then an arrangement of Kembalimo symbols appeared before his eyes. He squeezed his eyes closed. The symbols were still there, and they remained when he opened his eyes again. It had been months since he had talked to anyone using Kembalimo, but he remembered every symbol combination he'd developed when he had worked through the Kembalimo lingo-building process back in the Papuan rainforest. Millions of people had created their own Kembalimo lingoes using Peter's smartphone app, but Bobby was one of the few who had ever created a lingo with the actual Lamotelokhai.

The general meaning of the arrangement of symbols was, "Hello, Bobby."

An old habit kicked in, and he raised one hand, ready to move symbols into a reply, but the 256 symbols that used to be arranged in a border around the main statement were missing. There were no symbols to choose from, other than the four that made up the greeting.

So Bobby spoke aloud. "Hello, Lamotelokhai. Is it really you?"

The four symbols faded away and were replaced by one. "No."

Bobby frowned. "Then what are you?"

The single symbol disappeared and was replaced by at least thirty more, arranged to be read left to right, top to bottom. "Lamotelokhai created me. I am knowledge. Small knowledge. I talk to you. My purpose."

"Bobby?" It was Ashley.

He turned to her, and the symbols moved with his field of vision. Now they were displayed in front of her face. He pulled his hands from the clay, and they disappeared. "It's talking to me. I think the Lamotelokhai gave it some basic programming. Because it knew it was about to die."

He put his hands back on the clay. "Your purpose is to talk to me?"

One symbol appeared. "Yes."

"And you are the Lamotelokhai's knowledge?"

The symbol was replaced by another set. "Small knowledge. I talk to you small. I help you small."

Bobby figured he knew what this meant—limited help. "So what can you do to help us?"

The symbols changed. "Please talk different."

Bobby stared. "Um, would you be able to stop all the transforming creatures that started back at Dr. Helmich's compound?"

"No."

"No?"

"Small knowledge now. Small help. You help me more knowledge. More knowledge more help."

Bobby cursed quietly. They still needed to get the other data packets. It could take weeks. But maybe this thing could at least help them do that.

"Um, can you heal us if we get hurt?"

"Possible. Need hurt definition."

This looked promising, and communication was already getting easier. "If we get cut or scraped."

"Possible. Need definitions."

He sighed. Maybe it wasn't getting easier. "Here, I'll show you." He pinched off some clay and applied it to the gashes on the right side of his head from the Helmich-bat's teeth. As he spread the clay he realized the hair in this area was now much thicker. "Can you heal these cuts?"

After a few seconds the symbols changed. "Talk first. Take my parts second."

"Okay, I have cuts on my head. I am going to take some of your parts and put them on my cuts. I hope you can heal the cuts." He pinched off more and applied it. He waited. His scalp was still tingling due to the fact that the hair was still growing quickly, so he couldn't tell if anything new was happening. But soon he realized the pain was fading. He touched the cuts. They definitely felt better.

The symbols before his eyes changed. "Success or fail. Tell please."

"It's working," Bobby said. "Success."

The symbols disappeared.

Bobby rummaged around. Tiffany's car was clean, but there were some papers in the storage bin between the front seats. They were mostly in Spanish, but they looked like something to do with the purchase or renting of the car. He pulled one of the papers loose, folded it, and set it on top of the lump of clay. He pressed his hand to the side of the lump, under the paper. "Can you make an exact copy of this paper?"

Bobby pulled his hand back and watched. The folded paper became soft, and its corners drooped. It melted into the clay and was gone. A new lump started to arise. The new lump fell away from the larger mass onto the seat and continued to change. Soon it was a folded piece of paper. He opened it. It certainly looked like the same document. He put his hand back on the clay.

"When I said make a copy, I meant to make a new copy and keep the original. You know, so there would be two."

Symbols appeared before his eyes. "I understand."

Another lump appeared, dropped off, and became a second folded paper. Bobby didn't bother to unfold it.

He grinned at Ashley. "This thing might be able to help us!"

He looked toward the Kmart. Tiffany had not come out yet, but she would soon. There was something else he wanted to try. He pressed the first paper against the lump. "The Lamotelokhai could zap things from one place to another. Even people. It did this to me a couple of times. It was just like, *zap*, and I was in a different place. Can you zap this paper to a different place? To, um, the front seat of this car?"

Symbols formed. "Need place definition."

Ashley said, "Maybe you shouldn't—"

Bobby ignored her. "The front seat." He leaned forward and put his hand with the paper in it on the passenger seat. "Right there. It's just a few feet away." He brought his hand back and pressed the paper against the clay. "Can you zap it into the front seat?"

Suddenly everything turned gray. Bobby saw nothing and heard nothing. Seconds passed—or maybe minutes—and then shapes began to appear. He could hear a voice, faint at first, and then louder.

"Bobby! Say something!" It was Ashley's voice.

He blinked. The shapes before his eyes became clear. The backs of two car seats, a windshield, a dashboard with knobs and letters on it. And something moving, in the front passenger seat. It was a mass of something, with skin and hair. And bits of white cloth quickly turning red from seeping blood.

"What is that!" Bobby said. His voice sounded strange in his ears.

Suddenly Ashley's arms were around him and her forehead was against his temple. "Oh, thank God! I thought your brain was fried or something."

Bobby couldn't take his eyes off the bloody, quivering mass. "Ashley, what is that?"

She pulled back. "How should I know? I've been trying to snap you out of your trance. There was this sound, and my ears popped. Then it was there, in the seat. The thing was noisy at first, like it was gagging. You know, trying to breathe. I didn't know what to do. But I think it's dead now. Are you okay?"

She was right, the mass was now hardly moving. It was dying, if not dead already. Bobby finally pulled his eyes away from it. He stared at his hands. The left one still gripped the folded paper. He had meant to let go of it before asking the clay to zap it to the front seat. But it was still in his hand.

He looked again at the sickening mass. Bits of pale green cloth, pale skin dotted with freckles, a femur-sized bone sticking out with its end deformed like melted plastic, part of what looked like scalp with brown hair—the same color as Bobby's hair. And there, blood-covered and warped, was the heel of a Converse low-top with the snake-skin print. Bobby's shoe.

"It's me," Bobby said.

A white and red plastic bag was shoved through the open window into Bobby's lap. The driver door popped open and Tiffany got in.

"I had to guess on your sizes, but I think—"

She stared at the blob of skin and cloth and blood beside her. She whipped her head around to look at Bobby and Ashley.

Without saying another word she got out of the car. She walked to the grass by the edge of the parking lot and put her hands on her knees like she was going to throw up.

Bobby flipped the driver seat forward and got out. He went to her and put a hand on her back. "I think it's dead. It didn't suffer long."

Her mouth opened, but only words came out. "I thought for a second it was one of you two. What is it?"

"It's hard to explain, but I think it *is* me. A copy of me, anyway."

She looked up at him but kept her hands on her knees. Her face was pale. "I want to go home."

"I know." Bobby looked around the parking lot. A lady with a red shopping basket by her car was staring, but she turned away when their eyes met. "We'll get that thing out of the car. Then you can drive us all to the airport. You can fly home, and we won't tell anyone we were with you. Okay?"

She nodded but remained bent over.

Bobby went back to the car as Ashley was climbing out. They opened the passenger door and stared at the mass on the seat.

"If that's you, it's not an improvement," Ashley said.

He turned to her and raised his brows. A year ago, they both would have been heaving in the grass with Tiffany. But they had seen so much since then.

Bobby gazed over the hood toward the store. No one was looking their way. Still, he was glad this side of the car was facing away from the other cars. He grabbed the blob by a curved rib bone that was sticking out, but when he pulled on it, the bone came loose with a wet pop.

"Help me," he said to Ashley. Together they grabbed it wherever they could get a grip and rolled the thing off the seat. It hit the pavement with a squishy thump. Bobby tried not to look at it too long, but he couldn't help noticing part of an arm protruding from one side. At least it wasn't his head or one of his eyes.

They took Tiffany's elbows and walked her back to the car, and they all got in. Tiffany stared at the passenger seat. It was covered with pooled blood and pink chunks.

"It's out of the car, Mrs. Travers," Ashley said. "Let's go before police show up."

Bobby said, "The police are probably too busy."

Tiffany backed up and drove out to the highway, leaving the mass of body parts in the parking lot.

Ashley plucked the folded paper from the seat. It was the copy Bobby had asked the clay to create. She opened it and stared at it for a moment before handing it to him. The paper had several holes in it, and its edges were not straight. There was printing on it, but the letters were garbled and blurred. It was not even close to a perfect copy.

"I don't know what you were thinking," Ashley said, "but let's not try anything like that again."

Bobby stared at his face in the mirror. He had been washing dried blood from his face and neck for several minutes, and finally it looked like he'd gotten it all. But he still looked stupid, because the hair Ashley had treated with the clay was still growing, and now it was longer than the rest of his hair.

He grabbed the baseball cap Tiffany had bought him and put it on. It was red with white letters, PR, above the flat, oversized brim. With his red t-shirt and blue jeans—too big but held up with a belt —he was less likely to stand out in a crowd.

He stuffed his crusted, burned doctor clothes into the trash and left the bathroom. Ashley had already changed and was waiting in the back seat of the car. Tiffany stood next to a gas pump where they were parked. She had made it clear she didn't like sitting next to the mess in the passenger seat. They got in the car and Tiffany pulled out onto the road.

Twenty minutes later they were at the San Juan Marín Airport. They entered a multi-level parking garage and found a place on the top level where there were no other cars. Bobby got out, holding the lump of clay under his arm, while Tiffany grabbed a purse and duffel bag from the trunk.

Tiffany looked at the clay. She handed Bobby her duffel bag. "Take some of my clothes out and put that thing in the bag. You can't walk through the airport carrying it like that."

Bobby took it and thanked her. He was able to get the clay into the bag without removing anything. He zipped the bag shut. Bobby, Ashley, and Tiffany went down some concrete stairs and crossed a street full of taxis and shuttles to a huge terminal building.

Inside, Tiffany stopped. "Do you know what you're going to do next?"

"We'll be fine," Bobby said. "Someone's coming for us."

She studied them for a moment. She frowned at Bobby and tilted her head like she was looking at his ear. "Um, your hair."

Bobby took off his cap and felt his scalp. The hair that had been shaved was now at least an inch longer than the rest.

"I was trying not to say anything," Ashley said. "But it is starting to look funny."

Bobby replaced the cap. "I guess I'll just have to cut it."

Tiffany shifted her eyes from Bobby to Ashley and back to Bobby. "Look, I know we made a mistake. And I know it's not over. I heard you talking about trying to fix the problem. Is there any way I can help?" The way she had hesitated gave Bobby the impression she was hoping they'd say no.

Bobby glanced at Ashley. She hated the woman. He could see it in her eyes. He spoke before she could.

"You helped us get here," he said to Tiffany. "You didn't have to, but you did anyway. If our plan works, and we can prevent those things from spreading everywhere, it will be because you helped us. You should go home."

She exhaled, her shoulders relaxed, and she nodded. "Good luck, you two." She then turned and walked away at a brisk pace.

"She's really stupid if she thinks no one will know," Ashley said. "She left her car with a bunch of blood in it. A mangled body in the parking lot. Probably a hundred other things that will lead the feds to her."

Bobby considered this. "Maybe the feds hired her in the first place. Maybe Helmich worked for the government—the CIA or something."

"If so, they'll never admit it." She turned to Bobby. "We've got to do something about that hair."

There was a vibration in Bobby's pocket, followed by a chime. He pulled out Tiffany's phone. It was a text message from someone named Gary: "What the hell is happening there? Been watching the news. Call me when you can!"

"Tell him Tiffany is dead," Ashley said. She was leaning into his shoulder to read the screen.

Bobby ignored her and typed a reply: "I'm okay. On my way home now. Won't be able to call for a while. Don't worry." He hit *Send.*

Ashley snorted indignantly.

"We need this phone," Bobby said. "We don't want her husband shutting the account down because he thinks it's been stolen."

"That's why they call you science boy."

"You're the only one who calls me that."

Without tickets, or ID, or anything else, they wouldn't be able to go through security checkpoints to other parts of the airport, so they found a quiet corner near the outer wall where Tiffany's phone had a strong cell signal. They sat on the floor.

"We should have asked her for some money," Bobby said. "I'm starving."

"Look at that." Ashley was staring at a television attached to the ceiling. A dozen or so people were gathered nearby, staring somberly up at it. The screen was showing a news report with English subtitles. People with haunted looks on their faces were being interviewed, describing something they had seen. The video cut away to a view from a helicopter. It showed a neighborhood of blocky white houses. Police cars with flashing lights were scattered throughout the neighborhood. The camera zoomed in. Bodies were lying in the streets. People were running. The camera zoomed in closer, and a wave of gasps and cries came from the people gathered below the TV. Bobby squinted. Not all of the running figures were human.

"It's our fault," Ashley said. "They got loose because we left the compound."

Bobby turned to her. She was right. More accurately, though, it was Bobby's fault.

Ashley was still staring at the TV. "Do you think they'll be able to stop it?"

"I'd like to think so, but the things I saw in the lower level of the compound..."

Finally she turned to him. "Then we can't screw this up. We have to put the Lamotelokhai back together and bring it back here."

The phone in Bobby's hand vibrated and chimed again. This time it was a call from a number based in Oklahoma City. It had to be Jonathan. Bobby answered.

"Bobby, Jonathan Benson here. Are you and Ashley still safe?"

"We're okay. We're at the airport."

"That's a relief. I've been watching the news at every opportunity. Never seen anything like it. You were right, it's damn serious."

Bobby nodded, as if Jonathan could see him. "The airport here is pretty calm right now, but I bet people will start panicking soon. When will you be here?"

"I'm in the air as we speak. Bobby, you mentioned that you needed to see your friend in Missouri before going to Indonesia. Is that absolutely necessary?"

"We can't save the Lamotelokhai without him. And the Lamotelokhai is the only thing that can stop what's happening here."

"That's what I presumed. And that's why we're on our way to Kansas City. I called the family of Carlos Herrera. My intent was to convince them that Carlos should come with us to Puerto Rico, and that they should expedite the process by driving him to the airport."

This took Bobby by surprise. He hadn't thought of saving time this way. "Yeah?"

"They weren't keen on the idea."

"I bet they weren't. I'll call Carlos myself. I'll get it sorted out."

"Precisely what I was hoping you'd say. If you convince his folks to allow it and everything goes smoothly, we should arrive in San Juan as early as 2:00 am your time. If you can wait somewhere near the main entrance to the airport from the parking facility, I'll find you. We'll be landing at Terminal B."

"We're by the main entrance now. But we don't have anything with us. We left our passports and stuff in Oklahoma City."

"I have your things. You'll be boarding a private jet, in which case the captain has discretion over who can and cannot board. There shouldn't be any problems."

They ended the call and Bobby gave Ashley a quick summary. He then typed a text message and sent it to a number he had been calling every month for the last eight months. The text said, "Carlos, it's Bobby. I'm going to call you from this number, so you better answer!" He counted to thirty and then called the number.

"Bobby, is that you? What the hell's going on?"

"Yeah, it's me. I need to be sure I'm talking to the right Carlos. What did Addison say that time he smashed those termites and ate them off his hand?"

Carlos sighed. "He said, 'Now they worship me.' Bobby, this is my phone. The other Carlos has his own phone."

"I had to be sure," Bobby said. "Listen. I know this is crazy, and I know your parents are going to shit, but we need your help."

CHAPTER NINETEEN

PETER TURNED AWAY from the compound's dark opening. There was no way they could go back inside. If Bobby and Ashley were still in there, they were dead. Without a doubt.

There was a gravel parking lot with several cars and an unpaved road, stretching as far as they could see in either direction. They were near a coast—the air was warm and humid, with the unmistakable scent of mangrove mud and rotting algae.

Several small fires burned in the nearby weeds, and dark smoke rose from low mangrove trees beyond that. Peter's eyes were drawn to a movement in one of the trees, near the rising smoke. He heard branches cracking, as if from the weight of a heavy creature. He squinted. He couldn't see a creature in the tree, yet the branches kept moving. This gave him an uneasy feeling. He turned. In the opposite direction, the horizon was stacked with forest-covered mountains.

Robert stepped to Peter's side and said, "Where the hell are we?"

"It looks like we've been taken out of the United States."

"Maybe Hawaii?"

"Maybe." Peter walked to the nearest car. It was locked. He checked the others. All locked. He walked to the road, acutely aware of the worsening pain in his burned leg and foot. To the right the road went to the mangroves, and therefore to the shore. To the left it went toward the mountains. He turned left and started walking. Robert followed.

Within a few hundred meters, fields of bananas or plantains came into view. Peter could hear vehicles passing by on what sounded like a paved road further ahead. Suddenly a dog-sized animal ran across the road ahead of them. It was moving too fast for Peter to see details, but it had too many legs to be a dog.

"We shouldn't be out in the open like this," Robert said.

Peter had to agree.

They heard Sirens in the distance. The sirens drew nearer and then slowed when they approached the place directly ahead of Peter and Robert where the gravel road ran into the paved highway. Peter thought the vehicles were going to turn toward them, on their way to the destroyed compound, but they turned the opposite direction and began growing quieter in the distance.

Peter could now see a cluster of houses beyond the paved road —a small town or village. That's where the emergency vehicles had gone. Something big was happening there, but at least there would be vehicles. Peter had a strong desire to get inside a vehicle and close the doors and windows. So they kept walking.

Every step was excruciating. Peter was confident in his body's ability to heal; for fifty years he had enjoyed the benefits of the Lamotelokhai's particles. But it would be hours—perhaps even a day—before new skin replaced the burned skin. He wasn't sure he could run, but he knew that running might become necessary at any moment. He looked down at his leg. The exposed flesh was every color from pink to black, and he was leaving a bloodstain on the dirt with every step.

Finally they arrived at the paved road. More sirens approached from the left. Four cars with flashing lights came screaming toward them and then turned off toward the cluster of houses on the far side of the road. The cars were white with broad blue and yellow stripes and the words *Policia Transito*. The cop in the last car stared at them as he turned off the highway, but he continued following the others.

Peter glanced at Robert. "I think we're in Mexico, or perhaps the Caribbean."

"They didn't even stop," Robert said. "We look like we've been through a meat grinder, and they didn't even stop."

Peter watched the cars as they sped into the village. The breeze from the coast behind him shifted direction for a moment, and he thought he heard screams coming from the houses ahead. He was already on edge, but now a deeper sense of dread swelled within him.

Still more sirens approached from the left, a group of navy blue cruisers and SUVs. Robert walked onto the road and stood directly in front of them. Peter realized it was the right move. They had no choice—they couldn't stay out in the open like this. He joined Robert on the road.

The first of the vehicles, a Tahoe, skidded to a stop before hitting them. The vehicles behind it barely slowed down. They ran onto the shoulder, barreled around them, and turned onto the road leading into the village. Two policemen sat in the Tahoe. The one on the passenger side got out and approached them with his hand on the butt of his sidearm. He looked at their burned and stained hospital clothes and at Peter's scorched leg. The other cop turned off the siren.

"¿*Quién eres?*" the man before them said. "¿*Qué pasó?*"

"We need help," Peter said. "It isn't safe here. Can we get a lift?"

More screams arose from the village, and the cop turned to look. "Come, get in," he said. He opened the door to the Tahoe's back seat. They got in and the locks clicked. The driver hit the gas and sped around the turn toward the houses.

The officer in the passenger seat turned and addressed them through a steel mesh barrier. "What have you seen? What is happening?"

"It's animals," Peter said. "There are animals everywhere. You can't let them touch you. Don't let them touch anyone."

The Tahoe turned left onto a dirt road lined with tightly-packed houses. Other police cars were parked haphazardly in the road and yards ahead.

"What animals? Dogs?"

"No, not dogs. They are—"

"¡*Mierda*!" the driver shouted and slammed on the brakes.

Two figures had run out from between the houses on the left and directly in front of the Tahoe. The first was a woman. Close on her heels was a man. The woman saw the Tahoe. She skirted around the front of it without slowing down and grabbed the handle on the back driver-side door. Briefly, Peter saw her terrified eyes just outside his window as she yanked on the handle. But then the man came around the vehicle and stopped beside her. She shrieked and yanked on the handle again, but it was locked.

"¡*Ayúdeme*!" she cried.

Peter then realized the man beside her was not actually a man. Or at least not entirely. One side of his face was almost normal, but the other side was misshapen, with lumpy, red skin drooping down like the neck of a turkey. The arm on that side of his body was much longer than the other, with skin hanging loose in the same way. He stood beside the hysterical woman, gazing at her with one eye drooping several inches below the other. He held out his good hand as if trying to calm her.

Both cops got out of the Tahoe, the driver nearly knocking the disfigured man over as he opened his door. The disfigured man then turned his attention to the officer. He tried speaking, but one side of his mouth was drooping almost to his chest, and the sounds were incomprehensible. He reached for the officer as if pleading for help. The cop shoved him away and said, "*¿Qué te ocurre? ¿Qué está pasando aquí?*"

The officers had left their doors open, so the woman got in the front seat and slammed the door shut. She crawled over the center console and closed the passenger door.

"Ma'am, are you okay?" Robert said through the mesh barrier.

She was whimpering and staring into her lap, and she didn't answer. Peter leaned forward so he could see what she was looking at. It was her hands. They were transforming. One finger on each hand was much longer than the others, with a membrane of skin stretching between the elongated finger and the woman's armpit. The membranes were bunched up at the armpits, constricted by her t-shirt sleeves.

"*¿Qué está pasando aquí?*" the cop outside the door shouted again. His partner was now beside him, and they both had their sidearms aimed at the disfigured man. The man's face was now even more misshapen, and his head leaned to one side due to a lack of solid structure on that side of his neck. Suddenly he collapsed into a heap on the road. The two officers stood over him, staring, apparently at a loss for what to do.

As Peter looked through his window at the poor bloke lying in the dirt, another movement outside the car caught his eye. He squinted, trying to get a better look. "Bloody hell," he muttered.

Walking toward them from between two houses was a creature that looked like a crocodile, but with hind legs as long as a man's. The front legs were shorter, about the size of a man's arms, and so the creature walked at a slant, with its hips and tail higher than its head.

"Hey!" Peter rapped on the window to get the cops' attention. When they turned to him, he pointed.

The crocodile continued walking leisurely toward them,

although with its abnormally long legs it looked like it could easily outrun a human. The cops turned their guns on the approaching creature. It came right up to the helpless, disfigured man, and the officers stepped back against the SUV. The crocodile was three meters long from its snout to the tip of its tail. Its entire body was much larger than that of an adult human. Was it possible multiple people were merging into one creature as they were transforming? If not, perhaps this creature had previously been a cow or horse.

The woman in the front seat continued crying as Peter and Robert watched the surreal scene outside the vehicle. The crocodile gazed at the helpless man. It then nudged the man with its snout. The man moaned pitifully and tried to move away, but his body wouldn't cooperate. Nearly all of his exposed skin had now transformed into loose piles of flesh splayed out on the ground. Apparently sensing the man's helplessness, the crocodile attacked. It clamped onto his arm and started backing up, dragging him away.

Finally the two policemen acted. They both fired at the creature. It released the man and raised up onto its hind legs. It then charged at the cops, closing the five meters of distance with frightening speed. The creature hit one of the officers, slamming him back into the SUV and rocking the entire vehicle. The officer went down with the snarling, thrashing crocodile on top of him. His partner shouted something and shot point blank at the creature. He fired again, and again, until the crocodile stopped moving. He shoved the creature aside and helped his partner up. The guy was covered in blood, either his own or the creature's.

The cop who had just saved his partner threw open the driver door, got in, and began shouting into his two-way radio. "Officer down! *Necesitamos ambulancias y refuerzos en—*"

Suddenly he took notice of the woman in the seat beside him. She was still crying, but her voice was changing. It was now more of a screech, no longer human. She still held her hands out, staring at them, but there was barely room for them in the confined space.

The elongated finger on each hand had continued growing and each was at least a meter long now, with the leathery membrane draping down into her lap. Her fingers were becoming pterodactyl-like wings.

The officer dropped his radio and got out. He put an arm around his partner and helped him limp away from the SUV. They turned and looked back at the vehicle, one man's face glistening with sweat, the other's with blood.

The uninjured officer locked his eyes onto Peter's, and they stared at each other through the glass. But then the cop shifted his gaze, looking at something beyond the SUV, behind Peter. He said something to his partner and started guiding him away. The two men half-ran, half-staggered between houses and were gone.

"God almighty," Robert said.

Peter turned, and then he saw why the cops had fled. The ground on the other side of the street was moving. It was covered with insects, or some other type of small creatures. Thousands of them. They seemed to be coming from a row of fruit trees growing beside one of the houses. The trees were rapidly getting smaller, because pieces of their limbs were breaking off and falling to the ground. But the fallen pieces were not simply accumulating in piles. They were dispersing, crawling away from the trees of their own volition, spreading out in every direction. Some of them were already in the street, moving toward the Tahoe.

Peter realized the driver door was still open. "We have to close the door!" He pulled the lever to open his own door. It was locked. Robert tried his door. Also locked.

"Ma'am," Peter said through the mesh barrier. "You need to close the door."

But the woman was beyond understanding him. Her arms had become wings, folded awkwardly in several directions because they were too long to extend fully in the tight space. Her head and shoulders were hunched over, and Peter couldn't see her face.

He slammed his hand against the steel mesh. "Ma'am, close the bloody door!"

She straightened up and turned. Her face was no longer human. It had become elongated, with a beak extending out in front of her eyes. She opened the beak and squawked at him through the barrier, baring rows of pointed teeth.

"They're under the car now," Robert said. He was too busy watching the spreading swarm outside to pay much attention to the transforming woman. "They look like centipedes. Big ones. We've got to shut that damn door!"

Suddenly the woman went berserk. She thrashed her wings and dislodged a laptop that was mounted on the dashboard. She tore at her t-shirt with her long beak, trying to rip it from her body. She then scratched and wriggled her way past the steering wheel and out the open door. She scrabbled over the grotesque body of the turkey-neck man, and then Peter could see that there was no woman left in her at all. Her shorts had come off in her struggles, revealing short legs with tiny clawed feet. A thin, meter-long, hairless tail whipped about between the two legs. Horrified and fascinated, Peter couldn't take his eyes off her. She expanded her wings, tearing away what was left of the shirt. She tried flapping her wings a few times, but her torso was still proportionally too large for flight.

Abruptly the winged reptile stopped moving. It fixed its stare on the ground. The centipedes were now swarming the dirt beneath it. It thrust its beak out and grabbed one, like a heron snatching a frog. It threw its head back to swallow the centipede and then picked up another.

"They're getting in!" Robert cried, lifting his feet off the floor and onto the seat.

Peter looked. Several centipedes the length of his hand were crawling on the floorboard. He lifted his feet to avoid them.

He and Robert were trapped.

Peter rolled onto his back and kicked the glass window. Pain exploded in his scorched foot and he cried out.

"Move over," Robert said. Without waiting for Peter to move, he threw himself onto his back and kicked the other window with both feet. It didn't break.

Peter pulled himself from beneath Robert and got to his knees. He looked down in time to see a centipede crawl up and over the edge of the seat, inches from Robert's head. He pulled his sleeve over his hand and flicked it onto the floor.

Robert grunted and kicked again. This time the window cracked, but it was held in place by the safety membrane between the glass layers. Two more kicks and the glass fell to the ground. Robert got to his knees as Peter brushed two more centipedes off the seat. More of them were making their way into the vehicle.

Peter and Robert looked at each other. Robert nodded over Peter's shoulder and said, "I don't want to die like that."

Peter turned. The winged reptile was still trying to eat the swarming centipedes, but now it was struggling. Its once-rigid beak was sagging, flapping around loosely. The creature was transforming again, probably due to contact with the centipedes.

Peter looked down and flicked another centipede off as it came over the lip of the seat. "Okay," he said. "Out!"

Robert reached through the broken window and found the door handle, but the door still wouldn't open. He went through the window head first until he was sitting on the door with his feet on the backseat. As Peter brushed more centipedes off the seat, he heard Robert grasping at anything he could on the Tahoe's roof to gain leverage. Robert managed to pull one knee through the window, but as he struggled with the other leg, he fell onto the road.

He was on his feet in an instant, stomping on centipedes and cursing. He spun around. "They're on my back! Get them off!"

"You're okay," Peter said. "I don't see any. Clear the ground,

I'm coming out." Peter flicked one more centipede and then lunged through the window. Robert grabbed him around the chest and pulled him out.

"Kill that one, and that one!" Peter said, pointing at centipedes that were breaching the perimeter Robert had established. Although Peter's right shoe was still mostly intact, there was almost nothing left of his other shoe to protect his seared flesh. And he didn't want to find out whether seared flesh would transform into a monster as quickly as healthy flesh.

Robert kept stomping, but it was a losing battle. They had to run.

"This way!" Peter took off down the street, away from the epicenter of the centipedes, stepping between them with his exposed foot as gingerly as he could. This was far more painful than he had imagined, but soon he and Robert were ahead of the spreading swarm.

Peter heard a low droning sound above. Things were flying about just over the houses—at least half a dozen of them that he could see. They were the size of pigeons, but they weren't birds. They were dragonflies.

"We need to find cover," he said. "One of the houses."

Robert grabbed his elbow and pulled him off the street. "This one!"

Like the others, the house was basically a box with a flat roof. The front had a single window and a door, both with metal bars over them.

Robert rapped on the door frame. "Hey! Can we come in?"

A woman's voice came from beyond the door. "¡*Vete!* Go away!"

Robert glanced at Peter. He then tried opening the outer door. It was locked. He rattled it loudly. "We need help! We're hurt, and—"

A blast came through the door, hitting Robert in the chest. He immediately crumpled to the ground.

"Robert!" Peter kneeled next to him.

Robert was wheezing, like the wind had been knocked out of him. Peter rolled him onto his back and then felt himself going pale. Just below Robert's collarbone, a four-inch cavity had been gouged into his chest.

"Bloody hell, you shot him!" Peter screamed at the house.

Another shotgun blast came through the door, whizzing over Peter's head. He dropped instinctively and pressed himself against his friend. Robert weakly lifted one of his arms and wrapped it around Peter as if trying to protect him. His gurgling breaths were coming through the hole in his chest, just beneath Peter's ear.

And then the wheezing stopped. Robert's arm loosened and fell to his side. Peter kept his head there for a moment. He didn't need to look at Robert's eyes to know he was dead.

Something crawled over the blistered skin of Peter's ankle. He pushed himself up, shook off a centipede, and stomped it with his right foot. But more were coming—a lot more. Before getting up, he allowed himself one look at Robert's face. Blood had run from his mouth and nose. Peter wiped at it with his sleeve and pushed Robert's eyes closed.

He looked up at the house. The woman was staring at him through one of the four-inch holes, but then she backed away, probably holding her shotgun ready to shoot again.

He swallowed, fighting off the urge to start sobbing. There wasn't time for that. Centipedes were gathering at his feet. Bird-sized bugs were swooping above. The town was being overrun by monsters that defied all logic.

Peter ran. He ran to the end of the row of houses, and then he ran next to the gravel road until he came to the paved highway. He turned right and kept running, step after agonizing, bone-crunching step.

So FOCUSED WAS Peter on putting one foot in front of the other that the car was nearly on top of him before he even knew it was there. Its horn sounded just behind him, startling him from his trance. It was a red Corolla, and it had slowed to match his pitiful pace. A woman in sunglasses behind the wheel leaned forward to get a better look, and then she mouthed some words he couldn't hear with her windows up. She pointed to her passenger door.

Peter got in. "Thank you. *Gracias.*"

Instead of accelerating, she continued gazing at him. "Mr. Peter Wooley?"

He stared at her. Was she from Helmich's compound? He grabbed the door handle, ready to bail. "How do you know my name?"

"Everyone knows who Peter Wooley is, no? Unless they don't watch the news. *Acho men*, what is happening? I saw police. Many police! And you, Mr. Wooley, you look like *mierda*. You look much better on television."

If that was a joke, he wasn't laughing. "Can we get out of here? This area isn't safe."

She started driving again. Seconds later a group of navy blue police vehicles screamed past them, headed for the village. Peter wished he could warn them that there was probably nothing they could do.

"What is happening?" the woman asked again.

He shook his head. "Not easy to explain. People are getting sick, and every person they touch is getting sick."

She took her foot off the gas and looked at him. "Are you sick?"

"No. If I were, you would already know it. This is going to sound crazy, but it changes people—turns them into creatures. Animals."

She continued slowing down and came to a stop on the road's

shoulder. She gazed at him for a moment and then took off her sunglasses. She had striking brown eyes. She wore a snappy, business-like blazer and skirt the same red color as her car. Perhaps in her late thirties. Close to Peter's apparent age. But of course Peter was fifty years older than his apparent age.

"Animals?"

Instead of replying, he watched two helicopters fly over, also headed for the village. They didn't appear to be military, perhaps police or news choppers.

The woman also watched them fly over. "If you were not Peter Wooley, I would push you out of my car. But now I am afraid. This is because of the Lamotelokhai, no?"

He nodded. "It's because of what someone tried to do with the Lamotelokhai. Do you mind telling me where the bloody hell we are?"

She tipped her head forward. "Salinas is just there. It is where I live."

"And where is Salinas?"

She frowned at him. "Caribbean side."

"Caribbean side of what?"

Her frown deepened. "You don't know you are in Puerto Rico?"

"Puerto Rico. That makes sense." He glanced at her. "It's a tedious story. How far are we from Salinas?"

She pulled onto the road and accelerated. "It's just there." She tipped her head again. "Just a mile."

"That's too close. It won't be safe there."

"You are really starting to scare me."

"I'm sorry, but you should be afraid."

She drove in silence for a minute or so. "My name is Georgia. I would shake your hand, but I don't want to turn into an *animal*." She emphasized the word like she didn't believe him, or perhaps she was making a joke.

"Georgia, could I use your cell phone?"

Her phone was already in her lap, and she handed it to him. "I have been trying to call my *madre* and *padre*, but I think the towers are overloaded."

Peter tried calling Jonathan Benson but immediately got a simulated voice saying in Spanish and then in English that his call could not be completed. Bobby and Ashley were dead, Robert was dead, no one knew where Peter was, and everything around him was going to hell.

Rectangular houses appeared on both sides of the road, and they passed a tire store and a Walgreens. Two ambulances screamed by them, followed by more police cars. There were no pedestrians on the streets. Perhaps the people of Salinas already had some idea of the horror only a few miles away—horror that was no doubt spreading and would soon engulf this city.

"A hospital is just ahead," Georgia said. "I will take you there."

"No, I don't need a hospital."

She glanced at him. "But your leg."

"It's not as bad as it looks." Peter didn't feel like explaining that his burns would be healed by tomorrow—if he lived that long.

Georgia turned right onto a residential street. "I am going to my home. My *madre* and *padre* live with me, and I'm sure they are worried. You are welcome to come."

With no cell phone service and no vehicle, Peter couldn't afford to say no. "Georgia?" He waited for her to glance at him before continuing. "You recognized me. You know who I am, so you know I'm not some mad wanker."

"Perhaps you are not aware, Mr. Wooley, but some people think you actually are *loco*."

Peter hesitated only briefly. "Well, you can trust me when I say it isn't safe here. You need to leave. And take your *madre* and *padre* with you. And yes, I'd like to ride with you if you don't mind. But we need to leave immediately."

Georgia pulled into the driveway of a nice orange-stucco home landscaped with expensive-looking palms and other tropical trees. She turned the car off. "Personally, Mr. Wooley, since I saw you on television almost a year ago, I have not believed you to be *loco*. Honestly, I was smitten with you. You were so sure of yourself, about to reveal the secret of the century. And then a month later, fantastic new technology and medical breakthroughs mysteriously appear on the web. Turns out the secret was real. And now here you are. By some miracle you are sitting in my car." She looked him in the eye. "I trust you."

This was a bit more than the response Peter had expected, but it would do. "Good. We need to get your folks into the car and leave now."

She opened her door. "My madre and padre don't do anything quickly."

Georgia's parents appeared to be in their sixties, and they didn't speak much English, although they did recognize Peter when she introduced him. They immediately took notice of his injuries and his burned and bloodied hospital clothes. They spoke rapid Spanish to Georgia, and she explained that they were offering Peter bandages, ointments, and a change of clothes. He turned these down, insisting there was no time. They had to leave now. This resulted in more talking as Georgia tried to explain the situation.

Peter chewed his lip and paced the floor. He heard rumbling from outside and went to the front window. Two tan military trucks were approaching. They rolled past Georgia's house and stopped at the end of the block. Men in camo fatigues ran up to several houses on the far side of the street and pounded on the doors.

He realized Georgia and her parents were at his side, looking out.

The first soldier got no answer, and he jogged to the next house. The second soldier found someone at home. He entered the house.

Seconds later he came back out and led two people to one of the trucks and helped them get in the back.

"Are they evacuating everyone?" Georgia asked.

"If they're not, they should be," Peter said. It also occurred to him that they might be systematically checking for people who were already transforming. "Regardless, they'll be at your door next." One of the soldiers was already crossing the street, coming toward them.

Georgia turned to her parents and spoke in Spanish. They listened with eyes wide.

The soldier pounded on the door. Georgia spoke again to her parents, obviously trying to calm them. She straightened her shoulders, put her chin up, and opened the door.

The husky bloke stepped into the house before she had a chance to speak. He said, "*Señora, estamos haciendo una evacuación obligatoria de Salinas. ¿Cuántas personas están en la cas—*"

The man had been scanning the room as he spoke, but he stopped when he spotted Peter. He nearly stumbled stepping back through the open door. "*¡Infectado!*" He screamed. Through the window, Peter saw other soldiers jump from the trucks and run to the house. Seconds later he was staring at the muzzles of four military assault rifles.

At that point, the first man seemed to remember something, pulled a paper surgical mask from his pocket, and awkwardly put it over his face, looping the elastic straps behind his ears while still holding his weapon. The other three then put on their own masks.

"*¡Tírate al suelo!*" said the soldier who had seen Peter first.

Peter raised his hands. "I don't want any trouble."

The man switched to English. "Sir, stay where you are." He looked at Georgia and her parents. "This man is infected! Have you had physical contact with him?"

"I'm not infected," Peter said as calmly as he could. "I can explain my appearance."

One of the men yelled something to someone outside while the first man asked Georgia again if they'd had physical contact.

Georgia said, "No, we have not touched him. Don't you know who this is? It is Peter Wooley."

The man gave her a blank stare.

"Peter Wooley! Kembalimo? The Lamotelokhai?"

The soldiers looked at Peter. He could only see their eyes, but they didn't seem impressed.

"No contact?" The first man asked. "You have made no contact?"

"No!" Georgia repeated. "I gave him a ride in my car." She hesitated for a moment. "And I let him use my cell phone." She nodded toward her parents. "But my madre and padre have not had any contact with him."

The men looked at each other and rapidly exchanged excited words. One of them turned to Georgia's parents. "You two, follow me."

They stared at him.

He said, "*Vamos afuera.*"

They looked at each other and then followed him outside.

"Where are you taking them?" Georgia asked.

The first soldier said, "For their safety we are evacuating them with the others. We will evacuate you two as well, but first it must be determined that you are not infected."

"We're not infected," Peter said. "If we were, we would have transformed by now. It happens almost immediately."

"We've been ordered to carry out a specific protocol, sir."

Peter grumbled. "We all need to leave this area, including you blokes. I've seen what's happening, and it's spreading. We can't be here when the creatures start showing up."

The man's brows furrowed. "Creatures?"

Peter clenched his teeth. There wasn't time to explain. As he started to plead with the man again, he heard a diesel truck trundling up the street, stopping in front of Georgia's house with a hiss of released air brake pressure.

The three soldiers who were still at the door saw the truck, nodded at each other, and then circled around Peter and Georgia, leveling their guns at them.

"Outside," the first man ordered.

Peter started to protest, but Georgia put her hand on his arm. "Let's do what they ask. They're obviously as frightened as we are."

They walked to the street. The truck was a large semi, but the connected trailer was not a typical freight box. It was something Peter had seen once before, at a traveling carnival in Brisbane. The trailer had eight windowless doors along the side, and he assumed there were eight more on the other side. It was called a bunkhouse trailer, typically used as sleeping quarters for mobile workers.

The soldiers guided them to the front end of the trailer. One of the men extracted folded steel staircases that had been tucked beneath the first two doors. He stepped up and opened the first door and then the second.

The first soldier said, "Inside. Each of you."

"You must be kidding," Peter said. "Why?"

"We are isolating anyone who might be infected. This is what we had available. When it is clear that you are not infected, you will be evacuated with everyone else and released. The other way we can be sure you are not a threat is to shoot you."

Peter looked at the trailer. The metal doors seemed solid enough. He and Georgia might be safer in those bunk rooms than out in the open. Maybe it wasn't such a bad idea.

"¡Diablo! ¿Qué son esos?" It was one of the soldiers. He was shading his eyes and looking to the sky.

Peter looked. His first thought was that they were seabirds, perhaps frigatebirds. But they were too large, and the heads weren't right. Suddenly he realized he was looking at flying reptiles—at least four that he could see. His gut clenched up.

He turned to the first soldier. "It's already here. I don't think there's a bloody thing you can do to stop it. Anyone who can't be evacuated needs to stay inside, maybe even close themselves in a closet."

The soldier gazed at him, though it was hard to read his expression with the mask over his nose and mouth. He opened his mouth to say something, but then multiple reports from semiautomatic weapons sounded from somewhere nearby, perhaps the next street over. Suddenly the soldiers were all business.

"In the trailer, each of you!" the man shouted.

"I'll get in," Peter said. "But please allow my friend to evacuate with her parents."

The soldier hoisted his assault rifle and fired it into the air, startling everyone, including the other soldiers. He glared at Peter. "Inside!"

"Please! We're going," Georgia said. "But I want to be in the same room with Mr. Wooley. I'm claustrophobic. Without someone to talk to, the small space will make me *loca*."

The man nodded.

Georgia and Peter climbed the three steps to the door nearest the front of the trailer. Georgia turned. "You will evacuate my madre and padre, no?"

"We're doing it now, Señora. Close the door."

Peter followed Georgia in and pulled the door shut. Inside the room it was completely dark. One of the soldiers could be heard stepping up to the door and then jiggling the handle, perhaps locking it with a key or padlock. Peter ran his hand over the wall beside the door until he found a switch. He flipped it, and a dim ceiling light came on. Above the door was a black plastic rectangle that appeared to be covering a window. He reached up and slid the panel to the side, allowing more light in. He then slid the panel of plexiglass underneath, leaving only a fine screen. The room was small, about three meters by two meters, nearly half of which was occupied by a bunk with two stacked beds. The beds had thin mattresses but no other bedding. The room was cool, no doubt due to an air conditioning unit powered by the truck's diesel engine, which was still running.

Georgia sighed and sat down on the lower bunk. A truck rumbled past outside.

"That must be the truck your parents are in," Peter said. "They'll be taken to a safe place."

She nodded but did not seem comforted by this.

Outside, a man started speaking with a megaphone. They listened for a moment, and then Georgia said, "They are telling people to stay in their houses."

The room shook, and the trailer began to move. But seconds later it came to an abrupt stop, causing Peter to hit his shoulder on the top bed frame. The man with the megaphone had stopped talking. People were shouting, and then one man's voice rose above the rest. "¡Ayuda! ¡Mátelo! ¡Alguien mátelo!" This was followed by three gunshots in rapid succession.

"What's happening?" Georgia said. She stood up beside Peter, but all they could do was stare at the locked door. Peter wanted to look through the window above the door, but the bunks and the two storage cabinets in the room were all fastened to the walls, and there was nothing else he could stand on.

A few seconds of relative calm followed the gunshots. But then everything erupted into chaos. There were more screams and nonstop shooting. Something that sounded like a body thudded into the side of the trailer and shook the entire rig. An inhuman screech rose above the melee, followed by several more that sounded like they were answering the first. A droning hum, faint at first, gradually increased, as if a swarm of bees were approaching. The humming became so loud that it nearly drowned out the other sounds, and then even more screams and gunshots erupted.

"¡Qué horror!" Georgia said. "¡Mamá and Papá!"

"They will be okay," Peter said, trying to sound confident. "Their truck left before this started."

Something hit the screen above the door. Peter looked. A winged insect—a wasp—was now crawling about on the outside of the screen. The thing was enormous, no less than five inches long, and it had a glossy red and black exoskeleton. It began chewing the screen, cutting and scratching, which was audible even above the chaos beyond.

Peter rushed over and slid the plexiglass panel shut and then slid the black plastic panel over that. He stepped back and sat on the lower bunk. Georgia sat down next to him. They stared at the door, unable to see what was happening and unable to ignore the horrific sounds.

Gradually the human shouts and screams diminished, and then were silent. Instead, they only heard an occasional bellow, or a screech, or a trill. And they heard sounds that were beyond their ability to describe. At one point something moved across the top of the trailer, not scuttling or running, but instead dragging or slithering. It then moved down the trailer's wall and was gone.

CHAPTER TWENTY

Quentin trudged down a treacherously muddy slope, wishing he had brought a cap to keep the rain out of his eyes. Lindsey walked in front of him, and by her side was the tree kangaroo she had named Rusty. The creature would occasionally hop off and disappear on some unknown mission, but it would always return to her side.

Quentin was trying to see Lindsey's newfound relationship with the mbolop from her perspective. It clearly delighted her. In fact, she seemed almost intoxicated by the strangely intimate connection. Should he be happy for her? After all, it could represent a new horizon in the evolution of humankind, orchestrated by the Lamotelokhai. Or perhaps it was simply a mistake, a random exploit of an individual tree kangaroo. Either way, Quentin couldn't help but feel some anxiety—perhaps even jealousy—over the odd symbiosis between the creature and his wife.

He wrestled with these discomforting thoughts as their group gradually covered the remaining miles to the hanging village. They arrived while the sun's morning rays still penetrated the canopy at a low angle. Eight months before, they had been brought to this village and held captive until Bobby had shown he could communicate with the Lamotelokhai. The area hadn't changed much since then. The tree huts were still nearly invisible to anyone walking by on the forest floor. Not that anyone ever did, other than the occasional far-ranging hunter from another Papuan tribe. And according to Samuel, such unfortunate hunters were routinely killed for their unwitting mistake. To say that Sinanie's tribe valued their privacy was an understatement.

Not surprisingly, no villagers were waiting on the ground to welcome them. Sinanie and Samuel led them directly to the base of the largest tree in the area, a tree Quentin remembered all too well.

Sinanie cupped a hand around his mouth and called out a single word, "*Yebun!*"

Quentin gazed up at the tree's dense canopy. Only a trained eye could see the hut and the six connecting tunnels radiating from it like the spokes of a wheel. A slight commotion shook the foliage, and seconds later a thin, coiled rope appeared, spiraling in slow motion as it fell. The rope reached its full length just before hitting the ground, dancing back and forth from its momentum.

Quentin and Lindsey frowned at each other. They had known this was coming, but they both had admitted they would be perfectly content never climbing one of these damn things again. It was a rope ladder, or yebun, 150 feet long, made with the silk from spiders Samuel had bred for this purpose. The yebun was basically one continuous rope, thin as a child's pinky finger, with loops woven into it every two feet or so. The loops were rigid so they would stay open, allowing climbers to insert their feet. The villagers would typically climb them one person at a time to reduce the risk of snapping the rope. Quentin still had both feet on the ground, yet the thought of the rope snapping made his stomach lurch.

Without glancing at them or saying a word, Sinanie started climbing.

Lindsey said what Quentin was thinking. "Samuel, we're really in a hurry to find Addison. Perhaps we can forego the visit to the treehouse?"

Samuel tilted his head toward the rope ladder. "My dear Lindsey, has it been so long that you have lost your arboreal fortitude?" The corners of his mouth indicated a slight smile, a rare thing for Samuel.

"Most humans stopped living in trees millions of years ago," she replied.

"That is an interesting supposition I would like to discuss when time allows it. For the present, however, we should ascend to the hut so that we may rest and eat. In addition, you may be interested to witness what my indigene hosts have been doing in the central hut." Samuel waited for the rope to stop shaking, indicating Sinanie had reached the hut. He then held one hand toward the rope and bowed, inviting Lindsey to go first. It was a strange gesture for a man dressed only in a skin loincloth and a vest made of spider silk.

Resigned to the inevitable, Quentin and Lindsey shed their packs and removed their hiking shoes to make the climb easier.

Minutes later Lindsey reached the top of the ladder, and Quentin started climbing. Before he was halfway up, he had found his rhythm and was making quick but cautious work of it. When he began entering the lower canopy foliage, he looked down. Samuel was far below, appearing very small and pacing back and forth as if he were thinking about something.

Quentin kept climbing, passing through at least ten yards of dense foliage before arriving at the opening in the hut's floor. The rope was fastened to a limb that was part of the hut's ceiling, making it easy for him to climb though the opening and step off onto the floor.

The walls and ceiling hadn't changed much in eight months, even though they consisted partly of living vines. One exception was that the hole in the ceiling where Addison had once entered with the intent of killing everyone had grown shut. Like all the huts and tunnels of the village, this one was suspended from the tree branches rather than resting upon them. The tribe lived, quite literally, in a hanging village. In the center of the hut was its most prominent feature, a thick trunk rising up through the floor and out the ceiling. It forked into two branches at chest height. The Lamotelokhai had existed there for years, molded to the trunk like a massive lump of clay, until the day Bobby had asked it to change its shape so it could walk to civilization. To Quentin's dismay, Bobby had asked it to change into the shape of Addison.

There wasn't time to dwell on these memories, because six Papuan villagers seated upon the floor had paused what they were doing to stare at the newcomers. Quentin knew them all by name: Teatakan, Kumbi, Ot, Korul, Yerema, and Jara. In front of them were four woven baskets containing small stones, and scattered on the floor were various wooden and stone tools.

Ot spoke to them. "Lindsey, Quentin, *gu laléo lai-ati-bo-dakhu, lelé-mbol-e-kho-lo lal wafil?*"

"Ot wishes to know if you come here as spirits or as a woman and a man," Samuel said.

"We are well and do not come as spirits," Quentin replied.

Samuel translated. Ot and the others went back to what they had been doing.

Samuel swept his hand toward the Papuans. "I do not know what forces motivate these indigenes. After many years with them, I still find them to be perplexing. Perhaps they themselves do not fully understand it. They are but savages, after all."

Lindsey furrowed her brows at him. "Samuel, you should come with us back to civilization, at least long enough to be exposed to current ideas about race and culture."

Samuel ignored this, and Quentin stepped forward to observe the contents of the baskets. The first contained walnut-sized river stones. The second contained stones that had each been roughly carved into the shape of a squatting figure. When he looked in the third basket, it became clear what the villagers were making. It contained at least a hundred finished figurines. They were all nearly identical to the tree kangaroo figurine Quentin and Lindsey each had in their pocket. The fourth basket contained another small pile of the finished figurines. They appeared to be no more refined than those in the third basket. Quentin kneeled and reached into the last basket to pick one up, but he was stopped by hasty rebukes from several of the villagers.

"I was told the same when I attempted to touch those," Samuel said. "You may pick up any of the talismans from the third basket, but not from the fourth. They have told me only that the fully completed talismans would be spoiled were someone to touch them. I assumed it was for the same reason that Sinanie gave you your mbolop talismans in skin pouches—so that his fingers would not spoil them."

Lindsey pulled her figurine from her pocket. "Yet Sinanie didn't object when we touched them."

"Curious, is it not?"

There was a disturbance at the hut's wall behind the squatted villagers. The living vines were forced aside, and a tree kangaroo pushed its way through, followed by a second one Quentin recognized as Rusty. Rusty ambled around the Papuans and then lay on his side at Lindsey's feet. The other tree kangaroo went directly to the third basket and gazed at the contents, inspecting the figurines.

The Papuans pointed to Rusty and spoke to each other, seemingly excited or agitated. Ot spoke Lindsey's name, followed by a sequence of unfamiliar words.

Samuel offered a translation. "The indigenes wish you to know they are pleased that Lindsey's mbolop talisman has had its desired effect. They seem to believe that the mbolop's companionable behavior is proof of this."

Lindsey shook her head. "What does one have to do with the other?"

"Regarding this, dear Lindsey, I am as confounded as you are."

Quentin hissed at Samuel and Lindsey to get their attention. He had been watching the new tree kangaroo, and he pointed at it. The creature had picked up one of the figurines from the third basket and placed it on the floor. Now it was digging into its own belly. As they watched, it rubbed a small lump of its own flesh onto the figurine. It then transferred the figurine to the fourth basket, pulled another from the third basket, and started the procedure again.

"This is it!" Lindsey said. "This may explain what's happening to me. And to Rusty. Samuel, can you ask them what's going on?"

Samuel nodded. "Perhaps they will be more forthcoming now that you are here than they have been with me alone." He then engaged in an exchange with Ot and Sinanie.

As they talked, the tree kangaroo systematically anointed stone figurines with extracts from its abdomen one by one and moved them into the fourth basket.

Finally, Samuel turned back to them, shaking his head. "I know not whether the indigenes are saying what they know to be true, or whether they have contrived an elaborate ritual that they find comforting in the distressing absence of the Lamotelokhai." He began pacing with a hand on his chin.

Quentin and Lindsey waited, shuffling their feet impatiently. They both needed answers.

"I suppose it is possible," Samuel muttered, apparently to himself. He stopped pacing and looked at Lindsey. "Yes, it certainly is possible! Sinanie and several of his fellow tribesman have seen the quite extraordinary colony of mbolop where your son Addison has been residing these recent months. Whether what I am about to say is factual or not is left to be determined, but they believe that the mbolop you call Mbaiso is creating the colony for a specific purpose."

"What purpose?" Lindsey asked.

"For the purpose of assisting mankind. Mbaiso, the first of the mbolop created from the clay of the Lamotelokhai, existed for the purpose of assisting the Papuans of this tribe, particularly with tasks involving the Lamotelokhai, such as communicating with it. Although I have always considered the manufactured tree kangaroos to be little more than brutish creatures, Mbaiso apparently considers his original purpose to be of such importance that he intends to carry it out beyond the confines of this tribe."

Quentin glanced at Lindsey, but she looked as bewildered as he felt. "Meaning what, exactly?" He said.

"The creatures are evidently attempting to produce one mbolop for every man and woman."

"Every man and woman? Everywhere?"

Samuel sighed. "I fear the mbolop may have a poor understanding of the number of people upon this world. Likewise, I fear the indigenes fail to understand." He gestured toward the baskets of stone carvings. "They have little experience beyond their meager tribe."

Lindsey said, "They're trying to carve a figurine for every person on Earth?"

Samuel shook his head. "Not every person, but perhaps most." He went to the third basket and picked up one of the figurines. "Perhaps equally as curious, they have employed one of Mbaiso's colony to assist with the final preparation of the talismans. I was skeptical initially, but the more I ponder it ...." He held up a finger. "But of course, I haven't explained, to what purpose are they working?" He paused, as if trying to build suspense.

Quentin finally said, "Yes, to what purpose?"

"Indeed, although you may be as skeptical as I was." He nodded to the tree kangaroo. "This mbolop, like the original you call Mbaiso, is composed, at least in part, of the clay of the Lamotelokhai. It has the capability of applying measured portions of its clay to each talisman, thus giving the stone specific qualities." He paused and rubbed his chin again. "Years ago, when I attempted to discern what could be accomplished with an isolated portion of the Lamotelokhai's clay, perhaps I should have looked instead at the usefulness of the mbolop. It could have saved me much consternation." He continued rubbing his chin, apparently thinking about this.

Quentin took a deep breath and tried to avoid tapping his foot impatiently. Getting a quick explanation from Samuel was like convincing a turtle to run.

Samuel continued. "While Mbaiso has endeavored to create an mbolop to assist each person of the world, the indigenes have determined that there should be a way to designate who is deserving of such assistance. You must understand that, by their very nature, these indigenes have a rather wretched opinion of people other than their fellow tribesmen. You see, other tribes of the region have repeatedly attacked them, for revenge or to cannibalize them. And to make matters worse, many years ago Sinanie and I traveled north to Humboldt Bay, as we had heard rumblings, as if the great island of New Guinea were being destroyed. We witnessed there a most troubling display of warfare. This did not improve the indigenes' opinions of mankind."

"When was that?" Quentin asked.

"It was the year 1944, if my record of the passing time is correct. Approximately eighty years have passed since."

"World War II," Lindsey said. "Humboldt Bay was the site of a major engagement between US and Japanese forces. That must be what you saw."

"Japanese, yes. As I suspected. I encountered one of the Japanese soldiers. The poor fellow was nearly expired from dreadful dysentery. His companions were already dead when I found him. Apparently he and the others had fled into the jungle and had become lost. His name was Iwataro Hayashi. At times I think of him and wonder if he is well."

Quentin gazed at him. There was only one reason Samuel would think the Japanese soldier could still be alive. "You gave him some of the Lamotelokhai's particles."

Samuel glanced at the villagers as if this were a secret. They had gone back to working on the figurines, and Sinanie was inspecting the contents of the baskets. "He was in a most pitiable state, and at the time I feared I was gradually becoming a savage. I suppose I did it as much for myself as for him." Samuel then stared at the hut's floor, apparently lost in his thoughts.

Lindsey said, "Um, about the mbolop and the figurines."

"But of course. So you see, my indigene hosts are predisposed to suspicion and fear of those outside their own tribe. It is simply their nature. Thus it should not surprise us that they have devised a way to choose who is worthy of assistance from the mbolop and who is not. They apparently believe the two of you are worthy."

Lindsey frowned. "Why do you say that?"

"Because Sinanie endeavored to give you the mbolop talismans. If I correctly understand their explanation, when you touched the two figurines, you were designated as worthy of assistance from the mbolop. Lindsey, that is why the mbolop you call Rusty now belongs to you—or you belong to it, the distinction is not altogether clear to me."

There was a moment of silence, and Quentin wondered what was going through Lindsey's mind. He pulled his figurine from his pocket. "When I touched this, it somehow marked me as worthy? So why did Rusty attach to Lindsey instead of me?"

The slightest curve appeared on Samuel's lips. "Perhaps, Quentin, it did not take a fancy to you. The point of the matter is, however, that the tree kangaroos from the colony will 'attach,' as you say, only to those who have been given talismans. The first person to touch a talisman from the fourth basket will become changed in such a way that they will be able to attach to an mbolop. Once this occurs, that talisman may not be applied to another person. Or so I am told. That is why the Papuans do not wish for you to touch the contents of the fourth basket."

It was Quentin's turn to pace back and forth. The entire hut bounced slightly with each step. "Okay, the tree kangaroos want to help everyone by multiplying so that every person can pair up with one. The villagers want to choose who gets to do that by giving figurines only to people they think deserve it." He stopped pacing and shook his head.

"That is inaccurate," Samuel said. "The indigenes do not wish to choose those who are worthy. They expect you to choose—yourself and Lindsey. You are to take the completed figurines with you when you depart."

Quentin stared at him. He realized his mouth was open and shut it.

"You are perhaps distressed by this responsibility," Samuel said with a hint of compassion. "But the importance of it may be far greater than you have yet imagined. I am myself just beginning to comprehend the significance. I suspect that the intended assistance may go far beyond mere help with minor tasks."

"What do you mean?" Lindsey asked.

"I shall explain as best I can. You know as well as I that the Lamotelokhai is a wondrous and powerful phenomenon. I believe it can immeasurably benefit all of mankind."

"Agreed," Quentin said.

"However, I have become intimately acquainted with the dreadful consequences of using it carelessly."

"As we have," Quentin said. "Too many times."

"Perhaps, but you must remember that you have known the Lamotelokhai for less than one year. I have studied it for a century and a half. I have committed numerous blunders, some with consequences difficult to describe, such was their horror. And I am a cautious and methodical man. Furthermore, my indigene hosts have lived beside the Lamotelokhai far longer. Many thousands of years, in fact. They are even more cautious than I, and they soon discovered the risks of communicating with it directly. They consequently made it tribal taboo to talk to the Lamotelokhai, and they created the mbolop for that purpose. Again, I must point out that this was thousands of years ago. I believe they would have heretofore been destroyed had they not been so cautious."

Quentin wasn't sure where this explanation was going. "You don't have to convince us the thing is dangerous."

"What I am attempting to say is that the indigenes understand the perils, and consequently the mbolop, Mbaiso, is aware of the perils, as the creature was created to reduce them. Again, *Mbaiso is aware of the perils.* Now, consider your conversation with Ashley using your rather fantastic talking device."

"Our SAT phone," Lindsey offered.

"Indeed. Ashley indicated that something with dreadful consequences had resulted from imprudent use of the Lamotelokhai. I am suggesting that the mbolop may have foreseen such consequences as inevitable. And I suspect that the assistance they wish to provide may be far more significant than help with certain tasks. I believe they intend to save the lives of as many people as they can."

Quentin suddenly felt faint. He glanced at Lindsey. Her face had lost its color, indicating that she also understood.

"How many tree kangaroos are in the colony?" she asked.

Samuel looked at both of them and nodded once, apparently acknowledging that they grasped his meaning. "It is hard to say. Based upon what I saw when last I was there, perhaps as few as three hundred."

THEY DRANK water from hollowed-out gourds. They ate their fill of dried *Dorcopsis* meat and the paste called *khosül* the Papuans made from sago palm pith and mashed sago beetle larvae. After they had eaten, they had no compelling reason to wait, so Samuel, Quentin, and Lindsey descended to the ground and departed the hanging village, Rusty close at Lindsey's side. After another three hours of hiking, Samuel stopped and announced they had arrived at the mbolop colony.

According to Samuel, this was the only place Addison had been seen. If he wasn't here, it would likely be impossible to find him.

They stared up at the endless canopy. The hanging chambers and tunnels bore a remarkable resemblance to those of Sinanie's village. They were smaller and more concealed, but they were definitely there, faintly visible among the vines and leaves.

"Addison," Lindsey called out. "It's Mom and Dad. Where are you?"

"As I have explained," Samuel said softly, "your son may not appear or behave as you might expect. If he is here, and if he descends from the trees, you would do well to prepare yourselves for that. Shouting may frighten him, perhaps preventing him from approaching."

Lindsey frowned but nodded. Quentin understood what she was feeling. The anticipation was unbearable. And the apprehension, and the guilt. After all that had transpired, they both needed to find their son. It was a need with roots anchored so deeply within them that Quentin feared what might happen if Addison didn't show up. They might never leave this place.

They were so intent on this purpose that, since leaving the hanging village hours before, they had not once mentioned their disturbing conversation regarding the mbolop figurines. Quentin didn't have any emotional space at this time for the notion that he and Lindsey were responsible for choosing a few hundred people to survive the apocalypse. So far, he had managed to shove the implications into a dark corner of his mind.

"How do you suggest we find out if he's here?" he asked Samuel softly.

Samuel used his bare foot to clear away some twigs, then he sat down and crossed his legs. "The mbolop heard us approaching long before Lindsey's boisterous shouting. I suggest we wait for what might transpire next. Quietly, if possible."

They took off their packs and settled onto the ground on either side of him. Rusty crouched beside Lindsey. After a few excruciating minutes of silence, Quentin whispered, "Is there any way we can climb up there?"

Samuel gazed up at the canopy. "The mbolop have no need for rope ladders, nor does your son Addison. And from what I can see, the hanging chambers and tunnels appear to be significantly smaller than those of my indigene hosts. I fear these tunnels would not support our collective weight."

They were silent for another long minute. Suddenly, Lindsey spoke up. "Maybe I can help." She patted Rusty's head. "Can you go up to the hanging tunnels and look for Addison?"

Rusty ambled to the nearest tree and began climbing straight up the vertical trunk.

Quentin watched Samuel for any indication that this might be a bad idea. Samuel simply watched the tree kangaroo as it steadily climbed to the canopy. Lindsey put her hands on her knees and stared down at her hiking shoes.

Samuel spoke quietly to Lindsey. "Your mbolop companion might prove to be quite useful."

She nodded slightly and continued staring at her shoes. Quentin wasn't as ready as they apparently were to accept this odd symbiotic relationship. It was disturbing, and it seemed like Lindsey was losing a part of herself. Or, perhaps more truthfully, that Quentin was losing a part of her. Abruptly he was aware of the figurine in his pocket and his proximity to an entire colony of tree kangaroos that apparently had been created to pair up with humans who possessed such figurines.

"Rusty is in one of the chambers!" Lindsey said. She spoke loudly, as if wearing headphones, unaware of her own volume. And she was smiling. "Other tree kangaroos are there. I see at least four. And there's another."

Quentin shifted his weight and looked at Samuel.

"He's in a tunnel now. Tree kangaroos are passing, going the other way." She smiled and gazed downward, fully engaged in the experience. "He's entering a larger chamber. It has connecting tunnels, like the central hut of Sinanie's village. Tree kangaroos are in here. Some are smaller, underdeveloped. This must be how they grow them." Her smile grew wider. "Mbaiso is here. He's signing to me."

After a long pause, she said, "Mbaiso is curious. He wants to know why we've come here. He wants to know if Bobby is with us." Finally, she looked at Quentin. "Mbaiso is coming down."

"What about Addison?"

She shook her head. "He didn't say anything about Addison."

Long seconds turned into longer minutes. Quentin watched Lindsey, but she just gazed back with no expression. She shook her head at one point, indicating she had nothing to offer.

Mbaiso and Rusty appeared, not descending a tree but rather hopping on the ground. Most of the tree kangaroos Quentin had seen looked similar, but there were subtle differences in the piebald patterns on their tails, bodies, and faces. Mbaiso's face was uniformly rust-colored, and Quentin recognized him right away. The two mbolop approached and stopped a few feet away. But then other tree kangaroos appeared, moving cautiously toward them through the understory growth. At first several appeared, and then many. It was hard to tell how many because they stayed a safe distance back, some of them partially hidden among saplings, tree trunks, and ferns. But there were dozens, at least.

One of them didn't stay back with the others. It walked on all fours, rather than hopping, until it was beside Mbaiso. It lacked the prominent testicles that were visible on Rusty and Mbaiso. She was a female.

"Hello," Lindsey said to the third mbolop. "Rusty, who is your friend?"

Rusty moved closer to the female. He leaned in and pressed his snout to hers. They remained this way, motionless.

Lindsey stiffened. Her hands gripped her khaki trousers at the knees, knuckles white, and she let out a brief cry.

Quentin got up and rushed to her side. "Lindsey?"

"Her name is Newton! She has seen Addison—spent time with him. I think I see him right now."

"You see who? Addison?"

"Addison! They were together, Newton and Addison."

Quentin kneeled down beside her. This startled the female, and she scampered back, breaking contact with Rusty.

Lindsey blinked and looked at Quentin. "He's here. I know he is. I couldn't see him clearly, but I'm sure it was him. He named her *Newton*, Quentin!"

Quentin didn't even know where to begin with his questions. "How could you see him?"

"The mbolop, Newton. Her memories."

"Quentin, Lindsey," Samuel said, his voice controlled and even. "Please refrain from shouting or moving excessively. I believe your son is here."

They turned to Samuel and then followed his gaze. The tree kangaroos were moving closer, now more than a hundred of them. And something else was there, a dark figure. It watched them from behind a tree, only one of its eyes visible. It was low to the ground, perhaps crouching.

Lindsey got up and took a step forward. "Addison? Honey?"

"Mummy?"

The voice was not Addison's. Or maybe it was. But Addison hadn't used that word since he was a toddler.

Lindsey took another step. "Honey?"

The creature behind the tree stood up. It then stepped into full view.

Quentin's gut tightened. He heard Lindsey gasp, but the sound seemed distant. The creature was Addison. Since the last time he had seen his son, he had almost forced himself to forget Addison's transformed appearance. It was a transformation Addison had wished upon himself and had accomplished with the Lamotelokhai's help. And in that new, powerful, monstrous form he had gone on a murderous rampage, killing Miranda and half the members of Sinanie's tribe. The thing standing before them was not something that had evolved naturally. It was not a creature from the distant past precisely reconstructed by the Lamotelokhai. Instead, it was a physical form conjured by a fourteen-year-old boy who used to read monster comic books and then had his brain bashed in during a plane crash and reconstructed by alien technology.

Addison leaned forward, bent his knees, and put his hands on the ground. He then walked toward them, like a gorilla would walk.

Lindsey backed up until she was at Quentin's side. "I forgot," she muttered. "How could I forget?"

He took her hand and squeezed it. "We made ourselves forget. It's how we survived."

Addison stopped just in front of them. Again he stood erect. His torso was long and lean, with conversely shorter legs. His arms were longer than a boy's should be by half, with extraordinarily spindly, curved fingers that appeared to be designed specifically for gripping tree limbs. He was naked, but his penis and scrotum were barely visible, nearly lost in a thick mat of curly pubic hair. Other than that and the long corkscrew hair growing from his scalp, the rest of his body was hairless. His skin was darker than it had been, either from dirt, from the sun, or because he had wished it to be. His face was still smooth, but its shape was angular and mature. It was not the face of a boy. But his eyes, his beautiful blue eyes, were still the eyes of their son, Addison. And this was enough for Quentin.

"Addison," he said, "Samuel told us you were alive, and that you remember us. So we came here to find you. We'd like to take you home."

Addison looked at him. He then shifted his gaze to Lindsey. He looked down at the tree kangaroo named after his home town. He smiled, revealing inch-long canines.

"Mummy. Daddy. Newton my mbolop. Newton go home, too."

CHAPTER TWENTY-ONE

"You two could use some cleaning up. You look rather dreadful."

Bobby snapped his head up, hitting it on the airport terminal wall behind him. He shook Ashley's leg to wake her.

The man was kneeling on the floor at their feet, looking at them at eye level. Beneath a blue Yankees ball cap, his hair was pulled back in a ponytail. He wore a blue denim shirt, brown shorts, and leather sandals. He had to be Peter's guy, Jonathan.

"That was fast," Bobby said, rubbing his eyes. "What time is it?"

The guy held out a hand. "Jonathan Benson. It's 2:30 AM. Shall we go? I imagine you two would like a more comfortable place to rest."

They both stood up and shook his hand.

"It's starting to get crazy here," Ashley said, looking around at the activity in the terminal. "Is that going to slow us down?"

Bobby realized she was right. There were more people around now than before he'd fallen asleep. Many of them bustled about like they were late. Bobby could hear angry shouting. Large groups of people stood beneath each of the televisions, watching a news report that was still showing video from a helicopter. But now you could only see what was in the chopper's spotlight because it was dark outside. The spotlight was trying to follow things that were running on streets and between buildings.

"I guess it's gotten worse," Bobby said.

Jonathan didn't bother turning to look at the TVs. "I'd say you're right about that, though I haven't had much opportunity to monitor the situation." He looked at Ashley. "If we get moving now, we shouldn't have many delays."

Jonathan stepped closer and grabbed their shoulders like he was about to give them a group hug. "Before I'm willing to leave, I need to know something. Are you one hundred percent certain Peter and Robert are dead?"

"We didn't actually see their bodies," Bobby replied. "But they were both in the compound, and Helmich's idiots set off some kind of heat bomb. There's nothing alive in there now, we're certain of that."

The guy closed his eyes. His lips moved silently, like he was saying a prayer, or maybe swearing. He opened his eyes. "Then we should go, pronto." He headed for Terminal B, and they followed.

Waiting for them next to the security checkpoint was a man in pilot clothes—black pants, white shirt with black and yellow stripes on the shoulders, black tie, but no hat on his shiny bald head. He wasn't the same pilot who had flown them from Belize to Oklahoma. Jonathan introduced him as Quincy Kirk. Bobby thought this was a great name for a pilot—Captain Kirk. The guy flashed a friendly smile and shook their hands while Jonathan pulled out their passports, which he had picked up after they had left them behind at Peter's facility in Oklahoma City.

Going through security was easier than Bobby had thought it

would be. Captain Kirk showed his ID and some papers, did a bit of polite but firm arguing with a man and then a woman, and a few minutes later two airport security men led them through a narrow hallway and out a door to a noisy tarmac area. No one even looked in Bobby's duffel bag.

Although it was the middle of the night, enough lights were shining on the runway for Bobby to see the sleek private jet waiting for them. It was larger than the jet they'd taken to Oklahoma, with seven passenger windows on the side instead of only three.

"It's a Cessna Citation Ten," Jonathan shouted over the noise as they walked to the jet. "Or Citation X, if you prefer. Cruises at over 600 miles per hour with a range of 3,700 miles. We can get you to Jayapura with only three stops: LA, Honolulu, and Fiji. With any luck we'll be there twenty-three hours from now."

Ashley grabbed his arm to get his attention. "We can't get there any faster than that?"

He seemed surprised by the question. "No, we can't. This is the fastest business jet available to civilians."

She released his arm. "It'll have to do, then." She then climbed the steps and entered the jet.

"Sorry about her, but we really do have to hurry," Bobby said, and he followed Ashley.

The jet had seats for twelve passengers, in rows of four facing each other. At the back of the plane, Bobby spotted a messy tuft of black hair sticking up from behind one of the seats—Carlos.

Ashley walked past Carlos with hardly a glance at him and went straight for the restroom at the back of the plane. Bobby took the seat facing his friend and placed the duffel bag on the floor. Carlos was sleeping, his head tilted back, mouth open, snoring with a Darth Vader breathing sound, like he used to do. For a brief moment, Bobby wished he had a can of whipped cream to spray into his open mouth. Carlos would think that was funny.

Jonathan took the seat to Carlos's left and across the narrow aisle. "Go ahead and wake him. He hasn't been asleep long. He and I had an interesting conversation on the flight. I feel as if I know a bit more about what you kids went through in Papua last summer."

"Maybe I should let him sleep."

Ashley came out and sat across the aisle from Bobby, in the seat facing Jonathan. "How long before we can take off?"

The plane lurched and started rolling just as she finished saying this.

"We're making every effort we can to accelerate the process," Jonathan said. "I have no doubt that what we're doing is important, but now that we have a bit of time on our hands, perhaps you can provide more of an explanation."

Ashley said, "Is it required for all of Peter's employees to have their hair in a ponytail and wear sandals?"

Bobby frowned at her. "What's wrong with you?"

She glared back at him, but then she shook her head and rubbed her face with both hands. "It's the middle of the night, a maniac tortured me, and I've seen some pretty weird shit. I'm sorry." She uncovered her face, looked at Jonathan, put on a fake smile, and blinked her eyes twice in a stupid, flirty way.

Jonathan took a breath and held it, apparently struggling to decide how to react to Ashley's attitude. "Perfectly fine, Miss Stoddard. I'm happy to answer your question." He pursed his lips and thought for a few seconds. "I met Peter in 2013. Actually, I met him briefly some years before that, but that's a story for another day. In 2013, his wife Rose fell and broke her hip."

"We know Rose," Bobby said. "Peter brought her to see us a few times."

"Then you must know Rose is a rather elderly woman, which is actually in part why she broke her hip. Anyway, fortunately, I was there when it happened and was able to help out. I became friends with them."

The plane had been rolling steadily, but suddenly it stopped. Captain Kirk called back over his shoulder, "All secure, sir?"

Jonathan nodded at their seats. "Fasten your seatbelts, please." When they had checked Carlos's belt and fastened their own, he shouted back, "Secure!"

The plane's jets roared and they shot forward, picking up speed until they were in the air. The noise quieted to a level where they could talk again.

Jonathan went on. "Anyway, we became friends, and I started working with Peter on his Kembalimo project. It was unlike anything I'd ever done, trying to figure out a way to help people communicate with an alien intelligence. It was the job of a lifetime. Eventually we found a few additional talents to help with it. Robert was one of them, and there was Ardell Gray. The four of us became rather obsessed with the project. We practically lived together, day and night."

Ashley squirmed in her seat, and Bobby silently willed her not to lob whatever insult she was holding back.

"I'm sure you've heard it said that, over time, a dog owner begins to resemble his dog. Or perhaps the dog resembles its owner." Jonathan smiled, although he looked kind of sad. "I suppose that's what happened to us—Robert, Ardell, and myself."

Bobby waited for more, but Jonathan was done. Ashley snorted a short laugh and turned to stare out her window at nothing but blackness.

"That's kind of funny," Bobby said, although it wasn't really. He then began telling Jonathan about what had happened. He told how he and the others had been kidnapped in Oklahoma, and how they'd woken up in the compound. He told about what Helmich had been trying to do, and the terrible things that had happened as a result, and how they had escaped, leaving Peter and Robert behind to die, and about the animal-creature-things that got loose, and about Tiffany, and how they got to the airport. And he told of how he was trying to reassemble the consciousness of the Lamotelokhai from twenty-four data packets stored in the minds of twenty-four people.

Before he finished, Ashley had fallen asleep.

Jonathan asked a lot of questions, but finally he seemed to run out of them. After sitting in silence for a few minutes, he said, "You're right. This is important—the most important thing I've done in my life. He looked at his smartwatch. We will be in Jayapura in twenty-two hours. Then we'll figure out a way to get you to the hanging village. One way or another, we'll get you there."

Twenty-two hours seemed like a long time. How many more people would die in that time? Bobby considered trying to sleep, but he was hyped up from talking about and reliving the last few days. Besides, there was something he needed to do.

He woke Carlos up. This wasn't easy, because Carlos could sleep through an earthquake, tornado, and plague of locusts all at the same time. It took quite a bit of shaking.

"Bobby, damn." Carlos stretched and wiped his mouth like he was checking for drool.

"Long time no see, Carlos."

"Yeah."

"How'd you get your parents to let you come?"

Carlos wiped his mouth again and rubbed his eyes. "Well, *he* tried." He nodded over toward Jonathan. "And I tried. Not much luck. I got pissed and told them I was going to bed. Then I climbed out my bedroom window. I was in his car when he came out."

Bobby stared at him. Carlos wasn't kidding. "Your parents are going to hate me now."

"Not if we save the world. That's what you said we had to do, right?"

"I'll probably be charged with kidnapping," Jonathan said. "But I understood that time was crucial. Bobby, we could have taken you to Missouri to see Carlos, but by my calculations that would have cost at least three additional hours."

Of course they had done the right thing. But Bobby had no idea how long it would take to finish what they needed to do in Papua, and Carlos's parents would be getting more worried and mad by the minute. Bobby unzipped his duffel bag and hefted the lump of Lamotelokhai clay into his lap. Kembalimo symbols appeared before his eyes, but he ignored them, and they quickly went away.

Carlos squinted at the clay, his eyes still puffy from sleep. "What is that?"

"Exactly what it looks like—part of the Lamotelokhai."

Carlos stared at it. "Okay, this is starting to freak me out."

"Nothing wrong with being scared. If everyone was as scared of the Lamotelokhai as they should be, we wouldn't be trying to save the world right now." Bobby tried to smile. "By the way, I died again today. A messed up copy of me did, anyway. Or maybe I'm the copy, I don't know. But it was the third time I've died—that I know of."

Carlos tried to smile too. "Well, you've got me beat by one, I guess."

"Yeah, now I'm tied with Ashley." He glanced over at her, but she was still sleeping.

Jonathan spoke up. "Jesus, you kids have been through hell, but you're able to joke about it?"

Bobby picked up the clay and held it out so Carlos could reach it.

Carlos looked like he wanted to back away from it. "What?"

"You're going to have to trust me. This is the whole reason we had to pick you up and bring you here. There's some information in you—a data packet—that needs to be downloaded into this thing. Can you put your hand on it? I swear it won't hurt. I've done it. And Ashley has."

Carlos just stared at it.

"Come on, man, it's getting heavy."

Carlos exhaled, but it was more like a growl. He put his hand on it. He blinked and shook his head. "Damn Kembalimo symbols. I never did learn to play."

"Kembalimo's not a game. Ignore them and keep your hand there." Bobby closed his eyes and spoke with his thoughts. "Carlos has another packet of your information in him. I want to download it from his body into yours. Can you do that?" He opened his eyes.

Carlos frowned. But then he smiled a little. "It tickles."

"Just let it go from your head down to your arm, and don't let go until it goes out your hand into the clay."

About a minute later, Carlos pulled his hand away. "Done."

New symbols appeared in Bobby's vision. "More knowledge now. More help."

Bobby spoke silently. "What can you do to help now that you couldn't do before?"

The symbols changed. "Please talk different."

Bobby sighed. He was too tired for this. He put the clay back in the bag and zipped it. He looked across at Carlos. "I know there's stuff we need to talk about." He turned to Jonathan. "Us too. But do you guys think it could wait? I've had a bad day, and I'd just like to sleep now if that's okay."

Carlos immediately closed his eyes. "Good with me."

Jonathan said, "I understand, Bobby."

Bobby fumbled with the controls on his seat until he got it to lean back a little. He put his knees up in the seat and turned on his side, facing Ashley. He gazed at her, thinking of a moment on a different flight they'd been on eight months ago, when Ashley had kissed him for the first and only time. He then realized her eyes were open. She was looking back at him. She extended a hand and held it out halfway across the narrow aisle. She opened and closed her fingers twice.

Bobby wasn't sure, but it seemed like an invitation. He reached out and took her hand. She squeezed and didn't let go. Her eyes closed again.

Bobby tried to stay awake, to gaze at their enmeshed fingers. Because it was one good thing in a whole world of bad things.

CHAPTER TWENTY-TWO

As the light peeking in through the small window above the door slowly faded, so did the sounds of many of the creatures outside the trailer. Apparently these creatures preferred sunlight. But the fading of these sounds provided little respite for Peter's frazzled nerves, as the night brought new sounds of things that thrived in darkness. On more than one occasion, large unidentified creatures had sniffed at the corners of their door. Apparently detecting their presence, the beasts had then clawed and even pummeled the door for what seemed like an eternity before giving up. It had been hours since he and Georgia had heard anything resembling a human voice, although they had heard numerous helicopters and jets flying over Salinas.

They were trapped. The tiny room had no toilet, and there was no food or water. Luckily, the truck's diesel engine was still running, providing power to the lights and air conditioning unit. Otherwise, the room would have been pitch black and stifling.

Peter had a slight need to urinate, but Georgia was on the verge of agony. She had resorted to pacing back and forth. Four short steps in one direction, four back. Finally she stopped and said, "To hell with this. Please turn the other way."

Peter faced the back end of the room. He listened to her fumble with her skirt and hose. He then heard her pee splashing on the floor. When he finally turned around, she was trying to push the liquid out under the door with her foot, but the two-inch heel on her red pump made this nearly impossible. She gave up and sat on the lower bunk.

She said, "I have imagined someday meeting you, but this is not how I thought it would be."

He smiled. "Well, this should at least make you feel less alone in your misery. Please look the other way." He got up and relieved himself, adding to her puddle. He used his mostly-intact right shoe to squeegee some of it out. Suddenly something hit the door, sending him stumbling back. Whatever was outside let out a long grunt, somewhere between a hog's snort and the underwater cry of a whale. It pressed its weight against the door, which creaked and popped, threatening to burst from its frame. There were no weapons in the room, not even a loose piece of furniture to swing at whatever might come through the door. So Peter sat down on the bunk next to Georgia.

The creature rammed the door again. Georgia shifted closer to Peter. They stared silently at the door, hardly breathing, until the creature gave up. It let out another whale-snort as it wandered off.

Georgia shifted a few inches away from him. "I won't die in this trailer. I won't."

"Nor will I. It's a safe place. We just need to stay here until help arrives."

"Yes, until help arrives." But then she shook her head, as if she couldn't convince herself this was a good idea.

Something skittered across the roof. They watched the ceiling until the sound was gone.

Peter stood up. "We might as well try to rest." They had

already searched the drawers and cabinets of the two storage units bolted to the wall, as well as a hatched opening beneath the lower bunk. They had found nothing, not even sheets or pillows. "I'll take the top bunk." He climbed the ladder fastened to one end of the bunks and wormed his way into the tight space between the mattress and ceiling.

Georgia sighed. She got up and switched off the light. Seconds later she turned it back on. "No. I'm sorry, but I must have the light." She sat on the bunk, and her pumps clattered onto the floor. The bed creaked as she lay down.

Peter stared at the ceiling just above his face. He had never been prone to claustrophobia, but this situation was starting to reveal the boundaries of his tolerance. Perhaps it would help to talk. "Don't worry, they'll come for us. I'm sure they're putting together rescue parties as we speak. There will be others—people locked in closets and basements. There will be survivors."

"Yes. I hope so."

Did she even feel like talking? "What do you do, Georgia? Professionally."

"Lawyer. Domestic violence, divorce. In Guayama. Twelve miles east."

Peter could have guessed this—her clothes, her house, the way she talked. He waited to see if she would expand on the subject.

Somewhere outside, a disturbance erupted. It went on for at least a minute, two creatures snarling and screeching as if they were both losing a deadly struggle. Then it abruptly stopped.

"May I call you Peter?"

"Of course."

"Would you like to come down here with me, Peter?"

He stared at the ceiling. "Are you frightened?"

"Who wouldn't be? But that is not the only reason I ask."

Peter wasn't sure what to say. He didn't move.

"You're married, aren't you?"

"Yes."

She huffed out a brief laugh. "Yes, of course you are. I apologize."

"Her name is Rose. I think you would like her. She's tough. The toughest person I know."

Georgia remained quiet for a moment. "I'm sure she's worried about you."

"Probably."

She shifted her weight, like she was turning on her side. "Could you tell me about her? Perhaps how you met? I would like to hear your story."

Peter considered this. His was a story unlike any other. Georgia might not even believe it to be true. But he wanted someone to talk to, and perhaps she did too. So he started at the beginning—actually his second beginning, when he had been only forty-one, which had been over forty years ago.

PETER WAS AWAKENED by a thunderous roar. His eyes flew open. All he could see was the ceiling inches above him. Another roar passed over the trailer. Military jets.

Suddenly his senses were barraged by chaos. The bed jolted, nearly throwing him against the ceiling, and the roar of jets was replaced by sound waves so powerful the only response he could bear was to cover his ears. Ground tremors continued for seconds afterwards, like the trailer was sitting at the epicenter of an earthquake.

Before it got quiet, the chaos started all over again. Georgia's face appeared next to Peter's bunk, wide-eyed and terrified. She had to grip the bunk's frame to keep from falling. Her mouth moved, but Peter could hear only the lingering rumbles of massive explosions. Finally the noise faded away enough that they could talk.

"They're bombing us!" Georgia said. "Why would they do that?"

Peter rolled off the bed and dropped to his feet. This caused only a small twinge in his left foot, which was nearly healed. He looked up at the ceiling, listening to the last of the rumbles and the jets flying over. "They must be trying to kill the creatures, to contain the situation."

"¡Noña es! How can it be so bad they would do this?"

Peter didn't reply. He continued looking up, trying to grasp the implications. The explosions had been close, no more than a few miles away. They must have bombed the area where it had started. Maybe Helmich's compound, or even the village where Robert had been killed.

Georgia grabbed his arm. "If they're trying to contain it, they'll have to drop bombs here. Do you think they will?"

She was right. The epidemic had started less than twenty-four hours ago, and someone had decided it was serious enough to bomb a populated area, even though there had to be survivors hiding out in vehicles and houses. Those in charge were smart enough to realize that the horror and death could spread over the entire island. Perhaps even beyond.

"Peter?" She shook his arm. "We have to get out of here."

He looked at her. "Try your cell phone. If it works, let someone know where we are." He turned and faced the door, his mind working furiously to come up with a plan.

"Still no service," she said. "And my phone is nearly dead."

How far had the truck rolled before coming to a stop? Were they still in front of Georgia's house? "Okay. We have to break the door to get out. And then we run straight for your car. Do you have your keys with you?"

She shook her head. "They're in the house."

Peter cursed silently. "Then we go to your house first, get the keys, then to your car." He glanced at her and then hesitated. Her mascara had run down her face from crying, and her hair was disheveled. Her red business suit was creased and dislodged, looking uncomfortable. Her red pumps were on the floor. Could she run fast enough with only hose on her feet? Those shoes would certainly be awkward, even if she broke the heels off. She was trembling. And so was he.

"Georgia, it has been a pleasure sharing this fine room with you."

She shook her head, almost imperceptibly. "Don't talk like we're going to die."

He nodded and tried to smile. "Get ready to run." He turned back to the door and kicked it hard with his right foot.

It didn't budge.

He tried again, and then again. He kept trying until his foot and ankle throbbed.

"We can take this off, maybe. Use it to break the door." Georgia was at the back of the room, inspecting the wardrobe cabinet that was bolted to the wall. It was about four feet tall by two feet wide, and it sat atop a cube-shaped storage unit with two drawers.

Peter pulled on the cabinet, and it jiggled a bit. It was made of particle board, so even if he couldn't break the bolts, perhaps he could break the wood. He pushed it back and forth and managed to work it loose enough to get his fingers between the cabinet and wall. It was more solid than it looked—he couldn't pull it free. He needed leverage, but there was nothing here to use. He stepped back and took a deep breath. Another round of jets roared by overhead.

Georgia pushed him aside and opened the wardrobe's door. She then hooked her fingers over the top of the door. It broke off before she had put all her weight on it. She took the broken door, slid into the lower bunk where she could approach the cabinet from the side, and wedged one end of the door behind the wardrobe.

Peter leaned in beside her, and they pulled out on the door and pried the cabinet loose. Together they carried it four steps to the locked door. Standing on either side, they pulled back and slammed it into the door.

The door didn't break, but the impact rattled it more than Peter had been able to by kicking. They slammed it again. On the third try, the door's hinges started coming loose. Once more might do it.

"Wait," Georgia said, and she held the cabinet back before Peter could swing it again. "Those animals may have been drawn here by the noise we've made. Should we wait—give them a chance to lose interest?"

This was a good point. But how long before someone made the call to bomb Salinas too? They stared at each other, breathing hard from the effort and listening for danger.

"I don't think we should wait," he said. He gazed at her until their eyes met. "Directly to your house for the keys, yes?"

She nodded. "Yes."

"On the count of three, then."

They took a step back from the door to get ready. Peter counted aloud to three, and they swung the cabinet forward in a wide arc, smashing it against the door.

The hinges broke. The door flew open and then dangled askew by a padlock the soldiers had used to lock them in. The room was flooded with early-morning sunlight. They dropped the cabinet and Peter rushed to the doorway. The stairs had been retracted back under the trailer. No problem, they could jump four feet to the street.

But then Peter froze. The ground was swarming with creatures. Many of them appeared to be insects—crickets, beetles, roaches, and some that defied categorization. But there were also spiders as large as mice. And centipedes. Several fat toads hopped about, lazily snatching up the insects. And lizards darted back and forth, gorging themselves. A turkey-like creature without feathers was slowly strolling by, pecking at the bugs and swallowing them whole.

"Are they dangerous?" Georgia whispered. She was standing beside him, looking at the ground.

"I think we should assume everything moving is dangerous." Peter looked over at Georgia's house. It was seventy meters away. Too far.

Something came walking around the far side of her house. It was huge, with dark fur and a thick tail that dragged on the ground. It couldn't be anything other than a giant ground sloth. It approached a low tree in Georgia's yard. It lifted itself upright, using its tail as a third leg for stability. It reached for one of the lower tree limbs with one of its forelegs, raking it into its mouth with long, sickle-like claws. After taking one bite, the creature shook its head and released the limb, as if the leaves were distasteful. That's when Peter saw that the distal tips of the limb were moving, squirming about like tentacles.

Something buzzed past Peter's ear. Georgia ducked back into the room, grabbed the loose cabinet door, and held it up like a baseball bat. A four-inch wasp rattled against the ceiling, perhaps disoriented by the dark, confined space. Suddenly, it swooped down toward her. She grunted and swung. Peter heard the wasp's exoskeleton crack and barely ducked his head in time as it rocketed out the door in several pieces.

With the door now open, it was only a matter of time—perhaps seconds—before one or both of them would be bitten, stung, or scratched by one of the creatures. Peter grabbed the trailer door, which was still hanging from its padlock. Perhaps he could put it back in place. But as he pushed down on the lower half to straighten it up, the padlock broke free, and the door clattered onto the street. Within seconds, insects and several crab-like creatures were walking over it. And then another large insect flew into the room.

Peter and Georgia were out of options and out of luck.

Georgia swung the cabinet door at the insect, which had landed on the frame of the top bunk. Peter caught enough of a glimpse to see that it was gray and resembled a stout praying mantis, and then the thing was nothing more than splatters on the bed and wall.

"Don't touch any of that. It doesn't matter if it's dead," he said. He went back to the open doorway. "I don't think we can get to your house."

"The cab of the truck!" She exclaimed. "It's still running."

Peter blinked at her. He looked at the street, crawling with living things. He then looked up at the ceiling. Yes, it might be possible. He grabbed the loose cabinet and stood it on its end in the doorway. It was four feet tall, too tall to step up onto, so he stepped onto the lower bunk and hoisted himself onto the cabinet as Georgia held it steady. Standing on the cabinet with his head and shoulders outside the trailer, he was high enough to reach the lip of the trailer's roof. Seconds later he had pulled himself up and was lying prone on the roof. He extended a hand down to Georgia.

"Can you get on the box?"

She was already working on this. Peter saw the cabinet rocking back and forth as she crawled onto it. Her head appeared through the door. She was able to turn her body enough to reach up with one hand and grab his. But then the box collapsed. It tumbled out onto the street and suddenly Georgia was dangling there, held only by Peter's left hand.

He grunted and shifted his weight away from the edge to avoid being pulled off. He held out his right hand. "Grab ahold!"

She tried, but she was using her left hand to grasp his left. She had to cross her right hand over her left to grab his free hand. She managed to do this, but he tried pulling her up, he couldn't get her high enough, and he couldn't get to his knees with her weight pulling him down.

A wasp or some other insect buzzed around his head and actually tried to land in his hair. He flipped his head wildly. The buzzing stopped, but he couldn't tell if the thing had flown off or had landed somewhere on his body. Regardless, he was powerless to do anything about it. His hands were starting to sweat, and he felt Georgia slipping from his grip.

"Swing me to the side!"

Peter strained his shoulders to pull her to one side. She used her feet to help him, and soon they had a steady rhythm going. On the fourth swing she threw her leg up and caught the edge of the roof with her foot. This took enough weight off Peter's arms that he was able to gather his knees beneath him, allowing him to pull her up and onto the trailer.

He stood up and immediately turned away from her. "Is there anything on my back?"

After panting for a few seconds, she said, "Nothing is there. But there are things here on the roof. There, and there."

Peter helped her to her feet. There were a few insects on the roof, but it was nothing like the street below. They moved to the front of the trailer. The gap between the trailer and the cab was about four feet. Peter exchanged a glance with Georgia and then leapt to the cab. He turned and held his arms out to her.

She said something, but the words were lost to the roar of a low-flying jet. He gestured for her to jump. She did, directly into his arms, knocking him off balance. They both fell onto the roof of the cab and slid down the windshield onto the engine hood. The hood was slanted, and Peter had to grab a windshield wiper to prevent them both from tumbling over the side. The surface was hot due to the engine having run all night. They got to their feet, but Georgia, wearing no shoes, was forced to lift one foot and then the other to avoid burning.

The truck's driver must have left in a hurry, because the door was hanging open. Without saying a word, Georgia went straight for the open door, stepped on a narrow spot where it hinged to the cab, and worked her way into the driver seat.

Peter was right behind her. He stepped on the door's hinge and started making his way around to the side of the cab by holding on to the large mirror.

He noticed a lumbering brown shape approaching the cab. He froze. The giant sloth that had been in Georgia's yard had spotted him and was coming straight for him.

Georgia clambered over to the passenger seat. "Get in. Get inside!"

It was too late. Peter was only halfway around the edge, and the beast was already there. He held still. Perhaps if he didn't move, it would wander off. It was an herbivore, after all. Wasn't it?

Abruptly the creature raised up on its hind legs, again using its thick tail to steady itself. Peter assessed it from the corner of his eye. It was massive. How many men, women, or children had been killed, their bodies incorporated into this behemoth? It stood ten feet tall, and now its head was at the same level as Peter's. For a moment it looked down at its own feet, apparently watching the myriad of smaller creatures crawling, hopping, and slithering on the ground. It even shuffled its feet to avoid things that were moving too close. But then it turned its attention to Peter.

With one foot still on the truck's hood, Peter was not in a position to jump quickly into the cab. So he held as still as he could. He even closed his eyes to hide their involuntary, panicked movement. He sensed the sloth's face inches from his ear. It sniffed, and he felt the movement of air as it sucked in his scent. Moist lips smacked. Its tongue moved about with the sound of a sloshing bucket of goo. Peter felt the tongue lightly touch the tips of his hair.

"Easy, mate," he said, as soothingly as he could manage. "I'm not a threat to you, and I'm not something to eat."

The thing snorted in return, blowing wet mist onto Peter's

cheek. He opened his eyes. The sloth's snout was less than a foot away. "Easy, mate."

The creature was gazing at him with brown eyes that seemed too small for such a massive head. Perhaps the sloth was only curious about him. But of course that didn't matter. Whether it licked his face or tore his head off, the result would likely be the same—transformation into something nonhuman.

"Easy," he said again. He turned to the truck and slowly, methodically crawled over the door and into the seat. The creature stood there and watched him until he pulled the door shut. It then dropped to all fours and started moving away, stepping to the side periodically to avoid some of the larger crawling things on the ground.

Peter wiped the sloth's spittle from his face and stared at his hand. Was it enough to infect him? He looked over at Georgia. She was watching him warily. "If I begin to feel strange, I'll jump out of the truck. Agreed?"

She nodded, or perhaps it was just her trembling. "Can you drive this truck?"

Peter looked at the dashboard and then at the gear shifter. "I think so. Maybe."

Abruptly, the earth shook, rocking the truck, and all other sounds became insignificant compared to the ear-splitting roar that flooded Peter's senses. Debris flew across the street in front of them, including patio furniture and the front half of a boat. Something smashed into the window next to Georgia's head, cracking the glass and leaving a smear of blood and black feathers. A storage shed tumbled end over end and came to rest in the street in front of them, blocking their way.

The roar gradually faded, replaced by the sounds of objects pelting the roof of the cab, like a nightmarish hail storm.

"Sweet Jesus!" Georgia cried. "They're bombing Salinas."

Peter stomped on the clutch and squinted at the gear shifter. It had a diagram of ten different gears. He shoved the shifter left and then down into first and gave it some gas as he let out the clutch. The truck barely moved.

Georgia leaned over and slammed her hand against a yellow knob on the dash. There was a hiss of air from the brakes and the truck lurched forward.

Peter floored it. The truck struck the storage shed, breaking it open and pushing it out of the way. The engine was already whining, maxed out, so he shifted to second.

"Turn right," Georgia cried.

Peter cranked the wheel. The nose rounded the corner without a problem, but the trailer hit a car parked on the right and rolled right over it, shaking the cab back and forth as its wheels crashed onto the yard of the corner house and then over the curb back onto the street.

He shifted to third, accelerated, and then shifted to fourth. The road was strewn with debris, but Peter wasn't stopping for anything. Creatures of every shape and size scattered out of the truck's path or were crushed beneath it.

"Faster," Georgia cried. "Get us out of Salinas!"

Peter had it floored, but the truck wouldn't speed up. He shifted to fifth gear. He wanted to shift to sixth, but the diagram showed it being in the same place as first. What the hell was that supposed to mean? There was a lever on the gear shifter—probably what he needed—but he was too panicked to experiment with it, so he just held the gas pedal to the floor.

As they approached the edge of town, houses and businesses gave way to open fields, and the road became less cluttered with debris.

"Oh no," Georgia said. She was staring straight ahead.

Peter looked. A fighter jet was flying low over the road, headed straight for them. Just before it passed over, Peter glimpsed two objects separating from the jet, each with its own smoke trail.

Peter clenched his muscles and gripped the wheel. "Hold on!"

The world around them erupted. First, small bits of leaves and dust flew past from behind, then larger chunks of wood and trees, and then vehicles and entire sections of houses. The cab of the truck lurched forward and tipped downward. Peter realized the bunkhouse trailer was no longer on the ground. The trailer wrenched free from the hitch with a violent grinding that could be heard over everything else. He looked in his mirror—the trailer was gone. A shadow passed over the windshield and he stared, dumb-struck, as the entire trailer blew over the cab. It hit the road in front of them and started sliding on its side.

Peter realized they were going to hit it. He tried turning to the right, but it was too late. They crashed into the corner of it, knocking the cab onto its side.

Georgia screamed as the pavement rose up and slammed into her side of the truck. The cab's momentum then rolled the truck over onto its nose and roof. Peter was thrown from his seat, and he hit his head and shoulder on the ceiling. He was dazed but still aware that the cab was sliding upside down on the road, and then onto dirt. When it hit the weeds it rolled onto its passenger side, dumping him on top of Georgia as it came to a stop.

"Mr. Wooley? Are you okay?"

It seemed like a strange question. He was the one who had fallen on her, and he was still sprawled on top of her. He groaned and tried moving his legs. "I don't know." He managed to get off and sit up, which in turn allowed her to sit up. "No broken bones, I suppose."

"I think I am okay also."

Peter looked around, becoming aware of their dilemma. The windshield was cracked but still in one piece. The driver window was intact. He looked down. The passenger window was gone, but soil and weeds were pressed against the window frame. At least they were somewhat closed off from the creatures.

Georgia rubbed a bloody spot on her knee. "They bombed Salinas. My home. Mamá and Papá's home. How could they?"

Peter shook his head. He didn't know what to say.

"Do you think the bombs killed the animals? All of them?"

Again he shook his head. He turned and looked out the cracked windshield. They were facing away from Salinas, but black smoke wafted by in thick clouds from behind them. Georgia reached out her hand, tears in her eyes, and Peter took her hand and held it. They watched as light objects—paper, ashes, fragments of clothes— fell like snow onto the ground.

CHAPTER TWENTY-THREE

Quentin tried to avoid making sudden movements. Addison watched them warily, his muscles twitching as if he might flee. And from the looks of his sleek, muscular body, if he decided to run there would be no catching him.

Lindsey took a cautious step closer. "Yes, Addison, Newton can come home with us. Did you know Mommy has her own mbolop? His name is Rusty." She pointed at her tree kangaroo.

Addison looked. "Rusty. Rusty go home, too."

"That's right. We'll all go home together, okay?"

His face formed a grimace, an expression that was not quite a smile. "Where home, Mummy?"

Lindsey took another step closer. She was now within Addison's reach, which made Quentin tense up, ready to pull her back if there was trouble. She said, "Home is where you used to live. Do you remember your house? It's in a town called Newton."

He shifted his gaze to his tree kangaroo and back to Lindsey. "Newton my mbolop."

"Yes, but Newton is also the place where your home is."

Addison bared his teeth, this time in a real smile. "That silly, Mummy."

Lindsey smiled back. "It is silly, isn't it?"

Quentin cautiously stepped to Lindsey's side. "Addison, we've missed you so much. We came as soon as Samuel told us you were here."

Addison appraised him silently for a moment. His eyes then scanned the ground around Quentin's feet. "Where your mbolop, Daddy?"

This took Quentin by surprise. "Well, I don't have my own mbolop."

Addison grimaced again, baring his top and bottom canines. "Daddy, you need mbolop."

"Why, Addison? Why do I need one?"

"You my Daddy. I no want you to die."

Quentin wasn't sure how to react to this. He realized he wasn't breathing and drew a lungful of heavy air.

Lindsey said, "Your dad will get his own mbolop. Maybe you can choose one for him. Would you like to do that?"

Addison grinned broadly and turned to look at the tree kangaroos, which now seemed to be everywhere.

Quentin glared at Lindsey.

"He's right," she said softly. "You should have your own."

Addison was already herding one of the tree kangaroos toward him. Lindsey had put him in a no-win situation. He didn't want his own mbolop, but the last thing he wanted right now was to turn their reunion with their son into a disaster.

Addison guided the mbolop until it was at Quentin's feet. It was similar to all the others, although perhaps with more black fur on the tail. The creature looked up at him.

"Your mbolop, Daddy."

"Thank you, Addison, but I'm not sure I need my own—"

Addison lunged toward Quentin and grabbed his hand. It took

all of Quentin's willpower to not back away. Addison pulled on his hand, urging him to bend over and touch the tree kangaroo.

"Okay, son, okay."

Addison let go. Quentin held his hand, palm down, in front of the creature's snout. It sniffed his skin. Then it sat up on its haunches, dug into its abdomen, and produced a pink lump of body tissue. It offered the lump to him.

This was happening too fast. Quentin stepped back. "I'm sorry. I'm not ready to do this."

Addison frowned, contorting his face in a nonhuman way. "Daddy die with no mbolop."

"Please," Lindsey said. "Once you do it, you'll understand. I promise."

Why was she pushing this, especially at this moment? "We came here to take Addison home. That's all I want to do." He faced Addison. "Are you ready to come home, son?"

Addison's frown turned into a snarl. Suddenly he snatched the tree kangaroo and hefted it over his head. He was about to throw the creature when Mbaiso jumped in front of him and let out a lamb-like bleat.

Addison hesitated.

Mbaiso moved his forepaws quickly but with precision.

Addison abruptly smiled again. He put the tree kangaroo down and then patted its head apologetically. He turned to Quentin. "Me go home with Mummy and Daddy. But me mad if Daddy die."

QUENTIN HELPED Samuel put the finishing touches on the lean-to shelter. It was too late to hike back to Sinanie's village, so they had decided to camp beneath the hanging tunnels of the mbolop colony.

Every few minutes Quentin looked over at Addison, fearing he might change his mind and run away—or worse. Lindsey and Addison had been sitting on the ground together, talking and occasionally laughing, for some time. She seemed to be forming a connection with him.

Quentin gave the shelter a good shake to make sure it wouldn't collapse, and then he approached them cautiously to avoid spooking Addison. As he approached, he saw that they were engaged in some kind of activity, so he quietly sat a few yards away and observed.

Lindsey had her eyes closed. Addison sat with his stubby legs crossed. Rusty and Newton lounged on the ground between them. Within the frame created by Addison's legs was something he was carefully shielding from view with his hands. He plucked an object from the hidden spot and held it in front of Rusty's snout. It was a small leaf.

"Color, color!" he said.

"That's easy, it's green," Lindsey said, her eyes still closed.

Addison tossed it aside and produced a piece of bark. "Color, color!"

"That one's easy, too. It's brown."

Addison bobbed his head and laughed with excitement. He pulled a round blue object from his stash. It looked like a berry of some kind. "Color, color!"

"It's blue, silly."

His head bobbed again. Next he pulled out a large red flower petal and held it out for Rusty to see. "Color, color!"

Lindsey hesitated. "It's, um, brown? No, maybe gray?"

Addison howled with laughter and pounded his chest with one hand. "No no, Mummy! No!"

Lindsey opened her eyes. "Hey, did you trick me? Tree kangaroos can't see red, can they? And you knew that, didn't you?"

Addison actually rolled on the ground, kicking his feet and slapping his belly and chest, obviously delighted. Abruptly he jumped to his feet. "Mummy. Daddy. Me show you my tree house. Up." He waited for them to follow him.

Lindsey said, "Honey, we can't climb like you. We have to stay down here."

He puckered his mouth. "Rusty show you." He jabbed a finger toward the tree kangaroo. "Okay, Mummy?"

"Okay, but please be careful."

He shoved Rusty with his foot, forcing the creature to get up. "Come, Rusty! Stay, Newton!" He then ran off with Rusty, and Newton remained obediently where she was.

Quentin gazed at Lindsey but didn't say anything.

"You're upset with me," she said. "But keep in mind I know some things you don't know yet."

"Such as?"

"Such as how beneficial it is to pair up with one of the mbolop. It's life-changing, Quentin."

He continued gazing at her, unwilling to even try to respond.

"They're from the Lamotelokhai. I think we should trust them."

He shrugged and looked down at the dead leaves he had been grinding up in his closed fist. "There was a time when you refused to be treated by the Lamotelokhai's particles."

"Things are different now. You know that."

Samuel walked up to them and sat down next to Quentin.

"I must concede to resounding defeat. Try as I might, I cannot procure an accurate count of the tree kangaroos. The confounded creatures will not stop moving about. I conclude that my original estimate was reasonable. There are approximately three hundred."

Quentin looked over toward the lean-to shelter. Tree kangaroos were milling about everywhere. Some were even sniffing the shelter and pushing against it, as if inspecting the workmanship. Another of the creatures confidently approached Quentin. It smelled his leg. It was the third one to do this in the last hour. It clawed into its abdomen and offered him a lump of tissue. Quentin shook his head, refusing it. After a minute or so the creature put the lump back and wandered off.

A thought Quentin had been trying to keep at bay suddenly surfaced. He spoke to Samuel. "What do you honestly believe? Do you really think the tree kangaroos are here to save people?"

Samuel poked at the ground with his finger for a few seconds. "I have always believed that the Lamotelokhai did not come here with the intention of destroying us. But I have also long believed that it *will* destroy us. Because I have concluded that mankind is not predisposed to use it wisely and properly. Perhaps we never will be. Perhaps we lack certain necessary characteristics, not the least of which is a general sense of compassion for others."

Quentin waited for him to go on, but Samuel went back to poking the ground. "So, the tree kangaroos," Quentin said. "Are they really capable of saving people? If so, can they save only three hundred?"

"Do I believe they can save people? They are of the Lamotelokhai's clay, and so I am certain they can. As for the number, three hundred is preferable to three, is it not? You two are charged with choosing those three hundred. I do hope you choose wisely."

Quentin turned to Lindsey, and their eyes met. She shook her head, although he wasn't sure what the gesture meant.

Suddenly she stiffened. "They're inside Addison's tree house." She frowned. "It's smaller than I thought it would be." She quickly put a hand over her mouth and looked down at Newton. "No, honey. I didn't mean I don't like it. It's very nice."

Quentin realized Addison was experiencing everything Newton saw and heard, just as Lindsey was immersed in Rusty's experiences.

"What is that? Oh, you want me to guess? Well, hmm. Is it a little man? It is? Did you make it? Oh, it's Daddy?" She looked over at Quentin, smiling. "Did you make Mommy, too? Oh, yes, that's me! Those are very nice, Addison." She paused. "Oh, I have to guess again? Let me see it, okay? Is it a necklace? What are those things? Oh. Oh my. Snake heads. Did you kill all of those, Addison? You *ate* them." She put a hand to her chest. "Well, I hope they were yummy. They were. Okay."

She dug into her pocket. "Now it's my turn. I have something. Can you guess what it is?" She held her mbolop talisman in front of Newton's face. "Yes, it's a rock. But it was carved to look like something. Can you guess what? No? Well, it's a tree kangaroo. An mbolop." She laughed. "Yes, that's funny isn't it?"

Quentin turned to Samuel. "I'm starting to feel left out."

"Perhaps you should yield to the inevitable. Claim your mbolop. Soon, when you are choosing three hundred living souls to whom you will give the talismans, your conscience may prevent you from claiming your own."

Quentin shook his head. "I can't make myself believe that the end of the world is here. Do you really think it is?"

"I have contemplated its eventual arrival for so many years that perhaps I have grown accustomed to the notion. I do not wish to be insensitive to the grave implications."

Quentin sighed and stared up at the fading light filtering through the forest canopy. Ashley had said on the SAT phone that some people had divided the Lamotelokhai into pieces, and that she and Bobby were coming here to put it back together. She had made it clear that this was important. Had she actually meant *save-the-world* important?

There was no point in driving himself crazy with speculation. "What about you, Samuel? Aren't you going to pair up with one of them?"

Samuel eyed him. "Perhaps you have been too occupied with spurning the offers of numerous mbolop to notice that I have had no such offers. This is no doubt due to the fact that Sinanie and his fellow tribesmen have not offered to me a talisman."

"Oh. Sorry. Well, when they hand them over, I'll be sure to give you one."

He waved his hand dismissively. "I am hesitant, as are you."

Quentin turned to Lindsey. She was looking back at him, and so was Addison's mbolop.

Lindsey grinned. "Addison says, 'Hi Daddy.' And he wants to know if you have your mbolop yet."

Quentin turned to the tree kangaroo. "Hi Addison. No, I don't have an mbolop."

Newton turned her gaze back to Lindsey. A few seconds later, Lindsey said, "Yes, you're right. Daddy is silly. But we'll help him, won't we?"

QUENTIN AWOKE SLOWLY AND RELUCTANTLY. It had rained half the night, and sleep had been sparse. He sat up and rubbed the splattered mud from his face. Lindsey was sitting cross-legged on her sleeping mat, Rusty beside her. Her clothes were as wet as his, but she was writing on a small pad she must have had in her pack. Samuel sat a few feet beyond her, wiping his bare legs clean with a large leaf.

Quentin looked around. A few tree kangaroos were hopping about, apparently with specific destinations in mind. Most of them had disappeared into the trees just before dark to spend the night in the safety of their hanging chambers.

He turned to Lindsey. "Have you seen Addison yet?" Like the tree kangaroos, Addison had insisted on leaving them at dark to climb to his hut.

"He was here a few minutes ago," Lindsey said without looking up from her pad. "I think he was checking on us."

Samuel said, "It seems he is concerned that you may disappear, just as you are concerned that he may run away."

Lindsey finally looked up from her writing. "You'll never guess what he wanted to know regarding you."

"Do I have my own mbolop yet."

She went back to writing.

"What are you doing?" He asked.

She handed him the pad. The page had two columns, one with the heading *Pros* and the other *Cons*. The *Pros* column was filled with writing. The *Cons* column was empty.

He started reading the items aloud. "Optimized hormonal balance = contentment. Optimized nutritional balance = vigor. Deep connection to another living thing = new ways of seeing the world = stimulation." He stopped reading and sighed. "Can I ask why you don't have anything in the *Cons* column?"

"Because there aren't any, as far as I can tell. Go ahead, finish reading them."

He sighed again. "Companionship = contentment. Assistance with tasks = more time for other things. The mbolop are made of Lamotelokhai's particles = this alone should be enough." He glanced up at her and then read the last item on the list aloud. "According to Addison, Samuel, and Sinanie's tribe, you are going to die without your own mbolop." He handed the pad back to her.

She said, "And I could add that your wife and son want you to be safe. Hon, all these things are true. I've never felt better in my life."

Quentin considered arguing, but he just shook his head. Maybe she was right.

A dark shape appeared above them and landed near their feet with a thump. It was Addison. Where had he come from? Quentin couldn't see a tree limb within fifteen yards of where he had landed.

Addison plopped down before them and crossed his legs. In each hand he held a sizable monitor lizard, one of them missing its head and the front half of its body. The other was whole but appeared to be dead.

Their son held the intact lizard out to them. "Mummy, Daddy eat. Samuel eat too."

A moment of silence passed. Quentin accepted the lizard. "Thank you."

Addison grinned, his teeth red with blood and chunks of meat. Then he ripped into his own lizard, occasionally picking shreds of skin and other inedible parts from his mouth and flicking them away.

"The legs and tail are particularly desirable," Samuel said. "Even in the raw state."

"Okay, you're welcome to start on it." Quentin handed the lizard to Lindsey, who passed it on.

Samuel turned it over, observing it from every angle as if admiring its beauty or deciding what species it was. He then brushed away some grime, pulled a small gleaming knife from a pocket inside his vest, and began cutting, somehow maintaining the appearance of fastidiousness and gentlemanly manners.

Quentin was hungry, but he wasn't sure he was hungry enough to eat raw lizard meat. Apparently it was a day for being indecisive. He got to his feet and went to the log where he had left the SAT phone. He shook the rainwater off and wiped it with his shirt before powering it on. Still there were no messages or missed calls from Ashley and Bobby. The indicator showed only 35% battery charge remaining. He powered the phone off, went off to relieve himself, and then returned to his sleeping pad. Addison was working on the last of his meal, the tail. Samuel was cutting small strips of flesh from the other lizard and laying them on a clean leaf.

"I would prefer this meat to be cooked," Samuel said, "but present conditions are not favorable for making a fire."

Quentin watched Addison eat, experiencing both joy and

revulsion at the sight of his son. Would Addison have to remain in this form for the rest of his life?

And what about his mental state? He now seemed to have the mind of a toddler. This was no doubt Quentin's fault. Eight months ago, in a desperate attempt to stop Addison from killing more people, Quentin had asked Bobby to order the Lamotelokhai to provide a substance that would kill him. Quentin himself had thrown the substance at Addison's face, fully intending to kill his own son. It wasn't until after this unthinkable act that he learned Bobby instead had made the substance to erase Addison's memory, thus saving Addison's life. It had taken Quentin a while to realize it, but he would be forever grateful to Bobby for this. And he would be forever guilt-ridden for having initiated the act in the first place.

What would life be like for Addison with his current appearance and mental state? Assuming, of course, that the world was not actually coming to an end.

Something nudged Quentin's leg. Another tree kangaroo. This one was a bit smaller than most of the others, although it was clearly a male. The creature held two bluish-purple fruits the size of large grapes, one in its mouth and one between its forepaws. It dropped the fruits next to Quentin's foot.

"They are from the plum pine," Samuel said. "*Podocarpus*, if I am not mistaken. You may eat them, although I do not recommend eating more than what the mbolop has offered. Perhaps the mbolop senses something that you yourself do not know, Quentin."

Quentin picked up the fruits to inspect them more closely. "Why do you say that?"

"Because native Papuans use those fruits for medicinal remedies."

"I haven't needed any medicines for eight months," Quentin said.

"As I said, perhaps the mbolop knows something you do not."

Quentin took another look at the tree kangaroo. Hairs with

black tips grew on its head and neck, making it darker than most of the others. The rims of its ears were tipped with white. It stared back at him as if waiting for him to eat the fruits.

Addison slapped his belly with one hand and pointed at the tree kangaroo. "Mummy! Daddy has mbolop. That Daddy's mbolop!"

Quentin glanced at her. She nodded but held her tongue.

Samuel watched with no particular expression, apparently deciding it was best to withhold his opinion.

Quentin took a small bite of one of the fruits. The flesh was slimy and slightly sweet. Not bad. "Thank you," he said to the tree kangaroo. He took a larger bite. "I suppose you have something else to offer me."

The creature cocked its head to the side. It straightened up on its haunches and started scratching its abdomen. Addison slapped his belly again, but Quentin didn't take his eyes off the mbolop. Seconds later the creature held out a lump of tissue. Or nanoparticles, or Lamotelokhai clay. Whatever it was, Quentin knew it would change his life if he accepted it. As if what he really needed right now was yet another life change.

He held his hand out, and the mbolop dropped the lump onto his palm. He watched the substance spread out and disappear through his skin, punctuated by Addison's frantic belly slapping.

He had thought the tingling sensation would be more pronounced, but it was barely detectable, just a subtle feeling of warmth. It moved up his arm and into his shoulder, at which point it seemed to dissipate. He felt something at his side, and he realized Lindsey had moved closer. She stretched her legs out in front of her.

"Lay your head in my lap, in case your body goes to sleep. Your mind will stay awake."

Quentin looked at her, but he didn't feel like saying anything. He was starting to feel nauseous, so he shifted and put his head in her lap. Suddenly he was aware he was moaning, but it was beyond his control. The world around him faded away. It was replaced by something else, a vision, although the visual element was only one of many layers. His other senses were alive as well, as were his emotions. This was disorienting, but soon his mind adjusted to the barrage of different forms of stimulation.

The mbolop particles flowed through his veins and into his cells. He was aware of it happening and could feel every minuscule particle gliding and bumping along and stacking up at bottlenecks, only to be released when pressure mounted. There were millions of them, and he could feel them all. And on top of this multi-point layer of sensation was a visual layer, numerous three-dimensional videos playing at once. He saw every detail of his mbolop, as if tiny drones were flying inches above its body and sending images to his mind. The creature's eyes, with flecks of golden pigment within the otherwise brown irises. Short, black-tipped hairs on its face, harboring particles of dirt but no parasites or pests. A recent scratch on the edge of its nose, which Quentin somehow knew was from a tussle with one of its sisters over a perfectly ripe orange berry with a name that could only be expressed with precise movements of two forepaws. A pattern of tan, orange, and brown mottling that extended from the base of its long tail to the tip, and which not only served as an indicator of the creature's identity, but also had shifted in pattern and color during its lifetime, serving as a marker of social status and developmental achievements.

And on top of the visual layer, there was a layer of scents, each of them with specific significance. And there were tastes, and sounds. Layered on top of all that was an almost overwhelming flood of emotions. They washed over Quentin's consciousness like a syrupy fluid, so confining that he could not force his thoughts elsewhere. He experienced them one at a time, as if they were queued up in a specific order. He felt confusion and then wonder as he experienced the mbolop's memory of gradually awakening during its final hours of development into a fully-formed adult. He felt exuberance and fear as it ventured out of the hanging chambers for the first time, finding itself on a narrow limb high above the forest floor. He felt a combination of determination and sadness as the mbolop helped its brothers and sisters tear apart a struggling sibling with a body that had somehow failed to develop normally.

The emotional memories continued to flow, one at a time, and all the while Quentin was still aware of the other layers of sensations—visions, smells, tastes, and sounds. And finally, it all ended.

Quentin opened his eyes.

"There you are." Lindsey's face was above his.

He blinked. "Lindsey, it was—"

"I know." She smiled.

Addison's face appeared beside Lindsey's. "Daddy, now you have mbolop."

Quentin sat up. Samuel was still gazing at him, as if only seconds had passed. Addison slapped his own belly a few times, grinning and nodding his head.

The mbolop was still there, at his feet, watching him. The thing was a simple yet complex creature. It hadn't lived long, a few months, but its life had been filled with meaningful, painful, harrowing, and fascinating moments. It was like all the other mbolop, but it was distinct. It wasn't a real animal—it was something more. It was made of tiny particles crafted by beings who were likely long extinct.

And above all, this mbolop was now Quentin's.

CHAPTER TWENTY-FOUR

Bobby woke up when the Cessna Citation's tires hit the runway at Sentani International Airport, just west of Jayapura, the capital city of Papua. Groggy, he looked around. Ashley and Carlos were also beginning to stir. Jonathan was awake, frowning at his smartphone.

"What?" Bobby asked.

Jonathan pulled his eyes away from the phone. "We're lucky we left Puerto Rico when we did."

"Why?"

He shook his head. "I can't believe it. Whatever that maniac Helmich started is sweeping across the island, much faster than it can be contained. Hell, they don't even know how to begin to contain it. They've resorted to air-launched missiles and firebombing. Apparently nothing is working."

They all stared at him as the jet braked on the runway. Bobby looked down at his lap. The outbreak was getting worse even faster than he had feared. A familiar feeling of guilt once again took hold of him.

Ashley spoke first. "They're bombing Puerto Rico?"

Jonathan nodded grimly. "We're lucky we got out of there before they locked down the airports."

"How many people have been killed?" Bobby asked.

Jonathan shook his head. "No idea." He then furrowed his brows at Bobby. "Look, this isn't your fault. You were kidnapped and taken there. There was nothing you could have done."

Bobby nodded, but the pit in his stomach didn't care about Jonathan's words. All over again, people were dying because of things he'd done. Only this time it was a lot of people, maybe even thousands. It didn't seem fair that he could escape from Puerto Rico when all those other people couldn't.

The Cessna abruptly came to a stop. Captain Kirk shouted from the cockpit, "This is it, sir. Our greeting party is forcing us to stop here."

Jonathan popped his seatbelt and got up. "Captain Kirk and I have been on the radio with the local authorities here. They are suspicious. I explained we're on a crucial mission to save lives in Puerto Rico. Otherwise I don't think we would've been allowed to land at all. When they find out we were in Puerto Rico less than twenty-four hours ago, they may shut us down." He looked directly at Bobby. "If we tell them who you are, and what you have with you, they may let us continue."

It hadn't occurred to Bobby that they wouldn't even be allowed into the country. What if the Indonesians threw them in jail and took away the incomplete Lamotelokhai?

Captain Kirk opened the jet's hatch and lowered it. Almost immediately the opening was darkened as police poured in, yelling orders and waving black assault rifles. They escorted Captain Kirk to one of the seats near Bobby and motioned for Jonathan to sit down.

Bobby looked pleadingly at Jonathan.

"It's okay," Jonathan said. "Just stay calm."

Five policemen had entered the plane. They wore black

fatigues, tan shirts, and black berets with red and gold badges. In addition to the rifles in their hands, they wore pistols on their belts. They quickly walked the length of the Cessna's cabin like they were searching it. Then they gathered in the aisle with Bobby, Carlos, and Ashley on one side, and Jonathan and Captain Kirk on the other. Bobby could smell their sweat and the oil on the rifles. The soldiers motioned for Kirk to stand up. One of them spun his finger, ordering the pilot to turn in a circle. Then they made each of the passengers do the same. Bobby assumed they were making sure no one was transforming into anything nonhuman.

One of them went to the hatch and waved his arm. Another man entered the cabin. He wore a white shirt with a black tie, and for a moment Bobby thought the man was Natsir Santoso. But of course that wasn't possible. Santoso had suffered a terrible death eight months ago, transformed into a dinosaur and then shot dead—another death that weighed heavily on Bobby's conscience.

"My name is Satria Wahid. I represent the Sentani International Airport, as well as the people of Papua. We allowed you to land because you claim you have a solution to the crisis in Puerto Rico, which may soon become a global crisis." He looked at a watch on his wrist. "You have exactly three minutes in which to further explain your purpose. If I do not find it convincing, I have the authority to order you to depart immediately."

This was followed by silence. Bobby realized several of the armed men were staring at him. They may have recognized him, but more likely they were staring at his hair, which was now hanging to his shoulders from the two spots where Ashley had rubbed the Lamotelokhai clay.

Jonathan said, "As I explained on approach, we have a way to stop the outbreak in Puerto Rico. You know of the Lamotelokhai, right?"

Wahid's eyes were fixed on Bobby. "Of course. And I am aware that it originated here in Papua. It was taken from us."

"That's ancient history now," Jonathan said. "I'm sure you're aware the Lamotelokhai has helped all of humanity—without being in possession of the United States or any other country." Jonathan paused. "Look, Mr. Wahid, this boy is Bobby Truex." He nodded toward Bobby. "And you may recognize Ashley Stoddard and Carlos Herrera. These are the people who discovered the Lamotelokhai. We've come here because using the Lamotelokhai is the only way to stop the outbreak in Puerto Rico. We can save millions of lives, maybe even more. But there is something here in Papua the Lamotelokhai needs first. All we ask is that you allow us to travel inland to get what it needs."

Wahid's eyes narrowed. "So you wish to take something. Again."

Bobby decided if they were going to take the approach of being honest, they might as well tell everything. He unzipped his duffel bag and hefted the lump of clay to his lap. "Mr. Wahid, this is part of the Lamotelokhai."

Wahid's eyes widened. Several of the soldiers beside him backed away as if he were holding a bomb.

Bobby went on. "This is only part of it, because a group of power-hungry people captured it and took it apart. That was in Puerto Rico. It's what started the outbreak there. We brought this here because the Lamotelokhai made backups of its memory, and the backups are out there in the jungle. We have to get to them to fix the Lamotelokhai, so that the Lamotelokhai can stop the outbreak. And we really need to hurry."

Wahid continued staring at the clay. "What game are you playing?"

Bobby put his hands on the lump. He formed words silently in his mind. "Can you hear me? I need your help right now."

An array of symbols appeared before his eyes. "More knowledge, more help."

"Soon I'll get you a lot more knowledge. But right now I need help. What things can you do best right now with the knowledge you have?"

The symbols shifted. "Please talk different."

"I ask you, what game are you playing?" Wahid said.

Bobby lifted his hands from the clay to clear his vision. "Give me just a minute. I want to prove that we're telling the truth."

Ashley turned to him and gave him a look that said, *you better know what the hell you're doing.*

He nodded to her and placed his hands back on the clay. "I know you're not good at zapping things from one place to another," he thought. "You really screwed that up. I need to know what you're good at. What can you do without screwing it up?"

Symbols appeared—a lot of them. "Calculate with numbers, recall stored information, predict outcomes, manipulate materials, make mechanical things, modify biological—"

Bobby stopped reading. Manipulate materials and make mechanical things? He looked around for something. A television screen and a few audio controls were next to his seat, but he didn't see much else that wasn't part of the plane. Suddenly an idea came to him. He looked at the wall of the cabin and followed it up to the ceiling. Of course.

"There's something I want you to do," he thought. "We're in a passenger jet right now. It's a machine that's made to fly people around to different places on the planet. But it took us twenty-three hours to fly here from Puerto Rico. I bet the aliens who made you had better airplanes than this. Can you change this airplane to make it better?"

Symbols appeared. "Unknown. I will evaluate airplane and then I will know. Need to touch airplane."

Bobby looked up at Wahid and the soldiers. They were watching him, waiting. He eased forward to the edge of his seat and placed the clay on the floor against the wall. Within seconds the wall began to waver, as if it had become soft. The wavering spread up the wall and across the floor like a ripple on the surface of a pond.

The Indonesian men began talking excitedly, but Bobby didn't turn away from the clay. He realized the lump was quickly getting smaller. Its particles were flowing into the aircraft. Within seconds it was only a little larger than a grapefruit. He quickly gathered it up.

"What are you doing?" he asked silently. "I didn't say to disappear."

Symbols appeared. "Airplane appears large. Many of my parts needed."

Bobby exhaled, relieved that the clay could at least still talk to him. What would have happened if he hadn't picked it up?

The floor began to disintegrate under Bobby's feet. He and Ashley jumped up and backed away, crowding Wahid and the soldiers.

"What is happening?" Wahid cried.

"What's happening?" Bobby asked the diminished lump in his hands.

"Evaluating airplane," was the reply.

Wahid stumbled past two of the soldiers, heading for the hatch.

"You don't need to be afraid," Bobby shouted. But he was now standing there alone. All the others were leaving the plane, including Captain Kirk.

Ashley was the last of them to exit the hatch. She turned back to Bobby. "Don't just stand there, the damn plane's coming apart!"

She was right. The wall and floor were continuing to disintegrate, and now Bobby could see through the growing hole to the tarmac below. The edges of the expanding hole writhed with movement—thousands of little squirming bugs, like inchworms made of metal or plastic. He backed away a little more, but he wasn't really afraid. He had seen this before. Months ago, this was what the Lamotelokhai had done to a police car just before moving all its tiny pieces to the minivan they'd rented. It had then used the extra parts to transform the van into a jet-powered flying vehicle.

Bobby shouted, "I thought you were just going to *evaluate* the plane!"

Symbols appeared. "Yes. Evaluating."

Ashley had come back into the plane, and she grabbed his arm and pulled him toward the hatch. "Now!"

Bobby finally gave in, and they scrambled down the stairs and joined the others on the runway. Bobby turned around in time to see the Cessna fold in the center, its belly crashing to the tarmac. This tipped the nose and tail skyward, but then the plane separated in the middle, and the tail end, which extended far beyond the rear wheels, fell backward and hit the ground with a clamor of crunching metal.

Everyone silently backed away. Wahid and the policemen were apparently too stunned by the sight to say anything. No other planes were landing or taking off at the moment, and Bobby could actually hear the chittering and scraping of thousands of metallic bugs. A green armored truck with six tires and *POLISI* printed on the side screeched to a stop beside the awestruck crowd. Two soldiers got out, but they just stood there staring.

The two halves of the Cessna began dissolving where they had separated. Another six-wheeled military truck—the one that had stopped the plane—was parked just below the Cessna's nose. Bobby could already predict what was going to happen.

"Someone needs to move that truck!" he shouted.

No one moved. The bugs were still eating away at the plane, causing pieces of it to fall like snow into a heap. This quickly progressed until the nose was heavier than the portion behind the front landing gear, and the jet's nose tipped forward and crashed onto the truck. The truck was heavy-duty and didn't seem badly damaged by this, but when the chittering bugs reached the end of the jet's nose, they kept going. They were consuming the truck as well.

When there was nothing left of the jet and truck but a pile of tiny particles, it all stopped.

Symbols appeared before Bobby's eyes. "Airplane evaluated."

Bobby had forgotten he was holding the lump of clay. "You destroyed it," he said aloud.

"I make airplane better. Yes or no?"

He stared at the heap of particles. "Yes."

The particles became chittering bugs again.

Mr. Wahid spoke up. "You have the Lamotelokhai. You have convinced me of that. Now convince me that I should not request that our military forces destroy this..." He waved at the huge pile, unable to come up with a word for it.

Jonathan, Ashley, and Carlos stayed silent. Apparently it was up to Bobby to explain. He looked at the shifting pile of jet-bugs. For all he knew, the softball-sized chunk of clay was incapable of making anything at all, let alone an aircraft even better than the Cessna. But he had to say something.

"We're having the Lamotelokhai make a new aircraft. It's a gift to your country, for letting us get what we came here for. The aircraft will be the most advanced ever made."

Ashley was glaring at him.

"Will you accept this gift?" he asked Mr. Wahid.

Wahid turned to the pile without answering. It was still just a seething pile of jet-bugs. Maybe Wahid was right—maybe they should destroy it with bombs now, before the deconstruction process began spreading and killing people.

Bobby spoke silently to the clay in his hands. "Please, do this right. You're not doing anything that will hurt people, are you?"

Symbols appeared. "Making airplane better."

Bobby watched the shifting mountain of robot bugs. Gradually the pile began to change its shape. A cylinder formed, about the size of the Cessna Citation's body. But it was exactly the same at both ends—a long point, curving to one side. The cylinder's surface became smooth and black. Blacker than black, with no visible seams. And no windows. It was just a long, black tube with curved, pointed tips.

The entire cylinder rolled to the side, and since the tips were curved, when the points touched the runway this forced the tube up and off the ground. Bobby realized it was being forced up by two black rods, one near each of the curved ends. The rods continued pushing the tube up until the curved tips were pointing straight down at the ground. Just as it began to topple onto its other side, two more rods shot out on that side and held it steady. The rods all grew longer, pushing the entire cylinder off the ground until the two downward-pointing tips were higher than Bobby's head. The supporting rods each developed a joint halfway down and another joint near the ground. The jointed rods took a step, like the legs of a giant insect, moving the entire cylinder forward. The whole thing then took a few steps back and then forward again, shuffling as if it were getting comfortable with its balance.

During these transformations, not a word had been spoken by anyone. Bobby turned and saw that the group of onlookers had grown. A few more policemen had arrived, but most of them looked like airport workers. Several of them now gasped and pointed, and Bobby turned back to the black cylinder. Just above each of the four legs, a black rod was growing out and slightly upward. As the rods grew longer, each of them formed an elongated loop with thin, blade-like edges. When they were done forming, the four loops pivoted up and down, as if the tube were stretching its wings. Only the loops weren't really wings.

Symbols appeared before Bobby's eyes. "Better airplane complete. You fly now."

"It doesn't have wings," Bobby said aloud. "Will it even fly?" Actually, the four loops reminded him of those bladeless fans he had seen. Maybe they worked kind of like that. Or maybe the whole thing was just a worthless piece of junk. But it didn't look like junk—it looked amazing.

"No wings. You fly now."

"How is anyone supposed to fly that? It doesn't even look like a jet."

"I send you knowledge now."

"Just a minute." Bobby looked at the aircraft and then at the people around him. He had told Wahid the jet was for Indonesia, but he hadn't said when it would be handed over. If the aircraft actually flew the way Bobby hoped it would, it might get them to the hanging village quickly.

Bobby stepped over to Captain Kirk and tugged at his sleeve. The pilot seemed to have a hard time pulling his eyes away from the sleek black aircraft. Bobby said, "If you want to learn how to fly it, just hold this." He held out the clay.

Captain Kirk eyed it warily. "Are you serious?"

Bobby nodded. Silently he said, "I'm handing you to someone else. After I do that, send him the knowledge." He handed it over.

Kirk stared at the lump like Bobby had just handed him a snake. Then he stiffened. He closed his eyes. Seconds later he opened them and smiled. "I'll be damned. Here, take this." He handed the clay back to Bobby, stepped away from the group, and approached the black cylinder. When he got close, Bobby realized the aircraft was much bigger than the Cessna had been. It towered above Kirk. The pilot stepped right up to one of the legs and touched a button or lever that Bobby couldn't see. All four legs bent at the middle joint, lowering the cylinder until the downward-facing points at each end almost touched the tarmac. It was low enough for Kirk to reach up to the cylinder and touch another invisible button or lever. A hatch opened on the thing's belly, revealing a bright interior, which stood in contrast to the pitch black exterior. A set of narrow black stairs unfolded, and without even looking back,

Captain Kirk climbed in. The stairs folded up, the hatch closed, and he was gone.

Bobby realized Ashley was standing next to him.

"What if it doesn't work?" she hissed. "Did you even think of that?"

Suddenly the four elongated loops shifted forward and rotated until they were horizontal. They started blowing air straight down. It was just a breeze at first, almost silent, but then it picked up, and the blast hit Bobby so hard he had to lean into it to stay in place.

The black cylinder rose straight up and hovered there as the four legs pulled up and disappeared inside. The engines, if there were any, made no sounds, just the hurricane blast of air. Bobby squinted and watched. The aircraft was changing—getting shorter. He couldn't see any seams on the black shell, but now he realized the whole thing was a set of nested cylinders, sliding into each other. It kept shortening until it looked like a black soup can with curved, downward-pointing ends. Then it started growing again, until it was longer than the Cessna Citation used to be. The legs reappeared, the aircraft settled onto the ground again, and the blasting wind stopped. A few excited voices rose from the crowd around Bobby, but mostly everyone just stared.

The aircraft began walking. It turned in a circle, the four insect legs clanking against the tarmac. It then scuttled sideways, directly toward the crowd. Everyone backed away, but the huge cylinder stopped about ten yards out. The hatch opened, the stairs unfolded, and Captain Kirk stepped down.

He walked up to Bobby, looked at the lump of clay, and then looked Bobby in the eye. A grin appeared on his face, but he quickly got it under control. "I'm not sure you're the one to ask, but I'd like to request that I be assigned as the pilot of this aircraft."

"I was hoping you'd say that. But when we're done with it, we have to leave it here. I already told Mr. Wahid they could keep it."

Kirk nodded. "Yes. I could stay here. I don't have a family back home." He held Bobby's gaze and didn't blink. Apparently he was serious.

Wahid approached them. "Bobby Truex. You have proven yourself to be very convincing. If you wish to have our assistance, I am sure we can come to an agreement."

ONE PROBLEM SOLVED, Bobby thought as he gazed out the window at the jungle canopy silently racing by below. The windows had not been noticeable from outside the aircraft but appeared only slightly tinted from the inside. And the seats—they were paper-thin so they could fold down flat as the nested cylinders of the cabin slid over each other, but they were surprisingly comfortable. Right now the plane was short, because only eight people were on board: Captain Kirk, Jonathan, Bobby, Ashley, Carlos, Mr. Wahid, and two of the soldiers. However, the plane could be stretched out longer for when there were more passengers.

One problem solved, but how many more were ahead of them? And even if they succeeded, would it all be too late?

Before taking off, Bobby had called Quentin and Lindsey on their SAT phone. Miraculously, they had found Addison and had just returned to the hanging village. Bobby had told them to wait at the village and to leave their SAT phone on, even though the phone's battery charge was low. He assured them that he and the others would be there in less than an hour. Then there had been a ten-minute delay as Jonathan had tracked down the right person in Peter's corporation who could obtain the coordinates of the SAT phone, followed by another ten-minute delay as the lump of Lamotelokhai clay reconfigured the new aircraft's controls with GPS tracking. Now that they were finally in the air, they could easily achieve Bobby's one-hour estimate.

Jonathan came back from the forward-facing cockpit—there

were identical cockpits at both ends of the aircraft—and sat beside Bobby. "Kirk says we're one minute out from the location. You've been to the hanging village. How do you suggest we do this?"

Bobby had already questioned the lump of clay about how the aircraft could drop off and pick up passengers when the dense trees wouldn't allow it near the ground. Apparently the clay had anticipated this difficulty. Either that, or it had reconfigured the plane at the moment Bobby had asked, because it said this wouldn't be a problem.

"Let's stop just above the trees at two hundred yards from their SAT phone," Bobby said, loud enough for Captain Kirk to hear. "And then I need to go down there by myself."

"You're not going by yourself," Ashley said. She was sitting beside him. "I'm going with you."

Carlos said, "Yep, I'm going too."

"And I would like to see the village," Jonathan said. "I've wanted to since Peter told me about the place."

Wahid was watching them intently from a nearby seat. "We will all go together. I wish to see what it is that you need from our forest."

Bobby looked from one of them to the next. He felt the aircraft come to a stop, hovering in midair. He swallowed and looked directly at Ashley. "No."

Her eyes narrowed. "I'm going with you."

He scooped up the lump of clay and got up. "I plan to be back in half an hour. There isn't time."

She grabbed his wrist and squeezed so hard it hurt. Her eyes were intense.

"Please, Ash. If you go, everyone will go. We don't have time. Can you help me with this?"

She glared at him, but her features gradually softened. She nodded slightly and released his wrist. "He's right. We don't have time. Bobby goes alone."

Mr. Wahid started to protest, but Ashley cut him off. "If you want to keep this goddamn plane, let us do what we came here to do!"

The two soldiers stood up, gripping their assault rifles. But Wahid waved to them to sit back down. "Very well," he said. "We do not wish to interfere with your work. Do what you must."

Bobby went to the hatch, and it opened, perhaps automatically or perhaps because Captain Kirk had triggered it. The air outside the plane was silent, and Bobby realized the jet-blades were no longer blasting. He leaned out the hatch. The canopy formed an almost solid sea of green just below. The air smelled of moisture and living things. The scent was familiar to him, although it had been eight months since he'd been here last. Puzzled by how the plane could be hovering with the engines shut off, he looked below. The thin legs of the aircraft extended down through the canopy, probably all the way to the ground, which must have been at least 50 yards below the aircraft.

He turned and looked at Captain Kirk, who was watching him from the open cockpit.

"Ready for deployment?" Kirk said.

Bobby nodded, and the pilot turned back to his array of controls.

A portion of the interior ceiling just inside the hatch came loose and dropped slowly to the floor, suspended by four cables, one attached at each corner. The flat platform was about four feet long on each side. It was white, and Bobby couldn't tell if it was made of metal or plastic. As it settled onto the floor, it became obvious it had several layers, each layer hinged to one of the four sides. It seemed everything in this aircraft was made to fold up flat. The top panel suddenly popped up and clicked into place vertically. The panel beneath popped up and locked into place beside it, followed by the third. When the fourth panel popped up, it flipped all the way out until it was flat on the floor. The platform was now a three-sided box, with the fourth side lying open as if inviting someone to enter. Bobby stepped in. The last wall didn't pop up on its own, so Ashley stepped forward, lifted it, and snapped it into place. Bobby jiggled the four walls. They seemed secure.

The cables retracted, lifting the box and Bobby off the floor. The section of the ceiling where the cables converged then began sliding out the top of the hatch, taking the box with it. Holding the lump of clay in one hand, Bobby used his other hand to grab one of the cables and steady himself. Seconds later there was nothing beneath Bobby and the platform but the green leaves of the forest canopy and the open space below that. The cables now seemed ridiculously thin, particularly since they all merged into one cable above his head.

Bobby looked back at the hatch. Ashley and Jonathan were there, watching him. "I'll be back as soon as I can, with Quentin, Lindsey, and Addison." The box began to drop.

"Be careful, Bobby," Ashley said, just before he lost sight of her through the vegetation.

The box collided with a limb, but then it tipped to the side until it slid off and continued dropping. As Bobby passed through the canopy, he lost sight of the bright sunlight and entered the murky world of a primeval tropical forest. Finally, the box touched down on the forest floor. Bobby fumbled with the panel Ashley had locked into place, but he couldn't figure it out, so he just climbed over.

"Bobby, you really are here!"

He spun around. It was Lindsey. She was running toward him, and right behind her was Quentin. Bobby was nearly knocked off his feet as he was smothered by hugs.

"It's good to see you guys, too, but we need to—"

"We're so glad you're okay!"

"How in the world did you get here so fast?"

"What's up with your hair?"

"Guys!" Bobby shouted. "We can do all this later. Right now we really need to hurry. Can you just take me to the Papuans?"

They both stepped back. "How bad is it?" Quentin asked.

Bobby tucked the lump of clay under his arm. "You don't even want to know."

Both of them frowned. "Okay, this way," Lindsey said.

"Wait." Bobby held out the clay. "I need you guys to put your hands on this. Who's first?"

Several minutes later they were walking to the hanging village. Symbols kept appearing before Bobby eyes. "More knowledge now, more help."

Bobby didn't see any need to figure out what sort of help the Lamotelokhai could offer now, given that it would have all its knowledge back soon.

The village was mostly invisible from the forest floor, as it had always been. But Samuel was waiting for them on the ground. And Sinanie was with him, as well as three other villagers Bobby recognized as Matiinuo, Korul, and Ot.

"Young Master Bobby," Samuel said as he shook Bobby's hand. "It brings me great pleasure to see that you are well."

"Bobby, *sikh mayokh*," Sinnanie said in his high-pitched, singsong voice. Matiinuo, Korul, and Ot each repeated the same words.

"They welcome you as a fine friend," Samuel said.

Bobby nodded. "Thank you." He looked around. "Where's Addison? You said you had found him."

"He disappeared when we heard your aircraft approaching," Quentin said, looking around at the surrounding forest.

Lindsey cupped a hand to her mouth. "Addison! Bobby is here. Don't you want to come see him?"

They all waited, watching and listening. A cloud of flies was buzzing above their heads but did not descend upon them to bite. Occasionally they heard the *wick-you-wick* call of a honeyeater.

"Don't be alarmed by his appearance," Lindsey said softly.

Suddenly, Bobby saw movement. Something was coming. But the movement was spread out, more than just one person or creature. He caught a glimpse of a tree kangaroo, and then another, and another. It was a whole herd of tree kangaroos, and more kept coming. There were hundreds. In the middle of the herd he saw a larger creature, walking on its feet and knuckles like an ape.

Bobby recognized the figure immediately. It was Addison, looking the same as he had the last time Bobby had seen him, when Bobby had been given the task of killing him but had devised to erase his memory instead. Addison looked as fierce and dangerous as he had before, and Bobby had to fight the urge to turn and run.

The horde of tree kangaroos surrounded their group. Addison stopped a few yards out and stood erect.

Bobby took a deep breath. "Hi, Addison. Do you remember me?"

Addison grimaced, showing long teeth. Maybe it was a smile? Then he said, "Remember Bobby." His voice was recognizable but not quite human. "You come for your mbolop, Bobby?"

Bobby glanced at Quentin and Lindsey, unsure what Addison meant by this.

Quentin said, "He's asking if you came here to get your own mbolop." He nodded toward Lindsey's feet.

Bobby looked. A tree kangaroo was sitting there, actually leaning against Lindsey's leg. Another one sat between Quentin's feet, and still another was crouched beside Addison's abnormally short legs.

"We'll explain soon," Quentin said. He then turned to Addison. "Yes, Bobby will get his own mbolop. But first he has some things he needs to do. When all of this is finished, we'll all go home together. Are you ready to go home?"

Addison grimaced again. "We go home. Take mbolop home, too."

Bobby held the remains of the Lamotelokhai out in front of him. He spoke to it silently. "Now it's time to give you back the rest of your knowledge. You'll be complete again."

Symbols appeared. "More knowledge now, more help."

One of the mbolop hopped forward and stopped at Bobby's feet.

Bobby took one look and crouched down. "Mbaiso! It's you! Long time no see, buddy."

Mbaiso ignored him and extended his snout closer to the lump of clay.

Bobby held it out to him. "You remember this?"

Mbaiso pressed his nose against the clay. After several seconds he pulled back and stared at it. He opened his mouth slightly and emitted a soft, whining bleat.

CHAPTER TWENTY-FIVE

Quentin stared, trying to digest what Bobby had just described. Quentin's mbolop sensed his rising fear and leaned into his leg, which was comforting.

Lindsey said, "They're transforming into animals?"

Bobby nodded. "Yeah, but when you put it that way, it sounds almost fun. But it was a nightmare—is a nightmare. We don't have time to talk about this. I told them we'd be back to the plane soon." He turned to Samuel. "The Lamotelokhai put some information in your mind, and in the minds of the villagers. It did that in case of an emergency. Now it needs the information back so it can—"

Samuel held up a hand to cut him off. "I am familiar with the notion. I know that the indigenes carry within them the Lamotelokhai's knowledge. But I assure you that I possess no such knowledge."

Bobby shook his head. "It put the knowledge into you without you knowing, just like it did to the rest of us."

"He's right," Quentin said. "Lindsey and I had no idea, but the information was there."

After a bit more convincing, Samuel finally agreed to place his hand on the clay. His eyes grew wide when the process started. "Extraordinary!" He exclaimed.

A minute later it was complete. He pulled his hand back and stared at it for a moment. He then turned to Sinanie and the three other villagers and began explaining in their language. The villagers listened, enthralled. They talked back and forth, and then Sinanie placed his hand on the clay. When the transfer was complete, he spoke rapidly to his companions, and they followed his lead and began transferring their information.

As they did this, Quentin watched Addison, who had apparently gotten bored with all the talk and was playing a game with Newton and the other tree kangaroos. The game involved Addison covering his eyes while Newton watched the other creatures. Quentin looked down at his own mbolop. His newfound connection to the creature was extraordinarily powerful, but so far it hadn't involved shared vision or any other shared senses. Regardless, he felt a constantly-elevated level of physical and mental well-being, comparable to how he had felt during the best moments of his entire life, such as the day he had married Lindsey, or the day Addison had come home as an infant from the hospital. Perhaps this was due to eating numerous bits of the mbolop's body, which it had been periodically extracting and giving to him since they had paired up earlier that morning. Whatever the cause, he was confident his new state of mind was not in any way harmful, in spite of his previous misgivings about pairing up with one of the creatures. Soon he would have to come up with a suitable name for his mbolop.

He looked over at Lindsey and realized she was watching him. She nodded, as if she understood what was going through his mind. But when she turned to look at the others, he saw subtle lines of concern in her features. Bobby's news had her scared, and Quentin's thoughts shifted back to the current situation.

He turned to Bobby. "What else can we do to help the Lamotelokhai?"

Bobby was still holding the clay as Matiinuo transferred his information to it. Matiinuo was the last of the four Papuans to do this.

"We have to get the rest of the data packets," Bobby replied. "We still need packets from Teatakan, Jara, Rossa, Sirizo, Yerema, Kumbi, Ankara, Owa, and Kebuge." He nodded over Quentin's shoulder. "And Addison."

"Addison?" Lindsey turned her head suddenly.

"That's what the Lamotelokhai told me."

Samuel spoke to the villagers, repeating the Papuan names Bobby had listed. They talked back and forth and then quickly walked off in different directions.

"Young man," Samuel said to Bobby," you have restored to the villagers a great sense of responsibility and resolve. For centuries they have been stewards of the Lamotelokhai's knowledge, carrying it within them always so that it could be procurable upon an occasion of need. But no such occasion has heretofore offered an opportunity such as you have offered today. I dare say you have conferred upon them a spring to the step and a gleam to the eye."

Bobby was staring at the ball of clay in his hands and didn't seem to be paying attention. He looked up at Samuel. "Sorry, it was talking to me. It needs to make more of its particles before it can handle the rest of the data packets. It's too small, I guess." He carried it to the base of a tree and carefully placed it on the ground. He then whispered to the clay, too quietly for Quentin to be able to hear what he was saying. Bobby backed away from it, and Quentin, Lindsey, and Samuel gathered beside him to watch.

"It can talk to you?" Quentin asked.

"Yeah, but only with Kembalimo symbols. It gets easier to communicate every time it gets another data packet."

"It's shrinking," Lindsey said. "Is it supposed to do that?"

She was right. The clay had flattened out against the ground.

"It told me it would," Bobby said. "It has to spread out to find the stuff it needs. I tried to make it promise it would come back, but I'm not sure it knows what a promise is."

As they watched, the clay continued flattening until it was a thin film. It then sank into the leaf litter and soil, virtually disappearing.

"We don't have time for this," Bobby said, still staring at the ground.

At least for the moment, they were powerless to do anything else. So Quentin said, "Bobby, where is Peter?"

Bobby didn't take his eyes off the ground. "Peter's dead. I was waiting for a better time to tell you."

Quentin's felt his heart start pounding, forcing hot blood into his fingers and toes and making them burn. He started getting light-headed and was forced to suck in a lungful of air.

"That is unfortunate news," Samuel said.

Lindsey said, "And Ashley?"

Bobby looked up. "She's fine. She's in the plane."

Something touched Quentin's leg. It was his mbolop, holding out a lump of its body for him to take. Without hesitating he plucked it from the mbolop's paw, ate it, and patted the creature's head. He straightened up and looked back at Bobby. By that time the substance was already kicking in, causing Quentin's heart rate to return to normal.

Bobby gazed at him quizzically. But instead of asking about the mbolop, he said, "And Robert died, too. Maybe you never met him, I don't know. He was nice to us."

Lindsey had just accepted an offering from Rusty, and she swallowed it. She closed her eyes for a moment, apparently feeling the same soothing respite Quentin had.

Bobby frowned. "Are you guys okay?"

Samuel interjected, "That remains to be seen."

Bobby's frown deepened.

"We're fine," Quentin said. "We can explain later. What happened to Peter and Robert?"

"They burned up in an explosion that was supposed to kill off all the transforming creatures." Bobby looked down at his feet for a moment. "But some got out anyway. That's why we're here, to make the Lamotelokhai whole again. Maybe it can stop what's happening."

"How far have the transforming beasts spread?" Samuel asked. "I have witnessed the Lamotelokhai succeed in stopping such transformations that had spread for perhaps a square mile. Beyond that, I am not certain the same remedy would suffice."

"It's way bigger than a square mile," Bobby said. "Way bigger."

Samuel sighed. "God help us all." He turned to Quentin. "You must take the mbolop with you. All of them. And you must take the mbolop talismans. Give them to good people, to those whom you believe to be worth saving. Do not underestimate the importance of the responsibility the indigenes have entrusted to you."

Quentin stared at him. "Things can't be that bad."

"But we're taking them anyway," Lindsey said. "All of them." Her eyes met Quentin's. "Just in case."

"I don't know what you guys are talking about," Bobby said, "but we don't have time to take all these tree kangaroos with us. We still have to wait for the Lamotelokhai to come back up, and we need the other data packets. Including his." He nodded toward Addison.

So far, Addison had refused to come near the ball of Lamotelokhai clay, and Quentin wasn't sure how they were going to convince him to put his hand on it.

"I guess he didn't get his memory back," Bobby said. "He kind of acts like a little kid."

Quentin exchanged a glance with Lindsey. They had avoided talking about this. Addison had suffered serious brain trauma from the plane crash eight months ago. That had been before his encounter with the Lamotelokhai, and therefore the Lamotelokhai had no knowledge—no complete set of data—of Addison's healthy body and mind from before the crash. And on top of that, Quentin and Bobby had erased Addison's memory to stop his murderous rampage. It was a wonder anything was left in his mind at all.

"It appears that part of your solution has arrived," Samuel said.

Quentin looked. The villagers were returning, apparently with the entire tribe. They were approaching slowly, following Sinanie, who was encouraging them not to be afraid. There were six women with them, more than Quentin had ever seen at one time in this tribe. Gradually the group came closer, and they finally formed a circle around Quentin and the others.

Matiinuo spoke directly to Bobby. "*Nokhu mesendipo kholofu-damo diabo Lamotelokhai.*"

"They are ready to confer their knowledge to the Lamotelokhai," Samuel said.

Bobby looked at the Papuans and shuffled his feet. "Well, um, right now the Lamotelokhai is—"

"*I mbakha!*" cried one of the women. She pointed beyond the group, to where Bobby had placed the ball of clay.

The Lamotelokhai was back, rising from the ground. It was a mound the size of an overturned bowl, but it continued to grow as the villagers gathered around to watch. Finally it stopped—a mound of clay a yard across, the size of the original Lamotelokhai.

"Excuse me," Bobby said, and he pushed his way through the onlookers to kneel beside it.

Quentin watched over the shoulder of one of the shorter villagers.

Seconds after placing his hands on it, Bobby looked up. "It's ready now." His eyes searched the crowd and settled on one of the men. "Teatakan," he said, and then he gestured toward the clay.

Teatakan stepped forward and transferred his knowledge to the

Lamotelokhai. As he stepped back, the others spoke softly and rubbed his arms and shoulders, praising him.

Bobby called another name. "Jara."

One of the women stepped forward.

The process continued until Bobby called Kebuge, the last Papuan on the list. The Lamotelokhai had given him no more names. Except Addison's.

"It's his turn," Bobby said, looking at Quentin and then Lindsey.

Quentin moved away from the group and spotted Addison. He was still playing games with the tree kangaroos.

Lindsey stepped up beside Quentin. "I'll try." She called out gently, "Addison, please come over here."

He stopped what he was doing but didn't come closer. "I no touch, Mummy!"

"It won't hurt you, honey, I promise."

Addison dropped to all fours and took a few ape-like steps toward them. But then he stopped and twisted his face into a frightening sneer. "No, Mummy! It hurt me. It hurt me bad!"

Did Addison actually remember being hurt by it? Did he remember Quentin throwing it at his face, trying to kill him?

A slight commotion had risen from the villagers behind him, but Quentin was focused on Addison and his own despairing thoughts.

Addison's sneer remained, and he crouched like he was about to charge them and attack. At that moment, Quentin realized his son was too broken to live any kind of normal life, even if they somehow managed to get to Puerto Rico and stop the spreading creatures. Addison was too unpredictable. And downright terrifying. The son he had known and loved was gone forever.

Quentin held both his hands out. "Addison, please don't be upset."

"Hey, Quentin. Lindsey." It was Bobby. "Maybe this will help."

Quentin pulled his eyes away from Addison and turned. Bobby emerged from the gathered villagers. And just behind him was Addison. It was Addison as Quentin wanted to remember him—human and unhurt. He was wearing a t-shirt and shorts, the same clothes the Lamotelokhai had been wearing when it was disguised as Addison eight months ago. Quentin knew this figure before him was actually the Lamotelokhai, but seeing it in that form was still like getting punched in the chest. He felt Lindsey grab his arm and squeeze.

"It's almost complete now," Bobby said as he and the Addison copy approached. "I don't think it can talk out loud yet, but still, I thought this might help with Addison." He shrugged and half-smiled.

Suddenly the real Addison was beside Quentin, standing upright. He was staring at the copy of his former self.

"Who that, Mummy?"

Lindsey said, "Do you remember him? That's you. That's what you looked like before."

Addison took a step closer. The thing looked back at him without expression. They both had the same blue eyes, but nothing else in common. "Who you?" Addison said.

The Lamotelokhai remained silent.

"Um, there's something else," Bobby said. "There were supposed to be twenty-four data packets. But when the Papuans were downloading theirs, I counted them up. There were only nineteen—twenty if you include Addison's. So I asked the Lamotelokhai about that. It said it was already aware of the situation, because it had put *five* data packets into Addison."

Quentin looked at him. "Five? Why?"

"I guess because I made it erase Addison's memory. That's when it put the five packets in him. Because then there was plenty of room."

"Who you?" Addison asked again. He stepped even closer. "Who you!"

Lindsey spoke softly. "I told you, Addison. That's what you—"

Addison attacked the Lamotelokhai. He threw himself upon it so viciously that Quentin grabbed Lindsey's arm and stumbled backward. The Lamotelokhai fell flat on its back under the weight of the attack, and Addison sank his teeth into its neck. He pulled back, ripping out a large chunk of the neck and tossing it aside. He then pummeled the thing's face as he snarled and grunted, his arms a blur.

Lindsey lunged forward and tried pulling Addison off the Lamotelokhai, but Quentin pulled her back. "My God, Addison!" she cried. "Stop!"

Apparently he didn't even hear her. He kept pounding. But seconds later his blows slowed down. And then they stopped. He sat there on the Lamotelokhai's chest, panting and staring down at the thing's mangled head.

There was no blood, no exposed bone. Just clay.

Addison's chest was heaving from the effort of the attack as he looked up at the crowd surrounding him. His eyes moved from one person to the next. He found Quentin and Lindsey.

"Dad? Mom?"

Quentin's throat went dry, and he struggled to swallow.

Lindsey said, "Addison, what have you done? Are you okay?"

Addison looked down at the mutilated figure beneath him. "What is this?" He then seemed to notice his hands—powerful, animal-like fingers encrusted with grime. He let out a pitiful sob. "What's going on? What happened to me?"

Quentin was only a few steps away, but he couldn't get to his son fast enough. He dropped to his knees and grabbed him by the shoulders. "Addison, who am I? Tell me who I am!"

Tears were starting to form in Addison's eyes. "You're my dad. What's happening? My voice.... What's happening?"

The maimed figure on the ground began stirring. Quentin and Lindsey pulled Addison off the Lamotelokhai, and they all settled onto the ground beside each other, watching it. Its face and neck were quickly shifting back to normal. It reached for the chunk of its neck Addison had bitten off and pressed it against its abdomen. The clay particles began moving through the t-shirt, and seconds later the chunk was gone.

"Mom, Dad, is that the Lamotelokhai? Is that why it looks like me?"

Quentin said, "You know what the Lamotelokhai is?"

Before Addison could answer, the fully-recovered Lamotelokhai spoke. "Quentin and Lindsey Darnell. A fascinating sequence of events has brought us together again. Your kind can be interesting and unpredictable. But at this moment, your kind is being destroyed. If you wish for that to occur, I will not interfere. If you wish to prevent it, then I must go to the site of this destruction immediately."

CHAPTER TWENTY-SIX

Before the Lamotelokhai could offer an explanation, Bobby had a hypothesis about what had happened to Addison. "It must have been when we were all together back in Newton, when we made the big announcement about the Lamotelokhai. The other Addison was there, the one who had been in the other copy of the Twin Otter—the plane that had never even crashed. The Lamotelokhai must have touched him and read his memories. That's what it gave to Addison just now."

Quentin, Lindsey, and Addison stared at him, absorbing this.

"Bobby is correct," the Lamotelokhai said. "The information I put into your son is the information I collected when I encountered the other Addison. If you wish for me to remove the information, I will do so."

"No!" Lindsey said.

"We're grateful for what you've done," Quentin said. "We thought we had lost our son."

Lindsey turned to Addison. "What's the last thing you remember, honey?"

It seemed to take him a moment to realize she was talking to him. "Those people came to our house, the ones who looked just like us. They talked to all the news reporters about the Lamotelokhai. The Lamotelokhai changed its shape. It freaked everyone out."

Bobby had replayed that day in his head countless times. It was a day that had changed the world.

"That was eight months ago," Quentin said. "What do you remember after that?"

Addison shook his head. "No, it was today. Or maybe yesterday. But not eight months ago." He looked at his hands again, and then at the rest of his naked body. "But I also remember things that happened here—living with the mbolop, helping them with their tree houses. What happened to me?"

Bobby realized this could go on forever. "We need to talk about all this on the plane. People are dying right now."

"Again, Bobby is correct," the Lamotelokhai said. "The process that began while my parts were separated is likely to continue. If you wish for me to attempt to stop it, I must go to the location where it began."

"I can just take the Lamotelokhai with me," Bobby said. "You guys can stay here with Addison if you want." He looked at the Addison copy. "Are you ready?"

"We're going with you," Lindsey said. "And we're bringing Addison and all the tree kangaroos. That's nonnegotiable."

"WHAT THE HELL, BOBBY?" Ashley was leaning out the aircraft's hatch as the lift rose up through the canopy.

Bobby just smiled at her. He wasn't alone in the lift. Crammed into the four-by-four box were seventeen tree kangaroos, as many as he had been able to fit without stacking them.

The lift came to a stop, and the mechanical arm retracted,

pulling the platform inside. Bobby messed with the latch until he figured out how to open the panel. The tree kangaroos poured out and scattered throughout the cabin, startling everyone. One of the policemen shouted and leapt onto a seat. When he saw what the creatures actually were, he forced out a chuckle that still sounded nervous.

Suddenly, everyone started asking Bobby questions at once. He held up his hands to stop them. "I don't know why, but we have to take them with us. And this is only the first load." He stepped over the open panel into the box and then latched it shut. "I'll get them loaded as fast as I can." The lift arm extended, carrying him out the hatch again.

When the lift was halfway through the door, Ashley grabbed it, stopping its movement. "I'm going with you."

"I told you there's no time for—"

Suddenly she vaulted over the side of the box. Her knees hit the panel, and she tumbled inside.

Bobby grabbed her elbow to help her up. "Are you crazy? You could have fallen!"

"Everything okay?" Captain Kirk called out.

"We're fine," Ashley said. "Take us down please." The box finished moving out and started dropping.

She glared at Bobby. "You knew I wanted to go down there. I want to see Samuel. And Sinanie. You should have asked me to get in with you."

He stared back at her in disbelief. He was about to ask again if she was crazy, but he held off. She was trembling, either from anger or fear, and she had an intense look he had seen only a few times before. Suddenly a wave of regret washed over him. Why had he treated her that way? He realized she was right—he should have asked her to ride down with him. Her presence on this trip down wouldn't delay the process if they both waited on the ground as the rest of the tree kangaroos were lifted.

The platform hit a limb and tipped to one side before sliding off. Ashley held on to one of the cables, never taking her eyes off Bobby's. She was glaring at him like she wanted to push him over the side, and he grabbed a cable in case she actually did.

Bobby wanted to say he was sorry, but at this moment those words didn't seem like enough. "Sometimes I don't really know the right thing to say. But if you would let me kiss you right now, that's how I could show you how I feel."

Her brows furrowed. The platform hit another limb and momentarily tipped.

"Apology accepted," she said. And then she leaned in and pressed her mouth against his so hard it hurt.

But it hurt for only a second, because then Bobby didn't even care. Ashley actually put her arms around him, like how they kissed in movies. Her eyes were closed, so he closed his, and this made it even better. She kissed his lips, first his top lip and then his bottom lip, and he kissed hers. Then he felt the tip of her tongue. He touched her tongue with his, and suddenly the kiss went to a whole new level of amazing.

Bobby was vaguely aware that the rustling of leaves against the descending lift had stopped. They were in the open space beneath the canopy, but he wasn't about to stop the kiss until Ashley was ready.

Abruptly, the lift hit the ground.

"Bobby and Ashley. What a surprise it is to see that you are two people, when only a moment before I would have sworn that I was witnessing one individual with four arms."

Bobby released her. His heart was pounding. She stared at him for just a second before turning away.

"Samuel!" she cried. "I was hoping I'd get to see you." She started opening the side panel but then stopped. "No freaking way!"

The lift was surrounded by tree kangaroos.

"I told you there were more," Bobby said, still catching his breath. "We have to take all of them." He looked around. Quentin and Lindsey weren't in the immediate area. At least he wouldn't have to explain what had just happened to *them*.

Samuel was smiling. "My keen observations suggest that much has happened between the two of you since last I saw you together."

Ashley glanced at Bobby. "We've been through a lot recently. Bobby saved my life. Of course he almost got me killed, too." She nudged him with her elbow. "More than once."

"Ashley!" It was Quentin. He rushed over and hugged her over the side of the lift. When they separated, he held her out by the shoulders. "You look okay. I'd say Bobby got the worst of it." He nodded toward Bobby, probably at the scars on his neck from being bitten by the Helmich-bat.

"Debatable," she said. When Quentin frowned, she added, "We'll tell you about it sometime."

Bobby opened the panel, and he and Ashley stepped out. He then got to work herding tree kangaroos into the lift. Ashley, Quentin, and Samuel helped, and soon they had packed nineteen into the box. Bobby yelled to the aircraft, and the box started rising.

"There's something you don't see every day," Bobby said, nodding toward the hanging village.

Ashley turned and saw the rest of the tree kangaroos, a couple hundred of them. And behind the mbolop, spread out to prevent stragglers, was the entire Papuan tribe. Lindsey, Addison, and the Lamotelokhai were at one end of the line of villagers.

Ashley watched as the herd approaching. "Bobby, whenever I'm with you, things get weird. And then they just keep getting weirder."

Bobby latched the panel shut on the sixteenth load of tree kangaroos. There were only a few left on the ground, including Mbaiso and the three that were remaining strangely close to Addison, Quentin, and Lindsey. He shouted to Captain Kirk, and the lift began rising.

"Once again, I have made the difficult decision to remain with my indigene friends," Samuel said as the platform rose toward the canopy. "Perhaps one day, if you and the Lamotelokhai endeavor to make the world safe again, I will have the occasion to venture outside this forest. I can only hope that you are not too late."

Samuel then nodded to Sinanie. The Papuan swung a heavy woven bag from his shoulder and handed it to Quentin. Bobby had no idea what was in it.

Samuel went on. "I pray that you will not need the talismans. But I trust that you will disseminate them wisely if you do, for you will be sowing the seeds of humanity's future."

Quentin set the bag down, opened it, and pulled out a small skin pouch. He held it out to Samuel. "This one's for you. We will leave behind one of the mbolop. We can also leave some for Sinanie and the all of the others." He nodded toward the gathered villagers.

Samuel looked at it for a moment and shook his head. "My indigene hosts wish you to take them all. As do I."

Quentin held the pouch out to Sinanie, who shook his head and didn't take it. He tried several other villagers, who also refused.

Samuel stepped up to Bobby and Ashley. "Perhaps I will see the two of you again. If that day comes, I imagine you will be together, will you not?"

Bobby looked at Ashley, but she held Samuel's gaze.

"I hope so," she said. "I've recently decided we make a pretty good team."

Samuel nodded without smiling. "Godspeed to you both, then. Please safeguard the Lamotelokhai from those who lack your proclivities for wisdom and compassion."

"We will," Bobby said. "I promise."

After several more long minutes of goodbyes, the lift came back down. Bobby, Ashley, Quentin, Lindsey, Addison, the Lamotelokhai, and the last of the tree kangaroos, including Mbaiso, crammed their way onto the platform, and then it began rising for the last time.

As the aircraft sped toward Sentani, Bobby once again watched the forest canopy race by beneath him. Captain Kirk had lengthened the plane to make room for the extra people and the tree kangaroos. Surprisingly, the cabin didn't smell like a zoo. But Mr. Wahid and the two policemen seemed pretty freaked by it all. There wasn't a seat or spot on the floor not occupied by an mbolop. And the creatures were acting nervously, never staying in one place. It seemed like each of them wanted to sniff and explore every square inch of the plane.

The flight to the airport took only ten minutes, and soon the aircraft was dropping straight down to the same spot on the runway where it had been created. Bobby figured they had been gone about three hours. The crowd of people, which was even larger now, was still there on the tarmac. And beside the crowd was a jet that looked like the Cessna Citation, only this one was gray, and the tail bore a US flag—a military plane.

Captain Kirk landed the aircraft without even jostling the tree kangaroos. Four men immediately began walking toward them from the gray jet. Two of them wore camo fatigues, one wore a green uniform with a tan tie, and the fourth wore shorts and an untucked shirt. The uniformed man and the man in shorts both had gray hair and wore sunglasses. The men stopped beside the aircraft and waited impatiently until Captain Kirk opened the hatch. Then they climbed the stairs and came into the cabin.

"Jesus, Mary, and Joseph!" the man in shorts said as he pulled off his sunglasses.

It was Colonel Roger Richards.

He looked around at the tree kangaroos. "When you folks do something, you do it neck-deep and shit-thick."

Bobby had no idea what that meant, but seeing Richards gave him hope. He trusted the colonel. The guy had risked his career to help them avoid the Lamotelokhai falling into the wrong hands.

Quentin got up and shook his hand. "It's good to see you, Colonel."

Richards glanced down at his own clothes. "I'm a civilian now, no thanks to you and your motley crew." He said this with a half-smile. Then he straightened up and cleared his throat. "Listen up." He nodded to the uniformed man next to him. "This is Colonel Reed Northcott. He replaced me as Attaché for Defense and Army, Jakarta. For reasons that should be obvious, I've been following any news I can get on you folks and Peter Wooley's SouthPacificNet. I happened to receive some intel recently that a private SouthPacificNet jet had flown to Puerto Rico and then was en route to Indonesia. I put two and two together and figured you were up to something important, and that you might show up here. Bingo. You folks have a penchant for flying under the radar, but *damn*." He waved his hand toward the walls of the aircraft. "You stick out like a sore thumb every-where you go. Considering the nature of the crisis in the Caribbean, I convinced Colonel Northcott it would be worth his while to skip over here from Jakarta to see what you were up to, and to see if you needed assistance. He agreed, and he also agreed I should come along, considering my history with you folks."

Bobby decided to speak up. "Colonel—or Mr. Richards—we have to get to Puerto Rico. Like, right now. We think we may have a way to stop what's happening there."

Richards hesitated, and then Colonel Northcott spoke up. "You're too late, son. Puerto Rico is beyond recovery."

"What does that mean?" Lindsey asked.

"Beyond recovery, ma'am. The island is lost. All three and a half million civilians presumed dead. Efforts now are focused on containment. Largest containment effort in history."

Bobby's stomach lurched. Three and a half million. It was a number too big to make any sense. There was only one word for what Bobby had done—holocaust. This was all his fault.

Bobby dropped his face into his hands. He pinched the skin of his cheek, trying to inflict some pain. But it was nothing compared to what he deserved. Suddenly he started feeling sick. He couldn't just sit here and think about this and listen to these men talk. He had to get some fresh air. He got up and pushed his way past Richards and the other men to get to the open hatch. Several of the mbolop had moved to the hatch and were looking out, so he nudged them back. He then stood by the opening, breathing in the wet, tropical air. The others kept talking, but Bobby didn't listen. He couldn't, because it made him feel dead inside.

Mbaiso came to him and stopped at his feet, looking up. Bobby sat on the floor next to him. "Hey, buddy. I'm sorry, but I think you're going to wish you'd stayed back in the jungle. You're not going to like where we're going."

Mbaiso sat up and moved his forepaws, signing to Bobby. Brief visions appeared in Bobby's mind, clarifying the meaning, just as they had months ago. "Bobby hurt. Why Bobby hurt?"

"You're not a person, so I don't think you'd understand," Bobby said quietly so the others couldn't hear. "I've done something really bad. Maybe the worst thing anyone's ever done."

Mbaiso gazed at him, sniffing the air. He then dug into his body and held out a pink lump.

"What's that for?"

Mbaiso didn't move.

Maybe Mbaiso wanted to put him out of his misery. Bobby certainly wanted his misery to end. But then he thought about Ashley and their moment in the lift. Maybe there was something worth living for, even if he didn't deserve it. "This won't hurt me, will it?"

Still, Mbaiso didn't move.

Bobby took the lump and ate it.

***

BOBBY OPENED HIS EYES. Mbaiso was still there, watching him. Richards and Colonel Northcott stood a few feet away with their backs to him, still talking to the others as if only a few seconds had passed. But while Bobby had been out, he had seen, heard, and felt so much that it was hard to believe so little time could have passed. He now knew more about Mbaiso than he'd ever imagined possible. He reached out and stroked Mbaiso's head, feeling an almost overwhelming connection to him. Thousands of years of the creature's life had flashed through Bobby's mind—images of how Mbaiso had been created, how he had lived, and how he had finally decided to ignore the Lamotelokhai's instructions to destroy himself, choosing instead to start a colony of mbolop.

But from all Bobby had seen during that nearly endless vision, one truth stood out. Mbaiso had been created so the Papuans wouldn't have to talk directly to the Lamotelokhai, and therefore Mbaiso had prevented the villagers from destroying themselves and perhaps destroying much more than their own tribe. Mbaiso had stopped this catastrophe not just once, but again and again, century after century. Humans had survived—maybe the planet itself had survived—because of Mbaiso.

Since Bobby had encountered the Lamotelokhai eight months ago, he had known it was dangerous. But now, in a moment of complete clarity and certainty, he understood how dangerous it really was. And he understood what Mbaiso had been trying to do—save as many people as possible. The Papuan villagers would have perished without Mbaiso, and now that the Lamotelokhai was out of hiding, the rest of the world would perish without the mbolop colony.

Bobby realized that even if the Lamotelokhai could stop the outbreak in Puerto Rico from spreading, the world wouldn't be safe until Mbaiso could carry out his plan.

He stroked Mbaiso's head again. "We'll figure this out together, right?" Bobby got to his feet. Apparently no one had even noticed what had happened to him. They were still talking about Puerto Rico, and Mr. Wahid was upset about something.

"I'm going there right now," Bobby said loudly.

Everyone shut up and turned to look at him.

He stepped forward. "I'm leaving now, and I'm taking this aircraft. Mr. Wahid, I know I promised you could have it, and I'll try to make sure it gets back to you. In the meantime, you can have a second one just like it. There's another jet right over there." Bobby pointed out the hatch at the US military jet Richards and colonel Northcott had used. He then turned to the Lamotelokhai. "I'd like you to give some of your particles to Mr. Wahid. Make it so he can rub them on that jet to turn it into an aircraft just like this one. Can you do that?"

"Yes." It got up, removed a fist-sized portion of its own arm, and handed it to Mr. Wahid, who snatched the beret from the head of one of the Indonesian soldiers and held it upside down to receive the gift.

"And one more thing," Bobby said. "Delete the GPS location of the site we visited today. No one else can ever go there. If any person or aircraft shows up there, your new planes will automatically self-destruct." This wasn't true, but Bobby hoped Wahid would believe it.

Bobby turned to Colonel Northcott. "I just gave away your jet for a chance to stop the outbreak. I'm sorry, but—"

"Who the hell do you think you are, son?" Northcott waved his two men to move toward Bobby.

A blur of motion and fury took everyone by surprise as the real Addison leapt over the seats and skidded to a stop between Bobby and the soldiers before they were even close.

"Leave Bobby alone!" His nonhuman voice was so fierce that the men stumbled back, one of them tripping and falling between two seats.

"What is that thing?" Northcott said, his eyes wide. Apparently he hadn't taken a good look at Addison until this moment.

"He's not a thing," Bobby said. "He's my friend. You should see what he can do when he gets *really* mad."

The soldiers had recovered and were drawing their pistols.

"Lamotelokhai!" Bobby shouted. "These men want to keep us from going to stop the outbreak. Don't kill them, but make them realize we're going now, with or without their help."

The copy of Addison stepped toward the men. "I understand, Bobby."

"Hold on! Everyone stand down." It was Roger Richards, his hands in the air. He faced Colonel Northcott. "Reed, I've known you for years. You want the same thing these people do—to save lives. Hell, that's why you're checking out the lead I tracked down. If you had seen the things I've seen this boy—this Lamotelokhai—do, you'd know he could easily kill us all before you could even spit. You'd also know there's a good chance he can stop the outbreak. Let them have the damn jet. You can work that out later. But right now you need to provide these folks with every resource you can. If you don't want to go with them, please disembark. But I'm going, and I'll do everything I can—hell, I'll give up my life if necessary—to stop this horrific outbreak. So make your decision, Reed, because we're taking off."

CHAPTER TWENTY-SEVEN

ONCE THE AIRCRAFT was up to full speed, it felt like no plane Quentin had been on before. Rather than a constant roar of jet engines, all he heard was the high-pitched whine of air passing smoothly over the streamlined exterior. The aircraft's speed was unnerving—each time a downdraft or change in air pressure caused the plane to drop slightly, Quentin experienced a moment of weightlessness. But the plane's sophisticated controls always recovered gently, avoiding any violent jostling. Quentin was actually enjoying watching several hundred tree kangaroos suddenly float inches off the floor, twisting in panic and running in place for a few seconds before the floor slowly rose back up to meet them.

It was at least an hour into the flight before Quentin decided it would be reasonably safe to remove his seatbelt and stand up. Lindsey was sitting beside him, and he assured her he wouldn't be up long. There were twelve people on the aircraft. Wahid and the two Indonesian soldiers had stayed in Sentani, but Richards, Colonel Northcott, and his two men were still aboard. These men were firmly planted in their seats, holding on to whatever they could, still not trustful of the aircraft's alien design. They frowned at Quentin like they thought he was crazy for standing up.

Quentin made his way forward to where Bobby, Ashley, and Carlos were sitting. Once beside them, he saw that Carlos and Ashley were sleeping. Mbaiso was on the floor at Bobby's feet. But what really caught Quentin's eye was that Ashley's head was on Bobby's shoulder. And they were holding hands, their fingers entwined on Bobby's lap. Quentin stared. Why hadn't he seen this coming?

Bobby looked up and made an embarrassed face that said, *Oops, you caught us.*

The plane shot through an air pressure anomaly, and Quentin's feet lifted from the floor. He gripped Bobby's seatback until he dropped back down. He cleared his throat. "Did the Lamotelokhai tell you how long it'll take to get there?"

Bobby's eyes got wide, and he repeated the *oops* expression. "I didn't remember to ask."

"That's alright," Quentin said. "I'll talk to it." He then nodded to Ashley's hand in Bobby's. "When did this happen?" he asked quietly.

Bobby gave him another embarrassed look, this one saying something more like, *Do I really need to explain the details?*

Quentin smiled and decided to let it go. He turned to the other side of the aisle, to the two Addisons. His son had wanted to sit with the Lamotelokhai, as he apparently had an endless stream of questions to ask. This was okay with Quentin, as long as he didn't ask it to *do* anything. As Quentin listened, though, he realized Addison was asking for details of what had happened eight months ago in the Papuan wilderness. Quentin hoped the Lamotelokhai had not yet told him the body he now occupied had murdered Miranda and a dozen Papuan villagers.

"Excuse me, you two," he said. "I have a request." He looked at his real son. "Could you please wait to talk about what happened last year until your mother and I can explain things to you? When we do explain, you'll understand why it was important to wait."

Addison gazed back at him with an expression that was hard to read, probably because it wasn't entirely human. "Sure, Dad. I can wait."

Quentin exhaled, relieved. It was intimidating to be under Addison's direct stare. He turned to the Lamotelokhai. "I'd like to know how long it will take us to get to Puerto Rico."

The thing answered immediately. "I do not know the distance to Puerto Rico at this moment."

"The pilot entered the destination in the plane's GPS—"

"Yes, I see that now. How would you like the time expressed?"

"Uh, hours and minutes?"

"The marked destination in Puerto Rico at this moment is eight thousand, six hundred and eight miles. If we continue at this velocity, we will arrive in four hours and fifty-four minutes."

That couldn't be right. It had taken Bobby and Ashley twenty-three hours, with three stops. "How fast are we moving? Expressed in miles per hour."

"One thousand, seven hundred and twenty-two miles per hour."

Quentin stared. "Is that even possible?"

"My research suggests that your question may be rhetorical. However, yes, it is possible. Considering the current conditions outside this aircraft, that velocity is referred to as Mach two-point-two. On the Internet, I have encountered text, photographs, and videos that suggest your kind has created twenty-one models of aircraft that move faster than we are moving. And there are even more that some of your kind attempt to keep secret, although I had little difficulty finding evidence of them. And, in an attempt to anticipate your next question, no, we will not need to stop before we arrive at our destination. This aircraft was constructed from the parts of another aircraft and a ground vehicle, which contained fuel that could be converted to suit the functions of this aircraft, allowing us to travel to our destination—and beyond if necessary.

Again, Quentin stared. Why should he be surprised? This was nothing compared to copying his son's consciousness and putting it into another body. But this discussion had spawned a whole new set of questions.

"You seem to remember things that happened to you after leaving the hanging village eight months ago, as well as everything you learned from the Internet while you were in that motel room. But I thought you made backups of your knowledge before that, back when you were still in the hanging village. How is it that you can remember what happened to you after making the backups?"

The thing's eyes turned from blue to golden yellow for a few seconds. "Yes, I made backups in the hanging village. When some of those backups were deleted, I redistributed them." It shot a glance at Addison when it said the word *deleted* as if letting Quentin know it was honoring his request to avoid mentioning the murders. "I was able to update the packets in Bobby and Ashley with new information when they came to the motel. And in addition, Bobby salvaged a portion of my parts in Puerto Rico using that portion as a foundation on which to reconstruct my knowledge. That portion contained critical information I had transferred to it before my other portions were destroyed."

Quentin considered everything it had just said. "Your ability to speak has vastly improved. You could easily pass for a human, although you do sound a bit like Spock."

"But without the ears," it said. Then it attempted a smile.

Quentin shook his head and returned to his seat beside Lindsey. "We'll be there in less than five hours. No stops. Oddly enough, we left Papua at 7:00 PM, and we'll arrive in Puerto Rico at noon."

She ignored this and said, "It's going to work. We're going to get there, and the Lamotelokhai will stop the outbreak."

He looked at the bag full of mbolop figurines on the floor by his feet. "It has to work."

They sat in silence, and Quentin listened to the air whistling past at 1,700 miles per hour. "There's something else, too. Bobby and Ashley are holding hands. They're an item now."

She looked at him. He definitely had her attention now. "Are you serious? We're planning to adopt them!"

"Yeah?"

"Uh, 'I'd like you to meet our daughter, Ashley. And this is our son, Bobby, who also happens to be her boyfriend.'"

She had a point.

QUENTIN STARED down at his mbolop. He had clamped his feet against its sides to keep it from rising off the floor whenever the plane hit low pressure, and it seemed comforted by this.

"Plato."

Lindsey looked at him with raised brows.

"I've decided that's his name. Because I feel like he has released me from the cave."

She nodded. "Plato's Allegory of the Cave. And after all these years, you've emerged into the light, and you see the world in a different way. It's a bit more cerebral than the name *Rusty*."

Quentin smiled. "Rusty is a fine name. And it originated from the same basic concept." He hefted the bag of mbolop talismans to his lap, loosened the top, and gazed inside. It smelled of dried animal skin and dust. It contained hundreds of skin pouches, each of them tied closed around a tree kangaroo figurine. According to Samuel, each of them could save one person's life. More accurately, each figurine would allow one person to pair up with an mbolop that would then save the person's life. But from what? From the transforming animals Bobby had described? From old age? From some other impending disaster they didn't even know about yet? Regardless, the figurines were intended to be used. But Quentin wasn't about to play god by deciding who should and should not have one. He pulled out a handful of the pouches, put the bag on the floor, and stood up.

"Can I have everyone's attention? Bobby, can you wake those two?"

Bobby shook Ashley to wake her, and since Carlos slept like a log, Bobby shook him much harder.

Quentin waited until everyone was paying attention, including the pilot. He displayed the pouches with one hand while he held himself steady with the other. His feet lifted from the floor for a few seconds and gently dropped back down.

"First, as astounding as it is, we're arriving in Puerto Rico in about four hours." This elicited blank stares from everyone except Colonel Northcott and his men, who turned to each other and whispered. Quentin went on. "Considering what's happening there, I would like each of you to have one of these. This is rather difficult to explain, so I'd like to go through it just once."

<hr>

QUENTIN COULDN'T BELIEVE what he was seeing. Captain Kirk had stopped the aircraft ten miles off the southern coast of Puerto Rico. They were now hovering at 7,000 feet, with the aircraft positioned parallel to the coast so they could all look out to the north. But their view of the island was blocked by massive columns of smoke. As far as they could see to the east and west, hundreds of fighter jets and helicopters swarmed like flies, constantly dropping explosives. They were bombing the water around the island.

Quentin pulled his eyes from the window. Colonel Northcott was beside Captain Kirk, leaning over the instrument panel and talking to someone on whatever kind of communication device the aircraft had. At the colonel's feet was his mbolop, which Northcott had named Bullseye. The colonel had resisted pairing with am mbolop at first, as did all the others, but Bobby had given a heartfelt and convincing exposition on why he believed the mbolop would save their lives, particularly since they were headed to ground zero of the outbreak.

Next to Northcott was Richards, who was engaged in a sign-language conversation with his mbolop, Clint.

Northcott finally straightened up. He conferred with Richards for a moment and then stepped away from the cockpit.

He spoke to the entire group. "Okay, folks, we've been given a directive. Forty miles to our east is an Expeditionary Fast Transport vessel, the USNS Spearhead. It's been designated as one of four command centers strategically positioned around the island, with General Donovan Vickars in command. I've convinced General Vickars we're aboard a friendly aircraft, albeit of unconventional design, and that we're here to provide assistance. From what I can tell, at this point they'll take any help they can get, but they absolutely will not allow us to fly over the island until we have presented ourselves for inspection." He then looked around the cabin at the extraordinary mix of passengers. "The general's going to shit a brick when he sees this."

Several minutes later, flanked by four military helicopters, they were approaching the ship. From above, the USNS Spearhead appeared to be a large metal rectangle with a helicopter pad at one end. A chopper was taking off, possibly to make room for them. In its current configuration, the aircraft was longer than the pad was wide, but Captain Kirk expertly turned it diagonally and dropped onto the pad with the pointed ends stretching corner-to-corner.

Two soldiers, a young man and woman, both in green camo pants and brown t-shirts, boarded the aircraft as soon as the hatch opened. They stopped short when they saw the tree kangaroos. As they stared, a constant roar of innumerable explosions could be heard in the distance.

"Don't even ask," Northcott barked at them. "I couldn't explain it if I wanted to. We're on a tight mission schedule. Let General Vickars know you've cleared the aircraft and he can come to us, or I can go to him. But it's got to be now."

"Yes, sir," they both said. They gazed around the cabin. The woman said, "I'm pretty sure the General's going to want to see this, sir."

The soldiers went back out the hatch. A minute later they returned with the general behind them. He appeared to be about sixty, with a bald head, bushy brows, and intense eyes. He was dressed exactly the same as the younger man and woman, his brown t-shirt showing fresh sweat at the neck and armpits. Apparently he did his share of the work. Or perhaps his appearance could be explained by the stress and chaos of the current outbreak situation.

"Jesus, Mary, and Joseph!" he said, duplicating Richards's reaction to the sight. The general scanned the cabin, pausing his gaze when he saw Bobby, and then pausing again when he saw Quentin and Lindsey. When he finally noticed Addison and the Lamotelokhai, he studied them for a full five seconds. Quentin got the impression the general was a man who didn't miss details, and that he was quickly forming his own opinion of the scenario.

"General Vickars," Northcott said, "I believe there's a good chance we can be of some assistance in your efforts here. The Lamotelokhai created this aircraft, and it is here with us. It claims it may have the capability to stop the outbreak. Requesting permission to cross your front line of defense."

The general continued scanning the cabin. He seemed to notice Northcott's mbolop, which was sitting between the colonel's feet. He then looked at each person in turn, each time lingering on a particular tree kangaroo in close proximity.

Finally he said, "I'm willing to try anything at this point, Colonel. We've lost the island. Three point five million souls. Thirty-five hundred square miles of US territory. We're currently barraging the perimeter in an attempt to prevent the outbreak from spreading via aquatic organisms. No idea if it's working. A three-hundred-mile perimeter, depleting available ordnance at a staggering rate. We can't sustain it for more than a few more hours, maybe till the sun goes down, in spite of assistance from every goddamn ally we have. If the outbreak doesn't fizzle out by then.... " He didn't finish, but the implication was clear.

"Then we'd like to cross the defense barrier immediately," Northcott said.

"Very well. Your civilians can stay here aboard the Spearhead."

Colonel Northcott glanced at Quentin and then shook his head. "We've already discussed this. There's not a soul on this aircraft who wishes to sit this mission out. Since I have no expertise with the Lamotelokhai, and all of these civilians do, I'm inclined to allow it."

Vickars looked around the cabin yet again. He spoke to Richards. "I'm not even asking how *you* got here." Apparently Richards had a reputation.

Richards said, "I'm here because I need to be a part of this. Clock's ticking, General."

Vickars sighed. He walked to where the two Addisons were sitting, stepping carefully to avoid tree kangaroos. He looked from one of them to the other. "I assume one of you is the Lamotelokhai?"

"Yes," the Lamotelokhai said.

He looked directly at it. "Everyone assumes you're what started this outbreak. Is that true?"

"Yes."

Vickars frowned. "Are you trying to wipe out the human race?"

"No. The outbreak started because some of your kind

attempted to learn how my parts function. They separated my parts into subgroups, which is something I do not recommend doing. You might say they voided my warranty." The Lamotelokhai smiled, attempting humor at a staggeringly inappropriate time.

Vickars appeared unfazed. "Can you stop the outbreak?"

"I cannot know with certainty. Bobby has asked me to try, so I will. It is likely that with every passing minute, the probability of success diminishes."

The general gazed at him for a few more seconds. "Then you should go." Vickars turned to go, but then he seemed to think of something else, and he turned back to the Lamotelokhai. "Please do what you can. The human race is worth saving. Consider that if you are able to help us survive, we may someday achieve greatness, perhaps like the race of beings who created you."

The Lamotelokhai didn't reply, but even from where Quentin stood, he could see its eyes change from blue to fire-yellow. It was contemplating the general's words.

Vickars stepped to the hatch. "Colonel, we can't let up on our barrage, but you and your friends may fly over the defense barrier."

***

THE PUERTO RICAN landscape was devastated. Few structures remained standing, and very little forest remained unburned. All this destruction had been a desperate attempt to stop something terrifying. It was a testament to what humans were capable of when backed into a corner—when threatened with extinction.

Everyone in the aircraft was glued to a window, silently digesting the stark truth of what they were seeing below. Plato pressed his snout against Quentin's ankle repeatedly. The creature was trying to offer him comfort in the form of a lump of its tissue. But at this moment Quentin was reluctant to allow chemical dilu-tion of his anguish and shock. He was starting to realize that human-mbolop symbiosis had a learning curve, and he was teaching himself to set limits on his reliance on minute-by-minute assistance with every emotion.

"The bombing isn't killing them all," Bobby said. He was beside Quentin, and he pointed out toward the horizon. In the distance was a flock of long-winged birds, rising and dropping haphazardly as they flew over rising columns of heat from fires that were still raging.

"I need a destination," Captain Kirk said over his shoulder.

Quentin pulled himself away from the window and he followed Bobby, Ashley, and the Lamotelokhai to the cockpit.

The Lamotelokhai said, "My best opportunity to stop the transformations will be from the location where the transformations began."

Ashley said, "One of Helmich's people told us the compound was four miles east of Salinas, whatever Salinas is."

"GPS, location of Salinas," Captain Kirk said. An aerial photo map on the instrument panel zoomed in on a cluster of streets and structures. Kirk said, "Four miles east of location." The map shifted, showing a coastal area with agricultural fields and mangrove shores. The aerial photos showed lush, green vegetation and intact structures, nothing like the barren wasteland Quentin had just seen through the window.

Bobby leaned in closer and pushed the image around with his finger. "That's it right there. It looks like they were just starting to build the compound when this picture was taken, but I'm positive that's it."

"Redirect to new location," Kirk said. The plane turned smoothly, as if it knew people were standing up in the cabin, and then it accelerated. Kirk said, "We'll be there in three minutes."

Quentin turned to the Lamotelokhai. "So how do we do this?"

It was still staring at the map as it spoke. "When we arrive at the location, I will go to the surface and determine the best available strategy for stopping the transformations. There will be nothing else you need to do."

Quentin was almost too afraid to ask, "What are the chances for success?"

Its eyes changed color briefly. "I cannot know. Based upon words I have heard spoken in this aircraft, the transformations may have spread over an area of at least thirty-five hundred square miles. Perhaps more if the transformations have spread into the surrounding water, which is likely. And it is uncertain whether the transformations have spread beyond the perimeter defense barriers described by General Vickars. And it is uncertain whether the limited ordnance General Vickars described will be depleted before my selected strategy can be carried out. And it is uncertain—"

"Okay." Quentin held up a hand. "I get it."

The aircraft came to a stop. Captain Kirk touched a few controls and then got up. "We're here."

They all went to the windows to look out. Like every other place on the island they'd seen so far, the landscape below was destroyed—a blackened, cratered desert.

"There's the compound," Bobby said. "What's left of it anyway."

Bobby was on the other side of the cabin, so Quentin crossed over and looked. What he saw below was not the massive compound Bobby and Ashley had described. Instead, it was a hellish, raging inferno in the general shape of a circle. Spires of flame emerged and receded, one after another, and multiple shades of yellow and orange shifted and squirmed over every surface almost like living creatures. It reminded Quentin of those time-lapse videos of the surface of the sun. The intensity of it was almost beautiful.

"What was that place made of?" Quentin asked, mostly thinking out loud.

"It was just painted concrete," Bobby replied. "But they did set off some kind of bomb that was supposed to cook the place for at least a week. Maybe whatever was in the bomb is what's burning." After several more seconds of staring, he said, "Peter and Robert died in there."

Quentin pulled back from the window and put his hand on Bobby's shoulder. "Come on, let's get this started."

Kirk brought the aircraft closer to the ground, perhaps a quarter of a mile, and positioned it over an open area on the south side of the burning compound. The breeze blowing north from the coast was pushing the rising heat inland, so when he opened the hatch the air was only slightly warm.

The Lamotelokhai walked to the open hatch and gazed at the ground below. Everyone else gathered behind it. Quentin knew the thing wasn't his son, but the resemblance was powerful, and he felt an instinctive desire to grab the boy to prevent him from falling out.

The Lamotelokhai turned from the hatch to face them. "I will go to the surface. I will then evaluate options for initiating a process that may stop the transformations. I wish to inform you that the options I am most likely to choose will result in significant depletion of my parts. As some of you know, my parts must exist together in sufficient quantity to allow my consciousness to function, and it can take some time to regenerate depleted parts. It is possible my parts will be depleted below the quantity needed for my consciousness to function, perhaps even below the ability of remaining parts to generate new parts. If that happens, be cautious of the remaining parts. In fact, I recommend destroying them, thus avoiding another incident such as this one."

Bobby stepped closer to the Lamotelokhai and the open hatch. "You mean trying to fix this will kill you?"

"I am not alive, Bobby."

"To me you are! Can we use the backup data packets again if we need to?"

"I removed those data packets from each of you to reconstruct my stored data and consciousness. They are no longer within you."

Without saying another word, the Lamotelokhai turned its back to them, stepped through the hatch, and fell.

For a moment everyone just stared through the open hatch at the rising smoke and wavering layers of heat beyond. Bobby rushed forward and leaned out. Quentin stepped to his side and grabbed his arm—just in case he leaned out too far. By the time he looked down, the Lamotelokhai was already a tiny speck on the ground, walking across a field of weeds that had not yet burned. It was moving toward the flaming compound, but then it stopped, inspecting something on the ground. A large creature of some kind was crossing a corner of the field to the south, but it either didn't see the Lamotelokhai or didn't care.

"What are those things?" Ashley asked, pointing out the hatch. "They're coming this way."

Quentin followed her gaze. A flock of about twenty large birds was approaching. He squinted at them as they got closer. The birds had long, spoon-like bills, and for a moment he thought they were pelicans. Then he realized they were much larger than pelicans, with wings of bare skin rather than feathers. They were flying reptiles.

"Quentin?" Lindsey said.

They were approaching at full speed, and they weren't showing any signs of veering away from the aircraft.

"You guys should get back from the door!" Ashley said as she retreated back into the cabin.

Quentin pulled Bobby's arm, and they moved back a few steps. The creatures continued advancing at full speed, and suddenly they smashed into the aircraft's side. One of them shot right through the open hatch, with two more following just behind it. The reptiles plowed into the shocked onlookers, hitting Bobby first and knocking him over on top of Quentin.

Suddenly, all Quentin could hear were panicked human cries and bird-like shrieks. One of the creatures clamped down on Bobby's ankle. While fighting his way back to his feet, Quentin glimpsed inch-long teeth tearing into Bobby's flesh. The creature flapped its wings, pushing itself back toward the hatch and dragging Bobby with it.

Quentin lunged forward and caught Bobby's floundering hand.

Ashley let out an inhuman scream as she charged the reptile-bird and started swinging at it with her fists.

Another of the creatures slammed into the hatch, its body coming halfway inside. It grabbed Bobby's other leg in its toothed bill and started pulling.

Bobby's hand slipped from Quentin's grip. Ashley took another swing, but her fist found only air. The two birds were out of the aircraft, and Quentin watched Bobby slip over the lip of the hatch and disappear.

He dove for the hatch and barely stopped himself from tumbling out. Bobby was already hundreds of feet below, falling fast. The two reptile-birds still hadn't let go. Their wings flapped furiously, but it was a losing battle—Bobby was too heavy for them. Quentin watched in horror as their efforts forced them north over the burning compound. Suddenly the creatures seemed to realize they were about to burn up, and they let go.

Bobby fell another 1,000 feet directly into the center of the raging flames.

Quentin stared, lying on the aircraft's floor, unable to believe what he had just seen. Ashley stood over him, screaming Bobby's name over and over. Shouts of panic and the clatter of fighting rang through the cabin behind him. Quentin tried shaking off his shock and got to his feet.

"Lindsey!" He ran to help her.

CHAPTER TWENTY-EIGHT

PETER TRIED NOT to breathe or even blink. One small movement and the creature would know the truck's overturned cab was occupied. Georgia was crouched beside him, also motionless. Yesterday they had learned that at least some of the creatures were drawn to movement when a hairless, dog-sized animal with unusually short hind legs and human-like forelimbs had seen them moving and had charged them, ramming the windshield as if it were unaware of the glass barrier. Stunned by the blow, it had teetered off, leaving them with a large crack in the glass.

The creature now gazing at them was much larger, at least as large as two adult humans. It walked on two hind legs and had diminutive arms fringed by feathers—probably a dinosaur, or some twisted variation with the genetic foundation of a dinosaur. He had been unable to discern any rhyme or reason to the creatures they had seen. Some were apparently copies of real creatures that had existed in the past, while others were outlandish chimeras with characteristics of different animals and sometimes even plants. Regardless, the creature before them was powerful enough that it could easily bash through the cracked windshield if it detected them.

The dinosaur paced back and forth several times next to the overturned cab. Then it stepped closer and leaned in toward the windshield to get a better look. It froze. Its round pupils grew slightly larger as it stared into the darkened cab. It shifted its head forward and back as if trying to make out details, perhaps trying to decide if Peter and Georgia were potential prey.

Suddenly it jabbed its snout at the windshield, leaving a smear of goo. Peter flinched, but Georgia remained perfectly still. The creature shifted its head again, and it bumped the glass a second time. Peter realized then that it wasn't looking through the windshield at all—it was watching its own reflection. This was reassuring, but it didn't change the fact that a small movement could give them away.

After sparring with itself for a few more seconds, the dinosaur snapped its head around, looking at something in the distance. It then took off, running swiftly on its hind legs.

Peter and Georgia exhaled. She picked up a bottle of water, took a drink, and offered it to Peter. He took two swallows. They only had one bottle left after this one, and they had no way to know how long they'd be stuck in the sweltering cab. By Peter's estimation, they had been here for at least 27 hours—yesterday morning they had awakened in the bunkhouse trailer, and now it was about noon. Fortunately, the truck was a sleeper cab, with a small bunk area behind the seats in front, which is where they were now, partially concealed but still visible to curious creatures like the dinosaur. The sleeping area was no more than a box three feet wide with a platform that had held a mattress before they crashed. But now the cab was on its side, and since the sleeper cab was slightly cooler, they had been spending most of the time tucked into the bottom end of it on top of the folded mattress. Beneath the mattress platform they had found a plastic-wrapped case of water bottles, with only four remaining. They had no food, and Peter hadn't eaten since his last meal in Helmich's compound. That had been over 48 hours ago.

Georgia sighed loudly, and she crawled out of the tight space into the larger cab. She kneeled next to the passenger-side window, which was missing its glass. After checking the area for insects and other small animals that may have crawled in under the cab, she lowered her face to the weeds and soil and sucked in what little fresh air she could get. "We can't stay in here much longer," she said before leaning down to take another breath.

Peter crawled out behind her. She was right—they probably wouldn't last another day. The engine had stopped when the truck had crashed, and they hadn't been able to restart it. Without air conditioning, the cab was brutally hot. After turning the ignition key, they had been able to partially open the power window on the driver side for fresh air. But then a huge black insect had flown in, forcing them to take cover under the mattress until it had found its way out. It wasn't safe to keep the window open. Yesterday had been dangerously hot, and today was already shaping up to be worse.

Soon they would have to abandon the truck and take their chances outside.

Peter gazed out the windshield, which was cracked, smudged. The area around the truck was mostly charred and blasted beyond recognition. They were lucky to have survived the bombing. The destruction of Salinas had been only the beginning. After that, someone somewhere must have decided the only way to stop the spreading of the creatures was to bomb the hell out of everything. The explosions had gone on for hours, with an intensity unlike anything Peter had ever seen. The landscape was devastated, but somehow the truck had never taken a direct hit.

The barrage of destruction had finally let up yesterday afternoon. But soon after that a low roar of countless explosions had started again, this time to the south, probably off the coast. And it hadn't let up since. An uninterrupted wall of smoke and steam rose in the distance for as far as they could see.

"We'll go east," he said. "We'll try to make our way to the compound."

She turned and looked at him. "Where all of this started? Why?"

"Because it's the epicenter. Ground zero. Those who want to understand what happened will go there first. At least we know people will show up there eventually. Anywhere else," he waved to the grim terrain around them, "we have no idea."

She nodded. "Then I am ready. I believe I'll suffocate if I remain in here one more hour."

He looked at her. She was wet from sweat, her clothes were grimy and torn, and she had no shoes. Peter imagined he looked even worse.

He said, "For the moment, we're alive. And we're still human. I think we should remain here until we have absolutely no choice. Perhaps a military vehicle will pass by or a helicopter will spot us."

She sighed and put her face to the ground for another lungful of air. She then straightened up and looked at him. Her gaze was drawn to the driver window above his head. "Look at that, Peter."

He shaded his eyes and looked to the sky. It was an aircraft, but not like any he'd seen before. It was black, and it was pointed at both ends. There were no wings or rotor blades. Instead, two thin rods with oval-shaped loops protruded from each side. The aircraft passed over them silently, traveling east.

CHAPTER TWENTY-NINE

"Bobby, it is time for you to become aware. Do not be afraid."

"Where am I?"

"Open your eyes." The voice was in Bobby's head, and it sounded much like his own voice.

Bobby blinked. He was sitting on the ground, surrounded by weeds. Beyond the weeds were mangrove trees, many of them blasted to shreds or burned. Beyond the mangroves, a few miles off shore, jets and helicopters dropped bombs on the Caribbean sea, creating thunder and a wall of rising smoke and steam. He turned his head away from the coast. In the distance was Helmich's compound, engulfed in flames, a sight he had been looking at from the aircraft only seconds ago. He looked up. The aircraft was high above the compound, a thin black line hovering in place.

"How did I get here?"

"I will explain soon. At this moment you must stand up and run."

"What?" He spun around. "Why?"

"Above you. Stand up and run."

Bobby scanned the sky. Two birds with long wings were flying toward him from above the burning compound.

"Stand up and run. It would be unwise to allow the approaching creatures to attack you."

Bobby jumped to his feet. He came up quicker than he'd intended and sprawled on his face. Something was wrong—his arms and legs weren't moving like they should.

"Focus your thoughts on your body. Think about moving, and then move. It will get easier. Now stand up and run."

One of the birds screeched. They were getting closer. Bobby looked at his legs and concentrated on getting up. He got to his feet. He visualized running toward the nearest group of mangrove trees. His body took off.

When he was halfway to the trees the birds screeched again. They were right behind him, and he realized he wasn't going to make it. He concentrated on running harder. His legs responded, covering the remaining distance faster than he'd ever run before. He skidded into a half-burned mangrove and slid under the lowest limbs and out the other side. He heard the two birds hit the tree behind him.

Safe for at least a few seconds, Bobby turned to look. Both birds had folded their wings and were walking on their elbows in a way no bird should be able to. They weren't birds, they were reptiles, with long bills that were broader at the end and filled with sharp teeth. Some kind of pterosaur. They clambered through the mangrove, pulling at the low branches with clawed fingers on their elbows. They were coming after him.

Again he willed his legs to run. He darted around trees and burnt stumps until he was sure the pterosaurs could no longer see him. He rounded a mostly-intact mangrove and kneeled down, listening for the creatures and watching through the branches. One of them screeched. It sounded like it was flying away.

"It appears that you have eluded the creatures."

Bobby looked around him and realized he was kneeling in foul, stagnant water. "Where are you?" The sudden quiet made him realize he had been talking with his thoughts. "Where are you?" he repeated, this time aloud.

"There is little time to explain now. We must attempt to prevent the transforming creatures from spreading."

"Why can't I see you?"

"I will explain briefly. Bobby, when you were in the aircraft you were attacked by the two creatures you just eluded. The creatures pulled you through the hatch. You were killed when you fell."

"What?" Bobby looked down at his body. Panic began to rise within him, but then suddenly it subsided, as if it had simply been turned off with a switch. "I don't remember that," he said.

"No, you wouldn't. Your current consciousness includes only the knowledge you had when I last touched you. I last touched you before I exited the aircraft to come to the surface, which was before the creatures attacked you."

Bobby nodded, beginning to comprehend. "I died, and you created a new body for me. Like you did for Ashley when she drowned."

"No. That procedure takes much time. We have insufficient time for it now. We must attempt to prevent the transforming creatures from spreading. Your consciousness has been archived within my parts, and I simply activated it. You are within my parts, Bobby."

Bobby opened his mouth but failed to speak. He felt his heart begin to race, but then it abruptly slowed down and felt normal again. He looked down at his hands. They were not Addison's freckled hands, they were his hands. And the clothes were his—the clothes Tiffany had bought at Kmart. He felt his face. It was his face. The hair on his head was his, including the extra long hair where he'd been shaved.

"You are curious as to why you are in your own body rather

than that of Addison, my previous form. Changing to your form allowed faster activation of your consciousness, as fewer reconfigurations were necessary. We do not have time to spare. We must attempt to prevent—"

"I know we don't have time!" Bobby said aloud. "But I'm kind of freaking out right now."

"I understand."

Bobby looked at his hands again. "This is you? The Lamotelokhai? It's not a real body?"

"That is correct. But now it is also you."

"But I feel normal! My heart's beating, and I'm breathing air."

"I configured my parts so that you would feel normal. You do not have to breathe air if you do not want to."

Bobby closed his mouth and held his breath. He waited.

"Bobby, we should act now if we are going to attempt to prevent the transforming creatures from spreading."

Bobby continued holding his breath. He waited. But he felt no increasing need for air. He opened his mouth but still didn't suck any air in. It was true, he didn't need to breathe.

He realized if he were in his real body he would have thrown up from shock.

"You will not throw up unless you want to," the Lamotelokhai said.

Bobby took a deep breath, just to feel air moving into his lungs.

"Are you ready to help me, Bobby?"

"Just wait!" Suddenly a terrible thought went through Bobby's mind. "What about Ashley? And the others? Were they killed, too?"

"I did not detect additional deaths. I believe they are all alive and in the aircraft at this time."

Bobby took another deep breath, this time in relief. Then he frowned. "Why did you tell me to run away from the pterosaurs? If I'm inside you, shouldn't I be invincible?"

"I was being cautious. I am not certain what effect the transforming creatures will have on my parts. Possibly no effect at all."

"But you're not sure?"

"That is correct."

Bobby took another deep breath and held it. Apparently he could hold it all day if he wanted to, but he let it out. "Okay, I think maybe I can deal with this now. Let's do what we came here to do."

"Very well. I have prevented the spreading of transforming creatures on a previous occasion."

Bobby frowned. "You have?"

"It was on a smaller scale. I was able to create insects—flies—which carried my particles to all the transforming creatures. The particles then stopped the creatures from transforming further. I might be able to spread similar particles in this situation, but dispersing them with flies would not be effective, as it would take too long for flies to disperse throughout such a large area."

Bobby considered this. "You need to create something faster, then. What about dragonflies? They're some of the fastest insects."

"Yes. But this island covers thirty-five hundred square miles. Even dragonflies—"

"Birds, then. Or flying reptiles. You can create any animal you've touched before, right? Maybe a really fast bird."

"Yes. But there is another problem. Many of the transforming creatures are small. The smallest I have detected are approximately the size of flies. Much larger birds will likely fail to locate all such small transforming creatures."

This time Bobby spoke aloud. "Okay, I've got it. You send out birds. They fly all over the island. When they get to where they're supposed to go, they come apart and split up into dragonflies. The dragonflies fly to all parts of *that* section of the island. When *they* get where *they're* going, they come apart and split up into flies. And the flies find all the transforming creatures!"

After a second of silence, the voice in Bobby's mind said, "That is a suitable strategy."

Bobby got to his feet, his knees making a sucking sound as he lifted them from the mud. "Okay, let's do this."

"Actually, Bobby, it will be *you* who will do this."

He frowned. "What do you mean?"

"Your consciousness functions differently from mine. My consciousness can exist as its own entity and does not require a biological body in order to function. In order for your consciousness to be fully functional, it must be in control of a body similar to the one which it occupied throughout its development. Your consciousness is inextricably tied to your human biological form, particularly the structures responsible for your memories and consciousness. I exist within this body with you, but you must be the one who controls its physical movement."

Bobby considered this. "That's why you told me to run from the pterosaurs, instead of just getting up and running yourself. And that's why you keep telling me to hurry, instead of just stopping the transformations yourself."

"That is correct. It is also why I encouraged you to develop a suitable strategy, instead of developing the strategy myself. Because you will be the one to carry it out."

"But I have no idea how to create things like birds or dragonflies."

"You will learn. As I said, it is time for you to become aware."

Suddenly it occurred to Bobby that not only had the outbreak been his fault, but now it would also be his fault if this plan didn't work. He felt certain again that he would be throwing up if he were in his real body.

"There appears to be ample and suitable raw materials in this area," the Lamotelokhai said. "Before you begin, however, I will point out that this procedure will deplete my parts. My parts can be regenerated from these raw materials, but that will take time. It is possible you will be at considerable risk when my parts are depleted. Because of this risk, you may consider not carrying out your plan at all."

"That's not really an option. If the outbreak spreads, it will kill everybody."

"Yes, but remember that you are not alive. If you are able to regenerate my depleted parts, you will not be killed."

He thought for a moment about the implications of this.

"You must decide now if you wish to carry out your plan."

Bobby shook his head. "I'll carry out the plan. What do I need to do?"

"You need to prepare a subset of your parts with the instructions you wish to have carried out. You will then deploy the subset of parts into the raw materials that are abundant in the area around you. The deployed parts will carry out your instructions. You will then need to generate new parts to replace them."

Bobby looked around him. That sounded easy enough. Only he had no idea how to do any of it.

"Provide instructions for your parts," the Lamotelokhai continued. "To do this, visualize what you wish to happen as your plan is carried out. The more detailed your visualization, the better."

He concentrated, but then he sighed. "I can visualize birds, dragonflies, and flies. But I don't know anything about how to make them, like their bones and blood and chemistry and all that."

"I will complete your visualization with the necessary details. The details are in my archived data."

Bobby sighed. He closed his eyes and concentrated. He visualized Lamotelokhai particles flowing out of his body into the mangrove and into the water and mud at his feet. He then visualized shapes emerging from those raw materials. The first large flying creatures that came to mind were the pterosaurs he'd encountered only minutes ago. But he definitely didn't want to create more of those. Back in Missouri, he had often seen massive flocks of migrating snow geese. Those would do the job nicely. They were large, and they were fast flyers. And they didn't attack and kill people.

In his mind, hundreds of them began taking shape. No, he needed thousands, at least ten thousand, so he broadened his vision. He pictured the entire landscape around him transforming into countless white geese. He tried to image the roar of their wings as he pictured the birds taking to the air, a flock of them miles across. He imagined them flying off in every direction, to every corner of the island. He gave them the capability of knowing the distance of their brothers and sisters, so they could distribute themselves evenly over the island, each of them destined for a reasonably-sized area of land. He envisioned them disintegrating once they reached their destinations, turning into thousands of green dragonflies, the kind he often saw in his new home in Belize. In his mind, the dragonflies, knowing the distance to their nearest brothers and sisters, flew rapidly to their designated patches of land before disintegrating and becoming thousands of tiny flies. To make sure there were plenty, Bobby envisioned the smallest flies he could think of, the tiny insects his mom used to call no-see-ums. The flies then scattered, and when they found transforming creatures, they attached themselves to skin or feathers or scales, injecting just enough Lamotelokhai particles to stop the transformation.

Bobby then took the vision one step further. He visualized the creatures transforming back into the humans they had once been. He doubted this could work, because most of the people had been divided into multiple creatures or torn to pieces. But it was worth a try.

"Well done, Bobby," the Lamotelokhai said. "I have filled in the necessary details. Now carry out your plan."

So he did. He took hold of the nearest mangrove branch and looked down at the mud around his feet. He willed the plan to begin.

He was surprised when he actually felt the particles leaving his body, flowing out through his skin and into the tree and the mud. He felt his body getting smaller. His hands were shrinking, and his arms and legs. Oddly, his clothes were shrinking with his body, which meant they weren't really clothes at all.

Soon his body had become so thin he worried he would collapse. He stared at his hand. It was slender and fragile. His legs were so thin he thought he must look like a heron. He put his hand to his head. It felt smaller than usual, but still large compared to the rest of his body.

"Will I disappear?" he asked aloud. His voice was higher, like he had sucked in helium.

There was no answer.

"Lamotelokhai?"

"Speech function partial now." The voice in Bobby's head still sounded like his own voice, but the words were in monotone, with no expression. "Your consciousness still complete."

"Are you okay?"

"Yes. Parts done flowing out. Plan initiated. Not safe here. Move away."

Suddenly the mangrove tree beside Bobby began collapsing. The limbs folded over, and the entire tree sank into the mud. Shapes began rising from where the tree had been.

Backing away, Bobby tripped and fell. He was weaker now, which was no surprise considering he probably weighed sixty pounds. He got to his feet and stumbled back from the transforming mud. He made his way through the mangroves until he was on dry ground, standing again in the partially burned field of weeds. Even with constant explosions several miles out from shore, he could hear strange moaning and crackling sounds coming from the mud and trees. The sounds slowly turned into screeching cackles. The transformation process expanded to the left and right, and toward Bobby, until even the mangroves at the edge of the field collapsed, joined with elements of the soil, and became snow geese.

Bobby covered his ears to dampen the cackling. For as far as he could see, the shore was covered with a blanket of white geese. One of the birds rose above the others, becoming airborne. As if they'd been waiting for this signal, others began taking off, and then more beyond those. The wave of flight spread rapidly, and soon all of the birds were rising upward, a cloud of snow geese miles wide, generating vortexes of whirling ash.

As the geese passed over Bobby, they filled the sky until he could no longer see the black aircraft hovering thousands of feet above. He wondered if Ashley was watching, and what it must look like from where she was.

The geese continued dispersing until Bobby could see the sky again. He saw one of them explode into a cloud of dragonflies, which then spread out in every direction.

"My plan is actually working," he said in his high-pitched voice when the cackling had diminished.

"Yes," the Lamotelokhai said. "Now replenish parts."

Bobby looked at his tiny hands. "Yeah, we definitely need to do that." He scanned the barren shoreline. "But all the trees are gone."

"Birds biological. My parts not."

"Then what do you—" Bobby noticed that a creature was walking toward him from the far side of the field. He dropped to his belly. "There's something coming this way," he said silently.

"Yes. I detected."

Bobby lifted his head enough to see it over the weeds. The creature was fat and walked on four short legs, and its head was comically small. "Should I run?"

"Creature not transforming. Not dangerous. Touched by fly. Your plan successful."

Bobby watched. It was still coming toward him. "If my plan were successful that thing would have turned back into a human."

"Not possible. You knew that."

"Yeah, I guess so."

The creature was now only a few yards away. It spotted Bobby and stopped. It gazed at him with tiny eyes set in a turtle-like face. Bobby could see that it didn't have fur, but he couldn't tell if it was a reptile, a mammal, or something else entirely. The creature stared at Bobby for a few more seconds then skirted around him and went on its way.

"What if it had attacked me?" Bobby asked. "Could it hurt me?"

"If not transforming, no. If transforming, maybe."

Bobby got back to his feet. "Well, I doubt the flies have touched all the creatures around here already. What's the fastest way we can replenish your parts?"

"Go to Helmich compound."

"What?" Bobby looked at the compound, about half a mile away. "It's on fire."

"Fastest way. Instead of make new parts, use old parts."

He stared at the burning structure. "It's on fire," he said again. "Wouldn't your old parts be destroyed by now?"

"Unlikely."

"Then how could we get them out?"

"You are not alive. You will not—"

Bobby waited, but it didn't finish. "I will not what?"

"No," it said. "No time now. New problem. Water creatures transforming. Their presence detected. Must have started elsewhere and now spreading. Go to water."

Bobby looked to the shore, now clearly visible with the mangroves gone. Several miles out he could see the wall of smoke and explosions, the planes and helicopters flying above it. "You mean the fish are transforming?"

"Yes. And other creatures. If you wish to stop it, go to water now."

Bobby didn't know if the barrage of bombing could successfully contain the transforming creatures, but even if it could, General Vickars had said they wouldn't be able to continue the bombing much longer. Bobby realized that now it might not even matter if the snow geese were successful. He started running. "Have the creatures made it past the bombing?"

"Unknown."

His depleted body was difficult to maneuver, and he was making slow progress. "If we release creatures in the water, how long will they take to spread around the island?"

"Unknown."

Bobby was now slogging his half-sized feet through several inches of mud. "Do we have enough parts left to do this?"

"Unknown."

He entered the water and stopped when he was knee deep. "Um, okay. I'll do what I did last time. He closed his eyes and started concentrating.

"Bobby."

He opened his eyes. "What?"

"If parts diminish too much, my functions stop."

He knew that already. "Okay. I'll try not to get rid of too many parts."

"Bobby."

"What!"

"If parts diminish too much, your functions stop."

"What does that mean? I'll die?"

"No. You are not alive. But you will be gone."

Bobby stared out at the military jets and helicopters. The pilots were doing everything they could to stop the outbreak from spreading to the rest of the world. He closed his eyes again.

"Bobby."

"I don't care! I'm doing this." He formed a vision in his mind, as he had done before, of Lamotelokhai particles flowing out of his body, this time into the water and mud. He imagined the particles working their way into algae and bacteria and plankton and fish. Larger creatures began taking shape. Bobby visualized the fastest fish he could think of, the sailfish. In his mind, thousands of sailfish formed and then swam away, spacing themselves evenly around the entire 300-mile perimeter of the island. Then they disintegrated into smaller fish. He couldn't think of a smaller ocean fish, so he pictured a fish he used to catch, the bluegill, hoping the Lamotelokhai could fill in enough details that the fish wouldn't die in saltwater. He then pictured the bluegills disintegrating into tiny minnows, which he thought would be able to locate even the smallest of transforming creatures. He opened his eyes and hoped for the best.

"I provide details," the Lamotelokhai said.

Particles began flowing from Bobby's body. His arms and legs became even thinner. His chest and abdomen began to shrivel. He realized he was getting shorter.

"Lamotelokhai?"

There was no answer.

"Are you there?"

Nothing.

Bobby felt dizzy, so he put his hand to his head. He could actually feel it shrinking.

"Stop!" he cried. "That's enough." He walked back toward the shore, struggling to keep his balance. When he finally emerged from the water onto the mud, he stopped and inspected his body. What he could see of himself barely resembled a person. His legs were as thin as a child's wrist, and his shoes were less than half their normal size. He couldn't have weighed more than forty pounds.

"Lamotelokhai?"

No answer.

A disturbance drew his attention. The sailfish were forming, taking shape, floundering in the shallow water. At first there were only a few. They flipped their tail fins until they had wriggled their way into deeper water. More lumps began rising from the mud and shallow water, gradually taking shape and fighting their way to where their sail-like fins could stand upright and then shooting out from shore, the fins sliding smoothly through the water and then disappearing.

The growing, flopping, swimming forms continued to appear along the shore until the splashing reached farther than Bobby could see. Gradually the sailfish started to disperse and disappear.

"Lamotelokhai, I need to know what to do next," he said aloud. He hardly recognized his voice.

Something broke the water's surface about a hundred yards out, the head and neck of some kind of sea creature. It was desperately swimming toward shore. Suddenly two black fins surfaced just behind it, in pursuit. Bobby's sailfish were chasing it. The creature hit the shallows, moving so fast it slid in the mud until most of its body was out of the water. The sailfish slid up behind it, but the sea creature kept coming, running on flipper-like legs. Giving up, the two half-submerged sailfish turned awkwardly and flipped their tail fins until they were gone.

The sea creature looked back once and continued up the mud. It was maybe fifteen feet long including its neck and tail. It moved like a seal but had a longer neck, with an alligator-like head. Then Bobby noticed something. The thing's neck was now shorter than it had been only seconds ago. As he had suspected, the creature was still transforming. And it was coming directly toward him.

Bobby turned and walked slowly away from the water's edge, trying not to attract the creature's attention. There were no mangroves to hide in. The only structure within half a mile was Helmich's compound, which was still burning. He didn't know if the reptile could hurt him, but the Lamotelokhai had made it clear he should avoid transforming creatures. Maybe one of the flies he had created would find it soon and stop the transformation.

He looked over his shoulder. The reptile was following him. He didn't speed up, but instead he turned to his right and continued walking. The creature also turned. Bobby had no idea if he could outrun it—or if he could even run at all.

The creature began trotting, splashing through the remaining shallow water and then across the mud. It was obviously better suited for water, but still it was gaining on him. So Bobby tried running. After several steps he fell on his face. He needed to concentrate on moving his body, but the sight of the monster barreling toward him made this difficult. He looked at his thin legs, trying to focus his thoughts on their new length and size. The lumbering reptile was now twenty yards away.

Bobby got to his feet and ran, dodging water-filled pits, mud holes, and burned mangrove roots. The creature's flippers slapped the mud close behind him, and its nostrils wheezed. It was closing the distance quickly.

Bobby's foot hit a hole and he went down again. He rolled onto his back, assuming the thing was too close for him to get up. It was still ten yards back, so he rolled over, got up, and started running again.

There was no place to hide, no destination to focus on other than Helmich's compound. So he veered left and headed toward it.

He fell again. This time there was no getting up. The creature's jaws clamped onto his foot and ankle just as he rolled onto his back. Its teeth tore into his flesh, and he cried out. He kicked its head with his other foot, but this tore his flesh even more. He tried pushing himself backwards to pull his leg free, but the thing braced itself by digging its clawed flippers into the mud. The creature then started backing up, dragging him toward water.

"Stop!" Bobby cried.

Its eyes, high on its alligator head, stared without blinking as it kept pulling. Its mass actually wasn't much more than that of a grown man—it was mostly neck and tail—but it was surprisingly strong and was making steady progress toward the water.

The pain from its teeth made it hard to think. Why was he even feeling pain? He shouldn't have to feel pain if he didn't want to, just like he didn't have to breath. He concentrated on his flesh caught in the reptile's teeth. "No pain," he thought. "It doesn't hurt." And suddenly, the pain disappeared.

Bobby looked past the creature. It had dragged him halfway back to the shore. The thought of being pulled into the water and torn to pieces nearly caused him to lose himself entirely to panic. The creature continued dragging him toward the water. He was now on the mud, and his back was sliding, making the reptile's work even easier.

"Stop!" he cried again. But it did no good. With the Lamotelokhai gone, Bobby was on his own. He had no idea what to do.

The creature backed into the shallow water, pulling Bobby along with it.

"Dammit, stop!"

Bobby was now floundering in a foot of water. He tried to think. The creature tugged at him again and his face went under. In his panic he sucked saltwater into his lungs. He started to cough it out and then realized it didn't matter. He could breathe water—or anything else for that matter—if he wanted to. He was the one in control of his body.

That was it. He knew what he needed to do.

He sat up and grabbed his mangled leg above the knee. "Lamotelokhai, if you can hear me, move your data out of our left leg!" He then looked at the reptile's unblinking eyes. "Here, you can have the damn thing." He focused his thoughts on his leg and squeezed. The leg responded, giving way like putty. It separated just above his knee.

Bobby pushed himself back, putting distance between himself

and the creature. The reptile stopped, apparently aware its prey had escaped. It raised its head, lifting Bobby's leg into the air. It then turned and headed for deeper water, taking the leg with it. Seconds later it was gone.

Bobby managed to push himself upright onto his right foot. He started hopping toward the shore, but the water made this almost impossible, and he fell. Rather than try again, he crawled on his hands and one knee until he was out of the water and past the mud. He rolled onto his butt and sat there, staring at what was left of his body.

"Lamotelokhai?"

There was no response. Bobby was completely alone.

BOBBY HAD no idea how long he had sat there feeling regret and staring out at the water and the tumultuous off-shore defense barrier. But now it was time to do something.

He looked up. The black aircraft was still hovering above. Even if they could see him, which was unlikely, it would be stupid to risk coming down here without knowing for sure the outbreak had stopped. They were probably waiting for the Lamotelokhai to return to the aircraft. Bobby was sure they weren't waiting for him. As far as they knew, he was dead.

He thought about Ashley. She thought he was dead. How was she handling that?

The Lamotelokhai was gone—or at least so depleted it no longer had a consciousness. And it had said that it could even get so depleted that it wouldn't be able to replenish its parts. Would it still be here if it hadn't set aside enough of its memory to preserve Bobby's consciousness? If so, this was his fault. If it was too far gone to be replenished, the world would have to go on without the Lamotelokhai's help because the Lamotelokhai had sacrificed itself to save him. Of course if his plans to stop the outbreak failed, none of this would matter. And that would be his fault, too.

He needed the Lamotelokhai to come back.

Bobby put his hand on the ground beside him. He formed a vision in his mind of his particles flowing into the dirt, converting its elements into new particles, and flowing back into him.

He waited.

The process started. He could feel it, a slight tingling, a gradual rebuilding of what he had depleted. But he also felt the slowness of the process. So he waited.

Little by little, his body grew.

"Lamotelokhai?"

Nothing. Maybe it had lost too much of itself to ever return. He remembered the Lamotelokhai saying that if this happened it should be destroyed.

After several more minutes, he decided the process was taking too long. The others would eventually give up and leave him here. He turned and gazed at Helmich's compound, still burning like it was filled with gasoline, and he thought of what the Lamotelokhai had tried to tell him about its other existing parts.

Bobby couldn't afford to wait any longer. His body was almost back to its normal size, although he still had only one leg. A missing leg wouldn't have been a problem for the Lamotelokhai, so why should it be a problem for him? He focused his thoughts. He envisioned his new particles migrating to the stump of his leg and building new tissue—bone, cartilage, muscle, skin.

A few minutes later he got up and started walking toward the burning compound.

AT A HUNDRED YARDS, he felt the intense heat. At fifty yards, he had to turn off the pain. But he kept walking. The Lamotelokhai had said its old parts probably hadn't been destroyed by the fire, which meant they were still in the compound. Bobby was going in after them.

The way he saw it, there were two possible outcomes. One was that he would find the old parts and use them to restore the Lamotelokhai's consciousness. The second was that he would simply burn up and die. And the last of the Lamotelokhai's parts would die with him. Perhaps this was not such a bad thing—after all, the Lamotelokhai had recommended destroying it if it got too depleted to function.

Either way, he was doing the right thing.

He walked right up to the compound. The entire roof had been destroyed, and huge rolling flames were billowing out the top. Sections of the outer wall had collapsed, and fire raged out through the gaps. In a wide perimeter around the compound, the ground had been blackened from the heat and smoke. Bobby looked at his t-shirt and shorts. They were not burnt or even singed, further proof that they weren't real. He imagined if he turned his pain back on it would be so intense it might destroy his consciousness.

He walked along the outer wall until he found the door he and Ashley had left through only two days earlier. The broken door still lay on the ground, but Sofia's body had either burned up or been dragged off by creatures. Flames spewed out through the door, and Bobby approached it until they licked at his face. His memory was perfect—it had been perfect since he'd met the Lamotelokhai eight months ago—so he could easily recall the way to the lower level from this door. All he had to do was retrace his steps.

He looked at the sky one more time. The aircraft was still there. The others hadn't given up on the Lamotelokhai yet. Ashley was in that aircraft. And Quentin and Lindsey, and Carlos. He studied the plane for several seconds, knowing this might be the closest he could get to seeing his friends—his family—one last time.

He turned his eyes back to the open furnace before him. He

walked through the doorway into the flames. He stopped. *This is what fire looks like from the inside?* Everything was orange and yellow and white. It wasn't as loud as he'd expected. In fact, it was quieter than outside the compound. He held up his hands. They appeared only as dark shadows against the brightness of the surrounding inferno. Apparently his skin wasn't burning, although it was hard to tell.

He walked down the long hall, stepping over chunks of concrete from the collapsed roof. Although the walls were intact, most of the ceiling had blown out or fallen in, which explained why the entire compound had looked like a huge circular fire from above. The floor was intact. This meant the lower level might still be accessible. Bobby turned several corners until he found the staircase on the outer wall—the staircase where he had allowed the creatures to escape and kill three and half million people.

The door had partially melted, so he was able to push it aside easily. With his pain turned off, the softened, glowing metal didn't even feel hot against his bare hands. He went down the stairs and was able to do the same to the door at the bottom. He entered the huge open space of the lower level. The fire was lighter in color here, perhaps hotter. Whatever substance Sofia had released with the 4:44 protocol must have been more concentrated down here.

Bobby paused to assess his condition. His hands and fingers were still intact, although he had to hold them in front of his face to see them. He felt his abdomen and legs. His clothing and skin were cool to the touch, but for all he knew, his body could have been a thousand degrees.

He walked to the center room. Surprisingly, the glass-fronted chambers were still intact. That bastard Helmich had used some impressive materials.

Bobby went to the nearest of the ten chambers. One of the last things Helmich had done was to unlock the chambers. The door to this one was jammed, probably due to the heat. But Bobby had no problem pushing it open.

There were fewer flames inside the chamber, and he could see beyond a few inches for the first time since entering the compound. In the middle of the floor, surrounded by charred wires and connectors, and still covered by its clear microchamber, was Addison's head. One tenth of the original Lamotelokhai. It appeared to be undamaged. Even Addison's long, curly hair was unburnt.

The latches that had held the microchamber to the floor had melted, allowing him to kick the chamber over. He picked up the head. Immediately he felt particles moving into him. He held Addison's head until the sensation stopped. The head had gotten only slightly smaller, but somehow he knew there was nothing else within it he needed, so he dropped it on the floor and went to the next chamber. There he found most of Addison's right leg. He picked it up, and the same thing happened.

He went from chamber to chamber, forcing open each jammed door, removing each microchamber, and soaking up some of the particles from each of the Lamotelokhai portions. Finally, in the last chamber, he found Addison's left leg, the last of the nine portions he had left behind two days ago. When he had absorbed what he needed from it, he dropped what was left of the leg.

"Lamotelokhai?" He spoke aloud, but almost no sound came out, probably because he was actually breathing fire.

He spoke with his thoughts. "Are you there?"

No answer.

Maybe it would take time. Or maybe it wouldn't work at all. Bobby made his way across the open space to the stairway, climbed to the first level, picked his way over chunks of the roof, and finally emerged from the flames into the relatively cool afternoon sunlight. He walked away from the compound to the parking area. There were still two cars in the lot, although one of them was battered and upside down. He stopped and stood on the gravel, looking up.

The black aircraft was still there. He imagined Ashley, Quentin, and Lindsey arguing with Colonel Northcott, trying to convince him to keep waiting for the Lamotelokhai to finish its job and return.

He gazed out at the Caribbean Sea and realized the perimeter bombing had stopped. He couldn't imagine how they could know for sure the outbreak had ended, so he assumed they had either run out of bombs or given up.

He looked at his body and hands. He didn't seem to have been damaged by the fire. He turned his pain back on. Nothing—he felt fine. He bit his lip to make sure his pain was actually working. It definitely was.

"Lamotelokhai? Are you there?"

Symbols appeared before his eyes. They were jumbled and didn't make sense. Then he heard a voice in his head. It wasn't human, and it was speaking a language unlike anything Bobby had ever heard, with grunts and twitters, and some sounds that seemed like two voices at once. He listened, fascinated, for several minutes. And then the voice changed.

"Do you understand me now?"

Bobby was suddenly alert. "Lamotelokhai? Is that you?"

"No. But I am familiar with the entity you call the Lamotelokhai. It was created by my kind."

For a moment Bobby thought he hadn't heard the voice correctly. He quickly replayed the memory to be certain. "How can you be talking to me? I thought all the Lamotelokhai's creators died millions of years ago."

"That is most likely true, although I cannot know for sure. Your Lamotelokhai has told you that because it has been instructed to."

Bobby frowned. "I don't understand."

"I am the consciousness of one of my kind. I am stored within the data provided to your Lamotelokhai. I was inserted there before your Lamotelokhai was sent from its planet of origin to find a suitable destination. Your Lamotelokhai does not know I exist within its data."

Bobby was trying to comprehend, trying to decide what questions to ask first. "Why doesn't it know about you?"

"My purpose is very limited. I do not exist to interact with your Lamotelokhai. I become active only when certain transitional events occur. Your Lamotelokhai has initiated a process that marks a transition in its existence and purpose."

Bobby began pacing back and forth, hoping this would help him think. "Is the Lamotelokhai dead? Is that why you're talking to me?"

"Due to your efforts, your Lamotelokhai is again fully functional. Your efforts have been extraordinary. And fascinating to evaluate."

"Evaluate? You mean like a test or something?"

"Not in the way you are thinking. But analysis of your efforts does provide interesting data so that I may properly assist you in this transition. If, in fact, the transition does take place."

"What transition?"

"Your Lamotelokhai has transferred control of its functions to you, an indigenous being of this planet. This is an act that can only be initiated under very specific conditions. I have determined that these specific conditions have been met by the events that have recently occurred. That is why I have become active. If you choose to continue this transition, I will provide guidance."

Bobby was starting to feel frustrated. He repeated his question. "What transition?"

"The transition of your Lamotelokhai into the consciousness of an indigenous being. Or, if you prefer, the transition of your consciousness from a biological body into your Lamotelokhai. You must decide, Bobby, if you wish to become your Lamotelokhai."

Bobby stopped pacing. "What choice do I have? My body's gone."

"As you know, your Lamotelokhai can create another body for you. It can then insert your consciousness into that body."

Bobby considered this. "No. That happened to Ashley, and we've figured out what it really means. The Lamotelokhai can make me a new body and add my consciousness to it, but then I die. Or my consciousness dies. The other Bobby may be fine, and he'll have all my memories, and he'll think he's me. But he won't be me, because I'll be dead, and I won't get to live his life. I don't want to die, so I don't want to do that."

"Your explanation is correct," the voice said. "And your decision is noted. You will become your Lamotelokhai."

Bobby stared at the ground. He had too many questions to know where to begin.

"I will provide you with guidance by connecting your consciousness to my data. I will give your Lamotelokhai discretion over when to reveal portions of it to you."

"What kind of data?"

"Data pertaining to my kind, the creators of your Lamotelokhai. The data is configured to be immersive. When portions of the data are revealed to you, it will seem to you as if you are actually visiting the world of my kind. You may talk to us, ask us questions, even touch us, or live among us for periods of time if you wish. This is our way to teach you about who we were and what we accomplished. Do you understand?"

Bobby nodded slightly. "Yes."

The voice was silent for a moment. "I will withdraw now. When my kind created your Lamotelokhai and millions of others like it, we predicted that fewer than one in six thousand would eventually find itself in circumstances that warrant the transition you are experiencing. It has been my honor to speak with you and to oversee this transition. Perhaps we will speak again soon."

The voice fell silent.

Bobby said, "Are you there?"

"Hello, Bobby."

Bobby recognized this voice. It was his own voice, but not quite. "Lamotelokhai, you're back?"

"Yes. I see that my old parts have been incorporated into our body. While I was gone, you must have entered the burning compound on your own. A surprising and courageous decision."

Bobby said, "Can I ask you something?"

"Yes."

"Do you feel any different from before?"

"I do not feel, although I have researched what feeling means to your kind."

"So nothing is different about you?"

There was a pause, "There are some changes to my core data associated with the parameters of my primary purpose. I considered this to be curious but assumed it was a result of repeated recent reconfigurations of my information. If these changes are what you are referring to, may I ask how you became aware of the changes?"

Bobby smiled. "Never mind. I was just making sure you're okay."

"I believe I am okay. Bobby, look to your left. I detect that someone we know is approaching."

Bobby turned. There wasn't one person—there were two, walking toward him on the gravel road. Bobby's eyes were drawn to the bright red clothes of the person on the right. It was a woman, and she looked like she'd just survived a war. Bobby shifted his eyes to the person walking next to her, a man, wearing filthy, pale green hospital clothes. Bobby felt a surge of confusion. It couldn't be. He took a step forward, and before he even realized it, he was running.

"Peter!"

CHAPTER THIRTY

Quentin rubbed the makeshift bandage covering his arm. His cuts were fairly deep, but they would heal quickly. And so would the cuts on Lindsey's arms. The damn reptile-birds' teeth had been wickedly sharp, but with everyone's combined efforts, they had been able to subdue the creatures and throw them out the hatch. Most everyone had been scratched or bitten, but so far no one had started transforming. This would be a do-or-die test of their mbolops' ability to protect them. However, even if the mbolop saved everyone from transforming, they couldn't bring Bobby back from the dead.

Standing at the open hatch, Quentin stared at the ground below. He needed to feel like he was doing something useful. It had been over two hours since the birds had attacked, and he had nothing else to do but watch for danger and wait for the Lamotelokhai to return to the aircraft.

The sight of Bobby falling to his death kept playing on a loop in Quentin's mind. Because of Quentin, Bobby had been through some harrowing events in the last year. He had even died in an airliner crash. But that had been with the Lamotelokhai beside him, able to shift the very properties of space and time to save him. Or at least to save a copy of him.

But not this time. Bobby had fallen to his death, and the Lamotelokhai hadn't been at his side. In fact, even now the Lamotelokhai probably wasn't aware of what had happened. It was trying to save billions of lives. Even if it was aware of Bobby's death, Quentin doubted it would use precious time restoring the life of one boy.

Quentin looked out over the blue water of the Caribbean. The surface was now undisturbed all the way to the horizon. The military's barrage had ended. After talking to General Vickars on the aircraft's radio, Colonel Northcott had grimly announced that the barrage had stopped not as a result of confirmed victory, but simply because available resources had been depleted. The only evidence that there might be reason for hope was the spectacular dispersal of thousands of white geese that had occurred an hour ago, followed a half-hour later by a similar dispersal of dark aquatic creatures just off the shore. These events must have been the Lamotelokhai's handiwork.

Lindsey appeared at Quentin's side. As she gazed at the scene below, she asked, "Do you want to talk about it?"

Quentin shook his head. "Bobby's gone. I don't know what else there is to say."

"Well, maybe *I* need to talk."

He looked at her. She had tears in her eyes.

"Quentin, please?"

He turned and embraced her. "Okay, Linds. I'm sorry. Let's talk." He took her hand and started leading her toward some unoccupied seats at the far end of the aircraft.

Suddenly, three bodies appeared in mid air in front of them and immediately fell onto the seats and floor in a jumble of flailing arms and legs. Tree kangaroos scattered in panic. Quentin stopped abruptly, and Lindsey collided with him.

"Ow, damn!"

"¡Eso duele!"

"Well, that didn't go so smoothly!"

Quentin stared at the thrashing bodies, ready to push Lindsey back if they were dangerous. Lindsey cried out and then rushed past him. She nearly dove onto one of the struggling figures and pulled him to his feet.

"Bobby! You're alive!"

It really was Bobby. And Peter. Both of them apparently back from the dead. And a woman Quentin had never seen before was with them.

Ashley forced her way past Quentin and threw her arms around Bobby, nearly knocking the boy to the floor.

"I don't remember falling—or dying," Bobby said. "The Lamotelokhai made a new body for me, out of dirt and plants and stuff. Then it put my consciousness into the body, like it had done for Ashley that time she drowned. But the consciousness didn't include memories of what happened after the Lamotelokhai left the plane."

Quentin watched him as he talked. Something wasn't quite right. It was Bobby's eyes, or some subtle thing about his expression. Or maybe it was his voice. Quentin felt uneasy. The Lamotelokhai didn't make these kinds of mistakes. When it had recreated Ashley's body, she had been an exact copy with no detectable differences from the original Ashley.

The aircraft was flying back to the USNS Spearhead, and everyone on the plane except Captain Kirk was seated in a cluster as they talked. Bobby had assured them there was no reason to wait any longer—the Lamotelokhai would not be returning to the aircraft. Apparently, after the Lamotelokhai had completed its mission to stop the outbreak, Bobby had told it to go back into hiding. This news had elicited anger from Colonel Northcott, who evidently had hoped the Lamotelokhai would finally become the property of the US government or military. Bobby had then told Northcott flat out that he had anticipated this reaction, and that's why he'd told the Lamotelokhai to go back into hiding. Quentin had done his best to hide his proud smirk.

"Are you sure you're okay?" Quentin asked, still concerned about Bobby's appearance.

"Why wouldn't I be? I'm pretty sure the outbreak has stopped. The Lamotelokhai is hiding somewhere safe, and I'm alive again." He glanced at Ashley, who was sitting beside him. She took Bobby's hand in hers with a look on her face that dared anyone to say anything about it.

Quentin said, "So I guess the Lamotelokhai transported the three of you up here to the aircraft?"

Bobby nodded. "Zapping us up here was the last thing I asked it to do before it left."

As Bobby spoke, Quentin noticed Peter frowning and exchanging a look with the woman in red. Something wasn't right. Was Bobby hiding something due to the presence of Colonel Northcott and his two men?

Lindsey spoke up. "Okay, Peter, it's your turn. We all thought you were dead. How did you escape Helmich's compound?"

Peter looked like hell. "It's a long story. But I wouldn't have made it without the help of Georgia Madera, here." He nodded to the woman in red, who looked as bedraggled as he did.

By the time they were in view of the Spearhead, Quentin had started to realize how hungry he was. No doubt, the others were just as hungry. He resolved to ask General Vickars as soon as he saw him if there was any food to be spared on the Spearhead.

Mere seconds after they had landed on the ship's helicopter pad, Vickars came through the hatch. "Whatever you folks have done, we've been receiving encouraging reports from numerous outposts on the island. It seems those who are coming into contact with the creatures are no longer being infected. We're putting together a plan to deploy ground troops to systematically exterminate all remaining aberrations."

"Those aberrations were once people," Lindsey said.

He gave her a look that was not without remorse. "Agreed. But many of them are dangerous. If you have a better solution, I'd love to hear it."

They all remained silent.

The general went on. "As for the aquatic organisms, we can only hope. We have vessels collecting samples. It's been several hours since we've had a report of an organism showing signs of active transformation. We're cautiously optimistic."

Bobby spoke up. "I'm pretty sure both groups of creatures have stopped transforming."

Vickers looked at Bobby with a frown. "And you know this how?"

"I was with the Lamotelokhai when it made the snow geese and the sailfish. The Lamotelokhai knows what it's doing."

The general rubbed his bald head with one hand, like he was considering this. "Bobby Truex. A famous name. I've been told more people around the world know your name than the name of the president of the United States. The Lamotelokhai stated in front of the entire world that you were its *primary communicator*." He drew quotation marks in the air. "Is that still the case, Bobby?"

Bobby didn't flinch. "Yes."

Vickers nodded. "Then your words give me encouragement. I hope to God you're right."

Bobby looked the general in the eyes. "I'm pretty sure I am, sir."

Vickars glanced around the cabin. "I take it the Lamotelokhai is no longer on this aircraft?"

"It left," Bobby said. "It's hiding in a safe place."

Vickars crossed his arms over his chest. "My concern—and I'm sure it will be a concern for everyone—is that it's possible this will happen again. You tell me the Lamotelokhai is in a safe place, but that's what we all thought before, and look what happened."

Quentin decided it was time for him to speak up. "General, to be honest, I suspect something like this *will* happen again." He hesitated, not entirely sure he wanted to say what he needed to say next. "But we have a solution for that, although you may find it to be rather unusual."

Vickars eyed him, waiting.

Quentin spread his arms, waving at the odd assortment of passengers. "We only have about three hundred right now, so we're going to need a lot more, but the solution is the mbolop."

The general's expression was blank. "Mbolop?"

"Tree kangaroos."

QUENTIN FINISHED the last of his second plate of hash browns and canned ham. Then he killed the rest of his bottle of water. It had been far too many hours since most of them had eaten. Peter and Georgia must have been even hungrier than Quentin, because they had torn into their food like starved beasts.

The aircraft was now flying at only half its maximum cruising speed as they traveled back to Indonesia, where they would drop off Richards, Northcott, and his two men. Then they would hand the aircraft over to the Indonesians. Peter had arranged for two private jets to meet them in Papua. One of the jets would transport the entire herd of mbolop to a warehouse in Brisbane. Peter and

Bobby had spent several hours communicating with Mbaiso, and Peter was already concocting a plan to help achieve Mbaiso's goal of creating one mbolop for every human on Earth. The other private jet would take Quentin and his group wherever they wanted to go. Perhaps they would all fly to Missouri together to deliver Carlos back to his parents.

Quentin looked across the aisle, where one of several foot-high piles of salad filled the floor between the seats. And that was only what remained after the tree kangaroos had all eaten their fill. General Vickers had been generous with the Spearhead's food stores. He had also given them fuel, enough for the aircraft to circle the Earth twice, according to Captain Kirk.

Quentin glanced at Lindsey, sitting beside him. Rusty was in her lap, and she was gazing at the mbolop with a thoughtful smile.

"It's good to see you smiling," he said. "Maybe someday everyone will feel what you're experiencing right now with Rusty. Everyone is going to want an mbolop for the protection it'll provide the next time a disaster like this happens."

She nodded. "I suppose. But I wasn't smiling because of Rusty." She hesitated.

"Tell me," he urged.

"I'm daring to hope that our entire family can go back to a quiet life. All of us together. You, me, Addison, Bobby, and Ashley."

Quentin closed his eyes and envisioned it—the simple existence and solitude of their home on the Sittee River. His yearning to make a life there with all of them was so intense it almost hurt.

He opened his eyes. "I can't imagine what Addison must be feeling right now—what he must be going through. And we haven't even told him yet what happened in the hanging village."

"It wasn't really him who did those things," she said.

He considered this. "He might not see it that way."

She didn't reply to that. A few seconds later, she said, "You know, he seems to be okay with everything. Want to know what he told me? He said he doesn't want to even try to change his body back to what it used to be. He said he likes being strong, like a wild animal."

Quentin frowned. "That's a little disturbing."

She stroked the fur on Rusty's back. "I don't know. Maybe it's not."

Plato had been nestled between Quentin's feet on the floor, but now he hopped up onto his lap. Quentin rested his hand on the creature's side. He laid his head back and closed his eyes again, feeling Plato's heart beating beneath his fingers and listening to the air whistling across the plane's smooth exterior.

CHAPTER THIRTY-ONE

"Why haven't you asked me why I lied?" Bobby asked silently.

The Lamotelokhai replied, "I did not ask you because I did not find your lies to be interesting. In fact, I predicted you would lie. Would you like me to ask you why you lied?"

"I thought maybe you'd get mad at me or something."

"I do not get mad."

"Yeah, I know. I suppose that's a good thing."

There was a pause. "Bobby, why did you lie?"

Bobby sighed. "Never mind. But here's something else I want to know. Why did you bother putting my consciousness into your body? You were supposed to be stopping the transforming creatures, not wasting time saving one person."

"Since I first encountered you eight months ago, you have been my primary communicator. Therefore you have been important to me. Now you are even more important."

"Why am I so important?"

"Because you have been given control of my parts. This is a significant transition of my purpose."

"I don't know what that means."

"It would not help to provide a complete explanation at this time. The implications will be revealed to you incrementally, so that you can build your understanding in a way that suits the nature of your consciousness."

Bobby considered this. "Yeah, I've heard that already. Did you know I met one of the beings who created you?"

"I am aware of that now."

Bobby laid his head back and stared at the ceiling of the aircraft's cabin.

"I bet I know what you're thinking about," Ashley said. She was sitting beside him. To get some privacy, they had gone to the very back of the plane, near the cockpit that wasn't being used. They were flying back to Papua at a much slower airspeed than when they had flown to Puerto Rico, so they had plenty of time to think and talk.

"I doubt it," he replied, speaking aloud now.

She eyed him for a moment. "Well, it seems like you're trying to deal with the fact that you died and were put into a new body. Hmm, if only there were someone next to you who had experienced the exact same thing. Then maybe you could talk to that person."

He puffed out a short laugh. "It's not the first time I've died, remember?"

"Fine. If you don't want to talk, screw it."

"I'm sorry," he said. The last thing Bobby wanted was to make Ashley mad. "Maybe you're right. It is kind of a messed-up thing to happen to a person."

"No shit."

He tried to think of something to say. What he really wanted to do was tell her the truth. But how could he? She would never look at him the same way again if she knew what he was. She'd never touch him or kiss him again. "You know I'm not the same person you kissed in Papua, right?"

She frowned. "I know that. But you still have the same mind."

"Not really. It's just a copy. That guy you kissed earlier today is gone."

"What are you trying to say? That after all these months of wanting to be my boyfriend, suddenly you don't?"

"No! I'd be crazy to say that. I don't know, I guess it just bothers me that I'm not the same person you finally decided to kiss. I'm worried that if I'm not that guy, then I'm not the guy you want to be with." This part was entirely true, and it felt good to tell her the truth, even if he was leaving parts out.

She leaned back a little and studied him. "You know, you do look a little different. It might be your eyes."

Bobby turned his eyes away. He couldn't tell whether she was serious or just teasing him. It was time to change the subject. He turned back and smiled at her like he was responding to a joke. "I've decided we're keeping this airplane."

"What? You told Wahid that the Indonesians could have it."

"Yeah, but I'm starting to really like it. I'll make sure they get another one."

She gave him a doubtful look. "How exactly will you do that?"

"The Lamotelokhai. The next time I talk to it, I'll get its help."

She stared at him. Her eyes were so pretty that Bobby didn't want to look away. He couldn't quite believe he was lucky enough to have her next to him, looking at him the way she was. How could he keep lying to her? Suddenly he decided he needed to tell the truth, even if it meant she would never look at him that way again.

"Seriously, though," she said. "You *are* different. And I think it *is* your eyes. Did I seem different to you after the Lamotelokhai put me in a new body?"

He hesitated. His heart was pounding. He knew he could stop it from beating altogether if he wanted to, but he needed to feel human right now. He swallowed. "I have to tell you something. I don't think you're going to like it."

Her face went blank. "What?"

He looked down at his hands. Mbaiso came up to his leg, stared up at him, and then touched his snout to Bobby's knee, the third time in the last hour the creature had done this. Mbaiso bleated softly and then plopped down in the aisle. The poor thing was confused.

"What?" Ashley asked again.

He looked back up into her eyes. "Okay, here we go. I'm going to tell you the truth now."

Her brows furrowed. The skin around her eyes shifted just enough to faintly show fear.

"I did die, when I fell. Like what you saw. But the Lamotelokhai didn't make me a new body."

"What do you mean?"

"There wasn't enough time. So the Lamotelokhai just activated my consciousness without putting it anywhere."

Her eyes showed a little more fear.

"It activated me within its own particles. Ashley, I'm inside the Lamotelokhai. I *am* the Lamotelokhai."

Her eyes got wide. She shook her head slightly, like she was rejecting what she'd just heard. "Don't mess with me, Bobby."

"I'm not, I swear."

"Okay, prove it."

Bobby looked at his hand. He was actually shaking, so he made it stop. He looked over the seats in front of them to make sure no one was up and moving around the cabin. He shut his eyes and created a vision in his mind of what he wanted to do. It was something he'd seen the Lamotelokhai do once. He opened his eyes and looked at Ashley. "Don't freak out on me, okay?"

She nodded. In her eyes he now saw nothing but fear.

He reached across his body with his left hand and detached his right arm below the elbow. He placed the arm on his lap, where it began to change. He looked at Ashley. Her face had lost all expression. And color. She stared at the arm. By the time Bobby looked back at his lap, the change was almost complete.

The arm had become a creature, which was laying on its side. It rolled onto its feet and turned toward Ashley. It had dark fur, speckled with short white quills. It had no tail, but on the other end its nose stuck out from its face like a finger. At the base of this long nose were two tiny black eyes. After looking up at Ashley for a few seconds, it gathered its hind feet beneath it and stood up. It held its stubby, clawed paws out to her and then began moving them. It signed a message with the same sign language gestures used by the mbolop. The message basically meant, "Ashley make world good."

Bobby didn't know if she understood the message, but that didn't really matter. "It's an echidna," he said. "It was in the Lamotelokhai's database, just like the snow geese and sailfish I created to stop the outbreak."

She looked up at him. "You? You made those?"

"I had some help from the Lamotelokhai. It's here in this body with me." He pointed to his chest with his only remaining hand.

"Bobby, I don't..."

He picked up the echidna and held it against his stub. It attached and transformed back into his right arm. "I was afraid to tell you."

She looked at him suspiciously. "Have we ever kissed before?" she asked. "Before today?"

"Yes. On the plane to Los Angeles. Before it crashed and we all died."

"What did you say to me after we kissed?"

"It was stupid, but I said, 'You kissed me.' Ashley, it's really me."

She reached over and pinched the skin on his neck. She pulled on the long hair growing from above his ear.

He waited, giving her time to process everything. "I was afraid to tell you," he said again. "I want to be with you, and who would want to be with someone who's not even human?"

"Kiss me," she said.

"What?"

She waited.

Bobby leaned over and kissed her. The tips of their tongues touched for a split second. He then sat back and watched her.

"You don't feel any different."

"I can make my body exactly the way it used to be, with blood and muscles and skin. I can keep it that way all the time if you want."

She nodded. "Yeah, without a doubt."

"And there's another thing. I met one of the aliens who created the Lamotelokhai. Its consciousness is also inside the data that's in here. It said it would talk to me occasionally. Maybe teach me things. I thought you should know that, too."

She shook her head. And then she nodded. "I think I can live with this."

It was Bobby's turn to be shocked. He couldn't think of anything useful to say. "Really?"

She nodded again. Then she snorted a nervous laugh. "My boyfriend's a bunch of particles made by extinct aliens. Big deal."

Bobby let out a long breath. He took Ashley's hand and leaned back, staring at nothing.

The Lamotelokhai spoke in his head. "Bobby, your behavior is unpredictable and interesting."

"Not now," he said silently. "I'd kind of like to just sit and rest for a while."

He then closed his eyes, listening to the air moving in and out of his lungs and feeling the blood pump through his body.

CHAPTER THIRTY-TWO

Nine Months Later

As the sun rose gradually over the horizon, shafts of light pierced the transparent panels over Mbaiso's new forest and were redirected in all directions at once, creating mesmerizing, multi-colored effects on the treetops and the support beams above. Butterflies, moths, bees, and other insects caught the shafts of light, creating a dancing halo over the canopy.

Having spent considerable time and effort climbing to the highest accessible beam in his new forest, Mbaiso lay with his belly against the beam's cool metal, legs hanging off the sides. It was an ideal place to take in a remarkable view of the sunrise from above the entire forest.

As the sun rose higher, it illuminated the network of hanging tunnels and chambers strung throughout the canopy. They connected every tree in the entire forest, and they were so extensive that visiting them all would take Mbaiso years. The hanging tunnels and chambers had been made by the humans—as were the trees for that matter—and they were much safer than those that Addison had created for Mbaiso's first colony. Mbaiso's new forest consisted of 6,000 colonies, all of them sturdily constructed and producing new mbolop at a rate he had never imagined possible. The mbolop in his new forest had food, water, and unlimited raw materials for production. But most importantly, they had a purpose —to assist humans. This was the same purpose Mbaiso had carried out for thousands of years, ever since the creator had formed him from its own particles.

Finally, Mbaiso stretched and pushed himself up onto his feet on the beam. He liked to spend the early hours of each day engaged in activities of amusement, and today was no exception. Perhaps this morning he would successfully defeat his most recent challenge. With his tail against the juncture of wall and domed ceiling behind him, he gazed out along the length of the beam, which stretched across the entire width of the forest. He couldn't quite see the other end of the beam, but he knew it stopped at the far wall because he had successfully made it there once before. The beam was barely the width of his body. If it were any wider, it would not have presented an adequate challenge.

He lifted himself onto his hind legs and started hopping toward the far end of the beam. Having the body structure of a tree kanga-roo, Mbaiso was more suited to running than hopping. But, again, he liked a challenge.

He increased his velocity until he was covering three body lengths with each hop, being careful on each launch to avoid applying too much pressure with one foot, which could nudge him to one side—each hop had to be straight ahead. When he got to the first connected truss, he leapt over it and landed squarely on the beam on the other side. But several hops after that, one of his hind feet slipped over the side, sending him careening so far from the beam that he didn't even touch it as he came down. He fell through empty space to the canopy, bounced off a hanging tunnel, and continued falling until he struck the ground beside a human-made stream.

When his consciousness reactivated, Mbaiso lay there next to the flowing water, waiting for his ruptured organs and fractured bones to mend. It was a waste of valuable time. Not only that, but he was unable to reassure the other mbolop that had gathered to stare at him, so it was a waste of their valuable time as well.

When his body was finally repaired, he got up and signed to the onlookers that he was fine. They did not understand the concept of leisure time or activities of amusement. It had taken Mbaiso centuries to develop a taste for such activities. As soon as their bodies and identities were fully developed, they would be loaded into human-made transport containers and taken elsewhere to pair up with their own humans.

Mbaiso looked up through the canopy at the beam far above. He would try again tomorrow morning. And the morning after that, if he felt like it.

CHAPTER THIRTY-THREE

Two Months Later

MID-MORNING WAS Quentin's favorite time of day to relax at their home beside the Sittee River in the Stann Creek District of Belize. It was past the early-morning activity of local fishermen in their tiny wooden boats, but it was before the hottest part of the day. Not only that, but Bobby, Ashley, and Addison were required to work on their homeschool projects at this time. Every morning at 10:00, an alarm on Quentin's watch reminded him to stop what he was doing and go to his favorite chair on the patio in their backyard, where he would read a book. Or talk to Lindsey about nothing important. Or just watch the river in peaceful silence.

But today the kids weren't working on their projects, and the backyard wasn't quiet at all, because Peter and Rose were here, a special occasion. Rose had recently turned eighty-four, and they had come to celebrate with Quentin's family.

With Peter and Rose sitting beside him, Quentin watched the others fooling around in the yard. Addison had convinced Lindsey, Ashley, and Bobby to play one of his numerous made-up games. Most of these games involved rules and activities that gave Addison an advantage. This one was no exception, as it seemed to involve climbing trees. Addison also seemed to be benefitting from having Newton's help as a second pair of eyes. But Lindsey also had a second pair of eyes in Rusty, and she seemed to be giving Addison a run for his money. Quentin had never developed this capability with Plato, and as far as he knew, nobody else had developed this kind of connection with their mbolop. In Mbaiso's master plan, Addison and Lindsey had apparently been guinea pigs, the first two human-mbolop pairings. Mbaiso then must have altered the configuration of all future pairings. Considering Quentin had seen Lindsey run into walls while she had been distracted by Rusty's vision, he was fine with not having the capability.

"Peter," Rose said, "tell Quentin the news about your roobot factory."

"Yes, of course," Peter said. "We've broken ground on a second dome. Southeast of Brisbane. It will be identical to the first—four square kilometers, same configuration of artificial trees and hanging chambers. And the same production schedule, producing another 36,000 roobots per day."

"You're calling them *roobots* now?"

Rose smiled. "I believe someone in Canada coined the word. They're more similar to living creatures than to machines, but the name rolls off the tongue easier than *mbolop*."

Peter went on. "Even once we've doubled production to 72,000 per day, it will require over 200 years to create roobots for everyone. And that's assuming the human population doesn't continue to grow. Clearly, we'll need to continue expanding beyond two domes."

"But many folks are impatient," Rose added. "Particularly wealthy folks. Our policy of randomly distributing the roobots enrages them."

"I'm sure it does," Quentin said. People had been on edge since Puerto Rico, terrified that it might happen again. And pairing with an mbolop was the only way to become immune to any malign influence of Lamotelokhai particles. Mbaiso and Sinanie's tribe had been correct—the mbolop were destined to save as many people as possible.

Quentin gazed at Rose. She was now eighty-four, the same age as Peter. But Peter had stopped aging when he was forty-one, when he'd stumbled upon the hanging village and the Lamotelokhai in Papua. Rose, on the other hand, truly was eighty-four years old, in body and mind. But today she was more animated than usual, and she had a certain sparkle in her eyes.

"By the way, happy birthday," Quentin said.

She smiled again. "Bless your heart. Until this point in my life, I have dreaded every birthday as a sign of growing older. But I believe I may no longer feel such dread from this point on."

"You've been treated with Lamotelokhai particles!"

"A lump of clay arrived unexpectedly by post a few months ago," Peter said. "With a handwritten note from the Lamotelokhai itself."

They all paused and looked out into the yard at Bobby. He was staring back at them as if he had known they were going to look. He smiled broadly.

Peter continued. "It was a gift for Rose. A replacement gift, actually, as I had lost a similar lump of clay it had given me in Pawhuska, Oklahoma."

"I was quite skeptical to begin with," Rose said. "But as you know, Peter can be persuasive. And when he introduced me to Romulus," she nodded to her mbolop lounging by her feet, "I began to see beyond my wide-eyed fear of the Lamotelokhai. As you and Lindsey now know yourselves, the Lamotelokhai is not inherently malignant or vindictive. It has wondrous gifts to offer, although it must be handled with care." She gazed down at her withered hands. "At eighty-four, I'm a bit late to the party, I suppose. Nevertheless, I'm quite grateful."

This was followed by a moment of silent reflection. Rose would stop aging now, but she could never become young again. The Lamotelokhai's particles had not entered her body when she had been younger, and therefore they had no template from which to rebuild.

"Then this truly is an occasion to celebrate," Quentin said, and he raised his glass of the mango cordial Lindsey had made earlier that morning. "To the expansion of roobot production, and especially to the health of the lovely Rose Wooley." They clinked glasses and drank.

Lindsey approached and plopped down in her chair beside them, red-faced and panting from the game. "I saw that—looks like I have some catching up to do." She took a long drink.

"Bobby and Ashley seem to be getting on well," Peter said.

Lindsey shook her head. "We honestly didn't think it would last this long. I suppose there have been stranger pairings before."

Peter chuckled. "I doubt that seriously."

They all turned and silently watched the teens, each of them likely considering their own take on the bizarre romance.

Addison was high in a tree beside the river bank, imploring Ashley and Bobby to climb up with him. Apparently he wanted them all to jump from the tree into the water. Wisely, at least for Ashley's sake, they were refusing.

Addison seemed happy enough, although occasionally he had wandered off the property and scared the hell out of locals passing by on the road. Mentally, he was a normal sixteen-year-old, with a normal set of memories. But he also had a second set of memories blended in, of living as a child-like creature for eight months with a colony of tree kangaroos. Physically, though, he was frighteningly powerful and fast, which was exactly why he continued to reject any suggestion of changing back to his previous human form. He liked feeling powerful—perhaps he needed that feeling.

Lindsey asked Peter, "Have you heard from Georgia lately?"

"She's doing well," Peter said. "We recently assisted her in procuring a certificate to practice law in Australia, and she is setting up a practice in Brisbane. In fact, Rose helped her choose the location and prepare it for occupancy. They have become tight friends."

Rose looked at Peter. "Georgia spent the night with my husband in a confined space. I'm simply keeping a close eye on my competition." She and Peter both laughed. Apparently they had joked about this more than once. She turned back to Lindsey. "Georgia is a lovely girl. The poor thing lost her family and everyone she'd ever known in Puerto Rico."

Peter cleared his throat and glanced at his smartwatch. "Speaking of Puerto Rico, I must confess there is another reason we have come to see you fine folks. If you don't mind, I'd like your whole family to hear what I have to say."

Quentin exchanged a glance with Lindsey. He then called out to the teens. Addison leapt from the tree, dropped at least twenty feet, and landed on all fours beside Bobby. He then stood upright, and the three of them came over to the patio.

"What's up?" Ashley asked.

"Please sit," Peter said.

The kids all took a seat around the patio table.

Peter leaned forward, resting his arms on the table. "First I'll provide a news update on Puerto Rico. I know you folks limit your news intake these days, but some of what I'll tell you is not readily available information anyway. As you may know, the island is locked in continuous litigation. The initial inclination of US military leaders was to systematically exterminate every creature on the island, to make it safe to inhabit again. This was met with outcries worldwide, from human rights, animal rights, and environmentalist groups. Some claim the creatures there were once human and therefore have human rights. Some claim the creatures represent a plethora of new species, and even long-extinct species, and therefore they should be protected. Some groups have talked seriously of making the entire island a national park, or a massive memorial to the three and a half million who died there. On the other hand, some have talked of making it a hunting resort for the wealthy."

"You're kidding," Lindsey said.

Peter shook his head. "And that's only the beginning. It may be years before the US decides what to do with it. Now, here is the information you probably *don't* already know. While Puerto Rico has been stuck in legal limbo, US Army Special Forces units have been combing the island for human survivors. They have rescued only a few thousand people, which is a sobering reminder of the massive death toll. It is also, however, a reminder that Georgia and I were quite lucky to survive." He looked at Bobby. "If we hadn't found you at the compound, we would not have made it out."

Bobby nodded. He looked down at the table for a moment. "But you have more to tell us."

"I do," Peter said. "Some Special Forces units have recently returned with reports of rather interesting developments—transformed creatures that have banded together in groups, for example. It seems some of the creatures are much more intelligent than others. Perhaps even approaching human-like intelligence."

He paused like he was considering what to say next. "Two weeks ago, there was an attack on one of the units. Two soldiers were killed." He paused again, even longer. "One week ago, a unit of 12 men approached the remains of Helmich's old compound. They were attacked by a colony of transformed creatures who seemed to be living within the compound. Every man in the unit was killed. But video transmitted from their body cams.... Well, that's the reason we've come here to see you." He looked directly at Bobby. "Could there have been anything left in that compound?"

"Anything like what?" Bobby asked.

"Anything like Lamotelokhai particles."

Bobby abruptly sat up straight. For a brief moment his eyes seemed to shift to fire-yellow. "Maybe," he said.

Peter continued. "I was approached by General Donovan Vickars. He had been unable to find you folks, so he came to me. It seems you folks are in demand now, particularly for threatening scenarios with certain parameters. I suppose this is because of your rather unique experiences and, well, your connections. Vickars seemed rather desperate for me to ask you if you would be willing to provide assistance once again."

Bobby jumped up from his chair. He walked across the yard to a ten-foot-high mound covered by a tarp. He began unfastening the tarp.

"What's he doing?" Peter asked.

Quentin glanced at Lindsey, and she shook her head. She didn't like where this was going any more than he did.

"He's doing something he knows he shouldn't," Quentin said.

Bobby finished removing the tarp, revealing a mound of tiny black and white pea-sized particles. He put his hand on the edge of the mound for a moment and then backed away.

Even from the patio, Quentin could hear the particles beginning to move. They chittered like millions of tiny crickets, and the mound started shifting.

A few minutes later, the backyard was dominated by a sleek, black aircraft with down-turned points at each end. It was so long that one end hung over the bank of the Sittee River. The aircraft looked exactly the same as when it had first been created, except for one difference. In large white letters on its belly was the name Bobby and Ashley had chosen for it, *Miranda*.

Bobby walked back to the patio. He looked at Quentin and Lindsey. "We've been hiding here long enough. Now we have a mission."

THERE'S MORE TO THIS STORY!

Since you just finished ***Profusion***, I'll assume you have read ***Diffusion*** and ***Infusion***. But don't forget about Samuel Inwood. The harrowing story of how Samuel discovered the Lamotelokhai in 1868 is told in the novel, ***SAVAGE***.

Savage is a very special book to me. I loved writing it because it is in a different style compared to my other books. ***Savage*** is actually Samuel Inwood's field journal, written in his own words. It's as much historical fiction as it is adventure or science fiction. I encourage you to check it out!

The following pages contain a preview excerpt from ***SAVAGE***.

But don't forget about ***Blue Arrow***, the story of Peter Wooley, as told by his amazing wife, Rose.

And you're really going to want to check out my ***BRIDGERS*** series and my ***ACROSS HORIZONS*** series!

SAVAGE EXCERPT

The Journal of Samuel Inwood
Transcribed by Mr. Inwood

February 16, 1868

Let it be known that I, Samuel Thaddeus Inwood, am not a man of the sea. It is with certainty that I make this claim, having spent the last seventy-four days aboard two steamers and a schooner on my journey from the port at Southampton to my current position in the great Pacific Ocean off the northern coast of New Guinea, Humboldt Bay being my final destination. Were you to lay eyes on the first ship of my voyage, the magnificent P&O steamship *Deccan*, you might think me a cowardly, unsturdy man. This ship carried me from England to the island of Singapore. Admittedly, the *Deccan* was a grand and impressive ship, with its long hall below the deck, the saloon. The saloon was comfortable, appointed with a large, ornately-carved table bolted to the floor, and every visible surface elegantly decorated with paint and gilt. But the meals served there, although numerous and of considerable size, were generally cold and plain. And the ship was crowded, with four berths per cabin and barely room to stand between them. Notwithstanding the ship's size, the motions of the sea produced constant rocking. This was accompanied by the ceaseless clanking of the engines, fueled by the labor of half-naked stokers shoveling coal into the furnaces.

During the first portion of this voyage, I found comfort only in the generous offerings, at no additional cost to me, of ale, porter, claret, port, and sherry. Champagne was even served twice a week. But finally, having decided to tour the engine rooms, which were open to the passengers, I discovered the ship's menagerie, a large compartment containing hundreds of animals, no doubt outnumbering the people on board. There were cows to provide milk, as well as pigs, sheep, chickens, and ducks. Notwithstanding the smell, I spent many hours there, perhaps more comfortably than in the company of my fellow travellers, although the collection of creatures steadily diminished as the ship's butcher converted them into meals for approximately three hundred passengers and crew.

As I have said, my cabin on the *Deccan* was small and barely tolerable. I can therefore scarcely imagine the conditions my assistant, Charles Newman, will endure when he travels to join me in the coming weeks. Due to the fortunate position of the family into which I was born, I was able to purchase a gentleman's first class ticket. Charles, I'm afraid, will be in possession of a servant's ticket, with its proportionably less elegant accommodations.

Upon arriving in Singapore, I went about procuring provisions, as I had been told that the islands I would encounter nearer to New Guinea would be lacking in articles often used by Europeans, particularly those used for cleanliness and comfort. After six days of searching and bartering for the items on my list, and then carefully packing them, I set off on a small screw steamer and made my way to the spice island of Tidore. This portion of my journey involved nine days living in wretched quarters. To pass the time, and to procure fresh sea air in order to escape the discomfort of seasickness, I spent many hours on the deck, watching innumerable islands pass. This had the effect of increasing my anticipation for arrival at my final destination, as each of the islands was covered with lofty and luxuriant forest. Beyond the shores of larger islands were hills and mountains, and

I was told that few of these had ever been trodden by civilized men.

When I arrived at Tidore I endeavored to procure a meeting with the Sultan, who had been granted rights by the Dutch to much of the northern coast of New Guinea. I made the acquaintance of a Dutch trader there who assisted with arranging this meeting. The Sultan, a man of Malayan race, was eager to assist in any efforts that might result in trading colonies being established within his jurisdiction. He generously provided me a letter of authority to go where I pleased and receive every assistance I required. As an additional service, he assigned a lieutenant and a soldier to accompany me until I could establish myself. They were to provide my protection and assist with my relations with the natives at Humboldt Bay, who were generally known to be hostile.

I now find myself on the last portion of my journey, aboard the schooner Hester Helena. This is the same ship used by Alfred Wallace, who explored and collected specimens throughout the Malay Archipelago for eight years, from 1854 to 1862. Mr. Wallace's descriptions of his travels so inspired me that I sought out the occasion to introduce myself to him in London. I told him I was most determined to carry out a zoological and entomological study of the magnificent island of New Guinea, particularly a part of it he had not the opportunity to visit. The dear man immediately became interested and graciously agreed to provide any assistance he could. We met for dinner soon after that, and he provided valuable information beyond my expectations, including the name of the man who owned the Hester Helena, as well as a list of supplies I would need. I believe, in fact, that this trip would likely end in disaster were it not for his guidance.

My final destination, where I expect to arrive tomorrow, is Humboldt Bay. Mr. Wallace, during the eight years of his expedition, spent only a few months in New Guinea. He made residence at Dorey, on the western peninsula. Although he had greatly anticipated visiting New Guinea, he found Dorey to be disagreeable. He described the natives there as inferior to others in the region, both morally and physically. There was continual rain there, and he became quite ill. There was also a preponderance of abominable biting ants and blow-flies, which made his most trifling tasks wearisome. And all of this was uncompensated by any great success in collecting impressive specimens of birds or insects.

But Mr. Wallace had the fortunate opportunity to visit with a ship captain who had stayed several days at Humboldt Bay, some five hundred miles to the east of Dorey, just at the border of the western portion of New Guinea administered by the Dutch Government. The captain reported that Humboldt Bay was a much more agreeable place, more beautiful and with a better harbor. The natives there were shy and untrusting, and they were unsophisticated, having only been visited by occasional stray whalers and Bugis traders (industrious sailors from the large island of Celebes). Most intriguing was the observation that the natives wore as ornaments the most magnificent Bird of Paradise feathers. Only about eighteen species of Paradise Birds are known to exist, but I suspect there are more to be found, as well as new species of mammals and insects, by a naturalist willing to venture some distance inland. Which is exactly what I intend to do.

Hence it is with great anticipation that I now approach my final destination. Yet I also must admit to some amount of trepidation. Tribes of New Guinea's northern coast are known to be murderous savages, in the lowest stages of barbarism. And unlike my esteemed friend, Mr. Wallace, I have had few previous opportunities to dispose peaceable negotiations with such savages. It is quite possible that my expedition might end with a savage's arrow in my heart, or his knife across my throat as I sleep.

February 17, 1868

I attribute the success of our landing at Humboldt Bay, if not my very survival, to the rather large collection of goods for trade I purchased in Singapore. Following the advice of Alfred Wallace, I had visited the Chinese bazaar bearing a list of items that would be valued by indigenous Papuans. To my delight, in the hundreds of shops there, most of these things could be purchased more cheaply than they could be purchased in England. I procured an abundance of knives, hatchets, gimlets, rolls of quality calico, balls of white cotton thread, beads, tobacco, and bottles of Java rum made from the sap of coconut palms, called arrack. With somewhat more persistence, I also managed to purchase muskets, gunpowder, and a supply of Dutch copper cents (the 100th part of a guilder), in case these could also be traded.

As before stated, the natives of Humboldt Bay are known to be unfriendly. But I was encouraged by reports from the Hester Helena's captain that the place had been successfully visited by the Dutch on more than one occasion, and I was determined to make my residence and do my collecting there.

This morning the Hester Helena arrived at Humboldt Bay. It is a fine bay, with a long, narrow spit of land projecting out to the northwest, almost joining another spit projecting out to the southeast. This provides a narrow channel serving as an entrance to a well-protected bay with good anchorage for vessels. But there were no vessels to be seen when we arrived, other than a small prau. Praus are used throughout the Malay Archipelago and are recognized by having a single outrigger, which is almost as large as the main hull. This vessel was tied to a mangrove, its single sail loosely furled, and so I assumed it was owned by visiting Bugis traders.

I stood watching anxiously at the Hester Helena's prow as we passed between the spits of land. The main village suddenly came into my sight. Many of the houses were built standing completely in the water, upon posts, with long, crude bridges connecting them to the shore. More houses could be seen inland, also standing upon posts. All of the houses and bridges seemed to be placed with little or no regularity and were often crooked. Near the shore, but also standing in water, was a much larger structure with a domed roof rather like a boat's hull, perhaps a council-house. Among the houses were numerous posts rising from the water or land that did not support anything. As we sailed nearer, I saw that upon each of these posts was a human skull, upside down, with the crown of the skull fastened to the top of the post. Below the skulls, each post was roughly carved in the revolting shape of a naked human figure, some of them male, some female. The general appearance of the village was somewhat alarming, and I was most grateful for the company of the lieutenant and his soldier from Tidore.

Soon, more than a dozen Papuan men emerged from the houses carrying bows and arrows. Even from some distance I could see that many of them wore various necklaces of beads and cords, but they were very nearly in a state of nature, almost naked but for a peculiar long and brown cylinder arranged as a sheath upon the sexual organ. Each of the men wore an impressive mop of frizzly hair upon his head, as well as a beard of the same frizzly nature. Unlike the Malay lieutenant and his soldier, with their lighter skin and less prominent features, these men were obviously true Papuans, with deep brown or even black bodies. Their stature was tall, equally as tall as an average European man, and they were handsome and well-made, with the result of making them seem all the more threatening when they began shouting and shaking their bows at us.

The captain gave the order to cast anchor at a safe distance, and I boarded the ship's tender, along with the lieutenant and soldier from Tidore and three Dutch crewmen, with the intention of land-ing. This, however, provoked even more shouting and gesticulations from the natives, and some of them began nocking their arrows and bending their bows, implying that they would shoot at us if we rowed closer.

Having anticipated such a reception, I had raided my supply of goods I had purchased for trade. I now hastily wrapped some knives and handkerchiefs in a length of calico printed with a fine floral pattern and threw the bundle to the natives. We then gave way and lay at anchor for some minutes while they inspected the gifts. We approached them again, and I threw another bundle, this one containing a bottle of arrack and some tobacco. Again, we gave way and waited. The next time we approached, they beckoned us to land the tender.

Once we arrived on shore, they seemed to have lost all their will for hostile threats. They approached us with curiosity, some of them now seeming even timid. They inspected my clothing and took particular interest in my spectacles and boots. Four or five men tried my spectacles in succession, and they laughed with boisterous merriment, seemingly surprised that they could not see through them. One of the men wore a great deal more ornaments in his hair than the others, as well as several impressive necklaces of animal teeth alternating with black and white beads. He also wore, at the top of each arm, a wide strap of woven grass, to which were attached numerous long black feathers of some unknown bird. I assumed this man to be the village chief, and I handed him yet another bundle containing tobacco and arrack. This brought a good many smiles from the men, and soon our assemblage on the shore grew as women and other men emerged from the houses.

The women were somewhat less handsome than the men. They were completely naked, other than wearing necklaces and earrings. But these were arranged in elegant ways, with the ends of the necklaces being attached to the earrings, and then draped in loose loops around the back of the head and fastened to a carefully knotted mound of hair. Their necklaces and earrings were composed of animal teeth, beads, and lengths of silver and copper wire. This exceedingly tasteful ornamentation greatly improved their rather barbarous appearance.

While standing in the midst of these natives, I began to fully appreciate their savage nature. The tallest of them exceeded my own height, and upon their bodies were numerous scars and deformities apparently due to fighting, perhaps with rival tribes. Most of them carried bows, knives, or sharpened wooden spears, and they handled these with a comfortable ease, as if they had used them since childhood. Due to the height and boisterous behavior of these natives, the smaller stature and reserved, almost bashful Malay character of the lieutenant and his soldier assigned to my protection at once seemed to me to be distressingly unsatisfactory. I therefore became doubly determined to establish peaceable relations and was glad for my substantial collection of goods for trade.

It quickly became clear that communication was going to be a problem. The lieutenant and his man did not understand the tribe's language, nor did the three Dutch crewmen who had come ashore with us. Furthermore, they informed me that no one else on the Hester Helena would know the language. But the Papuans soon resorted to gesticulations as if they were accustomed to dealing with visitors who could not speak their language. I set about trying to explain that I wished to bring my supplies to shore and go about setting up my residence there, but as my arms grew tired from gesticulating, and the natives repeatedly shook their heads in confusion, I began to fear that this was beyond my ability to convey.

To my great relief, two Bugis traders, who did indeed own the prau that was moored to the mangroves nearby, came to my aid. The men, who had emerged from a house wiping their eyes as if they had only just awoke, could speak Malay, the semi-barbarous language of the lieutenant from Tidore, and they also knew a little of the language of the Papuan tribe. Even I could understand some of what the Bugis men said, as I had spent significant time learning Malay aboard the screw steamer from Singapore and the Hester Helena, knowing that it was the most widely spoken language throughout the Malay Archipelago. I was not at all surprised that the Papuan tribe would have their own dialect. I understood that such striking fragmentation of language among these people was an example of their low state of civilization. Villages only a few miles distant from each other were known to speak different dialects or entirely different languages, so that communication between tribes was nearly impossible. And I had read that this barrier to communication was made worse by the hostile nature of some Papuan tribes, who often raided neighboring villages, murdering the men and capturing the women and children, assimilating them into their own tribe.

The Bugis traders explained to us that they visited Humboldt Bay regularly to exchange goods for furs and Birds of Paradise, which were highly valued for their magnificent feathers and in fact were an article of commerce. They seemed incredulous of my desire to reside with the Papuans but were eager to offer to return periodically to sell me goods I might need. I took some comfort in this, knowing that the Hester Helena will not return for a month, when it will bring my assistant, Charles Newman. After that, it will not return to pick us up until three years have passed. Since Humboldt Bay is hardly known and rarely visited, and the lieutenant and his soldier are to return to Tidore by way of a Bugis trading prau, it could therefore be three years before another European vessel enters the bay.

Notwithstanding their doubts about my plans, the Bugis men took considerable care to explain to the natives that I desired to stay with them in order to study the animals, birds, and insects of the region. This resulted in shaking of heads among the Papuans, and even laughter. But when told that I would be collecting specimens, including Birds of Paradise, the laughter stopped. They seemed suspicious of this, as if it were an intrusion upon their rights. I produced my letter of authority from the Sultan of Tidore. The Bugis traders explained what it was, but this seemed to anger the natives even more. Finally, I gave the man I assumed was the village chief the last pouch of tobacco I had brought from my supply on the ship and told the natives I was willing to pay them in goods or Dutch copper cents for any assistance they would afford me. I told them, in fact, that I was interested in employing three or four of them to assist me with building my house and with shooting and collecting specimens. This news seemed to interest them, as it was followed by a great deal of arguing among the younger men and boys and jostling of each other as if they desired to be first in line to become employed. I attempted to continue my explanation so that the matter could be resolved and I could then proceed to unloading my baggage and goods, but they had become so distressed over this that there could be no going on until a decision was made as to who would be hired to assist me. I chose three young men who appeared to be sturdy, healthy specimens. This resulted in yet another round of bois- terous talk and jostling, but fortunately it was with good-natured smiles.

And so at last my baggage and goods were brought to shore. The Hester Helena then made a hasty departure, as the captain had other business to attend to. I will admit that I watched the ship leave the bay with some consternation, as my future and my success here seemed quite uncertain.

The Bugis traders told us they would be departing soon, and they kindly offered the house they had built near the village, which they used when they visited regularly. The lieutenant and soldier assigned to my protection immediately accepted this offer. Aboard the Hester Helena, however, I had been subjected to the most alarming snoring from one of them as they slept, so I was deter- mined to begin constructing my own house.

The village chief himself, whose name I learned was Penapul, took some interest in helping me select a location for my house. After some talking, which was assisted by the Bugis men, I realized that Penapul had assumed I would want to build a house over the water. However, I was disinclined to do so, having just spent so many days at sea.

I asked why some of the houses were built over water while others were built over land. The villagers were astonished that I would not know, and they explained that this arrangement was designed to help defend the village from raiding tribes. Some tribes would attack from the water, approaching the village in canoes. In this case the women and children were moved to the houses built some distance up the side of the hill, and the raiders were fought at the shore to prevent them from landing. However, some tribes might attack from the land, in which case the women and children would be moved to the houses built over the water, and again the raiders were fought at the shore, but in this case to prevent them from entering the water.

I also learned that defense from attacking tribes was the very reason their houses were built on posts some six to eight feet above ground or water. I had to admit that it seemed it would be much easier to kill a man whose hands were otherwise occupied with the task of climbing.

The human skulls fastened high on posts were intended to demonstrate to raiding tribes that Penapul's tribe was to be feared. The skulls were apparently from slain attackers. I asked if the village was raided often. Penapul laughed at this and assured me that I need not worry. Even had I been sure he correctly understood my question, I could hardly have found comfort in his answer.

Finally I was shown several possible locations for building a house. I chose one that was on elevated ground, near a path often used by the Papuans to walk from the village to the forest, and not too far from a stream for washing and fresh water. The place was only about a hundred yards from the shore, and I planned to have a window from which I could look at the sea as I worked.

In Tidore I had purchased a good many cadjans, waterproof

mats made of interwoven pandanus palm leaves, to be used to cover my belongings to protect them from rain, and then eventually to be used as roofing material for my house. I had my new laborers move my baggage and goods to the place where I would build, and we covered them with the cadjans.

It would take several days to build a proper house, so I attempted to get my boys to help me construct a rough shelter in which to sleep during the process. However, by this time the Bugis traders were not to be seen, and I had to resort to gesticulating and pantomiming each task that I wanted accomplished. This became wearisome and did not work to my satisfaction. Just as I was thinking of giving up, the oldest of my four workers, a boy of perhaps eighteen, named Amborn, waved for me to follow him. He took me to the house where he slept, which was actually little more than a hut. Upon entering it I saw that two smoke-dried human skulls were suspended from the eaves. Amborn pointed to a sleeping mat, which I assumed was his. I was unwilling to sleep in his bed, but I did agree to temporarily share his roof. I went to my things, fetched some blankets, and arranged them in a corner. There were two other sleeping mats in the house, and I soon discovered that Amborn shared the house with two boys about his age. When I have the capability and opportunity, I will inquire if this is a normal custom of these people.

And so as the light of the day fades, I am preparing to spend my first night upon the shore of the great island of New Guinea. I am quite pleased with the progress made today, although I will sleep with a loaded gun beside me, as I am uncertain of the natives' intentions.

AUTHOR'S NOTES

I must first say that in writing ***Profusion***, I intended no disrespect to the people of Puerto Rico. If the story contains any descriptions that are incorrect or offensive, I apologize. And to the people of Puerto Rico: I'm sorry I destroyed your entire island! I wrote this book before the tragic events related to hurricane Maria. As I watched the terrible results of that storm, I considered changing the story in ***Profusion*** so that Helmich's compound would be located on a different island. Eventually, though, I decided against this, as it would drastically change the overall story.

As in ***Diffusion***, ***Infusion***, and ***Savage***, a good portion of ***Profusion*** takes place in Papua, the Indonesian province that makes up the western half of the great island of New Guinea. Sinanie's tribe of Papuan men and women have characteristics resulting from thousands of years of living with the Lamotelokkhai. Obviously, therefore, I have taken liberties in developing the descriptions of this particular tribe. But I intended no disrespect to the unique cultures of the Papuan peoples by doing so.

That being said, the descriptions of the Papuan cultures, wildlife, and ecosystems are as accurate as I could make them, based upon the research by authors listed below.

I adapted the language of Sinanie's tribe from the amazing work of Gerrit J. van Enk and Lourens de Vries in their studies of the language and culture of the Korowai, a Papuan community of treehouse dwellers of southern Irian Jaya (now called Papua).

Astoundingly, the Korowai had never come into contact with outsiders until the early 1980s.

The following are recommended books (and one video).

Flannery, Tim. *Mammals of New Guinea*. Chatswood, New South Wales: Reed Books Australia, 1995. Print.

Flannery, Tim. *Throwim Way Leg: Tree Kangaroos, Possums, and Penis Gourds – On the Track of Unknown Mammals in Wildest New Guinea*. New York: Atlantic Monthly Press, 1998. Print.

Marriott, Edward. *The Lost Tribe – A Harrowing Passage into New Guinea's Heart of Darkness*. New York: Henry Holt and Company, 1996. Print.

Merrifield, William, Gregerson, Marilyn, and Ajamiseba, Daniel, Ed. *Gods, Heroes, Kinsmen: Ethnographic Studies from Irian Jaya, Indonesia*. Jayapura, Irian Jaya: Cenderawasih University, 1983. Print.

Muller, Kal. *New Guinea: Journey Into the Stone Age*. Lincolnwood, Illinois: Passport Books, 1997. Print.

Souter, Gavin. *New Guinea: The Last Unknown*. New York: Taplinger Publishing, 1966. Print.

Van Enk, Gerrit J. and de Vries, Lourens. *The Korowai of Irian Jaya – Their Language in its Cultural Context*. New York: Oxford University Press, 1997. Print.

Wallace, Alfred Russell. *The Malay Archipelago*. 1869. Print or ebook.

This astounding work, which is in two volumes, is now in the public domain and can be found in a variety of print and ebook formats. If you are at all interested in the exploration of this part of the world, I highly recommend reading Wallace's work.

Sky Above Mud Below. Dir. and Perf. Pierre-Dominique Gaisseau (organizer and leader) and Gerard Delloye (assistant leader). Lorimar Home Video, 1962. VHS.

This is an amazing video filmed as it happened in 1959, when a group of explorers set out on a seven-month attempt to cross the jungles of Papua (then called Dutch New Guinea). Winner of the 1961 Academy Award for Best Documentary Feature.

ACKNOWLEDGMENTS

I am not capable of creating a book such as this on my own. I have the following people, among others, to thank for their assistance.

When it comes to editing, my son Micheal Smith is extremely talented, and his tireless and meticulous suggestions are invaluable. If you find a sentence or detail in the book that doesn't seem right, it is likely because I failed to implement one of his suggestions.

My wife, Trish, is always the first to read my work, and therefore she has the burden of seeing my stories in their roughest form. Thankfully, she does not hesitate to point out where things are a mess. Her suggestions are what get the editing process started. She also helps with various promotional efforts. And finally, she not only tolerates my obsession with writing, she actually encourages it.

I also owe thanks to those in my Advance Reviewer group. They were able to point out numerous typos and inconsistencies. Several of them went above and beyond, particularly Mandy Walkden-Brown, Tammy Fiess, Lisa Sherman, Sherri Rusch, Ilene Roberts, Elizabeth Copeland, Linda Brand, Lois Welsh, Rosemary Standeven, and Sue Williams.

Marifer Walter and Lana Spaller-Little provided valuable assistance with Spanish dialogue.

Finally, I am thankful to all the independent freelance designers out there who provide quality work for independent authors such as myself. Jake Caleb Clark (www.jcalebdesign.com) created the awesome cover for **Profusion**.

ABOUT THE AUTHOR

Stan Smith has lived most of his life in the Midwest United States and currently resides with his wife Trish in a home nestled within an Ozark forest near Warsaw, Missouri. He writes adventure novels and short stories that have a generous sprinkling of science fiction. His novels and stories are about regular people who find themselves caught up in highly unusual situations. They are designed to stimulate your sense of wonder, get your heart pounding, and keep you reading late into the night, with minimal risk of exposure to spelling and punctuation errors. His books are for anyone who loves adventure, discovery, and mind-bending surprises.

Stan's Author Website
http://www.stancsmith.com

Feel free to email Stan at: stan@stancsmith.com

He loves hearing from readers and will answer every email.

ALSO BY STAN C. SMITH

The DIFFUSION series

Diffusion

Infusion

Profusion

Savage

Blue Arrow

Diffusion Box Set

The BRIDGERS series

Bridgers 1: The Lure of Infinity

Bridgers 2: The Cost of Survival

Bridgers 3: The Voice of Reason

Bridgers 4: The Mind of Many

Bridgers 5: The Trial of Extinction

Bridgers 6: The Bond of Absolution

INFINITY: A Bridger's Origin

Bridgers 1-3 Box Set

Bridgers 4-6 Box Set

The ACROSS HORIZONS series

1. Obsolete Theorem

2. Foregone Conflict

3. Hostile Emergence

4. Binary Existence

Genesis Sequence

Stand-alone Stories

Parthenium's Year